KYLIE CHAN

Bestselling author of *The Dark Heavens* trilogy

BLACK JADE

CELESTIAL BATTLE
BOOK THREE

DON'T MISS
BESTSELLING AUTHOR
KYLIE CHAN's
PREVIOUS BOOKS IN THE
CELESTIAL BATTLE TRILOGY

Also Available...

Books by Kylie Chan

Dark Heavens

WHITE TIGER
RED PHOENIX
BLUE DRAGON

Journey to Wudang

EARTH TO HELL
HELL TO HEAVEN
HEAVEN TO WUDANG

Celestial Battle

DARK SERPENT
DEMON CHILD
BLACK JADE

KYLIE CHAN

BLACK JADE

CELESTIAL BATTLE
BOOK THREE

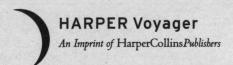
HARPER Voyager
An Imprint of HarperCollins Publishers

BLACK JADE. Copyright © 2016 by Kylie Chan. All rights reserved. Printed in the United States of America. No part of this book may be used or reproduced in any manner whatsoever without written permission except in the case of brief quotations embodied in critical articles and reviews. For information, address HarperCollins Publishers, 195 Broadway, New York, NY 10007.

Originally published in Australia in 2016 by HarperCollins*Publishers* Australia Pty Limited.

First Harper Voyager mass market printing: October 2016

ISBN 978-0-06232910-3

Cover design and illustration by Darren Holt, HarperCollins Design Studio
Cover images by shutterstock.com

Harper Voyager and ❭ is a trademark of HCP LLC.

16 17 18 19 20 QGM 10 9 8 7 6 5 4 3 2 1

Gentle Reader, this is the ninth book in this story. Although you can choose to start here, you may find it more rewarding to read the story from the beginning with the first novel, *White Tiger*.

In response to readers' requests I've added a list of characters at the end.

Note for parents/teachers

My books are sometimes shelved as 'Young Adult'. This novel contains adult themes that a less mature reader may find disturbing. Parental discretion is advised.

1

'So how does it feel?' John asked me.

I shook my head and turned on the spot. 'I keep expecting guards to come and march me into Court Ten to see Pao.'

John turned as well, facing the end of the causeway. The causeway no longer met the island; there was a moat between the two masses to stop demons from crossing from the demonic to the Celestial side of Hell. The White Tiger's Number Three, Katie, was on guard, holding one of the laser weapons that were the only way to destroy the hybrid armoured demons. This was a more polished version; not held together with duct tape.

'Dark Lord,' Katie said, saluting us. 'Lady Emma.'

'Hi, Katie,' I said.

'Any attempts at incursion since the Southern Bastion fell?' John said, approaching her. 'The phoenixes are preparing to retake the South. Is there any movement on the demonic side?'

She backed up a single step, then straightened and stood her ground as John neared. 'No, my Lord.' She looked from me to John, her face expressionless.

'Give me a moment,' John said, and the Turtle separated from the Serpent. Both of them slid into the water without leaving a ripple.

'You're marrying *that*?' Katie said.

'Oh, not you too,' I said.

'I mean, I've seen his human and Celestial Forms around the Heavens, and for an old guy he's okay, but ...' She took a deep breath. '*That?*'

'I'm a snake as well, Katie.'

'You'd have to be, to be attracted to it.'

I turned back to the water; I could sense him returning. 'He's the hottest damn thing on the planet.'

'I think your own serpent is,' he said, floating out of the water and recombining. Yin flowed out where the Serpent connected with the Turtle and disappeared into it where they touched. The cloud of yin dissipated and he landed lightly in front of us. 'No movement; the demons aren't aware of the Red Phoenix's plans. And you were correct, Emma. I think there's more but I can't see them.'

'More of what?' Katie said. 'Demons?'

'Yes,' I said. 'Planted like landmines. The one that took me to Hell was in the ground and invisible to all of us.'

'Fuck.' Katie scanned the battle-scarred landscape. 'I can't see anything.'

John stomped away over the ground, the Serpent writhing above the Turtle's shell. 'Let me have a look.'

'Holy fuck, that's disturbing,' Katie said.

John's Serpent looked back at us while the Turtle continued to search. 'Madam, you sound very much like your father.'

'If you mean I swear a lot, actually I sound like my mother,' Katie said, and grinned. 'English actress. They swear worse than Dad.'

'Oh yeah, I've met some,' I said. 'They use language that makes your father sound tame.'

'Emma, Three, here,' John said, and we went to join him.

Katie stood two metres back, then visibly rallied and stood next to the Turtle's head.

'Katie, I've seen you ride a horse headlong into a goddamn *tank*. I cannot believe the Dark Lord's True Form is freaking you out,' I said.

'Get used to it, Emma,' John said. 'Children tend to run screaming.'

'Katie's nearly two hundred years old.'

John's Serpent's head swung towards Katie, making her take a step back. 'You've never seen me before?'

'Dad allowed us to train with the Horsemen, but he kept us in the Western Palace where we'd be safe,' she said. 'It's only since Lady Emma pulled his whiskers out that he's given us equal access to the front line and field missions, and the opportunity to prove ourselves.' She poked her thumb into her chest. 'I wouldn't be Number Three otherwise.'

'Well done, Emma,' the Serpent said in its female voice. 'Katie, change to your own True Form and have a dig here.'

She put the laser on the ground, then changed to a snow leopard. She snuffled around on the dirt, then proceeded to dig.

'Yes, it smells weird,' she said. She stopped and snuffled again. 'Really disgusting, actually. Like bad meat.' She dug again, and her claws scraped on rock. 'There's a stone here.'

'That's not a stone, that's the head of a stone dem—' I began, but it was too late.

The demon surged out of the ground, grabbed Katie around the throat, and threw her away. It was made of stone, but not individual rocks floating together; it was more like a human-shaped creature of clay. It paused for a minute, then took three fast steps towards me.

I summoned Dark Heavens and filled it with shen.

John moved faster than was visible — the Serpent grabbed the demon by the head, the Turtle took its arm, and they ripped it apart. The stone reformed, taking the human shape again, and John surrounded it in a cloud of yin. It dissolved.

I ran to Katie. She was lying face down on the ground in human form.

'Uh, I think my neck's broken,' she said. 'I can't move.' She spat dirt. 'Fuck. Do me a favour?'

'Leave her, I can fix it,' the Serpent said.

'At least turn me over, I can't breathe!' she said, choking.

I turned her onto her back and her head flopped sideways. Her eyes glazed over and she stopped breathing, then disappeared.

'Damn, a hangman's fracture. I shouldn't have done that,' I said.

'She's Immortal, it's not a big issue,' John said.

'Talk to Pao. He'll keep her for ages since we sent her there.'

'I am,' the Turtle said in John's male voice, then added, 'Nope. He's holding on to her to punish us.'

'Bastard,' I said under my breath. 'Can the Tiger send another senior child down? We need someone to run this —'

Michael appeared next to John. He squawked and jumped back. 'Holy *shit*!'

'Oh, for god's sake,' I said with exasperation. 'It's not that bad!' I picked up the laser weapon and pushed it at him. 'Take this and guard Causeway Eight while Katie's stuck at Pao's pleasure.'

'Ma'am,' Michael said, edging around John to take the weapon from me.

'Talk to him, John,' I said.

'Is that really you, Lord Xuan?' Michael said.

The Turtle's eyes were full of amusement, but the Serpent showed its usual lack of emotion. John turned to face Michael and he took another step back.

'Wait a second,' I said with quiet wonder. 'You're enjoying this.'

'Oh my god, you are.' Michael grinned. 'Did it freak Katie out?'

'She used some language, yes,' the Serpent said in its female voice.

Michael's mouth flopped open. 'You're *female*?' He looked from John to me, his eyes wide.

'Cut it out, John,' I said. 'We need to see if there's more of them.'

'There are,' the Turtle said in John's male voice. 'I can't see them, but I can smell them.'

'Whoa,' Michael said. 'You know, you seemed really normal when I was part of the household in Hong Kong.'

'There's no need to be insulting,' John said.

Michael cocked his head. 'When I was living with you, it was all straight male turtle —'

'Straight?' John said.

'Perfectly aligned,' I said.

'Oh. Yes. I am,' John said.

'Are you gay female serpent as well now?'

'For an Immortal you ask a very mortal question, Michael,' John said in his male voice.

4

'Labels,' I said with scorn. 'You should know better. We are Shen, spirits incarnate. Our bodies are merely instruments for our spirits, and gender is a part of the instrument.'

John changed from his male to his female voice. 'You are attempting to label something that is the essence of the Tao. I cannot be labelled, categorised, analysed or comprehended, because I just *am*.'

'But are you two spirits?' Michael said. 'Are you two separate consciousnesses, one male, one female, or are you one combined mind? How does that even *work*?'

'I am yang and yin joined into yin,' John said with both voices, the sound resonating through the air.

'Holy fuck,' Michael said, his eyes wide.

'Stop playing with Michael and find the rest of the demons,' I said.

'What demons?' Michael looked around. 'There's nothing here.'

'They're in the ground, planted like landmines,' I said, pointing at the hole. 'One was in this, waiting, and when Katie dug it up it broke her neck.'

'Where is it?'

'I yinned it,' John said.

'Okay.' Michael turned to scan the island. 'And there are more?'

'I think there are about fifteen of them all over the island,' John said. He stomped between us and we followed him, dwarfed by his enormous shell. 'I can't see them at all, and they're almost impossible to smell unless I'm right on top of them.' He stopped. 'Yes. Take True Form and dig here.'

Michael changed to his golden tiger form and snuffled around on the ground. 'Can't smell anything.' He dug, sniffing at the ground at the same time. 'Nothing here.'

Simone appeared next to her father. 'Daddy, I have to be in class in ten minutes, and it takes at least twenty to make the trip back from Hell. What's so important?'

Michael stepped back and shook his shaggy tiger mane. 'I don't think there's anything here, my Lord.'

John concentrated on Simone, his turtle eyes half-closed.

She nodded, then turned and studied the island. 'Nope.'

'Just you then, John,' I said. 'What a pain.'

The Serpent separated from the Turtle and slithered in one direction, while the Turtle stomped in the other.

'Serpent,' I said.

'Turtle, then,' Simone said. 'Michael, stay with Emma.'

I followed the snake as it slithered across the ground, appreciating the way John moved with effortless, sinuous elegance. He was incredibly hot.

I can see your face, Emma, he said. *Are you really admiring my ass?*

Hell, yeah, I said. *When are we doing snake on snake? We still haven't tried that.*

I want you to be sure.

See this face? I said. *This is the face of sure.*

'Hold,' the Serpent said in its female voice. 'The Turtle found one.'

'Can Simone take it?' I said.

'Easily. She's yinning it. Done.' The Serpent moved over the ground again. 'There's one close by.'

The demon charged out of the ground five metres away and thundered between John and Michael to attack me. John slithered to it and grabbed it in his mouth, and Michael raised the laser weapon at it. John yinned it at the same time as Michael activated the weapon, and the laser went straight through where the demon had been and hit me in the throat.

I didn't feel it at first, then the pain struck and I couldn't breathe. Everything went grey and the ground spiralled towards me.

'Oh shit,' Michael said. 'God, Emma, I am so sorry.'

I wanted to tell him it was okay but the words wouldn't come.

The Serpent came to me and touched me with its nose. Everything went cold and dark. So cold. The cold was so intense that I wanted to scream, but no noise came out. I felt the Serpent's desperate concern as it healed me — it never wanted to lose me again. I touched its consciousness and we shared a moment of joined awareness, then the cold was gone and I shivered uncontrollably.

'You could have just let me die,' I said.

'And put you at Pao's mercy, right after we sent Katie?' John said. 'He'd keep you for a month.'

'He wouldn't do that, would he?' Michael said.

John changed to human and helped me up. 'How long was it last time?'

'Two and a half weeks,' I said. I shook myself out. 'That's three. Let's find the rest of them.'

John changed back to Serpent and looked out over the landscape again. 'Hold. We found another one,' he said. 'We're yinning it. Four.' The Serpent raised itself on its coils. 'We need to pick up the pace. The Turtle's winning.'

'Your other half is winning a competition with yourself?' Michael said with disbelief.

'I know. Can't have that,' the Serpent said, and moved off.

2

We stood next to the white marquee that had been erected on the lawn in front of the Gates of Heaven for the meeting with the demons. The red and gold banners on top of the Gates snapped on the spring Celestial breeze: some showed the character for 'Middle', as in 'Middle Kingdom'; others showed the character for 'Jade', representing the Jade Emperor; and a number had qilin and dragon motifs. John stood in his largest Celestial Form with his arms crossed over his chest, silent and apparently relaxed, but underneath he was thrumming with tension. I mentally touched him and we shared a quick moment of joint consciousness, easing each other's spirit.

'He's late,' Er Lang said from where he stood at John's right hand, also in Celestial Form.

'He always is,' John said.

'Do you think he'll stand us up again?' I said.

'Stand us up?' John said.

'Fail to show.'

'Oh. Probably.'

'This is becoming ridiculous,' Er Lang said.

'Can't you two see that he's holding us off with these endless negotiations while he hatches another army?' John said without moving.

Er Lang and I shared a shocked glance.

'How did the Heavens survive without me all these years?' John said, almost to himself.

'They didn't,' Er Lang and I said in unison.

'Look where we are now,' I said.

'Earthly overrun. South and West gone,' Er Lang said. 'Two hundred Red Warriors dead in their last aborted attempt to retake the South.'

John shifted and grumbled something unintelligible under his breath.

A small black-skinned demon appeared in front of us with an audible pop. He was naked, with a bloated torso and skinny limbs, and his oversized pink-rimmed penis hung down to his knees, swinging as he moved. He approached us with an evil grin that was unnaturally wide and full of pointed teeth, and held up an iPad. The Demon King's face was on the screen.

'Ah Wu, Er Lang,' the King said. 'I'll come up if you have something worthwhile to offer. Otherwise I'm staying here with my girls. So what's the decision? Surrender now so we can negotiate terms for my rule over Heaven, and I'll be kind to you, I promise.'

John glared at the King's image.

'Talk to me, Ah Wu, this may be your only chance,' the King said. 'Come on, it's just modern technology. I'm sure you have one of these as well.'

John uncrossed his arms. 'Your army is destroyed. Your force is a fraction of what it once was —'

'I could say the same about your own armies,' the King said with humour, interrupting.

'Remove all of your demons from the Heavens now, and we will cede the Earthly to you,' John said. 'You can have the Earthly, we'll retain Heaven, and Hell we'll split.'

'Uh, honey, that's less than I have now,' the King said. 'I hold the remains of the Western Heavens and all of the Southern Heavens. I'm replacing powerful people everywhere on the Earthly with my own thralls, and all the Little Brothers are helping me consolidate my rule.' He leaned into the camera and grinned. 'Great fun.'

'If you do not withdraw your remaining troops from the Heavens immediately, we will destroy them,' Er Lang said.

'You sure about that?' the King said.

'We killed nearly all of your forces, few remain,' John said. 'And we will retake the South soon. You haven't had time to hatch a new generation, and when you do, we will —' John stopped at a vibration through the ground.

'Yeah, about that,' the King said. 'You see, I have this magnificent fuck buddy who has a dick bigger than the little guy here, and he gives me all sorts of lovely things.'

The little demon's grin widened as the ground shook.

'And some of those lovely things are on their way now. If you don't draw a weapon on them —'

The rest of his speech was drowned out by the army of stone elemental demons that marched over the rise and approached the Gates — at least a thousand of them. Each was more than two metres tall and made of a loose collection of oval stones that walked on two, three or four legs, and had no discernible face. Some of the stones were recognisably the standing stones stolen from Europe.

'Man the barricades!' Guan Yu shouted from the top of the Gates, and disappeared.

Back, Emma, John said, and I retreated to the top of the Gates building.

The King continued to speak, unheard, as the stones marched up the hill towards the Gates.

John pushed his left hand out and yinned a hundred of the front demons, then drew Seven Stars.

The small demon holding the iPad scampered away, through the approaching stone demons.

John swung into the demons with Seven Stars, but it did nothing to them; the stones just separated to let the blade through, then reformed. They walked past him as if he didn't exist. He loaded the sword with energy, making the indentations light up, and attacked the stone demons — again to no effect.

The demon battalion that guarded the Gates came out of the left entrance and threw themselves at the stone demons, but again without effect. Every blow glanced off the stones, who disregarded our forces and marched towards the Gates in loose clusters with no organisation, slow and unstoppable. They walked through the marquee as if it wasn't there, ignoring the canvas as it caught on their legs and collapsed.

John changed to True Form, and his Serpent and Turtle separated. His Serpent slithered up to a demon, grabbed its head stone in its mouth, and pulled it off. He tossed the stone aside, vacuuming up the demon essence holding it together, then worked at the rest of the stones, dismantling the demon from the top down. The Turtle did the same to another demon nearby.

I changed to snake and flew down into the demons. I slithered up to one and dismantled it the same way. The Heavenly guard were still attacking the demons with weapons and energy, which did nothing.

'Call the Jade Emperor!' John's Turtle and Serpent shouted in unison, their mouths full of stone.

Guan Yu had shut the Gates behind the defending force, and the stone demons ran into the closed portal and piled against the Gates. With other demons already in the Heavens, the Gates no longer had their magical barrier properties and were knocked off their hinges.

The stone demons surged through and split into two columns on the other side. One column headed west and the other south, both continuing their unstoppable slow pace.

John's two animals and my snake continued to harry the demon force, but it was futile.

I had ingested so much demon essence that my mouth tasted bitter and acidic and my stomach burned. Now that I'd turned to the Celestial, demon essence tasted vile. I couldn't take any more in and stopped, but John continued to slowly dismantle the stones as they passed.

The two columns marched with mindless determination towards the fallen Southern and Western Bastions, disappearing into the earth with each step and leaving great gashes in the soil behind them.

Guan Yu ran down from the Gates to join us, his buzz cut glowing in the afternoon sun that reflected off the Gates' red walls.

'The Jade Emperor can stop this; he's stone,' Guan Yu said. 'Where the hell is he?'

'These are European stones, he may have no —' I began.

There was a sharp rattle of explosions and something slapped into me; a stinging blow. We spun to see that a group of twenty humanoids, armed with automatic weapons, had appeared further down the hill. They mowed down Guan Yu's demon gate defenders.

I felt pain and looked at my coils; I'd been scored by a bullet and was bleeding from between my scales.

The demons fired again as they approached, and John leapt in front of me to shield me. His True Form fell, shredded by the bullets.

Guan Yu's head exploded and he disappeared.

The next barrage felt like being put through a mincer, and I fell to lie on the grass next to the pieces of John's corpses. The demons marched over us and continued towards the Gates, some of them treading on me and breaking bones to add to my agony. I lay in pain as afternoon turned to night, gradually growing colder, and regurgitating blood and demon essence for hours.

* * *

I landed in human form in one of the holding cells for Court Ten, then spun and threw up into the cell bucket. At least it wasn't blood any more, but I still felt violently ill from ingesting so much demon essence followed by a vast amount of my own blood. I retched a few times and bent over the bucket, breathing deeply. When I had control, I wiped my mouth on the scratchy tissue paper, and turned to sit on the floor with my back against the cell wall.

John was in the cell across from me, asleep in True Form. The Turtle's snout was resting on the floor, and the Serpent was draped across its shell with its head sideways on the Turtle's. He looked exhausted and I was glad I hadn't woken him, but I couldn't help the warm rush of affection — he was adorable. I took more deep breaths and wiped my eyes.

The demon guard walked up to the door; a big humanoid in True Form, nearly two metres tall, green and smooth-skinned. She spoke in a whisper. 'Do you need anything, Lady Emma?'

'Emma!' John said from behind her. My view of him was blocked by the guard, then there was a crash and he was next to her in human form, holding the door of his cell and looking at it with bewilderment. He leaned it on the cell wall behind him, then studied me through the bars of my cell. 'I thought they had you. You were gone for hours. Did they capture you? You didn't negotiate anything with the King, did you?'

'It took me a long time to bleed out and die,' I said. 'I was left behind.'

'Unacceptable,' John growled. 'Someone should have checked —'

'John,' I said, interrupting him, 'there was nobody left to check.'

'I am teaching you shen energy suicide the minute we're back in the Heavens,' he began, then raised his head. 'Shit!'

The guard, Three-Fifty, bowed to him and put her arm out towards the stairs leading up to Court Ten. 'Celestial Highness. This way, please.'

John looked towards the stairs, then back at me, his expression full of conflict.

I put my hand through the bars of my cell and touched his cheek. 'I'm fine. You need to be released now so you can report to the Jade Emperor and retake the Gates.'

He covered my hand with his own, then grabbed the bars of my cell door and ripped it off its hinges. He placed it next to the other door he'd broken and gestured with his head.

'Not without you. Let's go.'

'Highness …' Three-Fifty began, following us as we strode up the stairs side by side.

'I will send someone down to repair the damage directly,' John said.

'My thanks,' she said.

We reached ground level, which was the back of Judge Pao's courtroom. Two guards were waiting to escort us.

'If you don't mind, I'd prefer not to be there when the judge sees you,' Three-Fifty said.

'If he gives you any grief about our actions, let me know and I'll have you reassigned to me,' I said.

'My Lady,' Three-Fifty said, and went back down the stairs.

We strode into the courtroom together, and the guards stationed themselves on either side of us. John stood in the centre of the room facing Pao and crossed his arms over his chest. I mirrored his pose.

'Lord Xuan, I have not yet released your latest dalliance,' Pao said. 'She is to return to the cells immediately.'

Dalliance! John said.

I know. Best one yet!

'We have decreed that Lady Emma is Our Consort,' John said. 'When We are wed, she will be Our Empress of the Dark North and joint Protector of Wudang.'

Pao scowled at John's use of the Imperial 'We'. 'Until then she is nobody,' he said. 'I decreed her Unworthy, and despite my wise judgement you Raised her yourself. And we all know how well that has transpired with your women in the past.'

John and I both stiffened at the mention of Peony, the Serpent Concubine, and Pao's face filled with satisfaction. *Touché.*

'Miss Donahoe is to return to the cells immediately,' Pao said. 'Guards.'

The guards moved to surround us and John raised one hand to stop them.

'Miss Donahoe is needed by my side. She is my equal and partner in the management of my realm, and I rely on her wise counsel.'

'You are vastly older than her, supremely more powerful than her, wiser and more intelligent than her, and in all ways more knowledgeable in the ways of war than her. This small human woman is profoundly not needed, except perhaps to pleasure you, and even then she is an unnecessary distraction when the Heavens are so threatened.'

John and I inhaled sharply in unison.

Mine, I said.

No, mine, John said.

Mine!

Please? he said. *I'm extremely concerned about the Gates and we need to get out of here.*

I bowed without looking away from Pao. *My Lord.*

My Lady. John changed to out loud. 'She is my equal in courage and spirit, and superior to me in will. And those are the only attributes that truly matter.'

Judge Pao sat glaring at us for a full minute, then picked up his brush to write the sentences. 'You are both released to the Heavens immediately. I suggest you waste no more time in reporting to the Jade Emperor.'

We turned to face each other, clasped hands, and John teleported us to the Celestial Palace.

'I'm more *stubborn* than you?' I said after we landed.

'It worked.'

'I surpass you in only one aspect, and that's *stubbornness*? Wow,' I said as we walked through the breezeway towards our Celestial Palace apartments.

'That's not a bad thing, Emma. You know I'm too soft.'

'And I'm too hard?'

'You weren't last night.'

I hissed with laughter.

'See? We complement each other,' he said. 'If I tried to explain to Pao how well we work together, he wouldn't understand. For him there is only "superior" and "inferior", and our mutual enhancement does not exist.'

'Say "synergy" and I'll divorce you,' I said.

'Sy...ner...gy,' he said, his voice a low rumble that echoed in the air. 'You'll divorce me before we're married?'

A Palace fairy appeared in front of us and we stopped so that John could speak to it.

'We wish to refresh ourselves before presenting to the Celestial,' he said. 'Is he in his quarters or his hearing room?'

The fairy silently told us to go to Er Lang.

'Doesn't the Jade Emperor want to discuss what happened at the Gates?' I said, incredulous.

The fairy quivered and rang like a bell.

'Okay, okay,' I said. 'Do we have to walk all the way over to Er Lang's?'

By the time I finished speaking, the Palace had already transferred us directly to outside Er Lang's office in the Elite residential quarters. A school class was audible nearby, with the children chanting a memory rhyme. All but five of the Elites were dead, and young families were occupying their rooms.

We went into Er Lang's office to find him sitting behind his desk, studying his computer monitor and looking grim. We sat across from him.

'Do they have the Gates?' John said.

'From all accounts the answer is yes. Everyone present was killed, and nobody can approach the area without being killed as well.'

'Guan Yu?' I said. 'He should know the details —'

'I will fucking *murder* that motherfucker, rip out his fucking entrails and fucking shove them up his —' Guan Yu roared as he entered, stopping dead when he saw us. He fell to one knee before me. 'My profoundest apologies, my Lady Emma. I did not realise you were present, and I sincerely regret burdening your ears with my filthy outburst.'

John's eyes were full of amusement. He shot a look at me, then leaned his chin in his hand and waited for it.

'Get the fuck off the floor,' I said to Guan Yu. 'We have much more important things to worry about than my delicate shell-like ears. For fuck's sake, man, we're all soldiers here and we need to know the status of the Gates.'

Guan Yu looked from John to me, then smiled with grim satisfaction as he rose and conjured a chair for himself. 'Very well. The King left about twenty of those stone fuckers in front of the Gates, with another twenty humanoid snipers on top, and anyone who tries to take them down is destroyed immediately. What the hell were you two … three reptiles doing that my people can't? You took them apart easily.'

'Eating them,' I said. 'But they made me sick after a while. Lord Xuan could eat more of them.'

'They tasted awful,' John said. 'What about the rest of the stone demons?'

'Yeah, they were sinking into the ground. What happened?' I said.

'They did sink into the ground,' Er Lang said. 'We couldn't follow their passage through the earth, but it's obvious they were travelling to reinforce the Southern and Western Bastions.'

'Shit,' John said.

'Can your children do what we did?' I asked John.

'They might.'

'I should round them up then. We can take them down together.'

Er Lang's expression filled with shock as he looked from me to John. Guan Yu's face was rigid with control.

'I know exactly what you are thinking and it is thoroughly beneath both of you,' I said. 'Look at me. I'm pure European. I know my genealogy back for two hundred years, and there isn't a single drop of Chinese blood there. Go further back than that and we run into the common-sense decree about ten generations.'

'Then why can you do it too?' Er Lang said.

'Because she used to be a demon snake, just like me,' John said.

Er Lang opened his mouth, but I said it first. 'I still am.'

'Conceded,' John said.

'So let me bring your children in,' I said. 'They might be able to do it.'

John rubbed his chin. 'Are you sure that's a good idea? Most of them live as humans. They've never met me and have no reason to put themselves in danger for us.'

'It's worth a try. They're family.'

'But they're *reptiles*.'

'So are we!'

'We need to take back the Gates, my Lord,' Er Lang said, and John winced at the use of the honorific. 'As long as Hell holds the Gates, travel in and out of Heaven is severely restricted. The two of you destroyed them easily; a group of ten reptiles with some ranged attackers should be able to retake the Gates.'

'I want to confirm that it will work first,' John said. 'I will send Ming Gui in to try, and if it works Emma can round up the other children. Anything else?'

Er Lang and Guan Yu didn't reply.

'Very well. I will summon Ming Gui, and we will meet close to the Gates in an hour to see if my reptile children can retake them for us.'

'You forgot your latest dalliance,' I said.

'Her too,' John said.

3

John, Martin and I approached carefully, but the minute we were within range of the Gates, there came a volley of sharp explosions from the building. John generated a circle of yin to absorb the bullets. Smoke rose from where the demons had fired at us.

'They're too far away for me to disable the weapons,' John said. 'Ming?'

Martin nodded and raised his right hand. A magnificent carbon-fibre-compound bow, a complex series of pulleys and balancing weights, appeared in it. He conjured an arrow, nocked it, and raised the bow. 'Simone will win another ten dollars,' he said as he loaded the arrowhead with shen energy, and let the arrow fly.

We were rewarded with another volley of bullets, which John absorbed again.

Martin summoned another arrow. He took aim, filled the arrow with energy, and fired.

'Incoming,' John said, and the ground trembled.

Martin passed the bow to John and took True Form: a sea turtle, four metres long, that floated slightly above the ground.

'Three,' John said.

I changed to True Form as well.

John conjured an arrow and shot at the Gates, using the left-handed bow with his usual flawless skill.

'Nice,' he said. 'You can hold the draw forever with this. These modern materials are so light for so much power.'

'Great for sniping, but too slow for battle,' Martin said, his flippers swaying.

The three stone demons approached us and Martin swam through the air to meet them, with John walking next to him as an escort. Martin raised his front end, bit the head off one of the demons, and vacuumed the demon essence into himself. He dismantled the rest of the demon and spat the stones away.

I joined him, dismantling the second demon while he started work on the third.

There was another volley of bullets and John dealt with them.

'How many more can you do?' John said, aiming another arrow at the top of the Gates.

'I think about three or four at the most,' Martin said. 'They taste *awful*.'

'All right,' John said, and lowered the bow. 'Let's go.'

He took a couple of steps forward, put his hand on the back of my head, and the Gates disappeared.

* * *

We sat together at the head of the U-shaped table in the war room on the Mountain. I checked my phone: three missed calls with no caller ID and no messages, which was supposedly impossible on one of Gold's specials. It was already five minutes past the time that John had asked his children to attend. I shot a wry glance at him and he shrugged.

A woman in her mid-sixties entered, round and tiny in black slacks and a dark blue silk jacket. She looked very much like the female human form the Turtle used when it wanted to avoid attention. She stood just inside the door and stared at us for a moment.

'It's all right, Grace,' I said gently. 'Come on in.'

She jumped as if she'd been stung and fell to one knee. 'Xuan Tian Shang Di.'

John, that was unnecessary. She's your daughter!

I didn't do anything; she remembered herself.

'You don't need to kneel,' I said, still gentle. 'He's your father. Come in and sit.'

Mother, actually, John said, and I glared at him. He shrugged again.

'You summoned me, Highness?' Grace said without rising, her head still bowed.

John stood so he could see her. 'Rise. Come and sit. This is not formal.'

She stood gracefully — she moved like someone much younger than she appeared — and sat, without looking at us, in a chair as far away as possible from John.

John sat. I rose, and the woman flinched. I went around the table and leaned on it next to her.

'How are you, Grace?' I said. 'You were under that stone's influence for a long time — is everything back to normal yet? Do you need anything?'

'My family were so glad to see me back,' she said.

A thirty-year-old woman came in. She was small but muscular and obviously trained in the Arts. She came to me and put her arm around my shoulders, saying with warmth, 'Emma. It's good to see you.'

Grace hissed under her breath and gestured with her head towards John.

The other woman squeaked and quickly fell to one knee. 'Xuan Tian Shang Di.'

John stood to acknowledge her. 'Rise.'

Both of them shot to their feet.

A young man walked in, saw John, and backed out again.

'All right, enough of this,' I said. I turned to John, who was still standing and looking bemused. 'You,' I jabbed my finger at him, 'disappear until I have everybody rounded up, and then come back in as something small and *not at all scary.*'

'Define "not at all scary".'

'Piss. Off!'

He raised his hands. 'Okay, okay.' He disappeared.

'I cannot believe you just did that,' Grace said with wonder, looking at where John had been standing.

'He does it deliberately, I swear,' I said, and stormed out to find the young man.

Fifteen people were standing in the courtyard and talking softly together. The air was full of the sharp scent of their anxiety.

'Hi, everyone,' I said loudly, and they turned and fell quiet. 'Thanks for coming. Lord Xuan's left the room. Please come inside and I'll tell you what's involved.'

They all hesitated, some moving from foot to foot with discomfort.

'Seriously,' I said, 'I threw him out. So come in and meet your brothers and sisters, and I'll explain why he asked you to come.'

They looked at each other, then a couple of young women went into the room, and the rest followed.

I went in last and stood at the head of the table. 'The reason we've asked you here is because you're the only ones who can retake the Gates of Heaven,' I began, and they listened silently.

About halfway through my talk, John appeared at the back of the room in his normal male middle-aged human form. He leaned on the wall and crossed his arms over his chest. Fortunately I had them so engrossed they weren't aware of his arrival.

'Any questions?' I said when I was finished.

Nobody spoke.

'Somebody ask me a question, please. I'm sure there are details I haven't covered.'

They still didn't say anything.

'Okay, I'll ask one myself. Miss Donahoe, who designs your clothes?' I sat on the table and crossed my legs. 'I'm glad you asked — I've been wanting to share my fashion and beauty tips for a while now. When I'm not in my sexy Mountain uniform, my eclectic fashion sense comes from Kmart. My complex daily beauty regime mostly consists of soap and water —' One of the women made a soft sound of frustration and I nodded to acknowledge her. 'Or Mena could ask me a worthwhile question.'

'You said they'd be shooting at us, but Lord Xuan would shield us,' Mena said. 'How much danger will we be in? I'm married to a stone, we have two human children together, and my husband's disappeared. How dangerous is this?'

'I won't pretend that you will be completely safe,' John said, and they all turned towards him. He strode around the table and stood next to me. 'I will be there to protect you, but if something unforeseen emerges — such as Western hybrid demons — there still may be risk.'

'These children need me,' Mena said. 'I'm all they have.'

'Then don't go,' he said. 'Up to five of you could leave right now and the mission would not be compromised. We had a test run and nobody was injured. The snipers can't hit you, and you will be destroying the stone hybrids, which don't fight back.'

She sat silently watching him, her mouth in a determined line.

'I must also warn you that if you have strong water alignment, you won't be able to see them,' John said. 'I can't. So if you're very strongly aligned — if both your parents are turtles, for example — then it might be best if you sit this one out.'

'Not being able to see them shouldn't be a major issue for a good practitioner,' one of the men said.

'Very true; and I can guide you,' John said. 'So this is your choice: stay or go. If you don't want to come, leave the room now. You will suffer no penalty, and I thank you for your attendance today.'

Mena, the single mother, still sat with her mouth in a grim line, but didn't say anything. Another woman fidgeted, but went still when John turned his attention to her.

'If you're not comfortable with this, then just say the word and you can go,' I said to Mena.

She shifted again, and looked away.

'Okay,' I said, and raised my hand behind me without looking away from Mena. 'You. Out.'

'Oh, come *on*, Emma,' John said with exasperation. 'This is *my* war room!'

I waved at him again, still focused on Mena. 'Out.'

'Humph,' he said, and there was a change in the air when he disappeared.

Grace giggled.

I looked around at everybody. 'Who wants out?'

Nobody moved.

'Mena, you don't want to do this,' I said. 'You can go.'

She didn't shift.

I sighed with exasperation. 'All right.' I looked down at the list in front of me and read out ten names. 'Everybody else can go.'

A couple of people rose and went out, obviously relieved.

'Mena, you weren't on the list,' I said.

'I want to fight them,' Mena said.

'What about your kids?'

'He was their *father*,' she said, distraught. 'I loved him. So many stones are gone. I know the demons took him, and they tortured him and experimented on him …' She wiped her eyes with a trembling hand. 'He's probably dead. And I want to make them *pay*! I want to grab those bastards in my mouth and I want to *eat* them. I want to take them apart and I want to destroy them.' The anguish was gone from her voice, replaced with cold fury. 'I'm coming with you.'

'No,' I said. 'Let someone else take vengeance for you. As you said, your children need you.'

'I'll bring a dead demon rock back for you,' Grace said. 'I promise.'

Mena looked from Grace to me, then nodded. 'Thank you. I will throw it into the deepest ocean in the farthest seas.'

'Last chance. Anybody who doesn't want to come, you don't have to,' I said. 'You can leave now.'

One of the middle-aged turtle Shen rose, nodded to me, and left.

'Twelve remaining,' I said. 'Good. We won't have to eat so many of these bastards that it makes us sick. Does anybody want to say anything before I let Lord Xuan back in?'

'*Let* him in?' someone said with amusement.

'Let's do this,' Grace said with menace.

You can come back, we're ready to go. Twelve of them.

Thank you, my dear lady, for giving me permission to re-enter my own damn conference room.

Weapons of choice when we're back from the Gates.

About time, he said with satisfaction, and reappeared with a smug smile on his face.

* * *

We arrived at the lawn behind the Gates of Heaven building, and stopped just out of range of the snipers. All of us were in reptile form: eight turtles and four snakes, not including both of John's reptiles and myself. A squad of Meredith's finest energy archers were with us.

This is the first time I have seen so many of my reptilian children together, John said. *Thank you for bringing me this opportunity.*

I was thinking of holding a reunion for all of you — I began.

And then you discovered that with the nature of our loose family bonds, nobody would show and it would be a waste of time, he said.

Yeah. Can you remember their names? I can't recognise anybody in this form.

Not even in human form.

Damn.

'Hold formation here,' John said. He rose above the ground and drifted towards the Gates, the Serpent's head writhing above the Turtle's shell.

The grass was greener and more lush closer to the Gates building; fertilised by the blood that had flowed there a scarce few weeks ago.

There was a flurry of gunshots from the top of the wall, and everybody hit the ground.

I have them, John said, and we all carefully stood again.

John's True Form reappeared next to me. His two reptiles separated, and the Turtle grew to five metres across.

'Archers on my shell,' he said.

The archers climbed up onto his shell, their faces a mix of bewilderment and concern. When they were all sitting, he gently rose into the air, with Meredith flying next to him on one side and the Serpent on the other.

'The rest of you wait here,' he said, and floated towards the Gates.

There was another volley of gunshots, but the bullets never reached us. We were too far back to see the archers fire, but the glowing arrowheads were clearly visible as they arched from John's shell towards the Gates. There was a reduced round of gunfire — obviously some of the snipers had been taken out — and an answering volley of arrows.

A single shot rang out.

'Incoming!' John shouted, and his Turtle plummeted towards the ground and landed next to us. 'Everybody off,' he ordered. 'Continue to fire at the snipers — they're on their way, protected by the stone demons. They're —'

The fake stone elementals stepped off the top of the Gates building, fragmented into piles of rocks on the ground, then collected themselves and headed towards us, faceless and menacing.

The archers fired arrows at the snipers hiding behind the walking demons, but there were still bullets for John to catch.

When the stone demons were ten metres away, I led the charge towards them. John hovered above us and took out the snipers with energy, aided by the archers who continued to pick them off with arrows.

I rushed up to one of the demons, dismantled it, and looked around. The other reptiles were more hesitant, but they quickly had the hang of it. An occasional shot rang out but John dealt with them. His Serpent dipped out of the air, picked up one of the humanoid snipers, and threw it at the wall of the Gates, where it exploded.

The reptiles had demolished about ten of the stone demons. They didn't fight back; they didn't seem to be intelligent or self-aware, they were just animated piles of rock. In perfect unison, they turned and walked away, heading down the hill away from the Gates. The reptiles followed, chasing them down to destroy them.

'Hold,' John said, boosted by telepathy. 'Don't follow. Come back. We've achieved our goal.'

The demon snipers continued to take shots at us from behind the stones as they retreated. The reptiles hesitated, then came back to us, some with obvious reluctance.

One of the snakes struggled at the rear with a large stone in her mouth. It was Grace, fulfilling her promise to Mena. A demon sniper took aim at her back and fired. It missed her, and she screamed with frustration through a mouthful of stone and spun to go after it.

'Stop!' I shouted. 'They're retreating. Let them go!'

The sniper raised its weapon to fire at Grace again, and one of our archers took aim at the sniper.

'No!' John and I shouted in unison, but it was too late.

The arrow sang through the air as the shot was fired. Grace dodged the bullet — snakes could move incredibly fast — and moved into the path of the arrow. It went through the back of her neck.

'No!' I shouted again, and ran to her, the other reptiles following.

'Stop right there!' John roared with the force of an imperative, and we halted. 'Meredith, stand guard. Everybody else, *back*.'

John recombined, took human form, and ran in to collect Grace. He picked her up, tossed her over his shoulder, and carried her back to us. We gathered around her as he laid her on the grass. The arrow was stuck in her serpent throat, in the back and out the front, and possibly through her spine or even the base of her brain.

'Please, you have to save her,' a young archer said, his face pale with concern. 'I shot her. I *shot* her! I'm here to protect the Celestial and I hurt one of our own.'

'It's all right,' Grace said. Her breath came in short wheezes and faded. 'I'm really cold. Why is it so cold?'

'Grace,' John said, softly and urgently, 'you must stay as snake. Don't change to human.' He looked up at me. 'Emma, help her to stay in snake form.'

'Can you heal her?' I said.

'Yes, but the arrow has to come out first. Grace, stay very still, and don't change to human. Emma, help her. Meredith, stand by with pain relief for when she changes back.'

'Something for the pain!' Grace gasped.

'After we pull the arrow out,' Meredith said. 'I can't do anything while you're a snake.'

I put my hands on either side of Grace's head and assisted her to stay in serpent form. It was a struggle with so much damage. Her body wanted to change to human to avoid the injuries from the arrow.

'Quickly, John,' I said. 'She can't hold it.'

Meredith put her hands on mine and both of us worked to keep her as a snake. John snapped the arrowhead off where it came out of her neck, and she screamed as the shaft moved inside her.

'Grace, you have to hold it,' I said. 'Don't change!'

We put more effort into keeping her in serpent form, but she slipped away from us. Her scales disappeared and her body stretched. Her face morphed to human.

'John, do it quickly!'

He grasped the shaft of the arrow and pulled it out of her neck, and she screamed again, now completely human. John tossed the arrow aside and shimmered into combined True Form. The Serpent put its snout against Grace where she lay, naked and pale, on the grass. John's dark healing energy hovered over Grace but didn't go into her.

'Too late,' he said. 'The arrow was in her spine, and when she changed it went into her brain. The change to human killed her.'

'You can cure anything!' I said, putting my hands on her chest to perform CPR, hoping that I wasn't squeezing too hard.

He lifted his head and spoke softly. 'I can't cure death.'

'Our only loss in the mission and it's from friendly fire,' I said, leaning back and wiping my eyes. 'We don't do friendly fire on the Celestial. We have eyes in the sky, we have telepathic communication. We're better than this!'

'It is the first in a while,' John said sadly, changing back to human and catching the young archer as he fell, stricken with guilt. He passed him to Meredith. 'First of many.'

He raised his head and concentrated.

Guan Yu appeared on the grass next to us and looked down at Grace's body. 'She will be given full hero's honours.' He looked around, then fell to one knee. 'I thank you all for returning the Gates to the Heavenly Host.'

The archer was sobbing, his head in Meredith's chest as she held him.

Guan Yu rose. 'Are they all definitely gone?'

John concentrated. 'All gone.'

'I will need replacement guards.'

'You may borrow some Elites from Er Lang,' John said, and Guan Yu disappeared.

John listened for a moment, then nodded. 'Er Lang's complaining that we just gave away all of his remaining Elites. I've told him he can hold an evaluation on the main court tomorrow morning.'

'Our students aren't ready for that,' I said.

'They never are. Meredith, escort the rest home,' John said.

He took my hand, and everything disappeared.

4

John, Er Lang and I stood at the edge of the main court on the Mountain and watched the Disciples run through the weapons drills in perfect synchronicity, with Liu at the front leading them.

Er Lang crossed his arms over his green armour and nodded. 'Good. I was worried you'd keep the training focused on disablement. It's obvious these are trained to kill.'

'Of course,' John said. 'The training isn't about technique any more.'

'You've brought them up to speed remarkably quickly.'

The God of War shrugged. It was what he did.

Er Lang leaned around John and spoke to me from under his green burnished war helmet. 'How's your training proceeding? There's a distinct possibility that the Jade Emperor will order you to join us in the Elites.'

'He'd better not,' John and I said in unison.

'I'm too new an Immortal and close to useless,' I added. 'I can't fly safely unless I'm in snake form, and I can't teleport at all. I did it a couple of times before I was Raised but now the skill eludes me. It's driving me nuts.'

'The Jade Emperor's probably blocked you from learning until after the wedding, so you can't change your mind and make a run for it,' Er Lang said.

'That makes sense,' John said. 'Decided yet?'

Er Lang ran his eye over the students. 'None of these are good enough.'

'I know that,' John said, his voice low, 'but you need to take some anyway. The Jade Emperor must be guarded.'

'Are they genuine volunteers?'

'They are.'

'Do you have sources other than the Earthly for Mountain cadets?' Er Lang said. 'Has the Tiger provided any Horsemen? Dragons?'

'Horsemen, yes; a good number came here after the fall of the West. We have a few Red Warriors who survived the fall of the South as well.'

'Most of the phoenixes are in the Northern Heavens regrouping for another attempt,' I said. 'They're more focused on winning their volcano back right now.'

'They won't do it,' John said without looking away from the Disciples.

'We know that, but they don't,' Er Lang said.

'What?' I said. 'How do you know?'

'We've seen it,' John said. 'They won't re-enter the South for at least three months, when this is all resolved. They will return to the volcano either in triumph or in chains.'

Er Lang nodded agreement.

'Then tell them to stop messing around and join the defence of the Celestial,' I said.

'Hope is important in these dark times,' Er Lang said. 'The Emperor will not take that away from them. I'll have the fifteen top physical workers and the top two energy.'

'Make it thirteen and two. The bottom two physical workers won't be good enough,' John said.

'None of them are good enough.'

'To survive your training.'

'Oh.' Er Lang hesitated, then said, 'Yeah, you're right. But it's not enough.'

'Nobody has enough,' I said.

* * *

30

Leo drove me to the two-storey house on Shek O peninsula that used to be a happy residence for David and Bridget Hawkes and their boys. The new staff were all demons.

The maid at the front door smiled and welcomed us in. Bridget was sitting stiff and nervous in the living room, while the David copy lounged on one of the armchairs.

He rose when I entered and saluted me; and I saluted him back. He gestured for me to sit in the other armchair, and Leo positioned himself behind me.

'Before we start,' I said, 'I'm holding a poison capsule in my mouth, that's why my pronunciation isn't perfect. Try to take me and I'm gone.'

'You sound like Leo,' the David copy said, grinning. 'Retarded.'

Bridget turned to him to tell him off for the offensive remark, then changed her mind and shook her head.

He's just trying to get a rise out of you, I said, and she jumped.

'None of that,' the David copy said. 'Out loud, or go home.'

'All right.' I leaned over my knees towards Bridget. 'I'm here, Bridget.' I took her hand, and she gasped for breath, trying to hold back the tears. 'Stay strong.'

'Thanks for coming, Emma.' She squeezed my hand and released it. 'I know how dangerous this is for you, but he won't tell me anything and I have to know. You're one of them now, so you must know.' She wiped her eyes with the shaking heel of her hand. 'Will I ever see David again? What's happened to him? The copy won't tell me anything and it's killing me. Please, can you tell me? Will my boys ever see their father again?'

'Oh, is *that* what this is about,' the copy said. 'You didn't need Emma to come for that, I'll answer for you. He's dead and gone, sweetie. We killed him, and you'll never see him again.'

She persisted. 'But what happened to him after that?'

The copy leaned back, crossed his legs and grinned. 'I changed my mind; this will be fun. Go ahead and answer her questions, Emma. Let's see it.'

'Do you remember when David tried to call me "Empress" and it didn't work?' I said to Bridget. 'He couldn't say it?'

'No?'

'Damn. Okay. The Jade Emperor's rulings are unbreakable. If he says I can't talk about something, then I can't talk about it even if I want to. And this includes what happened to David.'

'So where is he?' she said, obviously not hearing a word I'd said.

Hope in these dark times. 'If two people are destined to be together, then nothing will keep them apart.'

'So I have a chance of seeing him again?'

I couldn't look her in the eye. 'Not in this lifetime, Bridget.'

She hesitated, then, 'Perhaps in another lifetime?'

'I can't answer that.'

'I see.' She was silent for a moment, studying me. 'The David demon says you were Raised. They chose to make you an Immortal.'

'That's true,' I said.

The demon grew even more smug as Bridget continued. 'So why didn't anyone Raise David like they Raised you? Why just you?' She leaned forward and her voice filled with venom. 'What's so special about *you*?'

I flinched, and Leo put his hand on my shoulder. 'I can't answer that question either,' I said.

'There is a legend,' Leo said from behind me, 'that those who have spent their lives helping the less fortunate and working to make the world a better place, who have acted nobly and sacrificed much, are Raised to join the Immortals in Heaven.' Bridget opened her mouth to speak, but he interrupted her. 'Any who have lived a life of cruelty and selfishness, whether they are Immortal or not, are sentenced to be punished in Hell. It's ten levels of torture. When you're an Immortal, the torture can last for centuries.'

'That's not really true, is it?' she said.

'If the demons were to gain control of this system, they could hold all Immortals in the Pits and torture them for eternity,' Leo said.

'I don't see what ...' Her voice faded. 'That could happen to you?'

'We're not allowed to talk about it,' Leo said. 'We can share legends but confirm nothing.'

'Thank you,' I said.

He squeezed my shoulder and dropped his voice. 'I've had some practice at this.'

'But David isn't Immortal, he isn't down there being tortured, is he?' Bridget said. 'Oh lord, tell me he isn't Immortal!'

'David isn't Immortal.'

'So what happened to him? You said I'd never see him again in this lifetime.'

My phone rang with the default ringtone. I pulled it out and rejected the call; it had no caller ID.

'Sorry,' I said to Bridget.

'You Celestials make me sick,' the demon said. 'Stop dancing around the words. David's dead. Dead and gone. We threw his body into the ocean and the fish feasted on it. If he was very unlucky, a sea turtle went past and took a bite out of him as well. Hell knows, the Turtle caused him enough misery while the poor bastard was alive.'

Bridget jumped to her feet, sobbing. She ran out of the room and up the stairs.

'Show's over,' the David copy said. 'Go home and enjoy it while it lasts, Emma. If you're nice to the King, he may let you stay in the Heavens with your kids while the Turtle's in the Pits.' He rose and gestured. 'Out.'

Next time, turn your phone off before you speak to the grieving widow, Leo said as he opened the car door for me, checking around us.

I did turn it off before I went in.

He pulled himself behind the wheel. 'It rang when it was turned off?'

I took it out of my pocket and checked it. 'Yeah, and it's still turned off. I don't know what happened. That isn't my usual ringtone. Everything's gone strange on it.'

'You must have sat on the buttons.'

'It's one of Gold's specials. It doesn't have any buttons.'

He shrugged and headed back towards Wan Chai.

* * *

After I'd returned to my office, one of the Dragon's younger sons came to see me. It was Justin. He'd had a two-week relationship with Simone, before they'd quickly called it quits and decided to stay friends.

'Hi, Justin, how's things?' I said. I studied him: his Asian black hair appeared to have gold glints through it. 'You transformed? Congratulations!'

He winced. 'Nope, no transformation. The Archivist is adding me to the records. I'm the only full-blood dragon in history who doesn't transform.'

'How's university?' Then I remembered — all the students had been called up to the safety of the Celestial Plane. 'Sorry. So what are you doing here?'

He saluted me. 'I wish to apply for the position of Mountain demon master, if you will have me.' His face filled with quiet hope. 'Has anyone else applied?'

'Nobody, you can have the job,' I said, and he sagged with disappointment. 'You don't want it? Then don't do it.'

'I've been ordered.'

'Who ordered you?' I said sharply.

'Dad.'

I tried to control the ire in my voice; it wasn't Justin's fault. 'Did he say, "Do the job right this time or don't bother coming back"?'

He stared at me. 'How did you know? Wait.' Sweat broke out on his forehead. 'I will definitely do the job of demon master to the best of my ability, as he has ordered.'

'I'm not talking about demon master,' I said, my voice still sharp. 'He wants you to hook up with Simone.'

He sagged with dismay and wiped his hand over his eyes. 'I really like Simone. But ... not like that, and she feels the same way.' He looked away. 'I'm beginning to wonder if I'm really more into guys than girls. I tried to explain to Dad, and he threw me out and ordered me here.'

'Bastard,' I said under my breath. 'Go back to the East and tell him that the position's already filled.'

'I can't, ma'am. I've been ordered to stay here.'

'Yi Hao!' I yelled at the door.

'Ma'am?'

'Where's the Golden Boy right now?'

Justin squeaked.

'In his lab,' she said.

'Ask him to pop over, please?'

Gold came into the office in human form, accompanied by his child, BJ, who was in her usual teenage girl form. 'Ma'am? I'm awfully busy.'

I gestured towards Justin. 'Son of the Dragon. Postgrad IT student at Todai. He's been called home from the Earthly. Nothing to do, and he can't go back to the East at the moment. He's been working on the Dragon's stone AI. Need an assistant?'

Gold grinned broadly. 'Excellent.'

He turned to Justin and stopped. Justin and BJ were looking at each other as if they were the only people in the world.

'Maybe not,' I said.

'No, it's fine,' Gold said. 'Justin. Justin!'

Justin jumped, then stood and fell to one knee. 'Lord Gold.'

'Cut it out. Stand up. Can you teleport?'

'No, sir,' Justin said, rising. 'Absolutely no supernatural abilities whatsoever.'

Gold shrugged. 'No big issue. Can you carry him?' he asked BJ.

'Let me look,' BJ said.

Justin shivered.

'Yeah,' BJ said.

'Okay, you two, let's go sort out the file servers; and, Justin, you can share what you know about the new bio-storage technology. About time animals were used to store information as well as us stones.'

BJ held her hand out, Justin took it, and they all disappeared.

'You should have given him the job, ma'am, someone needs to do it,' Yi Hao said from her desk. 'There's half-a-dozen gardeners out there right now, standing around because nobody gave them an order to move to the next section.'

'Can you go and tell them?'

She sounded unsure. 'I can try. I was very much smaller than they are. I don't know what I am now.'

'Let me know how it works out — I'd be interested to see.'

'As long as you promise not to make me demon master.'

'You'd be perfect.'

'That's why I need your promise, ma'am.'

Gold and Justin reappeared next to my desk.

'Only if you're sure,' Gold said.

Justin fell to one knee on the other side of the desk, and I had to stand to see him.

'We passed more than fifty demons who are standing parked, doing nothing, and Lord Gold explained the situation to me. You really need a demon master, Lady Emma,' he said.

'Not so much we'll force someone to do it.'

'I volunteer.'

'Denied. Go with Gold.'

'I choose this, ma'am. Gold and BJ can run things. Let me do it.'

It was awfully tempting. 'Are you completely sure?'

He stood. 'I'll take up the post helping Gold with the IT after all this is over and you have a new demon master.'

'Gold?' I said.

'Let him do it. He's right, it needs to be done. BJ and I can handle the tech.'

I sighed with defeat, and Justin dropped his head with a similar emotion.

'Go report to LK Pak, the previous demon master,' I said. 'He will show you everything you need to know. Tell him that he is still to find a permanent replacement for both of you.'

Justin shook his hands in front of his face, obviously unhappy, but determined to do the job.

'I appreciate this, Justin,' I said.

He nodded, and he and Gold went to find LK.

Yi Hao came in and put some papers on my desk. 'It's the right thing to do,' she said as I sat.

'We need to win this, so everybody can be doing something they enjoy rather than something that traumatises them, wrecks their spirit, and could leave them dead.'

'Being demon master won't do that to him.'

'Being a soldier does it to everybody.'

'What about you, ma'am?'

I waved it away. 'All right, it does that to *sane* people, and I hate having to make them experience it.'

'You're doing the best you can, my Lady. It will all be over soon, one way or the other.'

I sighed as a grim foreboding filled me. 'That's what scares me.'

5

I walked through the tent city in the main court of the Northern Celestial Palace. Many of the refugees wore the red of the South or the white of the West: the Tiger's and Phoenix's families, homeless now that the Bastions had fallen. The stars came out above me as I picked my way between the tents, occasionally stopping to share a word of encouragement with the refugees. Many burnt small camp fires for cooking and heat; the late spring air had a chill in the evening. A phoenix in True Form lay on the ground in front of one of the tents, his feathers alight, providing a fire for the white-garbed refugees around him. They talked softly, sharing stories, and nodded grimly to me as I passed.

I reached the gate between the residential and administrative sections. The residential gardens and courtyards were also full of refugees. I turned right and went through a moon gate into the dragon tree courtyard, which contained more tents, then to the Imperial Residence, where the Tiger's more elderly wives were housed. I returned the DVDs I'd borrowed to the living room bookshelves, shared a few quiet words with the gracious wives, then went out, changed to snake, and flew to the Mountain to have dinner with my family in Persimmon Tree Pavilion. I landed near the pavilion and changed back to human to walk the rest of the way.

My eldest nephew, Colin — Jennifer's son, and brother to Andrew who had been kidnapped and tortured by demons — was waiting for me at the entrance with his Immortal stepfather, Greg. Colin had obviously been working out: he was no longer a pudgy teen; he was strong and muscular and moved with grace. He'd had a growth spurt too and was taller than me, with dark hair and eyes from his human father, Leonard.

'Hi, Colin,' I said. 'Is everything okay? You look serious.'

'Can I talk to you before you come in for dinner?' he said. He looked over his shoulder at Greg, who nodded. Colin turned back to me. 'In private.'

'Greg, can you take him to the Residence?' I said. 'There's nobody there.'

Greg nodded, put his hand on Colin's shoulder, and they disappeared. I changed back to snake and flew from Persimmon Tree to the Residence on the other side of the Mountain, again changing to human before I could freak anybody out.

They were waiting at the front door for me, and I guided them into the living room.

'Sit,' I said, gesturing towards the couches.

'No, I want to show you something,' Colin said.

'What?'

'Greg?' Colin said.

I watched them, bewildered, as Greg summoned a short Chinese-style sword and passed it to Colin.

'Oh, no,' I said. 'Not happening.'

'Watch this,' Colin said.

He went through the open doors into the Residence's central courtyard, then around to the training room. I followed him, and leaned on a wooden pillar next to the door.

'If you're planning what I think you are,' I began.

'Just watch,' Greg said from behind me.

Colin began a Wudang level-four short-sword set — the highest level — and I watched with admiration that quickly turned to alarm. He wasn't just good, he was brilliant.

'Who taught you this?'

'I did,' Greg said. 'Watch.'

Colin moved with deadly grace, performing the set close to perfection. His technique was nearly flawless.

'Holy shit,' I said under my breath.

As he reached the end of the set, he concentrated, generated chi, and loaded the sword with it, making it vibrate and glow. The weapon made a deep bass thrum that I could feel through the floor, and his hair floated from the static. He had generated much more chi than could be expected from a human his age.

'Holy *shit*,' I said even more softly.

I sent an image of Colin to John, who was in the Celestial Palace with the Generals.

Not surprising, considering his bloodlines, John said. *I wonder if the other boys are as talented as this? They're your family, Western serpents, after all.*

Colin reabsorbed the chi and his hair fell. He turned to me and put the sword away. 'Okay, you've seen what I can do. Now use me.'

'Colin, I can't —'

'Aunty Emma, I'm eighteen in three months. I'm the oldest of all of us. Andrew can do it — Greg's taught him as well — and it's helped him recover. Mark's too broken by what he went through and no amount of training will help him. David's showing talent, but he's only fifteen. I'm the oldest, I'm nearly of age, and ...' He fell to one knee and held the sword horizontally towards me. 'I would be honoured if you would accept my blade in the coming battle. I want to protect our family and avenge my brother and my cousin.'

My throat filled. 'Oh, Colin.'

'Don't you dare say no,' he said softly. 'I know exactly how talented I am — I could end up like you. There's a chance I can change to snake as well. I love the training more than anything I've ever done before — I feel like I was made for it. I want to protect our family and I'm an asset that you can't refuse.'

I wiped my eyes. 'Damn, Colin, I am so proud of you.'

He smiled shyly. 'Really?'

'Your mother and grandmother will kill me.' I looked up at Greg. 'Jennifer will divorce you.'

'She's too attached to being a Celestial Princess to ever divorce me,' Greg said without looking away from Colin, his expression full of pride. 'It's been an honour to train this young man, but he's already learnt all I can teach him …'

'What? You used to be the Tiger's Number One. No way.'

'Seriously. He needs to move up to training with the Dark Lord.'

'Please ask him to train me,' Colin said.

'Up you get, lad,' I said. I linked my hands behind my back. 'Do Andrew and David want to learn from us as well?'

'Who's "us"?' Colin said. 'If you mean Uncle John, absolutely! All of us do.'

You didn't tell them? Greg said.

I shook my head without looking away from Colin. *I'd prefer they never know. It's done and finished and I'm separate. No need to torture my family with what might have been.*

How much of his knowledge of the Arts did you gain? Greg said.

I will never be one with the Arts as he is, and my human brain doesn't seem capable of holding all of his knowledge, but the answer to your question is: a great deal. Don't tell my family.

Wait … do the family know you're Immortal?

I sighed and my shoulders slumped. *That will be hard. It's tempting to hide it completely from them — to age myself as the years pass and then pretend to die when I'm old enough — but I cannot live a lie. I hope I don't lose them when they discover that I've attained Immortality, something they probably never will.*

Now you know why so many of us disappear for a hundred years after we're Raised, he said.

I nodded. *But I don't regret coming back. I am needed.*

'You're talking silently — I didn't know you could do that,' Colin said. 'Who are you talking to? Uncle John? Can he train us?' He lunged towards the door, then stopped. 'Can I bring the other guys to learn off him?'

'None of you are of age yet,' I said. 'You need your parents' permission.'

'And don't look at me, I don't count,' Greg said.

'Dammit,' Colin said under his breath.

'Let's go and talk to your mother now,' I said. 'Then you can come back to the training room tomorrow morning, all three of you. I will teach you, not John; that will be much less scary for your families. Tell them that you'll learn from me for fitness and therapy, and don't mention that you wish to fight just yet. We'll deal with that when you're of age and can make that decision for yourself.'

Colin screwed up his face and opened his mouth to protest that he wanted to learn from the Dark Lord.

'Before you say anything,' Greg said, his voice full of warning, 'I think there's something you should know. Lady Emma, may I tell him?'

'Share the information with the boys only,' I said. 'I'll follow to Persimmon Tree in about ten minutes and we can talk to their parents over dinner. If they accept me training the lads, I'll see them back here first thing tomorrow morning.'

'Wah, Emma,' Greg said.

'It will pass with time.' I hesitated. 'I think.'

'Does it worry you?'

I shrugged. 'I'm still me. There's some of me in him too. Sometimes he loses his temper and sounds Australian.'

'Now that's something I'd really like to hear,' Greg said with humour. 'Come on, Colin, I have a story to tell you.'

'Don't tell my parents or sisters!' I said. 'They really don't need to know.'

He waved back at me without turning around.

'And thanks, Greg,' I added more softly.

He nodded and guided Colin out.

More students like you. Excellent, John said with relish. *I wonder which other youngsters we can round up to teach. How old is Greg and Jen's little boy? Fathered by a powerful son of the Tiger, mothered by one of you Western Serpents ...*

Only three years old!

Perfect. Are they planning to have a second one? If we could use modern medical technology to overcome the obvious problem you and your sisters have with carrying girls to term —

A breeding program? I said with fierce distaste.

He was silent for a moment, then, *And all it entails, I know. It's just that you're so damn powerful, Emma. The females of your line are much more gifted.*

And dangerous. Let's work carefully with these boys as we bring out their talents, because their demon nature will emerge and they'll need to control it.

This will be great fun, he said with satisfaction. *I hope I'm free to join you tomorrow morning.*

I shook my head and walked over to Persimmon Tree Pavilion.

* * *

Thirty-Eight had made a modern Western meal for the family and we all ate in the Pavilion's dining room, crammed around the ten-seater round table. Persimmon Tree only had three small bedrooms, so it was a crush with all the family. Two of the boys slept in the living room on futons that were rolled up during the day.

Jen and Greg sat with Colin and Andrew, her boys, and the little one they'd had together, Matthew, who stubbornly refused a high chair. Alan and Amanda's boys, Mark and David, were constantly needling each other. The boys had grown so much: Colin was close on eighteen, Andrew and Mark were both sixteen, and David had just turned fifteen and would probably have another growth spurt in the near future. My parents were glowing with good health and appeared younger than when they'd arrived in the Heavens; a side effect of living in the Celestial purity.

I relished the feeling of having everybody back with me; I'd missed them terribly while they'd been in hiding. Luckily they hadn't found it difficult to move to the Mountain while the Earthly was being overrun by demons; and they appreciated that they were safe with us. Knowledge that their friends on the Earthly were being replaced and that they themselves were a huge target was deeply distressing for them, but they kept a brave face in front of the children.

My father raised his pasta-laden fork and waved it at me. 'What's this about training the boys?'

'We want to learn!' Colin said, and Andrew nodded fierce agreement.

'I'll teach them myself, for exercise and health and energy,' I said.

'Rubbish,' Jennifer said. 'Colin wants to fight demons. He's been asking Greg forever to teach him.'

'It's your choice whether I fight demons, Mum,' Colin said. He lowered his voice. 'But when I'm eighteen and an adult, it's my choice.'

'There's too much of this violent snake thing in all of them,' my mother said. 'If I'd had the opportunity when I was a girl, I would have jumped at it as well. I think it's part of how we're made.'

'Don't try to stop me, Mum,' Colin said into his food.

'We'll talk about it later,' Jennifer said with quiet menace.

'And, Emma,' my father waved his fork again, 'you're Immortal and didn't tell us.'

I choked on my pasta.

'Does this mean that when you go out to fight, we won't have to worry about you any more?' my mother said. 'If you're killed by those horrible things, you'll just come back?'

'Uh ... yes,' I said.

'Good,' she said, and returned to cutting up little Matthew's chicken. 'About time. That's a huge relief. I swear, worrying about you has made my hair go completely grey.'

'Exactly,' my father said. 'And, Emma ...?'

'Yes?' I said, still pleasantly stunned at their reaction.

'When we found out you'd become Immortal, John offered to show us the methods you people use to gain Immortality.'

'*You people?*' Greg said with mock horror.

'Shut up, Greg,' Jen said without looking at him. 'You're one of them too.'

Greg buried his embarrassment in a deep drink of tea and filled their cups again.

'Anyway, John said that he'd be glad to teach us the physical alchemy or whatever-it-is techniques that you've used,' my father said.

'Uh ... good?' I said, not sure where this was going.

'How long can you hold horse stance?' my father said.

'Indefinitely,' I said, thoroughly confused. 'I meditate in horse stance sometimes.'

'Whoa,' Colin said quietly.

'Before you were Immortal too?'

'Uh ... yes. I mean, it was a complete bit— pain to learn. In more ways than one. It's unbelievably hard to gain that sort of strength. The training John put me through was non-stop suffering sometimes. But it was worth it in the end.'

'I knew it,' my father said triumphantly, and stabbed his vegetarian pasta. 'John said that horse stance is one of the most basic martial arts stances, and if we could learn to hold it indefinitely, then he could teach us the techniques to learn Immortality. But we have to learn horse stance first.'

'That makes sense,' I said.

'We tried it. Too hard,' my mother said. 'So painful!'

'It hurt too much, not worth it,' my father said.

My mother nodded and turned back to her own food.

'Oh,' I said, and sent a silent flow of information and gratitude to John.

Don't mention it, but it's completely true, he said. *You were willing to put up with the agony to learn the Arts. If someone wants to gain Immortality, they have to learn that it's not just a matter of sitting comfortably on a tatami mat looking stoned.*

I sent him a mental image of himself on a tatami mat looking stoned; it was how he looked when he meditated. He returned the image with me added next to him, my mouth hanging open. We exchanged a short burst of transferred images, each adding more and more vacancy to the other's expression, until I realised that my parents were staring at me.

'Sorry, I know, very rude, I'll stop.' I returned to my pasta. 'I'm glad you're all happy and safe.'

* * *

The next morning my entire family arrived outside the front door of the Imperial Residence.

'Our parents want to see what you do with us,' Colin said.

'I don't want to learn, but I'd like to watch,' Mark said.

'I want to learn!' Matthew said, his tiny face fierce.

'Okay,' I said. 'Let's go inside and you can watch for a while to make sure that everybody's happy.'

I guided them into the training room, with its gymnastic mats on the floor. Its third wall was the stone spine of the Mountain. My family sat to one side to watch, and I placed the three boys — Colin, his brother Andrew, and their younger cousin David — standing in front of me.

'David, can you do energy like Colin and Andrew?' I said.

'Wait, what?' Jennifer said loudly.

'They can do energy?' my mother said.

Thanks a LOT, Emma, Greg said into my head.

'I want to see them do energy!' Matthew shouted.

'Uh, I've been teaching them,' Greg said, rubbing the back of his neck. Jen was looking daggers at him.

'We asked him, Mum,' Colin said. 'It was my idea, and we all enjoyed doing it together, and he says we're some of the most talented students he's —'

'He's ever had — yes, I know,' Jennifer said.

She sighed with feeling, and opened her mouth to say something, but Colin interrupted her by loading his sword with chi and raising the glowing weapon. She stared silently at him, her mouth half-open.

'I will learn from the Dark Lord to be the strongest defender I can,' he said, his voice echoing with the energy, 'so that what happened to Andrew and Mark never happens to any member of our family ever again.'

Matthew cheered and clapped his hands.

Jennifer watched her glowing son, eyes wide, and when she spoke her voice was soft with awe. 'Okay.'

Colin nodded and released the energy, then turned back to me with his sword still raised in a ready position.

My phone rang in the pocket of my black Mountain uniform.

I took it out; another call with no caller ID. I answered it. 'Hello?' Nothing but static. I shrugged and put it away, with a mental note to talk to Gold about it.

'You can do energy as well?' I asked Andrew.

'I can, but Greg says I need more training to control it,' Andrew said.

David shook his head. 'I can't.'

'I want to learn!' Matthew shouted, and Jen hushed him.

John's Serpent walked into the room in female human form. She was taller than the Turtle's human form, nearly two metres, and lither and more athletic, but with the same dark eyes and sculpted face.

'How about I take the older boys, and Emma can teach little Matthew the beginnings of the modified energy set?' she said to my family.

They stared at her, confused.

'This is ...' I dropped my voice. 'Geez. Will it always be this hard to explain? This is the Serpent part of John. Where's the Turtle, John?' I asked her.

'Back at the office signing the orders for the supplies from the Earthly,' John said. 'Our guests are eating more than the Celestial can provide for them.' She smiled around at the family. 'But I want to see what the kids can do.'

My father pointed at John, then dropped his hand when he remembered. 'This is John? Half of John? How does that work?'

'Jonathina,' my mother said with amusement.

'I can only do it when the two halves of me aren't doing anything terribly complicated,' John said, coming to me and putting her arm around my shoulder. She kissed the top of my head to my nephews' fascinated horror. 'The Turtle's just signing Imperial Orders so I should be able to concentrate.' She smiled down at me. 'Start teaching Matthew the modified set. The Turtle's bringing Jade's and Gold's children to learn it as well.' She concentrated for a moment. 'Only five more requisitions to do, then I'll be right over.'

'You wanted the God of Martial Arts to teach you. You have her,' I said to the boys.

I turned to my sisters. 'Does Matthew have your permission to learn a modified tai chi set, Jen?'

'Out of the way, Emma,' John said, and I moved closer to the rest of my family. She summoned some training swords for the boys and handed them out.

'Modified in what way?' Jennifer said.

'It's simpler, which makes it easier for littlies to learn, and it takes advantage of the fact that small kids are so flexible. It's a way for them to keep that flexibility and gain strength without stressing their growing bodies too much, and at the same time gives them a good basis for energy work.'

'I want to learn!' Matthew shouted. 'I can do energy too!'

'Greg?' Jen said, obviously confused.

'It's not fighting, it's more like gymnastics. Really good for him,' Greg said. He put his hands under Matthew's arms and lifted him to his feet. 'Go and learn some kung fu.'

'Yay!' Matthew said, and ran to stand in front of me. He took a basic horse stance, thumping his feet on the mats, and put his little fists at his waist. 'I'm ready to learn!'

'Oh, he's so adorable,' my mother said.

'Don't start yet, Emma, I'm just outside,' the Serpent called from the other side of the room. 'Centre line, Colin! Tidy that up.'

The Turtle entered in male human form, with Gold and Amy's twins and Jade's three dragon daughters, also all in human form. The dragons were young teens, and Little Jade and Richie were both four, slightly older than Matthew.

The sight of Gold and Amy's kids coming to learn from us hit a memory inside me like a bell and my heart leapt.

The Turtle smiled into my eyes. 'I thought you'd react that way.'

He put his hands on the shoulders of the two smaller children. 'Jade and Richie, stand with Aunty Emma and Matthew; and, dragons, go to the other me.'

The Serpent saw their confusion. 'I mean me,' she said.

The three dragon sisters moved in front of the Serpent, and the boys made way for them. The girls were very similar in appearance to each other: slim, and taller than the boys, with oval faces from their mother and elegant grace from their father, the Blue Dragon.

The Serpent pointed at each kid in front of her in turn. 'Colin, Andrew, David, Emma's nephews. This is Frannie —'

'*Princess* Frangipani,' Frannie said, and straightened the collar of her black Mountain uniform.

John nodded. 'Princess Frangipani, Princess Jacaranda and Princess Bauhinia.'

'I'm Jackie and this is Hinnie,' Jacaranda said. 'Don't mind Frannie, she's stuck on the princess thing.' She shook hands with each of the boys in turn. 'Pleased to meet you.'

'Likewise,' Colin said. 'You don't look human … I mean, you look more powerful …' His voice trailed off. 'Sorry.'

'We're dragons,' Frannie said. 'Our mother is Princess Jade and our father is the Emperor of the East.' She lifted her chin. 'You don't need to bow.'

'Cut it out, Frannie,' Hinnie said. 'Yeah, we're dragons, and the Dark Lord and Lady Emma kindly invited us along for training.' She nodded to the Serpent. 'We're honoured by your attention, my Lady.' She spoke out of the corner of her mouth. 'And we line up now and *behave*, Frannie.'

'Boys in front, you're shorter,' John said, and the six of them made two lines. 'Now stay put, I'm merging. You'll like this.'

'Ooh, cool,' Hinnie said softly. 'We'll see the Xuan Wu!'

The Turtle raised his hand. 'Nobody move while I merge.'

'Give me a minute,' the Turtle and Serpent said in unison.

They moved to the far end of the room, and took True Form. The Serpent was a black snake four metres long; the Turtle was three metres long and two high. The Serpent coiled around the Turtle with its head facing the Turtle's tail, then turned its head to face the Turtle's. The Turtle looked back at it, the two heads moved together, and there was a flash of darkness as they became an immensely cold black hole in reality, then took John's male human form, taller and leaner now that he'd combined with the Serpent.

Matthew squealed and ran to his mother. He stood leaning on her and watched John for a moment, wide-eyed, then ran back to Little Jade and Richie and took the horse stance again, his face determined.

John shook his shoulders out, then went to the older kids and passed more small training swords around. 'All right, guard up, and let's start again from the beginning.'

'And I thought he was strange before,' Jennifer said softly.

Amanda's eyes were wide. Our eyes met and she opened her mouth to say something, then closed it again and shook her head, blushing.

Yes, I said to her.

She jumped, then her eyes went wider.

Yes, really. But he's usually two hot men when he does it for me.

An evil grin spread across her face. 'Tell me more later,' she mouthed silently.

I nodded, smiling back, and returned my attention to the small children. 'Okay, everybody, you see how Matthew's standing?'

'Call me Leo!' Matthew shouted. 'I'm a lion like Lord Leo. I want to be just like him when I grow up!'

I glanced at Jen, who smiled and nodded. Greg's face was full of pride.

'It's quite possible,' I said. 'Your dad is a tiger, after all. Okay, everybody, let's see you stand like little Leo here.'

'We're dragons,' Little Jade said as she moved into a similar position, her fists on her waist. 'Our mum's a dragon.'

'I'm a lion. I'm stronger!' Matthew said.

'Are lions or dragons stronger?' Richie asked me.

'Stay in that position, that's good,' I said. 'Strength doesn't come from what you are, but from the effort you put into it. The strongest one will be the one who does the most training.'

'That'll be me,' Little Jade said with conviction.

'We'll see,' I said. 'Now. Left hand out, like this. No, the other one, Matthew.'

'Leo!' Matthew shouted.

'Okay, Leo, other hand. Good. Now the right one. Left fist back to where it started at your waist, Richie, not waving around in the air. Turn it over, Jade. Well done.'

I didn't notice when the rest of my family went out and left us to it.

6

I greeted Michael with a hug as he entered the war room, and reached up to kiss him on the cheek, embarrassing him horribly. 'How's Clarissa?'

'She's fine, but I need to hurry home to her.' He winced. 'She had another small procedure done in the medical centre yesterday and I'm caring for her while she recovers.'

'We'll try to make this quick then,' John said.

Michael bobbed his head. 'I appreciate it.'

'I thought she was coming along well and didn't need anything else done,' I said.

'It was just a small procedure. She'll be fine in a few days.'

Understanding hit me. 'Oh, Michael, I'm so sorry. Are you both all right?'

'It's not a big issue.' He wiped one hand over his face. 'She's the important one, and we won't jeopardise her health for anything. It should never have happened anyway, and we'll make sure it never will again.'

'Go back to her when the main strategising is out of the way,' I said. 'Your father can brief you on the rest.'

He nodded. 'Thank you.'

'Is she walking?'

'Not yet.'

'John, should I arrange a time for Clarissa to see the Serpent?'

'Yes,' John said. 'She suffered because of us. We should have done this a long time ago.'

'See the Serpent? Why?' Michael said.

'He is blanking their minds!' I said, frustrated.

'I can't be spending all my time healing every minor injury on the Celestial after being away for forty years,' John said. 'We can offer my healing only to those in the most need.'

'Healing?' Michael said.

'The Jade Emperor's removed it from everybody's consciousness, but the Xuan Wu Serpent can heal anything,' I said.

'I know that, I saw it in Hell,' Michael said. 'Wait, I did know that. He is blanking our minds! What an ass.'

'It's the right thing to do,' John said. 'Emma will contact you when you're home and remind you — because you'll have forgotten by then — to make a time for Clarissa to see me.'

'Thank you,' Michael said. 'I can't believe he did that to us. If I'd known this before, we could have healed Clarissa and saved the baby.'

'Either way you could not have saved the child,' John said. 'The Serpent's healing is too intense for pregnancy. I must be very careful around small children.'

'It's our fault for not thinking of you soon enough,' I said. 'I'm sorry.'

'No, the Serpent's only been back a few weeks, and I'm glad Clarissa has the opportunity to be well again.' Michael lowered his voice with wonder. 'We may have a chance for a family, after all.'

'I'll do my best for you,' John said. 'South and Flute are here, let's do this.'

He gestured for everybody to sit at the war room table. John sat at the head of the table, and I sat next to him on his left, with Martin as Number One on his right. Each Wind had brought their Number One along, and the Dragon had brought both his Number One and the human avatar of the Tree herself.

'Their next target is the East,' John said. 'The Tree floats ten kilometres off the ground on the Celestial; the Palace Under the Sea is a kilometre below the surface on the Earthly. Their first target will probably be the Tree, as it's the Eastern Bastion. I've reviewed both Celestial and Earthly weaponry and there are a variety of ways to take down the Tree, but I may have missed some. We need to be ready for all of them and prepare our defence in advance.'

'Can they bring a human army up through the Gates, even when we still hold them?' the Tiger said.

'As long as the demons hold the South we cannot seal the Gates. With a large enough force they can overrun the Gate defences and bring anything in,' John said.

'Could flyers attack the Tree?' the Phoenix said.

'Too high for them, the air is too thin,' John said. 'Human drones could do it, but they can't carry enough of a payload to destroy the Tree. Aircraft are a definite issue. If he sends a fleet of jet fighters, the Tree is toast.'

'Toast?' the Tiger said.

John waved one hand towards me. I shrugged.

'I have no defence against any of these weapons,' the Tree said with misery.

'How likely is it that the King has fighter jets?' the Dragon said.

'Very likely,' I said. 'The Russian air force has been updating for a while, and they're selling off obsolete jet fighters complete with guided air-to-air and air-to-ground missiles. Demons are in charge of the Russian government; the European Demon King has replaced most of the senior leaders in Europe with his own thralls; and our Demon King is doing the same thing here.'

'Air-to-air missiles against the Tree?' the Dragon said. He put his forehead in his hand and the Tree patted his back.

I had an inspiration. 'How fast can a really quick dragon fly?'

The Dragon glanced up. 'Mach 3?' He leaned back and his expression went rigid. 'No.'

'It may be our only option, Ah Qing,' John said. 'Start training your Immortal dragons immediately in air-to-air combat.'

'I don't have enough Immortal dragons. I'll have to use mortal ones too.' The Dragon ran his hands up the back of his neck and flipped his long turquoise hair. 'I cannot ask them to do this!'

'I have no self-destruct mechanism,' the Tree said. 'I couldn't bear to be invaded and occupied by demons, Ah Qing.'

'Can you make a self-destruct device for us?' the Dragon asked the Phoenix.

The Phoenix hesitated, then said, 'What would happen if I blew you up, dear Tree? What would happen to your soul, your essence?'

'I don't know, it's never happened,' the Tree said.

'Trees aren't generally Immortal,' the Dragon said. He put his hand on the Tree's and she clutched it. 'I only hope she's different.'

'The best option is to evacuate me,' the Tree said. 'Don't worry about defending me. Take everybody off and I'll go as high as I can and still live.'

'You are the Eastern Bastion,' John said. 'We can't. There must be a garrison stationed on you, and a core group of the Dragon's family as a Celestial presence. Less than that and the Eastern defence is gone, and the demons can move straight up to take the North.'

'I don't like my chances,' the Tree said.

'I'll begin training dragon defenders,' the Dragon said. 'Do you have anyone who is expert in air-to-air, Ah Wu?'

John gestured towards the Phoenix.

The Phoenix nodded. 'We birds aren't as fast as you, but we can give you some tips.'

'Does the Tree have room for the Southern refugees?' I said. 'The phoenixes can help defend.'

'Oh, good idea,' the Phoenix said.

'I'll make room,' the Tree said. 'How about we swap some of our Western Palace refugees for the Southern ones you are housing?'

'Perfect. Talk to Jade,' I said.

The Dragon's eyes widened and his face went rigid, then his whole body heaved and he spewed a gush of blood and water onto the table. Everybody jumped to their feet and backed away as he shook with spasms and vomited again. The Tree held him and he leaned on her as the blood and water rushed out of him, then he collapsed quivering onto the floor.

The Tree knelt beside him and put her hand on his head, then looked around at us, desperate.

'There are —' she began, but John interrupted her.

'Depth charges on the Palace Under the Sea. Everybody who can, go now.'

Everybody except the cats and the phoenixes disappeared.

'Can you breathe underwater?' the Tiger asked me.

'Don't know, never tried.'

I went to the Dragon and helped the Tiger and the Tree to lift him and carry him out of the meeting room. He came around, shook us off, and disappeared.

The order came through from the Jade Emperor: the Palace Under the Sea was losing its Celestial protection against the deep-sea pressure and all aid was needed to assist the evacuation.

'There are air-breathing wives and children down there!' I said, changed to snake and flew out the window.

I was much slower than any of the other Celestials and it took me fifteen minutes just to reach the Gates. When I flew down onto the Earthly and made it to the Sea of Japan, the Celestials were bringing the last of the residents out of the water. I checked around: dragons and water-breathing Shen were carrying humans limp in their arms, but they didn't number anything close to the total human population of the Palace Under the Sea.

I flew to the Dragon and the Tree. He was floating in True Form, holding a woman and five children on his back, and the Tree was carrying another child piggy-back on hers.

'Can I help? Can I do anything?' I said.

'Move back!' the Dragon roared. He grabbed me with his front claw and dragged me fifty metres backwards. *Everybody back! At least a hundred metres from the centre!*

The sea rose in a dome that grew to a hundred metres wide, the water rushing from its silver surface. As the dome rose, it became apparent that it was a sphere of energy containing a bubble of air. John floated in the middle of it in Celestial Form, his arms out and his hair writhing with a life of its own. A hundred humans and twenty demon servants were sitting in the bottom of the bubble, clutching each other and obviously terrified.

'That's not all of them,' the Dragon said. 'There's still about twenty kids and a hundred demons down there.'

The sphere rose higher in the air and the Celestials gathered around it.

How far to land? John said.

A hundred and fifty ks, the Dragon said.

Too far. Find something. Quickly! John said.

'What do we do? What do we do!' the Dragon said. 'Not enough wood left to work with. Metal and fire aren't here. Ice is busy. Shit! Help me out, Emma — where can I put them?'

Can you build an ice floe for them to sit on? I asked John. *Solid water?*

No. This is all I can manage.

True Form? Sit them on your back?

Good idea. I can carry about half of them.

'He'll drop them in the water and take True Form to carry half of them,' I said. 'The rest will have to tread water and we'll take turns ferrying them to land.'

'They can't swim!' the Dragon said.

'Dear Lord, how many can't?'

'Nearly all of them!' the Dragon wailed, his voice full of panicked tears. 'What do we do?'

The Tree appeared in True Form in the air above us, her massive root system blocking the sun.

'Yes!' the Dragon yelled with triumph.

The dragons and Shen that were carrying people flew up onto the white and blue paved expanse around the base of the trunk. John floated his bubble past the roots of the Tree, hovered it above the pavers, then made it disappear. The humans and demons tumbled out, and John floated down to stand on the paving with them.

The Dragon ran to John, jumped up on his hind legs and hugged John's Celestial Form. 'Thank you, Ah Wu, you saved so many of my beloved children.' He fell onto all fours. 'We need to rescue the others. Did you put them into a bubble as well? Are they all right? Hurry and bring them up!'

John's face went grim. 'I'm sorry, Ah Qing.'

'No.' The Dragon changed to human form and leaned on John, who held him. 'My children. There are still twenty ...' His voice broke. 'So many dead. So many children dead. How could they do this? They were *children*!'

John pulled him into an embrace and the Dragon let go into his shoulder.

'I am so sorry, my friend,' John said.

'It is not your doing, you saved so many of them,' the Dragon said, choking with tears. 'How did this happen? Who —'

The Tree shook, and a golden glow like a sunrise shone over the edge of the platform, making ripples of light shimmer on its foliage far above. The Dragon pulled back and looked around, his face full of joy.

John and the Dragon took off over the edge of the Tree's platform. I changed to snake to follow them. An enormous dragon had floated out of the water; he was more than three hundred metres long and shining gold, glittering in the sun. He held a bubble in his front claws that contained the Blue Dragon's remaining children and fifty demon staff. Jade's three daughters were there too, in dragon form. I hadn't known they were visiting their father, and they were too young to survive the deep-ocean pressure. The King of the Dragons himself had saved them.

The Dragon King carried the children and servants, still in their bubble, up to the base of the tree, then released them onto the pavers. John and the Blue Dragon landed next to him as he changed to human form: four metres tall and wearing gold and green Imperial robes, but still with the head of a dragon.

Jackie ran to him and hugged him around his knees. 'Yeh Yeh!'

He hugged her back and touched his snout to the top of her dragon head. 'As if I'd let anything happen to my littlest grandchildren.'

'Thank you,' she sobbed into his robes. 'It was awful. So dark ...'

Qing Long fell to one knee in front of the Dragon King. 'Long Shang Di. I thank you most sincerely for saving my beloved children. I am forever in your debt.'

'They are my children too, little one,' the Dragon King said. He raised his snout and nodded to John. 'Xuan Tian.'

John nodded back. 'Long Huang Di. Did you see who did this?'

'A Chinese navy ship,' the Dragon King said, his voice full of bewilderment. 'They dropped the charges, then headed north. Why did they do this?'

John's face went hard. 'A navy vessel. Found them.' He leapt into the air and screamed northwards, leaving a contrail behind him.

'Go after him,' the Dragon King said. 'Stop him before he does something he'll regret and more die.'

The Dragon and I both changed and took off after him together.

John, I said. *John, they're humans, you can't hurt them.*

He didn't reply and I picked up speed. The Dragon whistled past me and pulled me with him at breathtaking velocity. The two of us landed on the ship after John did.

The crew were on battle stations, fully covered in flame-retardant equipment and armed. John stormed up the stairs to the bridge, knocking aside anyone who tried to stop him and filling all the guns with water to make them useless. The Dragon and I took human form and ran up behind him.

John crashed onto the bridge, looked around, then thundered up to the captain and grabbed him by the throat.

'John, you can't —' I began, desperate.

'I won't,' John said, cutting me off. 'You know me better than that, Emma.'

'Innocents have died,' I said. 'Remember what happened at the Celestial Palace?'

'I have control,' John said as he stared, furious, into the captain's eyes. 'Who ordered you to drop those charges?'

One of the crew pulled out a revolver. John held his hand towards the officer without looking away from the captain. The armed man stiffened, then crumpled to the floor. John raised his hand, flicked his wrist and the rest of the crew froze.

'Now,' John said to the captain, his voice like ice, 'you will tell me exactly who gave you the order to drop those charges, and where I can find them.'

'Who are you?' the captain said. 'Are you Korean? Where are you from?'

John's face became fierce. 'Who gave you the order?'

'Do what you like to me, I won't give out security details of the People's Navy's military exercises.' The captain's eyes glazed over and he went limp in John's hand. 'Admiral Hu, on board the *Liaoning*,' he said, as if from a million miles away.

'Where is the *Liaoning*?' John said.

'I need the map to show you,' the captain said.

John released him and he moved to a computer screen and pulled up the navigation charts. He pointed. 'There.'

'Scale,' John said.

'Here.'

'Fifty. Seventy. North northeast. How big is the *Liaoning*?' John said.

'It's their aircraft carrier,' I said.

'Got it,' John said.

The captain snapped out of it when he saw me. 'Wait, who are you? What did you use on me? How did you get on board?'

He reached to pull his weapon and John tapped him between the eyes. His expression went blank.

'You think the admiral on the *Liaoning* is a demon replacement?' the Dragon said.

'I'm damn sure he is,' John said.

'Let's go,' I said.

'With pleasure,' John said grimly, and the three of us flew off north northeast.

7

The *Liaoning* was an ex-Russian aircraft carrier that the Chinese navy had bought, stripped under the pretence that it would be a casino ship in Macau, and then refitted and brought into service as a 'training' ship. John hovered above it, and we joined him.

'How many aircraft can this thing carry?' the Dragon said. 'If they throw them at the Tree ...'

'They're only at the flight testing stage; the pilots are still learning how to land on it,' I said. 'But the Russian sister ship carries eighteen fighter jets and seventeen helicopters, and is being refitted to carry another thirty fighters.'

'Holy shit,' the Dragon said.

The ship's deck was clear of aircraft. Around its edge stood what appeared to be an honour guard of the crew in their white dress uniforms. The admiral and a couple of officers stood in the middle.

'Why aren't they attacking?' the Dragon said. 'They're just waiting for us.'

'They're waiting for me,' John said.

'A trap?' I said.

'No, they do this sometimes when they know I am after them. A duel.'

'With you?' I said. 'He'll lose.'

'With honour.'

'Unless he cheats,' I said.

'They do that sometimes as well. Watch my back, Ah Qing.'

'My Lord.'

John spread his arms and floated down to land on the deck ten metres from the demon admiral, with the Dragon and myself behind him as support.

'Eastern Heavens,' John said without looking away from the demon.

'My Lord,' the Dragon said.

'Is the Tree secure?'

'She's already back in the Heavens. All clear.'

'Good. Emma —'

'You just concentrate and take it down,' I said. 'I can't miss this opportunity to gain more information on the *Liaoning* and what we may have to face if they control it. The Dragon can send me to Court Ten if necessary.'

'I have your backs,' the Dragon said.

'Very well,' John said, and stepped forward to speak to the demon.

The demon saluted us Western-style, and, as one, the crew of the ship saluted as well, their feet ringing against the metal hull as they stomped on it.

'Number Nine,' John said. 'It's been a while.'

'Xuan Tian,' the demon said. 'I hoped it would be you.' He nodded to the Dragon. 'Emperor Qing Long. I am profoundly honoured.'

'How can you say that when you just tried to murder my children?' the Dragon said.

'I did not factor in your incompetence when I attacked,' the demon said. 'You had to know we'd do this eventually. Why weren't you prepared? You should have been ready for us and had an evacuation plan in place.'

The Dragon gestured with his head towards the sailors surrounding us. 'What did you tell them?'

'You're in league with the American woman here. You've been experimenting with mind-control and mind-altering substances, and they're not to believe anything they see. I've told them that this is a personal matter of honour between the Dark Lord and me and they will not interfere.'

'I'm not American, I'm Australian!' I protested.

'Ah, yes, Australia, America's little lapdog. Where Chinese students are routinely beaten and killed by racist neo-Nazi skinheads, and terrified refugees are put in concentration camps to be raped, tortured and murdered. Thank you for clearing that up, it makes it so much easier.' The demon turned to John and saluted again. 'I have a request, Highness.'

'No,' John said.

'Give me a one-on-one with Seven Stars and they can have free run of the ship while we do it. Every single crew member is up here. You can go right through and look at everything.'

'Why?' I said.

The demon grinned at me. 'To be destroyed by the Seven Stars Sword of the Three Platforms, wielded by the Dark Emperor of the Northern Heavens himself for the first time since he returned? It's more honour than I deserve.'

'I agree,' the Dragon said.

'Is it worth it, Emma?' John said.

I hesitated, then said, 'Yeah. This is the only aircraft carrier in the region, and the demons have control of it. Knowing exactly what they have on board would be invaluable.'

'How many stone Shen died to block our vision of the interior?' John asked the demon.

'Two hundred and ten.'

'Holy shit,' I said.

'The Jade Building Block was not one of them, do not be concerned. The King is holding it. He has plans for it.'

I wiped my eyes. 'I'm concerned for all the stones. Every stone lost is a tragedy.'

'I really don't understand you Celestials sometimes,' the demon said. 'They're just rocks.' He turned to John. 'Do we have a deal?'

'You'll compromise your security so you can fall to Seven Stars?' the Dragon said.

'Demons have *turned* to fall to Seven Stars, Highness. The honour of dying to that sword, wielded by the Dark Lord himself, is unmatched.'

'Then turn,' I said.

The demon shrugged. 'The result is the same, so I will die with my loyalty, my allegiance and my honour intact.' He spoke to John. 'They can go wherever they like if you will do this for me.'

'Is he telling the truth?' I said. 'They'd really give that much to die to Seven Stars?'

John hesitated, then said, 'Yes, he is. It's true.'

'What a pain in the ass.'

'You have no idea.'

'You watch his back, I'll have a look around,' I said to the Dragon.

'No. Go with her,' John said without looking away from the demon admiral. *She hasn't learnt shen suicide yet. Be ready.*

Oh, wonderful, the Dragon said. *I can see this ending with both of us dead and Emma in their hands.*

I'll keep it busy. Watch her back.

I gestured with my head towards the bridge tower. 'Let's go.'

John took full ugly Celestial Form and drew Seven Stars. The admiral changed to his demon form — two metres tall, green and scaled — and summoned a Chinese-style two-handed broadsword, a rare and specialist weapon. John's face didn't show it, but he was delighted to face a talented practitioner with a weapon similar to his own.

The sailors around the edge of the ship made loud sounds of astonishment.

You call me the second you think anything's strange, I said to John.

I'm the strangest thing here.

Conceded, I said, then, *Gold.*

Ma'am?

I'm in the Sea of Japan on the Liaoning. *I need you as soon as you can be here.*

Accessing ... Turn on the GPS on your phone.

I pulled my phone out of my pocket as the Dragon and I ran up the stairs to the top of the bridge island. There were twenty-seven missed calls with no caller ID, and it dawned on me that it could be my stone trying to contact me. I turned the GPS on, and when we reached the surprisingly small bridge — less than ten metres across and two metres deep — we stood and waited.

Hurry, Gold, I said, checking out the window.

John was keeping the demon occupied with a well-matched battle, and the sailors were fiercely cheering them on. It would be ugly when John won.

Sealed. Can't go in, Gold said. *Leave your phone somewhere close by and I'll use it to extract the data I need.*

I don't want to leave it, I said. *I think your parent's been trying to contact me — there's a bunch of calls with no caller ID.*

Really? he said with delight. *Leave it there anyway, it's connected to the network. I'll check the logs later.*

I rifled through the cupboards full of charts and binders of operating procedures, and found one with just enough space to jam my phone in.

'Teleport us into the hangar bay,' I said to the Dragon. 'It's the large open area under the main deck.'

The Dragon put his hand on my shoulder, but nothing happened.

'Shit,' he said, and spun to the door. He tried it and it was sealed. 'Move back.' I moved to the other side of the small bridge and he used all his strength on the door. 'Shit!'

I looked down through the window. 'Ah Qing!'

The three aircraft elevators lifted onto the deck, each of them carrying ten huge black-skinned demons. The human sailors took off when they saw them, running to the aft of the ship in panic.

The Dragon took True Form, squashing me against the comms panel and knocking the breath out of me. He rammed his head against the glass of the bridge with no result. He pulled back and tried it again, making the whole bridge shake, but he couldn't break the glass. He changed back to human, and I sagged, gasping for breath now I was no longer crushed against the console.

The black-skinned demons charged John and overran him. He fought them with Seven Stars but the blade did nothing.

John changed to True Form, the Serpent and Turtle together, and generated a cloud of yin around himself that destroyed the demons. It destroyed the deck as well, and John plummeted through the hole.

'There'd better not be a Celestial Jade cage under there!' I shouted.

There was a roar like a jet engine and the ship shuddered in the water. The infrastructure trembled again and the ship rocked as if it had been hit. The sound lowered in pitch and John rose out of the hole, his True Form larger, darker and more menacing. Yin floated in a cloud of destruction around him as he rose, shredding the metal of the deck at the edges of the hole and causing a mini tornado of metal shards around him.

He pulled the yin into himself, then drifted sideways above the deck with the Serpent's head and body writhing above the Turtle's shell. He landed lightly on the deck and stood menacingly in front of the defiant demon admiral, who had moved back from the hole but was now standing his ground.

Are you okay? he said to me.

We're stuck in the bridge. The way out is blocked.

Ah Qing, send her to Court Ten, John said.

'What about you?' I asked the Dragon.

'I'll send myself directly after,' he said.

Not until I see you safely destroy this demon, I said to John. *Is there a jade cage under there?*

No, just many of those hybrid demons.

Damn, I would have liked to know how many aircraft are in there.

I'll come and open the window for you, then I'll keep it busy while you go down and have a look.

'It appears that our friend Number Nine had a fast hard lesson in exactly how powerful the combined Xuan Wu is in True Form,' the Dragon said. 'He must have been promoted after Ah Wu separated.'

The Serpent lifted from the Turtle and flew towards us. *Back up*, John said, and we moved away from the window. The Serpent produced a circular cloud of yin and slowly moved it towards the window. At the same time, the demon rushed the Turtle with its weapon raised.

The Serpent looked away from us, distracted, and the yin shot through the window. The Dragon knocked me to the floor with one arm, then held me down with his foot as the cold yin flew straight into his head. He sucked it into himself, then bent and gasped with effort, still holding me down with his foot.

'Let me up,' I said. 'You're giving me more of a beating today than any of the demons.'

'A moment,' he said, then released me. 'Sorry. My control isn't as good as Ah Wu's. There was a small chance it would escape me.'

I climbed to my feet. 'I understand.'

I leaned over the console to check the deck below through the hole in the glass. John had recombined and the demon was attacking his heads, but the combined Turtle and Serpent were way too fast for it. The human sailors were gathered at the rear of the deck, watching with their mouths hanging open and loudly discussing what they were seeing.

The Dragon put his hand on my shoulder and we teleported out of the bridge to a position floating just above the bow of the ship.

You really are magnificent, you know that? I said to John.

That's not a word often used to describe my True Form, he said, and changed back to Celestial Form. He swung Seven Stars at the demon's black-scaled head and the demon ducked, then tried to break through John's guard into his abdomen. John twisted the sword down faster than the eye could see and swept the demon's blade away.

For fuck's sake, stop playing with it, the Dragon said. *Finish this and let's go. That thing doesn't deserve this kindness. It broke the rules and tried to kill my children!*

I said I'd destroy it with Seven Stars and I'm a creature of my word, John said. *Go through and make sure I didn't leave anything behind*. He blocked the demon's sword again and took a couple of steps back to float over the hole in the deck. The demon followed him and both of them hung suspended over the empty space, still striking at each other. *As soon as it's dead we leave.*

'Pah, it's more than it deserves,' the Dragon said. 'Let's gather your information then get out of here.'

I changed to snake and we flew towards the hole together. The storage hangar under the deck was five metres wide and twenty long, only just large enough to hold the aircraft. It was deserted.

'Sense anything?' I said.

'Ah Wu has broken the stone seal; I can see inside.'

'How many aircraft?'

'None.' The Dragon pointed aft. 'What's supposed to be down that end?' He tilted his head. 'Towards the front of the boat it's divided into rooms; below us are more rooms full of machinery; but that way there's just one big room and it's six decks high.'

'Normally that would be the senior officers' mess and quarters,' I said. 'One really big room? Let's have a look.'

The Dragon nodded and took Celestial Form in his silver and blue scaled armour. 'Have you made one yet?' he said.

I changed back to human, then concentrated, grew, and pulled my armour to me. I didn't have a Celestial Form as such, it felt too pretentious; but being bigger and stronger always helped. I held my hand out and summoned Dark Heavens.

'Really not good enough, Emma. You can do a much better battle form than that, and you need to assert your individuality by getting your own damn sword,' the Dragon said.

He stopped at the bulkhead between the hangar bay and the aft room, put his hand on the door, then took the handle and turned it. It wasn't locked so he pushed the door open. We went through to a raised platform composed of steel grid suspended above the six-deck-high space. Below us stood hundreds of the black-skinned demons, silent and obviously parked. They needed the large space because they were close on five metres tall and all had leathery wings.

'Majesty, Lady Emma,' said a male voice with a cultured English accent. It came from our left, behind the open door.

The Dragon pushed the door closed to reveal a smaller black-skinned demon standing behind it. I raised Dark Heavens, and the Dragon shifted position, readying himself.

The demon raised both clawed hands. 'I will not harm you. I haven't been ordered to.'

It was the usual black-skinned Eastern-Western hybrid, two metres tall with long limbs, but its head was more of a bulge above its torso than a true head, and it had no neck. Its face made me step back: it was grotesquely small and disproportionate to the size of its head.

The Dragon made a small sound of disgust.

The demon bowed. 'I apologise for my appearance, although I probably shouldn't as I have no control over the way I'm made. Don't try to attack me. You know you can't hurt us.'

'Are you in charge?' I said.

'No, I just mind the door. I think they forgot to tell us you were coming. We're not ordered to do anything.'

'Most strange,' the Dragon said.

'Want to turn?' I asked the demon. 'I can give you a good home on the Mountain.'

It shrugged. 'I appreciate the offer, but that is too far from my Centre. We are being shipped —' It raised its head. 'You have permission to wander through, but if you linger anywhere I must move you along. So I ask you to go back through the door; there's nothing else here but us.'

'What would happen to all of you if we were to sink the ship?' I said.

'Please don't do that, Lady; it's a very long walk to shore.'

Its voice had the ring of truth. The Dragon opened the door and we went out of the room and back down the narrow metal corridor.

There are hundreds — I began.

One at a time, not both together! John shouted in my head. *I'm facing a single-digit demon here!*

The Dragon and I shared an amused look. He gestured towards me to speak first.

There are hundreds of those black demons in the aft of the ship. Can you destroy them after you take out Nine?

I'd have to yin them and that would probably sink the ship.

Damn. We couldn't risk hurting the human crew. Even if they evacuated the sinking ship, some could still be lost. *Finish up and let's go.*

We swept through the rest of the ship and found no aircraft or other demons, just evidence of residence by the human crew. The Dragon carried me and we returned to our position floating over the bow of the ship.

John was keeping the demon busy without damaging it, and the demon was blowing heavily with effort. John blocked a blow from the broadsword, pushed it down and to the side, and slammed the pommel of Seven Stars into the demon's face. The demon reeled back, stunned, and John swung and took its head off. It exploded into black streamers.

John put the sword away and strode to the aft of the ship. The Dragon floated us forward to land on the deck, and we followed John. He stopped in front of the sailors, still in Celestial Form.

The crew had been sitting on the deck, bored with the long fight. Now they jumped to their feet and all of them crowded away from him. He enhanced his voice to make it as intense and majestic as the rest of him.

'You have witnessed a battle between the Shen of the Heavens and the demons of Hell,' he said, and their faces filled with wonder.

One of Nine's officers stepped forward and turned to speak to the sailors. 'Don't believe what you see and hear. Remember the admiral said —'

His voice was choked off as John picked him up by the collar of his uniform and lifted him high above the deck, his legs dangling.

'It is wise not to believe your eyes and ears sometimes. But if I were to drop you right now, hitting the deck would definitely hurt,' John said.

He spoke to the sailors, still holding the officer. 'I apologise for the damage to the ship, but your admiral was on the wrong side.'

Some of the sailors were starting to believe John; it was in their faces. They were thrilled and terrified.

'I am Zhenwu, Supreme Emperor of the Northern Heavens, the Destroyer of Demons,' he said. 'I have just destroyed your admiral. Think on that, and think on the nature of the creatures that stand in the space below us.'

He lowered the officer to the deck. The officer staggered but remained on his feet, then took a few steps back and glared, furious, at John.

John turned away. 'Let's go.'

Stay human, Emma, the Dragon said. *I'll give you a lift.*

The Dragon raised us ten metres and changed to his most massive True Form, a fifty-metre-long dragon. He produced a glowing nimbus of shen energy around us that reflected off his scales and made shifting patterns of light on the grey deck of the ship. The sailors shaded their eyes and made loud sounds of astonishment.

John floated up next to us. 'Make sure you are on the right side in the coming battle, humans,' he said.

Then the three of us shot straight up so fast that the breath was knocked out of me.

8

John summoned a cloud, floated to stand on it, and put his hand out to pull me in to join him. He held me close, my back against his chest and his arm around me, as he carried me through the interface between the Earthly and the Heavens.

The air became sweeter and purer as we arrived in the crystalline sky of the Celestial Plane. We went straight to the Tree, and landed on the large open area around her base, already covered with the refugees from the Palace Under the Sea. They mobbed the Dragon when we landed, all talking at once, and he changed to human form to embrace his wives, children and grandchildren.

John shrank to human form and went to Jade and Yue Gui. They were standing to one side with Gold, who was projecting an array of names and numbers in front of him.

'We need to protect the Tree at all costs,' Yue Gui said. 'If the Eastern Bastion falls, we won't have enough space to hold the remaining refugees.'

'We don't have enough space now,' Gold said, studying the list scrolling in front of him. 'The food will run out soon, even with the supplies we're purchasing on the Earthly.'

Jade was watching the list as well. 'We have to move some to the Earthly. There's no other way.' She glanced at us. 'I'll start chasing humans out of the Earthly Follies.'

'Not secure enough,' John said. 'The demons are well aware of the locations of the Follies. Without me down there to protect the buildings, the demons will probably destroy them as soon as they're occupied.'

'Destroy the buildings?' Jade's eyes widened. 'They would too.'

'The hotels,' Gold said. The list changed to known properties owned by the Four Winds. 'The Tiger has a variety of hotels scattered throughout the world. If he can give me the locations of all of them, we can accommodate many people there.'

'Jade?' I said.

'We can do it,' she said. 'Gold, can you find me a stone to do the room allocations?'

'There's an international computer system that will do it,' Gold began, then, 'Never mind, the demons will be in it. We'll have to set up false identities for everybody. I'll see what I can do.' He made a soft sound of frustration. 'We don't have enough people to organise everything!'

Someone screamed and we all turned to see. The Dragon was standing rigid, his arms out and his eyes wide as he stared down at himself. Smoke billowed from his abdomen, and everybody stepped back. We ran to him as flames spurted from his blue robes.

John put his hands out and summoned a bubble of water, and laid it against the fire. Flames continued to spray from the Dragon's abdomen within the bubble.

'Not me. Not me!' The Dragon jabbed one finger up to the left. 'Save her!'

'What?' I said, and looked where he'd pointed.

A dot of light, too bright to focus on, was causing smoke and shooting flames from the Tree's trunk.

'What is it?' I said. I turned to the Dragon; the same flames were coming from him, inside the water bubble. 'Ah Qing, what is it?'

'I don't know,' the Dragon wailed, then collapsed into a ball on the ground. 'Save her!'

The spot of light was moving across the Tree, cutting through her. The smoke billowed in large clouds and her bark popped and sizzled.

'What's happening?' Jade said, distraught. She fell to sit next to Qing Long and put his head in her lap. He clutched at her. 'Ah

Qing, talk to us.' She brushed her hands over his face and bent over him. 'What's hurting you?'

'Hold me, Jade,' he said. 'It burns.'

'It's a laser!' I shouted. 'John, take True Form and put yourself between the Tree and the source.'

'Won't that kill me?' John said.

'Probably, but it'll give us time to work out how to block it.'

'Where's it coming from?' Jade said. She put her hand over the flames on the Dragon's abdomen, then jerked it away. 'Why is there no beam to see?'

John took True Form and flew up to the Tree. He positioned himself in front of the spot of light and it hit him instead. He generated a circle of yin to absorb it.

How long do we have? I asked him.

Ten minutes at the most before I lose control of it and do more damage than the laser.

'It's a laser beam!' I shouted at the Tree. 'Move away from it.'

The Tree's branches thrashed as she shifted, and the ground moved. People were knocked off their feet, and tiles clattered from the roof of the Dragon's Palace. The point of the laser skidded across the Tree's trunk and disappeared.

'I can't believe I didn't think of that,' the Dragon said as Jade helped him to his feet.

John changed to human form and floated down to join us. 'Are you all right?' he asked the Dragon.

'Give me a moment ...' the Dragon said, and collapsed again.

'No,' Jade said, and knelt next to him. She gathered him in her arms and held him as smoke came from his robes.

The Tree screamed and tilted sideways as she moved again. The buildings trembled but none of them fell. The point of the laser shifted on her trunk, then moved across her and resettled to its original spot, resuming burning a hole through her. She kept moving and the laser followed her, leaving a trail of black charring across her trunk. It was seriously damaging her: there were deep furrows in her wood where it hit.

The Dragon moaned with pain and Jade sobbed into the top of his head.

'They have some way of tracking us,' Gold said. 'How do they know where it is?'

'Tree!' I shouted. 'Down. Lose altitude.'

The Tree's branches thrashed again as she plummeted towards the ground, then stopped, knocking more people off their feet.

I staggered and righted myself. 'The laser cannon generating this is probably at the Western Palace — the Tiger was building something like it,' I said. 'If you can go low enough, the curve of the Earth will block the beam.'

'What beam? There isn't any beam!' Jade said.

'That's how it works,' I said. 'You can't see it.'

The red dot reappeared on the trunk.

'Further down!' I yelled.

We screamed towards the sea's surface again and stopped. The horizon was now visible over the edge of the Tree's platform. We all waited with our breath held for the dot to reappear, and it didn't.

Jade helped the Dragon to his feet again, and he embraced her. They stood silently, holding each other.

John grabbed my hand and we clicked together, sharing our consciousness. I passed all the information I had about the laser cannons to him and he nodded, then released my hand and turned away.

'Gold!' he said. 'Straight line beam, now below the curve of the earth — you saw it cut across the tree. Can you triangulate it?'

'Diameter of the Earth …' Gold said. 'Accessing. Processing.' His expression cleared. 'Yeah, you're right. The source is where the Western Palace used to be.'

The Dragon pulled away from Jade. 'I must go,' he said to her. She nodded. 'Go.'

He kissed her and turned to John. 'Ah Wu?'

'Let's go,' John said.

'Faster if you don't come along, Emma,' the Dragon said.

'I'll stay here and help sort out the refugees.'

John changed to True Form, and the two of them rocketed into the air, moving so fast that the ground recoiled beneath us.

'Can the hotels carry all the refugees?' I asked Gold.

'The Northern Heavens are full, we don't have a choice,' Yue Gui said. She looked pensive. 'I wonder if the Grandmother would help?'

'We'll find a way,' I said. 'Defending them is another issue.' I felt a vibration through the breeze. 'What's that?'

'I don't …' Gold said, but Jade's face went strange.

'My lizard ears hear a sound,' she said. She changed to dragon form and flicked her tongue, much the same way I did in snake form. 'It sounds like …' She changed back to human and yelled, 'Insects! Move everybody inside!' She raised her arms and strode through the crowd. 'Everybody inside — there are insects coming!'

The refugees rushed to the buildings that clustered at the base of the Tree. A few children cried with alarm, and adults lifted them and carried them to safety.

'Dragons and any who can fight, out on the concourse with me!' I shouted, and summoned Dark Heavens. I turned back to see the sky; it appeared to be clear. 'Can you see anything, Tree?' I said.

John, come back. There are insects, I added silently.

Already, he said.

'There,' the Tree said above us, her leaves rustling.

The insects became visible: a dark cloud like a flock of birds. The buzzing grew louder and more intense.

I glanced behind me. A small group of dragons — only twenty or thirty — stood in True Form, together with Gold in his battle form. The King of the Dragons had transformed as well, and towered over the rest of the group. I backed up to be with them.

John appeared next to me in True Form, and the Serpent separated from the Turtle. The Dragon floated above us in True Form as well.

'There are thousands of them,' the Dragon said softly.

'I know,' the Dragon King said. 'We won't have time to evacuate everybody before they arrive.'

The Blue Dragon spun in the air and headed towards the buildings at the base of the Tree. The Tree's branches thrashed and we dropped again. She moved sideways as well; she was taking us to land so that when she fell she wouldn't kill the mortals. Unfortunately her motion carried us towards the insects rather than away from them, and the buzzing became almost maddening in its intensity.

The black cloud thickened — they were right on top of us — but then they weren't.

I realised with shock that the lack of contrast in the light had fooled me. I'd thought the insects were twenty centimetres long and close to us, when actually they were twenty metres long — and some were three or four times that length, with grotesquely elongated pulsing white bodies and multiple sets of double wings down their backs.

They followed the Tree towards the ground, blackening the sky above us. The dragons leapt into the air to fight them.

The smaller insects, each a metre long, flew to the Tree — thousands of them. They latched onto her trunk and she screamed again as she turned into a black mass of shining wings and shells.

The dragons attacked the insects, but immediately fell, limp and unconscious — the insects had deadly stingers. The remaining dragons threw energy from the air at the insects, but it had no effect.

A dozen larger insects — sixty metres long from mandibles to stinger — floated above the ground, their many pairs of wings humming. The dragons attacked these instead.

One dragon ripped off an insect's head, but the body remained hovering. The white pulsing abdomen split open lengthwise along its belly, and a mass of writhing worm demons tumbled out onto the ground. All of the bigger insects had now split, and hundreds of worms, each two metres long, squirmed over the ground in a puddle of toxic goo. The dragons landed to fight them.

I ran to them with Dark Heavens, and the worms closest to me raised their front ends to spit poison. I couldn't avoid all the poison, but it didn't matter. I swiped as best I could, taking heads off as the green burning slime hit me. A gob of goo hit my left eye, and the side of my face melted away, blinding me in that eye. I blocked the pain and continued to attack.

John had taken human form to fight with Seven Stars and swung the loaded blade next to me. We killed more than a hundred of the worms, cutting them to pieces that continued to wriggle, but the rest were gone. They'd burnt a hole through the paving and tunnelled into the earth around the Tree.

John and I shared a look.

'Do you need help with that?' he said.

'No, I have it.' I wiped the poison off what remained of my face with my sleeve. The dragons who'd fought the worms lay on the ground, motionless. 'Save the dragons.'

'It's too late for them. I'll heal everybody still alive when this is done.' He pointed up at the Tree. 'We have bigger things to worry about.'

The insects were eating her. They had opened great holes in her trunk and it was only a matter of time before she fell. The Dragon was gone; he'd carried as many children as he could but there was still a huddled group of more than a hundred terrified mortals cowering next to his Palace.

A great cracking sound erupted beneath our feet and the ground trembled.

John changed back to True Form and grew until each of his two animals was fifty metres long. The Turtle stomped to the terrified people and they cowered away from him.

'Onto my back,' he said. 'Climb on!'

People screamed and scurried away from it, but the Serpent grabbed them in its mouth and lifted them onto the Turtle's shell.

I ran to help, picking people up and hoisting them so they could climb up to the edge of his shell, three metres from the ground. Blood dripped from the wounds where the poison had burnt holes through my skin, but I fought the weakness. I lifted a young woman holding a screaming child, her face white with fear but full of determination. My remaining vision blurred and I forced myself on; I could succumb to the poison later. Right now there were people to save.

The ground shook again and tilted. The top of the Tree leaned as her trunk splintered away from the hole the insects were eating. A ridge appeared along her base, running three hundred metres from her trunk, popping out the pavers. The ridge grew and expanded, and a great root, covered in worms, surged out of the ground.

I felt more than heard the sound of the wood separating, and more roots surged into the air. The ground tilted, and the people who weren't on the Turtle slid away from us over the smooth pavers.

The top of the Tree fell with a vast crack that made the ground shudder, and John's Turtle lifted off the ground to stay horizontal and hold its passengers.

I tried to change to snake, but the poison was blocking my ability. I slid down the slick turquoise pavers as the top of the Tree separated from her trunk. The canopy caught on the ground around her base, then tumbled into the water with a splash so huge that the spray stung my wounds. The remains of the trunk pivoted out of the ground, with the insects still gnawing on it.

The tiled surface tilted further until it was nearly vertical and I slid off. I turned onto my back to see John's Turtle hanging in the air above me as the enormous remains of the Tree fell, surrounded by a cloud of wreckage from the shattered buildings.

The people who hadn't made it onto John's back were falling around me, the debris crushing them as they fell. The Serpent swam through the air, trying to catch them, but only managed to grab one man in its mouth and make it back up to the Turtle before we hit the water.

The impact was like hitting concrete and the pain was intense. I was *never* —

* * *

— jumping off a building to commit suicide, it was way too painful. I'd died instantly; a change from the usual drawn-out suffering. Broken neck, from the feel of it.

I looked around and saw the familiar minimal comfort of a cell attached to Court Ten. I rose from the pallet and went to the bars. The other cells were full of dragons in human form, some of them curled up in the corners and weeping.

'Hey, Three-Fifty,' I called.

The demon guard approached the cell and nodded to me. 'Dark Lady.'

'How many mortals did we lose?'

'One hundred and sixty-seven, Lady.'

'Thank you.' I turned away to sit on the pallet and put my head in hands.

'We did our best, Emma,' one of the dragons called from across the corridor.

'And we have a hundred and sixty-seven reasons for our best not being good enough,' I said. 'The East has fallen.'

They were all silent at that, except for the quiet sobs of the Immortal dragons who had lost family and friends.

I rolled onto my side on the pallet and closed my eyes, surrounded by softly weeping dragons. I thought of my own little boy, alone with those monsters in the demonic side of Hell.

Frankie. It's your mother. I will always love you.

I sensed a sharp intake of breath, the desperate hope for a better life, and then his rejection of the possibility that anything good could happen to someone as undeserving as him.

You are a wonderful little boy, Frankie, and —

You are not my mother. He raised the barrier and blocked me.

* * *

I was woken by banging and yelling, and looked around, disoriented. I was still in the cell — not surprising. Judge Pao had a large number of us to work through and I was probably a long way down the list.

The demon guard charged up to the door of my cell and opened it, panting and out of breath. I didn't move, fearing that Judge Pao was trying me out again. It hadn't worked either of the times he'd tried it before though ...

'Lady Emma,' the guard said, gasping. She looked back up the hallway, then turned to me and held out a sword, hilt first. 'We're under attack again — there's an army of them. Hundreds. And those black fuckers.' She pushed the sword towards me. 'Help us!'

I jumped up, summoned my armour and Dark Heavens, and grew so that I had to duck to fit under the ceiling.

'Don't mind the sword, I'll use this,' I said. 'Show me where to go.'

The dragons and Immortals from the Tree were being released, the bamboo doors of the cells echoing as they were thrown open. The demon guard turned and ran back up the corridor, with me following. There was shouting above, but no clash of weapons.

I followed the guard up the stairs that led to the back of Court Ten. We raced out onto the island at the centre of the Celestial side of Hell. The guards were standing at the end of the causeway, facing an army of demons. The demons had filled in the gap in the causeway using the corpses of their own kin that hadn't dissipated when they were destroyed.

John appeared next to me in human form. 'They said there were black ones? I can't see any.'

Both of us looked around at the group accompanying us: mostly dragons from the Eastern Palace that had been killed by the worms and insects, together with the Celestial's demon guards.

'Cynic!' John and I yelled together.

I gestured towards John — he did the talking when we were both thinking the same thing. He had more authority.

Cynic floated in human form towards us. 'My Lord? My Lady?'

'Go up and see if there's anything more coming,' John said.

She changed to a ten-metre-long green dragon and shot into the air.

The demons moved into position, ready to attack, and the Celestial defenders readied themselves behind us.

There was a commotion and Judge Pao stormed through the group to stand next to us. He was holding his sword, and accompanied by Marshal Meng, the guardian of the City of Hell.

'You have yet to be judged and should still be in your cell,' Pao said to me.

'I can go back if you like.'

'You have special dispensation,' Pao said.

'Oh, thank you so much.'

Cynic landed lightly on the ground next to us. 'There's a group of about twenty of those black things on its way.'

She telepathically projected an image of them: the Eastern-Western hybrids that had no difficulty travelling anywhere on the Planes, marching up the causeway a hundred metres behind the army we were facing.

John concentrated, calling reinforcements, and Simone and Martin appeared next to us.

John and I had the same thought at the same time. He spoke to Simone and Martin; I turned to speak to the rest of the group.

'The Dark Lord, the Crown Prince and the Princess will handle the black-armoured demons,' I shouted, boosted by telepathy so all could hear. 'We will handle the ordinary demons on the causeway. Keep well away from the armoured ones, they'll use yin —'

I was cut off by the demons on the causeway running over the corpses of their brothers to attack us.

John, Simone and Martin shot into the air, heading out to fight the armoured demons. I moved back to stand with the vanguard of the defenders.

Hold, I said as the demons ran towards us. When they were right on top of us, I yelled and we engaged.

We stood shoulder to shoulder and fought them. Pao wasn't as skilled as any of my trained Disciples, but he fought valiantly, his black face full of determination.

My vision was full of a mass of weapons heading towards us, and in the heat of battle all style was forgotten. We slashed at each other and I defended, sometimes clumsily, and often missed my attacking strikes. I worked in a team with Pao on one side and a dragon on the other, helping them as they watched my flanks, and we pushed forward over the ground that was slippery with demon essence, destroying the demons in front of us.

I blocked a strike to my head, and it bounced off my blade into the dragon next to me. She fell, and someone moved up to take her place. I ignored a couple of lucky hits to my shoulders, but one particularly strong blow nearly took my left arm off. I blocked the pain and continued to fight, but the attackers were thinning.

Then there was nothing in front of us; we'd broken through their lines.

I took a deep breath and threw energy at some of the remaining stragglers, blowing them up. The energy backlash from destroying them sizzled through me and my arm was healed; an advantage of being in Court Ten where our bodies were energy-based extensions of our spirits.

There was an explosion on the causeway fifty metres in front of us, and the unmistakable whistle of a rocket-propelled grenade going overhead. I felt the shockwave more than heard it.

9

The demon guard came to the door of my cell. 'Your turn, ma'am.'

'How long have I been here?' I said.

'Only forty-eight hours.'

'I thought I would have a shorter sentence for helping to defend Court Ten.'

She opened the door of the cell. 'You did. You're one of the first out.'

'Why? What happened?' I said as I followed her up the stairs and into the two-storey Court Ten building.

I stopped when I reached the top of the stairs. Court Ten was gone. Two of the four walls were left, and only reached a couple of metres above the ground before they became splintered remnants. Five craters where the bombs had hit dotted the ground where the building used to be, and the stone floor of the courtroom was rubble.

'He was right,' I said.

'Who?'

'The Jade Emperor. So where has the Court moved while we rebuild?'

'We don't have the resources to rebuild; we'll have to win this war first,' the demon guard said. She gestured with her halberd. 'Pao's conducting his hearings in Court Nine. No mortals are being sent to the Pits anyway, so we might as well make use of it.'

We picked our way through the destruction and went through the doors of Court Nine, two hundred metres away at the end of its own causeway. The courtroom was unadorned except for Judge Pao at his desk on the raised dais and the small group of spectators sitting on benches to one side. Relief rushed through me when I saw John. Although they'd told me we'd won, it had still been lonely without him.

I missed you too, John said, and we shared a sad smile. His face was gaunt with stress — he hadn't been eating or sleeping well — but the special smile that showed he was glad to see me always lifted my spirits.

I knelt in front of Judge Pao in my white prisoner's garb and lowered my head. I needed to be out of there and back into action as quickly as possible, and aggravating him would only be counterproductive.

'Lady Emma Donahoe,' Judge Pao said from the dais above me.

'This small Shen is present and honoured,' I said, my head still bowed.

'You are to attend me in my office immediately. Escort the prisoner,' Judge Pao said, and he rose, walked down off the dais and through the door behind him.

I was stunned, and the guard had to take me by the arm to pull me to my feet. She pushed me to follow Judge Pao out of the courtroom, and we went up the external stairs to his private office in his quarters on the floor above. The guard guided me into the office, and I fell to my knees on the rug in front of the empty desk. This was new.

Judge Pao came in holding a teapot and some cups. He gestured towards me with them. 'Up. Sit. Lord Xuan, you too.'

I rose and sat on one of the visitors' chairs. John appeared next to me.

Pao sat behind his desk, put the cups out, and poured. I tapped the surface of the desk next to my cup in thanks.

'So what do we do?' Pao said. 'The East has fallen. It's only a matter of time before they move on the North. Can you hold them?'

John lifted his teacup and studied it. 'We will make our last stand on the field outside the capital of the Northern Heavens.'

'What are our chances?'

John put the cup down, rubbed one hand over his face and looked away. 'Not good.'

'If they win the North, they'll go straight to the Celestial Palace.' Judge Pao poured more tea into our already-full cups. 'The Celestial will fall.'

'I will fight to my last breath —' John began.

'We all will. All civilian staff must be evacuated from Hell now, Lord Xuan. They are at desperate risk of being thrown into the Pits if the Heavens fall.'

'As soon as I can find Jade I'll send her to make the arrangements,' John said.

'Jade's missing?' I said.

John nodded. 'Did she come through the Court, Honourable?'

'She is in my cells now,' Pao said. 'I suggest you relieve her of duty. Two of her youngest daughters — Princesses Frangipani and Bauhinia — died in the fall of the East. It has broken her.'

'No,' I said, and leaned my head in my hand.

'Before you ask, no, they weren't Worthy, but even if they were — I am no longer Raising Celestial Worthies. They are better served by being reattached to the Wheel rather than living with the possibility of an eternity in the Pits.' He tapped his teacup on his desk blotter. 'We may as well close the Courts. I will sign a blanket Edict that all Immortals are immediately released, and all mortals are returned to the Wheel.'

'Will the Edict still apply if Hell falls?' I said.

'Of course not,' Pao said. 'Lord Xuan ...' He hesitated, turning his cup in his hands. 'How will we minimise the suffering of the innocent when everything falls apart?'

'I don't know,' John said, almost a moan of pain.

'What does the Celestial say? He does not answer my calls.'

'He says nothing,' John said. 'He meditates. He ponders. He wanders his Palace, which is full of innocents who are at risk, and he remains silent. No orders, no suggestions, no plans.'

'He sees the worst.'

'He sees something that fills his visage with so much grief that it breaks my hearts to look upon him,' John said. He straightened. 'We will. Still. Fight.'

'Go and fight, Celestial Highness,' Pao said. 'Fight with your Lady and your children by your side. Fight with your black-garbed Disciples. Fight with the host of Heaven. All of us are behind you.'

John put his hand out to me and I took it. He teleported us to the Mountain. We landed in the administrative section and headed straight to John's office. I changed my white convict's robe to a black Mountain uniform on the way, and John nodded appreciation. Three weeks before I hadn't been able to do that.

'Welcome back, Lady Emma,' Zara said as we went through her anteroom.

'Thanks, Zara. Call Yi Hao for me, will you?'

John sat behind his desk and checked his email. I stood on the other side and flipped through the documents on his desk, reviewing what had happened while I was in Hell. He finished and put his hand out, and I took it. We linked up and he gave me a quick update on the three days I'd been away. I was the fifth one back. The Dragon had been held for forty-eight hours for losing his Bastion, had been released first and hadn't been seen since.

John gave me a quick summary of his trip to the remains of the Western Heavens with the Tiger, to look for the laser weapon. They'd found a huge prefabricated steel building over where the Tiger's lab had been.

We went invisible and attempted to infiltrate, he said. *They could sense us. The minute we were close, alarms went off and they tried to destroy us with a spray of bullets. I don't know how they managed to detect us — we were both invisible and silent!*

Infra-red sensors detecting your body heat, I said.

Oh, he said, understanding. *So I should have gone in as a reptile with cold blood?*

Warm enough to move is warm enough to be detected. Did you see what's inside?

The Tiger says metal. A great deal of metal. He melted it to slag. All of it, the building as well.

Good.

On his return, John had met with the Generals and they were gathering every remaining warrior the Celestial had in the Northern Heavens to make a final stand on the field outside the city, next to the lake. The Generals had demanded that John move his centre of operations there.

I agree with them, I said. *Why are you still here on the Mountain?*

He ignored me, and continued to bring me up to date. The dragons were doubling up in the refugee camps, but the accommodation was full. The latrines were overflowing, and even in the Celestial purity the sanitary facilities were struggling. We needed Jade back as soon as possible.

I interrupted him. *We need to find someone else to do the refugee housing. We're taking Jade off duty.*

Right. Yes. Food was running low, rationing had been introduced. And now John and I had to pack and move everything to the Northern Heavens for the last stand.

I released his hand and nodded.

Yi Hao came in and I turned to speak to her. 'Pack up my office, we're moving to the Northern Heavens. Tell Smally to pack my private things as well.'

Yi Hao nearly ran into Jade as she went out. Jade fell to one knee in front of us, her face fierce with grief. I knelt in front of her and took her hands, and she embraced me, sobbing into my shoulder. She wept for a while, then pushed me away and rose.

'I'm returning to duty,' she said.

I opened my mouth to argue with her, but she raised her hand, her face still swollen and wet with tears.

'I need something to do. Something to keep me occupied. I need to keep —' She lost it again, gasping and unable to speak, then found her voice. 'I need to keep busy! I need to help. We have … we have … by the Heavens, how many dragons do we have that need homes?'

'Jade,' I said, guiding her to sit in the other visitors' chair, 'you just lost two of your daughters. You need to spend time with …' I struggled to remember which ones had died, furious at myself for not knowing.

'Jackie,' Jade said, unsurprised. 'I know that everybody saw them as a little clump of troublemakers, but to me they were unique and special and they were my darling little girls.'

'We taught them martial arts a few weeks ago,' John said. 'Frannie had a great deal of potential for energy.'

'Hinnie was very forthright, and although she wasn't the most talented, she was obviously willing to put the work in,' I said.

Jade was nodding, and John passed her a box of tissues.

'Both of them are gone, and Jackie's left,' I said. 'Her heart must be broken to have lost two sisters who were like a part of her. You need to be with her, because both of you have lost more than we can possibly understand.'

'I need to keep occupied, my Lady,' Jade said. 'If I sit around at home I will drift into depression. That has happened before when I lost family. I need to keep *busy*!' The last word was a cry of anguish.

'Meredith is outside,' John said. 'If she gives you the all clear, you may continue.'

'The Blue Dragon is also outside,' I said. 'Maybe you should spend some time with him and Jackie together?'

'If I had never agreed to the custody arrangements, they would still be alive!' Jade cried, hoarse with grief. 'It's his fault they're dead. He didn't protect them.' She gestured angrily with one hand. 'Send him away, I beg you, my Lord. I have no desire to see his selfish face.'

'If you want to resume your duties, you must work with him to arrange refuge for his subjects from the East,' John said. 'If you can't work with him, then it would be best if you didn't do it at all.'

She stared at him for a while, tears still running down her face. She mopped them with a tissue and nodded. 'I will overlook his failure for now, because our fellow dragons are in greater need. This is too important for my personal feelings to be in the way.'

'As I said, Meredith must give you the all clear,' John said. 'Now go and speak to her, and tell the Dragon to come in.'

'My Lord,' she said. She rose and saluted him, then me. 'My Lady.'

She turned to go, her green robes flowing around her. She stopped at the door and glared at the Dragon. He opened his mouth to say something to her, but she made a loud sound of disgust and stormed past him and out of the office.

The Dragon hesitated, looking after her, then came in. He was holding something like a baby, wrapped in the folds of his robe. As he neared us, it became apparent it was a fifty-centimetre-high tree sapling with a slender stem, bare roots, and a bushy gathering of leaves at its top.

'It took me nearly a full day, but I found one,' he said.

'You managed to salvage some of the Tree?' I said, relieved.

'No,' the Dragon said. 'She's gone. This is one of her children.' He bent with grief for a moment, then straightened. 'This is the only one that survived; I fished it out of the ocean. Can you help it?'

The leaves shifted and seemed to form a face, then they drifted apart again and were just a random pattern. The tree spoke with a voice like a child's whispering: 'I have been doused in salt water for days. I cannot be saved.'

'Ah Wu?' the Dragon said.

John generated a bubble of water and placed it over the plant, washing it clean. The sapling shivered within the water, then shook itself. John released the water and the tree faded again. John changed to Serpent, so big that the transformation knocked me off my feet and slammed me into the wall. The desk toppled over, scattering its contents.

'Are you okay?' John said in the Serpent's female voice.

'Yeah, no damage,' I said, wriggling out from under its coils. 'I think you broke your desk.'

'I know, Zara will kill me.'

It touched its nose to the sapling and the tree changed from yellow to green, a subtle transformation.

'Stop,' the Dragon said, his voice full of urgency. 'Enough.'

John changed back to human and turned his desk right way up. He concentrated and the papers that had been on it flew back to land haphazardly on its surface. He bent to pick up the Ninja Turtle figure and carefully placed it next to the monitor.

'Thank you, Dark Lord,' the tree said. 'But three days in salt water ...'

'I know,' the Dragon said. 'You need nourishment. Take it.' He held his arm out so the robes pulled away from his forearm.

'Highness,' the little tree said, 'you are one with us and we will not harm you.'

The Dragon put the tree on top of his arm. 'Do it. You are the only one left.'

'I cannot.'

'I did this for your mother, and I will do it for you. It will connect you with the forest, child, it must be done. You are the last one. Do it!'

The tree's roots grew and lashed out like whips, wrapping themselves around the Dragon's arm, then piercing the skin to bury themselves into it. We both stepped forward, but he raised his hand to stop us, his face fierce with pain. He staggered, and John and I helped him to sit. The tree's roots ran under the skin up his arm, and he jerked as it penetrated his chest and spread through him.

His face went blank and he looked up at us. 'Ah Wu. Some Shen are killing a tree. They've taken a tree to Europe and they will sacrifice her to open a portal.'

'Stop them, Lord Xuan, they are planning to kill one of us,' the tree said.

'How close to the grove are they?' John said.

'They're halfway there; she's fighting them every step of the way.'

'We have to stop them,' I said.

'I know. Do you need someone to remove the little tree when it has fed enough?' John asked the Dragon.

'No,' the Dragon said. 'I've summoned my Number One. He will find a safe place to put it once it's killed me.'

'Very well,' John said.

* * *

He took my hand, and teleported me to a location floating above the ocean. Both of us took True Form: him the two creatures, and me a serpent. His Serpent separated from the Turtle and I took its place, wrapping my coils around its shell.

Ready, I said, and the three of us dived into the ocean.

We reviewed the troops as he swam. Less than five thousand left to defend the Heavens. We shared the horrible knowledge that if the tree died and its sacrifice worked, a portal into the European Heavens would open. We could spring a surprise attack on the demons and dramatically increase our chances of success.

As he swam, we worked together to select a force of a thousand of the finest soldiers in the army, and mobilised them to the far west of the Western Heavens, ready to move if the way to the European Heavens was opened.

After three hours of liaison with our staff, we ran out of things we could do remotely and instead silently shared the sensation of underwater travel. He was in his True Form, the Serpent whipping through the water beside his Turtle, and his quiet joy at being whole and in his element eased my own spirit.

The Serpent changed to male human form: taller and leaner than the John I'd known, but with the same dark eyes and noble face. He swam to me and settled to sit cross-legged on the Turtle's shell, carefully moving my coils to make space. I wrapped my serpent body around him and he stroked my scales, the tips of his fingers sending ripples of pleasure through me. He pulled my serpent head down and smiled into my eyes. He stroked his hand over the top of my head and down the side of my neck, and I leaned into his touch. He pulled me closer and I rested my chin on his shoulder as he held me, his Turtle thrusting through the water beneath us.

He changed to Serpent and his coils slid cool and silken around me. We twined against each other, the feeling delicious on my scales.

You won't lose control of the Turtle? I said as we both moved down to lie on his shell.

I may be forced to stop for a short time when things become very interesting, both of him said in unison.

I hesitated. I'd never done this before — serpent to serpent — and I wasn't sure how the mechanics …

Relax, the Serpent said. *Slide. Sssslide.*

We slid over each other and the sensual movement on my scales ignited something deep inside me.

Yes, wonderful, you're there, he said. *Taste it.*

I flicked my tongue and tasted the essence in the water around us. It tasted of me: cool and musky and ready. And of him: sweet and wild and full of the freshness of the ocean.

Good, right species. If I was the wrong species it would be most traumatic for you. I haven't done this as snake in a very long time.

Turtle only?

I have more powerful urges, the Turtle said beneath me, making his shell vibrate and driving me to greater need.

I wrapped my coils more tightly around the Serpent, knowing that I needed to position myself correctly. Snakes only had a single opening and I wondered how …

Now I need you to trust me, he said with both voices. *Don't be afraid*. His head was next to mine and he flicked his tongue again, touching my scales. *I know it looks —*

'Holy shit!' I shouted, quickly disentangling myself. The scents that had filled the water around us dissipated. 'There's *two* of them? Those spines make the Turtle's organ look *tame*! No way will *both* of those things fit inside me.'

'Didn't you know? You used to own a snake.'

'Monty never grew big pink cactuses!'

He changed to human. 'Perhaps I should have warned you.'

'That has to hurt like hell, John. Hasn't a female serpent ever warned *you*?'

'Most of the time I am a female Serpent, Emma. And the experience is extremely pleasurable, believe me.' He ran one hand down the side of my body. 'When the species is right, the body of the female is built to accommodate the body of the male. Everything slides into place and locks and it's …' Even though he was in human form, his scent filled the water again, and I couldn't help but flick my tongue to taste it. 'It really is very good. Trust me.'

'Just like you trusted me,' the Turtle said beneath us.

'You stopped swimming,' I said without looking away from the Serpent.

'Oh,' he said with both voices, and the Turtle swam again.

'But there's *two*,' I said.

'I only use one.'

'What, and jerk off with the other? That must be hard with no hands.'

He bent to put his forehead in his hand and his shoulders shook. *Thank you*, he said as he laughed silently, probably for the first time in weeks.

I coiled up beside him and put my head in his lap, and he stroked me between the eyes, scratching behind my eye ridges and below my jaw where the most sensitive spots were.

'Do you want to try again?' I said.

'I can't perform unless your scent fills the water. And I don't think you're in the mood now.'

'The big pink cactus things can't emerge unless I make the scent?'

'That's right.'

'We can try again later,' I said.

'It might be better to stick to human form.'

'No,' I said, raising my serpent head. 'That was very good until the cactuses came out. I really do want to try again.'

He stroked my head. 'I promise it's worth it.' He dropped his voice. 'And your snake form is so damn hot — I've been wanting to do that for ages.'

'How far left to go?' I said.

'We're nearly there.'

I settled my head in his lap again. 'Then we should stop fooling around and prepare.'

'We have to stop anyway. Simone is flying to catch up with us when we reach France.'

'France?'

'This grove is in western France, near the Spanish border. Old Gaul.'

'Send Simone home. She shouldn't be involved in this,' I said.

'We may need her.'

'She shouldn't be fighting.'

I'm probably the most powerful thing on the Celestial apart from Daddy right now. If we can break through into the European Heavens, you'll need me, Simone said.

'You're too young.'

Simone's voice filled with grim pleasure. *You forget who my father is, Lady Emma. I'm not a child. I am adult spawn of the reptile God of War, the Destroyer of Demons. It is in my nature to be a warrior.*

'You're changing into something darker and more destructive,' I said. 'This isn't you!'

Yes, it is, she said, the grim pleasure even more pronounced. *I'm not changing, I'm growing. This is who I really am.* Her voice went back to a cheerful young woman. *I just sensed something out there. Daddy?*

John was silent for a moment, then said, 'Move to the side. I want to merge.'

I shifted and he changed to Serpent form, then combined beneath me. I wrapped my coils around his Serpent and clung to it while the Turtle carried us through the water.

'I have it,' he said. 'I smell death. A great deal of death. The tree — Sang Ye, Sang Shen's sister — she's mad.' The Turtle raised its head and moved with more force. 'We have to stop her, she's infecting the forest.'

After ten minutes of frantic swimming, he surged out of the water and flew. Simone came into view next to us, flying in Celestial Form in her dark blue robes and armour, with her twin swords on her back and her immensely long black hair streaming behind her.

Hang on, John said, and he gathered himself and shot forward so fast that the breath was knocked out of me. His Serpent held me as we streaked towards the mountains between France and Spain, Simone easily matching our velocity.

I smelled it before I saw it: decay and destruction.

A spiralling whirlwind of darkness full of black leaves rose a hundred metres into the air in front of us. The trees in the forest below thrashed in a gale that wasn't there. The trees weren't just dead; they were rotting where they stood, black goo dripping off them.

Sang Ye stood in tree form in the middle, seemingly untouched, but her branches writhed in the wind. The Shen who had tried to sacrifice her lay with their bodies decomposing into the dark sodden earth. The trees on the edge of the contaminated area died, their leaves falling, then turned black in an expanding circle around her.

'The only thing I can think of is to yin around the edge and create a firewall,' John said. 'Any other ideas?'

'That's what I was thinking as well,' I said. 'As long as Simone has enough control to run it around the edge without it getting out of hand.'

'We'll have to move fast, it's growing,' Simone said.

'Emma, go down to land and wait for us,' John said. He turned in the air towards me as he changed from True to Celestial Form.

'At least a hundred metres from the edge, and keep well back from it. Stay snake.'

Simone's Celestial Form grew and darkened, the stars within her robes becoming bright pinpoints floating around her. She dropped feet-first towards the earth, then banked to the edge of the black trees and started to yin behind them. I turned and flew well back to land on a small hill overlooking a farmhouse. There were sheep in the field, but no other signs of habitation. The wind picked up, blowing cold across me, as the god and goddess yinned a firewall around the heaving branches of the blackened forest. The smell of decay was even stronger and I resisted the urge to flick my tongue.

Okay, John said. *Come to the edge.*

I lifted off the ground and drifted closer to the contaminated area. A swathe of empty, yinned earth, twenty metres wide, circled it. The trees on the inside dripped black goo from their bare branches, their leaves spinning in the localised wind. The darkness was still spreading; the damage moving through the earth across the yinned gap. We didn't have much time.

She's not answering, Simone said, her voice raw with pain. *She's gone.*

The three of us flew up and over the decaying forest until we were in the eye of the whirlwind of leaves. The trees thrashed below us, seeming to reach up to destroy us.

There's a portal, Simone said with wonder. *We're in!*

You wait here while I go in, John said. *Destroy her after I've gone through.*

Simone didn't reply.

You're not strong enough to destroy her?

Simone shook her head.

Okay. Back up while I do it, John said.

No, Simone said. *I'll dash through the portal, you destroy her. Easiest.*

John was silent for a while.

I'm Immortal, Dad, and we hold Hell.

I really don't like this. Give me a minute.

We waited as the leaves thundered around us.

I see no major losses in the future, he said. *Take very special care, please.*

On my mark, she said. *Go.*

She swept down to the portal so fast that she was invisible.

John dropped at the same time and sent a concentrated column of yin straight into the middle of the blackened trees. The trees stopped thrashing as ice spread from the centre of the forest outwards, covering them in a coat of glittering crystals. The whirlwind weakened and the leaves fluttered to the ground.

The portal disappeared and there was complete silence.

John floated down and landed in the cleared space where Sang Ye had stood. He checked the area, then gestured for me to join him. I flew down as well and landed next to him, and changed to human — the ice was bitterly cold against my snake belly.

Simone? I said.

Nothing.

'Can you sense her?' I asked John.

'No,' he said, staring where the portal had been. 'But she may not be able to contact us. We'll just have to wait.'

10

After two hours of sitting on the damp ground, the sun was gone and I couldn't control the shivering. I was too new an Immortal to be unaffected by the cold.

'I've been summoned,' John said, his voice full of pain. 'The troops are two hours away. I'll station a squad here and have them wait for her.'

'Do I have the JE's permission to remain?'

'Yes. But wait at the chain hotel nearby; she'll contact you if she comes out. There's no need for you to freeze to death.'

He was right. I'd suffered through a cold night with no shelter before and wasn't in a hurry to repeat the experience. We flew to the small hotel and checked me in. The Eastern European woman behind the desk was astonished when John appeared to speak fluent Estonian, and she gave us a free upgrade.

When we were in the room and the door was shut, we wrapped around each other.

'I'm sure she's fine,' I said into his shoulder. 'She's Immortal.'

He pulled me tighter. 'Try to rest.' He moved away to speak to me, still with his arms around me, his dark eyes full of the deep connection we shared. 'I don't sense anything bad in the near future; she may just be stuck.' He looked away. 'I can't delay any longer. We've run out of food for the refugees in the Northern

Heavens and need money quickly to pay for supplies. I'm the only one who can sign the documents to sell the securities on the Earthly. I have to return.'

I pulled him down for a long kiss and he held me like he'd never let me go.

'Trust her,' I said. 'We've given her all the knowledge and wisdom we could. Now we must trust her to do what's right. She's probably smarter than both of us put together.'

'My Turtle agrees with you. My Serpent is offended,' he said, quickly kissed me again, and disappeared.

I sat on the bed and switched on the television. As usual, there were nearly a hundred cable channels and nothing worth watching. I tried to meditate, to avoid the horrible images of what could be happening to Simone alone in that unforgiving place full of demons. I missed my stone; it could provide me with updates from the network and always gave valuable advice in difficult situations like this. I wished I'd asked Gold for a new phone before we left so I could check my messages.

Two hours later I gave up. Perhaps I should take a shower, and try to wash my clothes with the hotel soap.

I rose and walked from one end of the room to the other, feeling alone and helpless. There wasn't room for a tai chi set. Meditating was ineffectual. I didn't have the strength to contact people back home by telepathy. Simone was out there alone and —

Emma? Daddy?

Simone! John roared in my head, then lowered the volume. *Are you okay?*

Wow, loud, she said. *I have it open. Hurry up!*

I threw myself out the door and rushed to the dead forest.

Simone gave a running commentary as I flew in snake form. *I went for kilometres all around the portal and didn't find anything. I didn't want to call that city guy — what was his name?*

Semias, I said.

Yeah, him. I was worried someone else would hear if I called him. I see you, Emma. Her voice became strained. *I don't know how much longer I can ...*

She was standing inside the shimmering portal as I swooped

towards her in snake form. A roar like a jet engine sounded some distance away: John at full speed.

Hold it open, John said, and streaked through the air above me.

He didn't stop at the portal; he took me behind the neck and dragged me through it. He stopped on the other side, put me down, and hugged Simone fiercely.

'Let it go,' he said.

The portal closed with a sound of metal scraping over ice.

We were on a wide grassy plain with a forest at the edge. Above us, high sweeping clouds brushed the night-time Heavenly sky. I looked up with wonderment. Enormous oval crystals, the smallest the size of a bus and the largest big enough to carry a city, hung in the air at different altitudes, some of them immensely far off the ground. Cities with glittering towers had been built on the islands, and silvery suspension bridges hung like delicate webs between them. The moonlight glinted off the crystals, causing rainbows all around us. The air was fresh with the fragrance of the living earth and I breathed deeply, flicking my tongue to taste it. This was Heaven, my Heaven, the place I'd come from.

'I feel the same way,' Simone said. 'I suppose it's because I'm half-European.' She concentrated and the portal opened again, then closed. 'Cool. I have it.'

'What's the word?' I said.

'I say "cool" all the damn time,' she said. 'But you're with Daddy anyway — he'd know if I was a copy.'

'She was just making the point that you still say it too much,' John said. 'But I don't think you do.' He raised his head as if listening. 'I can sense a great many demons about a hundred kilometres away.'

'I can't sense any demons,' Simone said. 'I went out looking — don't worry, I was really quiet — and I didn't find anyone. I can't sense that Semias guy, I can't sense any demons, it's like the whole world is empty.' Her voice caught. 'The towns on these floating islands are very beautiful, but there isn't a single living thing here; it's like they have no soul. I went out as far as I could but it's just so *quiet*. I've never been completely by myself like that before.' She wiped her shaking hand over her eyes. 'So I came back and I couldn't open the portal! It took me ages to work it out, and I was scared I was stuck, and I was alone. It was awful.'

'Never forget you are Immortal and Court Ten is always an option,' John said. 'Now open the portal and go out. I'll reconnaissance here. Open it once an hour, on the hour —'

She didn't let him finish. 'I don't know if I can open it from the other side, Daddy.'

'All right, you go out and I'll open it from this side.' He held his hand out. 'Show me how you do it.'

She took his hand and I quickly put my snake chin on her shoulder to watch as well. She opened the portal and John's eyebrows creased.

'I have no idea what you just did,' he said with wonder. 'Do it again.'

'God, Simone, you're twisting reality through four dimensions,' I said with similar wonder as she closed and opened it again. 'That must have been so challenging to learn, and it only took you a couple of hours.'

'I can't even see it!' John said.

'I saw how it worked as I came in,' she said. 'It's difficult, but I have it. It's like a three-dimensional maths graph in my head, but the graph is kind of back to front and the stuff that's further away is closer at the same time.'

'In four dimensions,' I said. 'I know some Earthly physicists who would give anything to see what you just did.'

'I can't hold it for much longer,' she said.

'Let it go,' John said, and released her hand as it disappeared. 'Emma, I can't see a damn thing. I have no idea what she's doing.'

'Can you do it, Emma?' Simone said.

'No way. It'd break my brain. I wouldn't even try.'

'Oh, come on, you know you're smarter than me. You're smarter than just about everybody.'

'Humph,' I said. 'Don't underestimate yourself. Remember who one of your fathers is.'

'The Serpent is female, so it's one of my mothers.'

'Whatever. Have you found anything, John?'

John's eyes were unfocused; he'd been searching the area while we talked. 'I need to travel north and see what's there. I think it's demons but I'm not sure.' He snapped back. 'Can you open the portal anywhere, or does it have to be here?'

'Here,' Simone said. 'Something about the alignment of the crystals in the sky affects the Celestial Harmony.'

'Both of you wait here —' He saw Simone's expression. 'Never mind. Let's go.'

He took Celestial Form, summoned a cloud, and I rode with him in my larger human form. Simone flew next to us in her usual human form, wearing a pair of jeans and a tatty sweater with a Harry Potter owl on the front. After twenty minutes of travel John slowed and reduced altitude. We edged over the top of a range of hills and John stopped. He hid us from view, and we approached the demons.

It was all I could do to contain my astonishment. It looked like a traditional army encampment, but with no sleeping tents or cooking fires. The demons stood unmoving in neat ranks, and there was a cluster of marquees at the end of the rows on the far side, which obviously held the administrative support. The demons covered the plain, an orderly unmoving engine of destruction.

Those humanoids are close to level sixty, John said. *They have ten battalions to one brigade — by the Heavens, there are a hundred thousand demons here.*

The cohort on the aircraft carrier was nothing compared to this, I said.

I know, he said. *There's another thousand armoured demons acting as centurions, stationed at the end of the rows of humanoids. We are in serious trouble.*

There's more on the far side, Simone said, rising higher and moving away to see.

Another twenty or thirty thousand toxic and ranged support troops: flyers, dogs, worms and slimes, John said.

There's no way we can defeat them, Simone said. *What do we do?*

Pre-emptive strike, John said. *I'll bring the other three Winds and as many Number Ones as we can gather, and we'll yin yang them.*

You can't use yang and yin at the same time — Simone began. *Never mind — one then the other.*

Can you take them all out? I said.

Maybe about half with a couple of Number Ones along, then the other half if they don't move. You'll need to help as well, Simone. Let's go back and call everybody.

My phone doesn't work up here! Simone said.

Of course not, there's no network, I said. *Your phone probably went flat searching for a signal. I'd say the Demon King's set up a small network using Gold's tech that they stole from us, but it's localised onto their main strongholds.*

Open the portal and I'll summon them, John said. *If you're not sure whether you can open it from the other side, we'll wait this side for them.*

Okay.

* * *

Twenty minutes later we arrived at the portal and hovered above it. Ten big armoured demons were standing at the location, guarding the Demon King, who was in their centre looking smug.

'Shit,' Simone said. 'Now what?'

Don't you dare use Seven Stars on him, I said. *If you destroy yourself now to take him out, that army will still conquer our Heavens.*

John floated closer until he was directly above the King, who didn't move. John put his hands out, palms down, towards the King and generated a concentrated column of yin that made the demon guards fall back. The yin snapped off, leaving a crater in the ground below the Demon King's feet. He floated above it, exactly where he'd stood before John attacked him.

One of the demon guards drew his weapon to retaliate, but the King waved him down.

'It was worth a try,' the King said. He gestured towards John. 'Let's talk.'

'Stay here,' John said to us, and floated down.

'You know what comes next, Ah Wu,' the King said when John was standing in front of him. 'Save your people a great deal of anguish and end it now.'

'I know. I will return and advise the Celestial,' John said. 'We will be in touch shortly.'

'This is why I love you so dearly, Turtle,' the King said. The demon guards shifted away from the location of the portal. 'You have seen how merciful I am prepared to be. Go talk to the Jade Emperor and I will wait for your call. If this can be resolved without more conflict I am prepared to be *extremely* merciful.'

'I thank you,' John said.

The portal opened.

'Go through,' the King said. 'I won't stop you or harm you. I've achieved my goal.'

Simone and I hesitated, floating above the open portal.

'Go through,' John said without looking away from the King.

We swept down, through the portal, and landed on the blackened ground next to the destroyed trees. John followed us and the portal closed

'Wait a few minutes, give him time to leave,' John said.

We stood silently in the dead forest.

It seemed forever before John spoke. 'Can you open it from this side?' he asked Simone.

Simone concentrated, then stopped and walked in a small circle. She crossed her arms in front of her chest and concentrated again. She stepped back and put her hands out towards the location of the portal.

She shook her head. 'It's like it's locked or something.'

'He closed it behind us,' John said. 'We must return to the Celestial and tell him we have no chance of victory.'

'We can yin and yang them when they come out to attack us,' Simone said.

'We have enough to take out about half of them, Simone,' John said. 'Then the Four Winds will be exhausted and the remaining demon soldiers will overrun Heaven. The refugees need to be moved into hiding on the Earthly, because once the demons occupy Heaven no civilian will be safe.'

'We need to hide Simone as well,' I said.

'Simone blazes like a dark sun. She cannot be hidden,' he said.

'The civilians come first,' Simone said.

'The best we can hope for is to hide the mortals,' John said. 'Mo Wang made no attempt to stop us when we came here; he wanted us to see his strength. The King can be merciful when the mood takes him.'

'How is that merciful?' Simone said. 'We'll lose. All of us will end up in the Pits!'

'Not if we can negotiate something,' John said. 'But now we know what our chances are, and we have time and opportunity to move the weakest somewhere safe. It is a kindness.'

'Don't you dare offer to go into that fucking cage,' I said, my voice low. 'I'd rather be lying dismembered in a pool of blood with you, than alone in a golden palace with you in a cage.'

'When the time comes I do not think we will have a choice,' he said. He changed to True Form. 'We need to head back quickly. Come and sit on my shell and I'll carry you.'

As soon as we entered the Asian Heavens, my head filled with voices.

We need the Dark Lord to sign the transfer of the securities, Jade said.

And the cistern's overflowing with sewage — there isn't enough water, Meredith said.

Nothing for breakfast tomorrow. We can't even make congee because there's no rice.

I know that having no laundry detergent isn't as major as …

Without his medication his heart will …

Five babies that need formula …

The last of the antibiotics …

The voices went silent.

'Thank you,' I said.

'A brief respite,' John said. 'We'll deal with all of them as soon as we've spoken to the Celestial. Then we need to arrange a safer place for everybody. I've asked Gold to contact the Grandmother — she may be able to help.'

'I'll head home and start organising things,' I said.

'No. I want you with me when I speak to the Jade Emperor. He can order me around but he can't bully you,' John said.

'I'll go to work on it. You two talk to the Jade Emperor,' Simone said.

'You are wonderful, Simone,' I said, and she grinned without humour and flew away.

The huge red gates of the Celestial Palace opened for us, and we were greeted by chaos in the main square. It was full of refugees, sitting outside their tents sharing stories, listening to music with headphones, or silently pensive. Others walked between the stacked belongings, carrying water or plastic takeaway boxes with the meals the Palace was providing. A couple of men were arguing loudly close to the wall, and some Elites rushed to quell the altercation. Some who saw us fell to one knee, but others sat silently on the pavers, their eyes turned inwards.

John, still in combined True Form, nodded his heads to those who acknowledged him as he strode through the cleared corridor up the centre of the crush. Nobody approached us, and some cringed away from John, intimidated.

He changed to human before we entered the Hall of Supreme Harmony. It was also full of refugees, this time the elderly and mothers with children. Babies cried, their wails echoing off the clerestory windows above. A few laughing children played tag along the corridor through the mattresses lined up on the floor. Women called our names as we passed, and both of us nodded a response.

The Imperial Elite Guard Cloud was waiting on the other side of the hall to escort us.

'Where is Er Lang?' John asked her.

'He is with the Celestial, Highness.'

We went through the smaller gardens and courtyards, again full of refugee humans, to the Jade Emperor's private quarters. The echoing voices went silent as we stepped through the moon gate into the empty courtyard outside his Residence. The Jade Emperor and Er Lang stood together under a peach tree.

We stopped and fell to one knee in front of the Jade Emperor, then rose. He guided us to a gazebo next to a small pond, and we sat around a ceramic outdoor tea table.

'Majesty,' John said.

'Lord Xuan. You have news?'

'Simone found a way into the European Heavens.'

'Good!' Er Lang said. 'Can we move in? Did you find any demons there? We can attack them before they attack us!'

'There are a hundred thousand troops there, each of them equal to one of ours. There are a thousand black-armoured demons, and another twenty thousand support troops. We cannot win. We need to begin the negotiations for surrender, because if they march on the Heavens many innocents will die.'

'Are they active? Or just parked?' Er Lang said.

'Parked, but not dormant.'

'Can we fly in and drop a nuke on them? Take them out in one go?'

'The portal is closed. The Demon King allowed us to enter to see the size of his force to spur us into surrendering without a fight.'

'We can't!' Er Lang said, shocked.

'We should. We have no chance. We need to negotiate terms for surrender,' John said.

'There must be something pre-emptive we can do! They're just standing there, a sitting target, and you want to surrender before they even move?'

'Majesty,' John said, addressing the Jade Emperor, 'we need to start negotiations to protect the mortals and keep non-combatant Immortals from the Pits. If the demons march on the Heavens, we will lose. We may be able to salvage something out of this now, if we do not fight.'

The Jade Emperor hadn't moved during this entire exchange. He just sat, pale and withdrawn, looking at the table. We waited for a reply.

After a couple of minutes I prompted him. 'Majesty?'

He glanced up at me. 'Yes, Lady Emma?'

'Lord Xuan suggests we begin negotiations for surrender.'

'I know.'

'Do you want me to initiate proceedings? I can manage it,' John said. 'I will do my best to salvage the dignity of the Celestial —'

'We will not surrender,' the Jade Emperor said. 'We will fight.'

All my breath left me in a long rush. 'That's suicide.'

'Ready the defences on the plain outside the Northern Heavens. We will face them there.'

The three of us were silent for a moment, then realisation hit us at the same time and our expressions filled with wonder.

'What aren't you telling us, Majesty?' Er Lang said.

'We have a chance?' I said. 'You think we can still beat them?'

'Prepare the defences, Generals.'

'Are you sure, Majesty?' John said. 'Unless there's something you're not telling us, there is no way we can win this. You must tell me if you have a secret weapon that will ensure success.'

'I cannot tell you.'

Relief filled me. 'You know something. We'll win!'

'Majesty?' John said, still unsure.

The Jade Emperor rose and nodded to each of us. 'Prepare the remaining troops for a last stand outside the Northern Heavens. The demons will attack in five days.'

He turned and walked into his Residence without saying another word.

'What the *fuck* is wrong with him?' John asked Er Lang. 'We can't possibly win. Even if he pulls an army of fucking qilin out of his ass, there's no way we can beat them. The Winds and their children can yin yang about half of them, I can destroy another few thousand before I go down, and then the Heavens will fall.' John looked from Er Lang to the Jade Emperor's pavilion. 'What isn't he telling us?'

'He has to know something that he can't tell us. Something that will bring us victory,' I said.

'Er Lang?' John said.

Er Lang leaned his elbows on the table, his expression grim. 'I've never seen him like this. What we just saw is the most communicative he's been in weeks. It's like he's given up and doesn't care. I'm not sure he knows what he's doing.'

'He's the goddamn *Jade Emperor*, guys,' I said. 'He knows *everything*.'

'That may be the problem, Emma,' John said. 'Imagine if every future you saw was full of suffering. Every single one.'

I paused at the implications. 'Can his mind handle it?'

'Exactly,' Er Lang said. 'Is death preferable to imprisonment by the Horde? Maybe he thinks it is. Maybe he's deliberately leading the army to their deaths because the alternative is worse.'

'But they're *mortal*,' I said.

'Even so.'

'Can we negotiate a surrender anyway?' I raised my hands. 'Never mind. The answer came to me immediately: we must follow his orders.'

'We can only hope that you're right and victory will be ours through circumstances only he can predict,' John said.

'What do you two see?' I said.

They shared a look and their expressions said it all.

'My family are on the Mountain,' I said, my throat thickening. 'If they defeat the army at the Northern Heavens, they'll tear straight through the Mountain to the Celestial Palace and destroy everything.' I wiped the tears away. 'My family have nothing to do with this, and the boys are just children. Matthew's only three years old. I hate to think what the King will do to them to have his revenge on us.'

'The Grandmother may be able to protect them,' John said. 'Her location is remote, isolated and sparsely populated.'

'You're right,' I said, relieved. 'The Australian desert is huge. The demons will never find them if we hide them there.'

'Isn't the extreme climate dangerous?' Er Lang said.

'Not as dangerous as staying here,' John said.

'Good point.' Er Lang rose. 'We have five days. I'll work on the remaining troops; you organise a refuge for the non-combatants. I'll be in touch if I need anything.'

11

'The Grandmother and Gold are in your office,' John said as we flew back to the Northern Heavens on his cloud. 'Can you talk to her while I sell these securities? It needs to be done before the banks close.'

'Leave it with me,' I said.

He pulled me around so my back was on his chest, held me close and kissed the side of my neck. I put my arms over his and held them. We shared the closeness until we approached the Palace of the Northern Heavens. When it came into view, he released me and straightened, pulling his dark forbidding persona around him. I composed my face as well, and we tried to be as cold and regal — and as confident — as possible as we landed, then stepped off the cloud and strode through the refugees in our own Palace complex. He headed to the Hall of Dark Justice to handle the paperwork, and I went to the administrative offices next to the main court to see Gold and the Grandmother.

They were sitting in the visitors' chairs; Gold in his tan suit and the Grandmother in a brown and gold tie-dyed shift.

I knelt and bowed my head. 'Grandmother.'

'Emma, dear, don't do that,' she said. 'Up you get. You just saw the Jade Emperor, how bad is it?'

'Gold, go out,' I said.

Gold opened his mouth to protest, then closed it again. 'That bad?'

I raised my hand. 'Sorry. Some of the Dark Lord's bad manners still linger. But it would be better if the stone network didn't hear this.'

'Out,' the Grandmother said. 'I'll let you know as much as I can once we're done here.' She glared at him. 'You have a big mouth, Gold, you know you do.'

He looked about to protest, then smiled wryly. 'You have a point. But I want to know your plans for keeping my children safe.'

'You'll be a part of them. Right now, let us sort this out,' I said.

Gold rose, saluted me, bowed to the Grandmother, and went out.

'He's probably eavesdropping anyway,' I said, sitting behind the desk and indicating my computer's microphone.

'If he is, he'll be in two pieces,' the Grandmother said. 'Now tell me how bad it is. I heard that Simone broke into the European Heavens. What did you find?'

Simone, I said, contacting her telepathically. *Did you tell anyone what we found in the European Heavens?*

Dear god, of course not, she said with horror.

Thanks. Need-to-know for now, please.

Of course! Geez, Emma.

'We found a hundred thousand big humanoid troops, a thousand armoured centurions, and a support army of twenty thousand worms, slimes and dogs,' I said out loud.

The Grandmother puffed out her cheeks. 'You can't beat that. They'll overrun you.' She leaned her elbow on the armrest and rubbed her chin. 'That's why you asked to speak to me. You're hoping I can shelter the people who are hiding here.'

'And the ones in the Celestial Palace. We have a hundred thousand mortal refugees, Grandmother, and when the demons win —'

'*When* they win? What did the Jade Emperor say? If they're going to win, you need to negotiate something now.'

'That's what we said. The Jade Emperor's ordered us to fight. Here. In five days.'

'He needs his bloody head read. Thousands of humans will die.'

'Can you shelter them, Lady? I know our homeland. There are stretches of the Great Sandy Desert where a hundred thousand people could disappear with no difficulty whatsoever.'

'Not any more. You know that fuss they made about immigrants? How they created a special security force to combat them? They filled the media with xenophobic propaganda about how Australia's being overrun with illegal Asian immigrants ...'

'Oh, dear lord, our refugees are all Asian.'

'Exactly, dear. He's been ahead of you all the way.'

'But that's just the borders, the coastline. If we fly them into the Red Centre —'

'There's an army of humans there waiting for you. They *train* them there, just to keep an eye on me. They have helicopters patrolling the desert. Your refugees would be found and sent home to Asia, straight into the demons' hands.'

'I need to find somewhere safe for these people to go!' I brushed my hair back and retied my ponytail. 'Are the Australian Shen talking to you? What about the Australian Heavens?'

'Like all Shen, they're bound by the Earthly laws of the land they oversee. The government of Australia was voted in fair and square, and their laws say that no refugees are allowed. Like the rest of the Shen, they're waiting to see who wins this and they don't want to be involved.'

'Do you have any suggestions at all, Grandmother?' I said, my voice weak.

'How about the desert of Western China?'

'Patrolled as well. Heavenly and Earthly.'

'Then you leave them where they are and fight to defend them.'

'And gamble with their lives that the Jade Emperor hasn't lost it and wants to send everybody to their deaths.'

'Let me look.' Her eyes unfocused as she looked into the future, and her face went grim. 'Too complicated. Too much suffering and death. All I see is death.'

'If anything comes up, please let me know. Any place not watched by the demons. Anyone who'd be willing to provide them with sanctuary. Anything.'

'I will.' She rose, and I did too. 'You were right. Gold doesn't need to know any of this.'

'Thank you.'

She came to me and gently clasped my upper arms, kissing me once on each cheek. 'I'll keep looking. I know how important this is. Let me talk to my Elders.'

'I appreciate it,' I said, but she was already gone.

'Gold?' I said loudly.

He came in and saluted me. 'Top-secret meeting finished?'

'Ask the Grandmother,' I said. 'You were arranging accommodation on the Earthly for some of the refugees. How many can the hotels take?'

'About twelve hundred.'

'Move them in. The most vulnerable — mothers and children — first. You have five days.'

'What happens in five days?'

I went to the doorway to speak to Yi Hao. 'Is the first one the baby formula?'

'Yes,' Yi Hao said.

Gold persisted. 'Are you sure you can't tell me more? We have Lord Xuan to defend us. The Horde don't have a chance.'

'That's right. But I still want those mothers and kids out of here before Saturday.'

'What about your family? What about *my* family?'

'I'm giving you the most important mission I ever have, Gold —'

'Wah, he's still in there,' he said, his eyes wide.

I continued, ignoring him. 'I'm trusting you with the lives of my family. Find somewhere safe for them. Somewhere so remote the demons will never find them. The hotels owned by Celestials aren't anonymous enough. Hide your family too. Make them invisible.'

'Can't your family go to Australia? They're Australian citizens.'

'The demons are waiting for them.'

'That's why the Grandmother can't take our refugees,' he said, understanding.

'Exactly.'

'What happens in five days? They'll attack? We have the Dark Lord. Everything will be fine.'

'How much of the future can you see, Gold?'

'Hardly anything. I'm a very small Shen.'

'So am I. So just keep saying that we'll be sure to win — the last thing we need is panic. But have those mothers and children out of here before any attack happens.'

'My Lady.'

'I need a new phone as well. What was on the log — all those calls?'

'Just random strings of data, white noise. I ran a few decryption algorithms against them and found nothing. I think there's a glitch on my Celestial network but I don't have time to track it down.' He held his hand out and a phone appeared in it. 'Here's a new one for you.'

'Thanks.' I raised my voice to speak to Yi Hao. 'Let the baby formula woman in.' I lowered it again to speak to Gold. 'We need the formula in a big hurry — I'll probably have to head down to the Earthly and buy it myself. Any Asian person buying retail milk powder in bulk in Hong Kong is likely to be lynched after that Mainland run on it.'

'Good idea. Take a demon with you to carry the shopping, and stock up on medicine and antibiotics as well.' He saluted me and went out.

* * *

The minute Simone, Smally and I arrived in the Heavens with the trolley of formula and drugs, we were mobbed. Simone used energy to push the people back and stood guarding, keeping them at bay.

Yue Gui came out of the offices and strode across the square to us. As the crowd parted to let her through, a little green dragon took advantage of our distraction, raced up to the pile of supplies, grabbed one of the cartons of baby formula, and ran.

'That's for human babies!' I shouted after her.

'Stop her. I'll handle this,' Yue Gui said.

Simone and I pushed through the people to chase the dragon. She moved too fast to follow, flitting through the air a couple of metres above the ground.

'That's formula for human babies!' I shouted again, but she ignored us.

She went straight to the medical centre and changed to human form of a fifteen-year-old girl. She ran through the centre of the packed patients to a dragon in True Form lying prone on a blanket next to a hospital crib holding a tiny baby.

'Ah Ma,' the girl said to the dragon.

The dragon raised her head. 'Is that milk for your sister? Tell me it's milk for the baby!'

'It is!'

'Thank you, Lady Emma, I owe you my daughter's life.'

The dragon tried to rise but didn't make it. She collapsed to lie on her side, panting.

'Ah Ma had a very difficult delivery in human form,' the girl said, taking one of the pre-made bottles out of the carton.

She looked around and Simone held her hand out. 'I'll warm it for you.'

'She's stuck in dragon form, the internal injuries are too severe,' the girl said. 'She was recovering in the Palace Under the Sea when it fell. One of the other mothers helped out with Bebe, but she didn't have enough milk for ours and her own.' She bent to speak to the dragon. 'Can you do it, Ma Ma?'

'You do it, I might hurt her,' the dragon said. She put her front claw on the girl's knee. 'You are a good daughter, Ah Gau.'

Ah Gau stroked her mother's claw, then picked up the baby and sat in a chair to nurse her. Simone checked the temperature of the milk on her wrist, nodded, and handed it to Ah Gau. The baby was on a drip and didn't respond when her sister tried to feed her. She lay limp with her eyes open.

'Eat, little one,' the mother dragon said, her voice soft and desperate. 'Don't give up now.'

'She won't take it,' Ah Gau gasped. 'She's too weak.'

Simone knelt in front of them. She took the baby's hand and concentrated. 'She's ice-cold. Come on, we won't let this defeat us.'

A silvery nimbus of energy floated around her, then surrounded the baby. The baby squealed, then threw her mouth open and wailed. Ah Gau tried to put the teat into her mouth and she fought it.

'Put it on her cheek next to her mouth,' the dragon said. 'There's a touch reflex.'

Ah Gau tried it, and when the teat touched the baby's cheek she turned her face towards it. They had a small tussle, with the baby becoming more and more agitated as she reached towards the teat, until Ah Gau had it positioned correctly and the baby latched on and sucked enthusiastically.

The mother dragon gave a huge sigh of relief and her head flopped onto the floor.

I checked the box: enough bottles to last the baby at least another couple of days, when I could do another run.

'Your daughter will be fine,' I said to the dragon, and stopped. She was lying unmoving with her eyes half-open. Even without touching her I could see that her chi, her breath of life, was gone.

'Ah Ma?' Ah Gau said.

Simone knelt and put her hand on the dragon's side, then took it away and shook her head.

Ah Gau wept over the tiny baby as she continued to give her nourishment. I put my arm around her shoulders while Simone notified a couple of demon staff to take the mother's body away.

My phone rang and I yanked it out of my pocket. No caller ID. I rejected the call.

* * *

Jade was in my office when I returned. She closed the door and stood on the other side of the desk. She was pale and drawn, and her eyes were red. I didn't ask her if she was okay because I knew the answer.

'What can I do for you, Jade?'

'I need you to talk to Jackie. She won't go with your family.'

'Can anyone order her to go?'

'She's not of age. She hasn't pledged allegiance. Only the Jade Emperor himself would order her, and I won't ask him. So can you talk to her for me?'

Jackie stormed in, wearing a pair of jeans and a T-shirt. She fell to one knee and saluted me, then rose. 'Lady Emma, my mother needs me.'

'You won't be safe here. Go with them,' Jade said.

Jackie put her arm around Jade's waist. 'I will not leave you alone after we just lost my sisters.'

'But you won't be —' Jade began.

'I miss them so much,' Jackie said, the tears flowing down her face. 'We need to stick together, no matter what happens.' Her voice thickened. 'You're all I have left!'

Jade pulled her into an embrace and they both let go, clutching each other.

'Okay,' Jade said. She pulled back and wiped her eyes. 'You can help me.'

'Just keep me busy,' Jackie said. 'If there's anything you need done, Lady Emma, let me know.'

'I will.'

They went out, leaning on each other.

12

It was a crisp spring night when my family and Gold's gathered at the top of the Celestial stairway.

John divided, the Serpent took female human form, and she went down the stairs. She came back up accompanied by Amy's father, Richard Wu. He looked in his mid-fifties and was stout with a strong New Zealand accent.

He stood at the top of the stairs and gaped up at the main gates to the Celestial Palace. 'I finally make it to the Celestial Palace and I don't have a chance to go inside and look around.'

Amy and Gold's children, Little Jade and Richie, ran to him and hugged him.

He picked up Little Jade and kissed her on the cheek. 'How are my best grandchildren?'

'We're learning kung fu off Aunty Emma!' Richie said, pulling at Richard's trousers. 'We're really good, we'll fight the demons if they try to attack us. Hiya!'

He performed the first few moves of the modified set I'd been teaching him, making loud martial arts noises.

'I'm glad I have you to protect me,' Richard said, jolly.

'Were you followed?' Gold asked him.

'I don't think so. The streets were deserted.'

'We'll change everybody's forms just to make sure,' John's Turtle said.

'There's an awful lot of us,' I said.

'We can handle it,' his Serpent said. She gestured for Gold to approach, and put her hand out. 'I'll give you the pattern and we can work together.'

Gold hesitated, and John gestured impatiently again.

'It's okay,' I said. 'It freaks me out as well.'

'Get over yourselves, it's just me,' the Serpent said.

'John, that's harsh,' my mother said, scolding. 'What if Emma suddenly changed into a man? How would you feel then?'

'What, like this?' the Serpent said, and the air became pearlescent around me.

My sisters collapsed laughing.

Ignore them, I think you're gorgeous, the Serpent said.

She took Gold's hand and they concentrated together.

My family changed into a Maori family group, dark-skinned but with similar faces. The Turtle changed to his European male form, and the Serpent changed to a tiny middle-aged Chinese woman — the same form we'd taken in Beijing when I'd been absorbed by him. She smiled into my eyes and somehow she was still my John. I wanted to give her a huge hug — she was adorable — then she went steely-eyed and she was all Dark Lord.

Gold turned into a pretty Chinese woman with long hair and dimples, and grinned at Amy, who was in male Maori form. Two of the boys had been changed to slender mixed-race women.

'Okay,' Gold said loudly. 'After we go down the stairs, you can talk to each other but don't use names. There's a van waiting for us in the Great Eagle Centre car park. When we reach the airport, I'll handle everything. Richard?'

'We're flying to Wellington,' Richard said. 'It's a nine-hour flight. We have a big house outside town on an acreage that Gold bought for us.'

We went to the bottom of the stairs, and my parents stopped and stared at the chaos. The area under the building that had held the elegant nine-dragon wall was a mass of construction work, and all the traditional features — the wall, the dragon fountain and the qilin statues — were gone. It was dark except for the dim light of neon signs outside shining through the canvas barriers that blocked the construction from public view.

'What happened here?' my mother said.

'A demon took over the company that owns the building. He was a copy of one of the human executives,' I said, leading them through the destroyed Chinese garden and out through the construction barriers, unguarded this late at night. 'They took the wall down and offered it to the government. A demon copy who'd taken the place of a senior government official said the wall had no cultural value and they didn't want it. It's in pieces in a warehouse in Lam Tin.'

'What about the dragons in the wall?' Amy said, distraught.

'They refused to leave,' John's Serpent said. 'I had to order them to abandon the wall.'

'We have to keep a guard at the top of the stairs because the demons try us all the time,' I said as I led them towards Great Eagle Centre. 'The demon executive is replacing the Chinese garden here with a copy of a Western one in New York.'

'Classy,' Jennifer said, her voice heavy with sarcasm. 'Matthew's half-Chinese and his heritage is being thrown away.'

'We tried to buy the wall but they wouldn't sell it to us,' Simone said. 'As soon as we defeat the demons, we can bring everything back.'

'Good,' my mother said.

Gold guided everyone to the car park under one of the twin towers next to the waterfront in Wan Chai. The van waiting there was actually a minibus, big enough to carry all of us.

'I'll patrol above,' the Johns said in unison, and disappeared.

'I'll drive, you ride shotgun, Gold in the back,' Greg said to me.

I put my hand on his arm to stop him. 'Whoever's bigger should ride shotgun and be ready to defend them. That's you.'

He hesitated, and looked from Gold to me. Gold's face didn't shift.

'You know you are,' I said. 'I'll drive. You two guard.'

He nodded once, and I went around to sit behind the wheel. He sat on the front passenger side, summoned his sword and placed it at his feet. Gold went into the back of the bus with Amy and their children.

I eased the bus down the narrow steep ramp, out of the car park and onto the four-lane main road through the centre of town, then turned west to take the Western Harbour Tunnel for a direct route to the airport. The traffic was intermittent this late at night. The children in the back were excited and shared their knowledge of the brightly lit Hong Kong landmarks as we drove, but the adults were alert and nervous. We swept through the tunnel and out into the complex network of raised expressways that ran through the newly reclaimed West Kowloon. We ran into a traffic jam halfway there, and the waiting cars dodged between the lanes to try to squeeze through faster.

'Is everything okay?' my father said from the back, his voice thin with concern.

'This isn't unusual,' I said.

'Will we miss our airplane?' Little Jade said.

'No, we have plenty of time,' Greg said.

When we reached the blockage, a jolt of panic shot through me and Greg stiffened in his seat. It wasn't an accident causing the pile-up, it was a police roadblock. They'd put a portable barrier across the road and were letting cars through one at a time, checking them as they did.

'Any demons?' I said softly.

'No. All human. May be legit,' Greg said.

Gold?

Accessing, Gold said. *They're looking for fugitives from a foreign tour group who are infected with something like Ebola ... They've been warned to be very careful but to take the group unharmed ...* He spoke out loud. 'They're on to us and they're diverting us!'

The police came around to the driver's side to speak to me.

'Through,' one of them said. 'Then pull over.'

I hesitated, looking at him. We could easily take all of them out and continue to the airport ... and they would have a small army waiting for us when we arrived. I followed the policeman's directions and took the bus around the barrier to park it on the other side.

'Stay here with the kids, Jen,' Greg said, and he and I exited the bus to speak to the police. Gold stepped out as well, and the three of us faced off against half-a-dozen nervous policemen.

The door of the bus opened and John came out in his normal middle-aged male human form, wearing a Western-style suit and tie. The policemen weren't fazed by him; obviously they were all humans with no demons at all.

John strode up to the senior police officer and fixed his dark gaze on him. 'You will let them through.'

'Of course,' the policeman said. 'My mistake, you can go.' He straightened and spoke to us with force. 'No, you can't. We want to talk to you. Stay here.'

A middle-aged man in the uniform of a high-ranking police officer emerged from a large black car nearby and sauntered over to us. It was a demon in the form of Superintendent Cheung, my contact in the Hong Kong police. He was dead and replaced. Everybody I touched died. My throat filled.

'You didn't kill him, Emma,' John said softly.

'If he'd never met me, he'd still be alive.'

'He came after me first, love.' John's voice gained an edge of an Australian accent; he was closely linked to me. 'He thought I killed Michelle. Chin up.'

We stepped forward to speak to the Cheung copy.

'Back, Gold,' Greg said, and Gold edged nervously away to stand in front of the bus.

The demon stopped in front of us and put his hands behind his back. 'Lord Xuan. Lady Emma. Prince Bai Jin.' He nodded to Gold. 'Lord Gold. I take it that the Lady's family is in there?'

'Make any attempt to harm them or hold them and I will take your head and the head of every other demon here,' I said.

'I understand the threat, my Lady, but I am the only demon here. The others are all human police doing their jobs for me as police superintendent. I'm not here to hurt your family. I'm just here to gently suggest that you take them back home and don't try a stupid stunt like this again. Go home, everyone.'

'They won't be safe,' I said.

'Let us negotiate something,' John said at the same time.

'Dad wants them where he can see them,' the demon said. 'If they do not attempt to hide themselves or attack us, we will not harm them. They will be very useful.' He gestured towards the bus. 'Now take them home before they all go for a drive in a police car to our headquarters and find themselves in detention. The police have good reason to believe that they are illegal immigrants on forged passports. The photos on their passports show white people.'

I hesitated, looking at him, then at the human policemen surrounding us. I could take them all down single-handedly, and John could easily destroy the demon.

But these were innocent humans being controlled, and I wasn't a murderer.

'Immigration and security at the airport have been alerted and they're waiting for you,' the demon said and linked his hands behind his back again. 'They'll never make it onto their plane.'

'What can I offer you to let them through?' I said.

'I have my orders, my Lady. I'm a demon. I must obey the King as you must obey the Jade Emperor. We are merely puppets that dance for them. So take your family home, and hope they are not called to join the dance.'

I made a loud sound of frustration and turned away to look into John's eyes. He gestured with his head and we headed back to the bus. The policemen made no move to impede us as we reboarded. They opened the metal railings blocking the two sides of the expressway and stopped traffic so I could pull the bus onto the other side of the road and head back to Hong Kong island.

'What if we went over the Eastern Harbour Crossing?' my mother said.

'They're waiting for you at the airport,' I said. 'Your passport photos look nothing like your current forms. We can only cloud their minds so much; if they know what to look for, you are in serious trouble. You'll be detained as illegals.'

'I will arrange transport to have you carried to New Zealand by some dragons or something,' John said.

'Good idea,' Greg said. 'I can carry some too. We'll move you somewhere safe.'

'What's the matter, Mummy?' Matthew said. 'Aren't we going on the plane after all?'

'No, we'll do something much more fun,' Jen said with forced cheerfulness.

Amanda made a soft sound of terror.

Four hours later, we all met outside Persimmon Tree to try again. John changed to his combined True Form and the Serpent separated from the Turtle. Greg summoned a large cloud and his family — Jennifer, Matthew, Colin and Andrew — stepped onto it. I hoisted the rest of the family — my parents, Amanda and Alan, Mark and David — onto the Turtle's shell, then changed to snake.

'My Serpent will take the left flank. Don't be afraid, the snakes are me and Emma,' John's Turtle said as the Serpent slithered up to guard the other side of him. 'Are we ready?'

'We have nothing to hold on to!' my mother cried.

'You don't need to hold on,' the Turtle said, and lifted into the air.

I flew up to guard its right flank and Greg protected the rear on his cloud.

We flew down off the Mountain, with Matthew making loud crows of delight until Jennifer hushed him. John swam through the air, his flippers making curling patterns in the clouds. We reached the Gates and slowed. A squadron of flyers — each three metres from nose to tail — was waiting for us on the Heavenly side.

Greg flew his cloud to the edge of the Turtle's shell. 'Everybody off,' he said.

Jennifer carried Matthew off the cloud, and the boys followed. Greg dismissed the cloud and took Celestial Form: three metres tall, wearing a white robe with gold armour, and with golden hair to his waist held in a topknot with a small gold crown. He summoned his sword, the Gold Meteor, and nodded to us.

'You are so cool, Daddy,' Matthew said softly.

Greg grinned down at him. 'You'll be just as cool one day. All of you.' He turned back to the demons and his face hardened. 'Three on the right.'

'Two on the left,' I said.

'And all the rest for me,' the Serpent said.

The Turtle dropped to settle on the grassy hill before the Gates; it couldn't hold my family in the air while the Serpent fought the demons.

We rushed them and they came for us. I grabbed the demon on the left by the neck. The one next to it opened its mouth to bite me and I used the one in my mouth to block the blow. The flyer missed me and latched onto the one I was holding. I worried them from side to side, then dropped them and watched with satisfaction as they fell, stunned and locked together. I flew down to finish them, ramming my nose into them and destroying them.

Over a hundred armed humanoids carrying swords swarmed out of the Gates building, heading towards my family. The Turtle gently levered everyone off its shell, then stood its ground in front of them. I moved as fast as I could to help it.

'Greg, down!' I yelled.

'What?' Greg shouted, then dropped as well, the flyers following him. 'Where the *fuck* is Guan Yu?'

Greg, the Serpent and I stood in front of my family, who were cowering behind the Turtle's shell. The flyers swooped down, attempting to grab my sisters, but the Turtle knocked them out of the sky with blasts of shen from its mouth.

The demons from the Gates stopped three metres from us, a mass of sharp pointed metal. One of the larger ones stepped forward, opened its mouth to reveal its tusks, then took a deep breath and shot a blast of demon essence — black with pale blue energy around its edge — straight into the Turtle's head. The Turtle imploded into a black hole in reality, leaving my family undefended, and the Serpent disappeared as well.

One of the flyers swooped down, grabbed my sister Amanda, and dropped her into the group of demons.

'Amanda!' I screamed, and slithered towards them with my head raised.

They pushed her to the front where we could see her: seemingly untouched, but rigid with fear. One of the demons held her with its hand around her throat.

'Back off or I will kill her right now,' it said.

'Mum!' Mark wailed behind us.

I changed back to human and raised my hands in surrender. Greg put his sword on the ground in front of him and raised his hands as well. The demon grabbed Amanda's arm and pulled it behind her, so strong that it seemed effortless. She dropped her head and whimpered.

'Don't hurt her,' I said. 'We surrender. We concede. Take me instead. I'm the one you want. I'll send them back home, just don't —'

The demon jerked Amanda's arm and her shoulder cracked. She screamed and collapsed in its grasp, sobbing. Both of her sons screamed as well. Alan tried to run to her and I put my hand out to stop him before he passed me. He fought me, pulling away, and I had to hold his arm tight to stop him from throwing himself at them.

'Alan, she needs you!' I said.

He made a loud sound of frustration and stood next to me, trembling.

'Please,' I said. 'Trade me for her.'

'If you go home now, nobody else will be hurt,' the demon said. It shook Amanda, making her scream again. 'Just stop trying to take your family out, okay? When we win, we'll need them to make sure you don't do anything stupid.'

It pushed Amanda towards us and she fell into Alan's arms. Mark and David loudly protested behind me; Greg was stopping them from running to their mother.

'The next time you try to run away, we'll do this to one of the *children*,' the demon said. 'Dad's waiting for you to meet him and discuss terms. He won't wait much longer. Now go home.'

* * *

That afternoon I was sitting alone in the living room of the Imperial Residence in the Dark Palace of the Northern Heavens, staring at the contact list on my phone while I waited for John to be returned from Court Ten. The phone started to play music without me touching it: smooth jazz with a velvet-voiced woman singing about smoke and whisky. It was the sort of music that my stone adored. I checked it, but there was no call to answer. It was just playing music that I'd never put into it.

My parents came in and I quickly turned the phone off, then rose to hug them.

'Are you okay?' I said, sitting them on the other sofa. 'Is Mandy all right?'

'She's resting comfortably,' my mother said. 'Meredith gave her energy healing and her shoulder should be okay in a couple of weeks.'

'Will she see me now? I need to apologise.'

'No, you don't,' my mother said. 'But you should stay away for a while anyway.' She smiled without humour. 'That was quite a scare, wasn't it?'

'What happened to Guan Yu?' my father said. 'The guy that guards the Gates?'

'They killed him. He's in Court Ten as well. They've taken the Gates.'

'How did they know we were there?' my mother said. 'Both times we tried to go through and they were waiting for us.'

'They didn't know,' I said. 'Now they have control of the Gates, they've been watching them. Big Shen like John can go down directly, but smaller Shen like me and Greg, and humans like you, have to use the Gates.'

'Humans like *us*,' my mother said.

'Emma ...' my father said, and trailed off.

'I know. This is all my fault,' I said, looking down at my hands.

'We want you to be brave, sweetheart,' my mother said. 'And if it comes to us or the rest of the Heavens, choose the Heavens.'

I glanced up at her. 'What?'

'If they're blackmailing you with our safety, and they threaten to torture us, just take us out of the picture,' my father said. 'You mustn't let anything stop you from doing what you have to.'

'I can't do that!'

'If you have to, you have to,' my mother said. She took my hand. 'If we are the only thing stopping you from fighting these monsters, then we want you to remove us so you can concentrate.'

'I will never do that in a million years,' I said. 'If I did that, I would be as bad as them.'

'We won't make you promise,' my mother said. 'But if you need to make the hard decision, we are right behind you.'

'God.' I ran my hands through my hair. 'We think this might be what the Jade Emperor is doing to everybody. Killing you all because the alternative — being toys for the demons — is worse than death.'

'If that's the case, then I agree with him,' my father said. He rose. 'We'll leave you to it. We just wanted you to know how we feel.'

'Thank you, but it will never come to that,' I said. 'And it's beside the point, because if they threaten the children then I will have to do anything they say. I may, in a fit of madness, be able to remove you from the equation, but I could never do it to a helpless child.'

'We wouldn't expect you to,' my father said.

'We're behind you, Emma,' my mother said. 'I'll let you know when you can see Mandy. She can't be mad at you forever.'

'And in the meantime, take care of yourself, honey,' my father said. 'Let John do some of the work.'

They kissed and hugged me again and went out.

I sat back on the sofa and picked my phone up from the coffee table. I scrolled through the names in the contact list, selected 'George', and pressed the call button.

'Ah Wu,' the Demon King said with pleasure. 'I was worried that the idiot Jade Emperor thought you had a chance of winning and was about to throw you all into the Pits. Please, tell me where we can meet and sort this out so nobody else is hurt.'

'It's me,' I said.

His voice went richer. 'Emma, darling. I'd say about time the brain of the outfit was in charge, but I know how damn sneaky his Serpent is. So where do we meet?'

'The French restaurant on the top floor of the Hong Kong Marriott,' I said. 'Seven pm?'

'Good choice. I just replaced the CEO of that hotel chain two weeks ago,' the King said. 'I'll have the staff pull the finest vintage out of the cellar. Will Simone be coming as well? I'd love to see her.'

'No. Just me.'

'Oh well, can't have everything … Wait.' He was silent for a moment. 'Just you?'

'Yes.'

'Without Ah Wu?'

'Yes.'

He wheezed with delight. 'Holy shit, are you coming to me behind the Turtle's back?'

'Seven o'clock. French restaurant. I want to talk to you about my family,' I said, and hung up.

13

I fiddled with the strap of my bag as I stood under Central Plaza in Wan Chai, waiting for a taxi; it had been a while since I'd needed to carry one. After nearly twenty minutes I was at the head of the queue, and the first taxi drove away without picking me up.

'Racist,' I huffed under my breath.

The next taxi was driven by a man with a kind face who let me climb in.

'Peak. One Black Road,' I said. 'Off Mount Austin Road.'

'Wah,' he said, pulling away from the kerb. 'Your Cantonese is really good.'

I smiled. 'Everybody says that. Been here all my life.'

'Which King's your favourite?' he said, turning up the Cantopop on the radio.

'Leon!' I said with enthusiasm.

He chuckled. 'You're old. He's one of the old Kings.'

'I know,' I said, settling back in the seat and trying not to sneeze from the intense cold of the air conditioning combined with the overpowering lemon scent from the air freshener that didn't quite cover his stale cigarette smoke. 'I'm an old gweipoh.'

He glanced at me in the rear-view mirror and I tried my best to look like an innocent old gweipoh. I was still too new an Immortal to change my shape, and every year had left its mark. I was twenty-eight when I first started working for John, and now I was forty-three. When I'd learnt John's true nature I thought we'd never be together, or have the chance of a family, have children of our own —

I pushed the thought away.

When we arrived at John's building, I gave the driver a generous tip for being nice to the old gweipoh. I stepped out of the car and stared up at the building, full of nostalgia. We'd had some good times there, just the five of us — John, Simone, Monica, Leo and me.

I hefted my bag and went up to the entrance. The security guards didn't know me and sat watching me suspiciously from their post.

I'm downstairs, I said to Leo. *Buzz me up, will you?*

I have to come down and sign you in, Leo said. *Be right there.*

I tried to look casual as I waited and the guards watched me. It wasn't until Leo came out of the lifts that I realised — the guards hadn't seen me call up to the flat. No wonder they were so suspicious.

'We've had to increase security. Nobody goes up to the top floor without an escort,' Leo said as he signed me in. 'We've been constantly tested since we arrived.'

'How big?' I said as I followed him to the lift. The sound of the doors opening — that particular whining tone followed by a mild clatter — gave me another pang of nostalgia.

'Biggest was level forty-five or thereabouts — nothing we can't handle.' He crossed his arms over his chest and watched the lights above the lift door. 'They settled down after a couple of weeks, but we don't take any chances.'

We exited the lift, and Leo tapped the keypad next to the metal gate, opened the gate and door, and stood back to let me in.

Buffy and Er Hao were in the living room, with a collection of toys that any child would be proud to own. Er Hao stood and bowed to me, smiling, and I gave her a hug.

'Er Hao. I hope these men aren't working you too hard.'

'It is my pleasure, ma'am. But remember that I am yours and one day hope to return to you.'

'I'll never forget.'

Through the large picture windows the view over the south side of the island, to the ocean, was obscured by pollution haze. The presence of so many demons in the territory had made the pollution thicker and more poisonous. The government had stopped releasing the pollution figures as they were always an unhealthy level of toxicity.

I went down onto one knee. 'Hello, Buffy.'

'Hello, Aunty Emma,' Buffy said, not looking up from her Lego. 'Where's Aunty Simone? I want to play with her.'

'Next time,' I said, rising. 'Can I talk to your dads for a while?'

'Ba Ba is away,' she said.

'What, again?'

'He'll be back soon,' Leo said. 'Come into the dining room and wait for him.' He turned to the door. 'Oh, he's back already.'

Martin came in the front door and knelt so that Buffy could run to him.

'Ba Ba!'

He kissed her on the cheek and stroked her hair, then pulled her in for another hug. He saw me and his eyebrows shot up, then his expression went rigid with restraint. He rose and, still holding Buffy's hand, went to Leo and embraced him.

Then he turned to me. 'I won't stop.'

'That's not what I want to talk about,' I said. I gestured with my head towards the dining room. 'Can we?'

Leo and Martin shared a look, and Martin gave Buffy to Er Hao. We went into the dining room together. Martin had replaced John's ink paintings of sea creatures with his own work: Western-style watercolours of Hong Kong scenes. He'd also framed some of Leo's novice calligraphy and hung it proudly among them.

'You're needed in the Heavens, Ming Gui, and constantly doing this is wasting everybody's time,' I said. 'Give it up, and try again when it's all resolved.'

'You said that wasn't what you wanted to talk about,' he said.

'I've been given an order; I have to fulfil it.' I sighed and leaned my elbows on the table. 'I've been avoiding you so I don't have to bring it up, but now I'm here the imperative's taken over.'

'The Jade Emperor has forced you to interfere?'

129

'He has.' I saw his face. 'He hasn't forced me to order you. He just wants me to talk to you.'

'We need to be married before it all falls apart. We must ensure Buffy's future. You know how important this is to us. I'll keep petitioning him until he allows it.'

'I do know. I support you.'

'So tell the Jade Emperor to let us marry!' Martin said with frustration.

'I did. He said to stop petitioning him, because the answer is "No" and you're costing the Heavens dearly by constantly throwing yourself under the executioner's blade.'

'Did you notice he didn't say that the answer will *always* be "No"?' Martin said.

'Yes, I did. He told me that he can't say more.'

'If we weren't a same-sex couple this wouldn't be an issue! We could have a quick quiet ceremony and secure the future of our child.'

'It has nothing to do with that.'

'He's never permitted same-sex marriage, Emma. If you and Father asked him, he'd let you marry in a second.'

'He didn't.'

'He —' Martin stopped. 'What?'

'We asked him and he wouldn't let us. He won't let us marry until this is all over and finished, same as you.'

'He has a blanket ban on marriages?' Leo said.

'No. Just us. Other people are marrying their partners all over the Heavens for the same reason we want to — to ensure the care of their children and the distribution of their property. He's picking on you two and me. And probably on your father as well.'

'*Why?*' they said in unison.

'Wish to hell I knew. He just said no, and if I asked again he'd execute me, same as you. So we have to trust him and stop asking.'

'Do you trust him with what's about to happen?' Martin said. 'There are nearly a hundred and fifty thousand of them, and five thousand of us. He's throwing four thousand mortal soldiers to their deaths, and a thousand Immortals into the Pits.'

'Do we have a choice, Ming Gui?'

He studied me searchingly. 'Are you still in there, Father, and didn't tell us?'

'No, Martin, it's just residual time ripples. I'll be like this for a while.'

'Freaky,' Leo said.

'You have no idea,' I growled.

'Leo and I will be first to be sent to the Pits, leaving Buffy orphaned,' Martin said. 'This King detests our entire family. We must protect the children.'

'I know. That's why I'm here,' I said. 'I want to know what my chances are.'

'Chances of what?'

'Killing the Demon King. The Horde will probably fall to bits without his leadership. I want your opinion as to whether it's doable.'

'Only with Seven Stars,' Martin said.

'Then why hasn't John destroyed the King with it already?' Leo said.

'You were there when he explained it,' I said. 'It was the demon attack when they drugged the Serpent.'

'He did his thing where he blocked out the conversation. I didn't hear anything,' Leo said.

'He does that?'

'Sometimes,' Martin said. 'He's even done it to me two or three times.'

'He's never done it to me,' I said.

'That's because he trusts you completely,' Leo said. 'So what's this thing about Seven Stars?'

'Are you sure he should know?' Martin said. 'Father made me vow not to tell anybody.'

'Leo should know.' I turned to him. 'If John uses Seven Stars on this King, he'll absorb the King's demon essence and turn back into a mindless nature spirit.'

'He's done that before,' Leo said. 'You're Immortal. You can wait. That's not a good enough reason.'

'He wouldn't return. He'd stay an animal permanently. And that much demon essence could easily make him revert.'

'Revert to what?'

'Father was immensely powerful turtle and snake demons before he combined and turned to the Celestial,' Martin said.

Leo was silent for a long time. Then he said vehemently, 'It's not worth it.'

'Seven Stars is the only thing that can destroy this King, Emma,' Martin said. 'Don't waste your time trying with energy. It won't work.'

'What about the Murasame?' I said.

'Oh,' Martin said.

'It can?' Leo said.

Martin nodded.

'It's in the centre of Hell,' Leo said. 'You'd have to go right down to the bottom of Hell, and talk your son into giving it back to you when he has no idea who you are.'

'Yep,' I said.

Leo grinned. 'Can I come too?'

'That's why I'm here.'

'Me,' Martin said.

'Both of you,' I said. 'Simone can mind Buffy with Er Hao. Heaven knows, the child has enough toys to keep her occupied for a couple of hours while we go find my sword and bring it back out.'

'I'm in,' Leo said. 'We may be able to stop this before it starts.'

'Me too,' Martin said. 'But I must have Father's permission.'

'He may order you not to go,' I said.

'He is my Emperor and I am his Number One. I won't go behind his back.'

I looked from Martin to Leo. Leo's face was full of pride.

'It's a matter of honour, Lady Emma,' Martin said.

'All right, I understand.' I checked my watch. 'We can talk to him as soon as he's home from Hell. Right now I have a meeting to go to.'

'Don't try to negotiate with the Demon King,' Martin said. 'He isn't trustworthy.'

I rose to leave. 'Too late.'

* * *

I nodded to the restaurant's receptionist. 'I'm here to meet with George Mo.'

The receptionist checked the booking, saw the character for 'Mo' — demon — and looked up, confused. 'His name is a very bad word, very bad luck, very bad.'

'That's the good luck version of his name,' I said.

'Why?'

'You don't want to know. Keep away from him.'

She paled and nodded, shut the book, and led me into the main area of the restaurant. Floor-to-ceiling windows overlooked the latest ugly reclamation on Hong Kong harbour, and the pollution haze effectively blocked the view of the other side of the water.

I stopped when I saw who was sitting with the Demon King. A couple of Mothers, his Number One Andy Ho ... and John.

John's expression mirrored my shock, then he lowered his head and smiled grimly. I nodded to him and sat next to him.

The Demon King poured some red wine for me. 'You wanted to talk about the same thing, so I thought I'd do it all at once. One more to come ... and here she is.'

Simone stopped when she saw me and John and her expression went rigid. She sagged and sat at the table as well, on the other side of John.

'Let's hear the offers, one at a time,' the King said, swirling the red wine in his oversized glass. 'Ah Wu, you first.'

'We discussed me going into the jade cage in True Form. If we lose, I'll do it. I'll go into a cage if you promise to keep Emma and Simone safe.'

'Done. Emma?'

'I'll be a mother for as many little serpent babies as you want. Just guarantee my family's safety.'

John stiffened but didn't say anything.

The King saw his reaction and smiled. 'Just your immediate family?' he asked me.

'Simone's like a daughter to me. Her too.'

'Not Ah Wu?'

John remained completely unmoving.

'No,' I said without looking at him.

'So … I could do what I like to him? I can torture him in the jade cage until the end of time?'

'If it keeps Simone safe, yes.'

Simone dropped her face into her hands but didn't say anything.

The Demon King's blood-coloured eyes were full of amusement as he looked from John to me. 'I don't know, he's been tortured so many times that he's used to it. It would be so much more fun to play with your family instead. You've been burnt, you know what it feels like. What if I sent your family to the Hell of the Red-Hot Grates?'

I stiffened as the horrible images raced through my head, and a rush of nausea surged over me. Both the Mothers smiled with satisfaction.

'I'll do anything,' I said. 'Just don't hurt them.'

'Would you take their place on the grill?'

I hesitated, then raised my head and looked him in the eye. 'Yes.'

'More efficient to roast them over the coals though.' The King gestured towards John with his glass. 'See his face?'

I glanced at John. He'd darkened and withdrawn even more. I looked back at the King. He was enjoying watching John's reaction … to my reaction.

'You'll make my family suffer,' I said, 'purely to break Lord Xuan's heart?'

'So much fun,' the King said jovially. 'Torture them, torture you, torture him.'

'Don't hurt them,' I said, desperate. 'I'll do anything. Have your babies. *Anything*.'

John shifted uncomfortably but didn't speak.

'You can't have any more babies, dear,' the King said kindly. 'I have a better idea. When I win I'll be too busy to spend all my time with Frankie — how about you go back to being a nanny? For me? Care for my darling son, and I'll keep your family unharmed. How about that?'

'Done,' I said with relief.

John looked away and rubbed his hand over his face, obviously relieved as well.

The King turned to Simone. 'And you, Princess?'

'Do I have anything you want?' Simone said. 'We need to establish a value position before we start any sort of bargaining.'

'I don't know. It depends what you want to bargain for.'

'I want you to call it all off, leave the Heavens and the Earthly and go back to Hell,' Simone said. 'What could I give you in return for that?'

'Humph.' The Demon King leaned back and took a sip of wine. 'Once again Simone outshines both of you. You already consider the Heavens lost, and you're negotiating your lives away for the safety of half a dozen. She is focused on the bigger picture and puts both of you to shame.'

'I completely agree,' I said. 'But I know my value, and it isn't enough to send you back to Hell.'

'Is my father enough value?' Simone said. 'Would you trade your withdrawal from the Heavens and the Earthly for Xuan Wu in the jade cage?'

'You hear that, Ah Wu?' the Demon King said. 'They're quite happy to throw you into a cage to be tortured for eternity if it means they'll be free of me.'

'If it puts you back in Hell, the deal sounds good,' John said, his voice low.

'You'd make a magnificent Demon Queen,' the King said to Simone. 'I would relinquish the Heavens if you were to pledge your loyalty and allegiance to me.'

She stiffened and her eyes went wide.

'You demons don't have queens,' I said.

'For her I could make an exception. How'd you like it, Simone? Ruling Hell by my side? We'd be a formidable team, matched in power by your father and stepmother in Heaven. Wait,' he raised his hand, 'don't make that face. I know Hell's a —'

'Pit,' she finished for him.

He smiled. 'Yes. But what if you were to rule all the Earthly as well? How about that? Queen of the whole damn world? I'm sure we could do a better job of running things than those idiot humans.'

'You'd abandon your attempt on the Heavens if I did that?'

He gazed at her over the rim of his glass. 'I'd seriously consider it.'

'Is that a genuine offer? I'm not that smart or powerful. You already rule Hell, you've taken the Earthly, and you're close to taking the Heavens. Why would you trade that for me?'

The King gestured towards John with his wine glass. 'You're his daughter. It would tear his heart out if I possessed all three of you. Having his son calling me "Mummy" every day and both of you unwillingly in my bed every night would drive him insane.'

John bent his head into his hands, then straightened, took a deep breath with his eyes closed, and tied his hair back.

'Everything you do seems to be aimed at hurting him.' Simone looked from John to the King. 'Is there something personal between you two that I'm not aware of?'

John didn't move but his expression darkened even more.

The King thumped his wine glass on the table. 'You didn't have to take her when you ran! She was happy with me. Now she won't even talk to me.'

'No mother will ever leave her child when she escapes a bad situation, George,' I said.

He rounded on me. 'You did!'

I winced. He was right.

Who is he talking about? Simone said, bewildered.

'Simone just broke the rules, the parley's over,' the King said. 'Go home and write your offers as contracts, sign them in blood, then send them down to me at my office in Beijing. I probably won't even use them. I'm so close to winning that you don't have anything of value to me.' He dropped his voice. 'Except, perhaps, Simone.'

He and the rest of the group disappeared.

'Who was he talking about?' Simone said.

'Yue Gui,' John said. 'I'll tell you the whole story when we're home.'

'You don't need to,' she said. 'It's obvious what happened. Let's go.'

I waved to attract the attention of one of the wait staff. 'Cheque, please.'

Simone leaned her chin on her hand. 'That's a ridiculously expensive bottle of wine and he left us to pay for it.'

'Don't do it, Simone,' John said. 'Promise me you won't even think about it.'

'You want my word?'

'I would appreciate it, yes.'

'Then promise me you'll never enter a jade cage in True Form.'
John was silent.

'We're going to lose, Dad,' she said, her voice very soft. 'I can
see it.'

'Can you see past that?'

'No. There's no clear future after the Heavens fall. There's a
huge crossroads right there. A point where a vital decision is made.
And I have no idea who makes the decision or what the result will
be.'

'Is that what you see too?' I asked John.

He nodded. 'We must keep fighting and not surrender, Emma.
The future is never fixed.'

The waiter brought the folder with the bill and I flipped it open,
then slipped my credit card in to pay for it. 'They ate before we
came. Five thousand, four hundred dollars. Assholes.'

My phone vibrated in my pocket and I pulled it out to check the
caller ID. It was Gold, so I answered it as I handed the folder to
the waiter. 'Emma.' The phone shrieked in my ear and I flinched
and jerked it away. 'Dammit! That's the third time today.'

I checked it: the phone's screen had turned to static. Some
garbled words came out, then it shut down completely.

'You keep dropping it, I'm not surprised you've broken it,'
Simone said.

'I have never cracked the screen,' I said. I rested my elbows on
the table as I restarted the phone, and everything came back up
looking normal. 'Gold says there may be a glitch in the network.'

'My phone doesn't have a problem,' she said. 'Daddy?'

John shook his head.

The waiter returned with the folder. 'Sorry, the card doesn't
work.'

'Oh, okay,' I said, and pulled out another card. 'Try this.'

Once the Heavens fall there's nowhere safe for anyone, Simone
said to me. *Do you think the King will trade everybody's safety
for both of us?*

'Simone, how many times do you have to be told to talk out
loud?' John said.

'Sorry.'

'All three of us may be sufficient, but I doubt it,' John said; he'd heard her anyway. 'Making us suffer is a minor benefit compared to setting up your little brother as Jade Emperor to rule everything.'

The waiter returned and stared at John when he heard what he'd said, then snapped out of it and handed me the folder again. 'Sorry, this one doesn't work either. Do you have cash?'

My phone rang and shrieked again, vibrating so hard it jumped off the table. I caught it before it hit the floor. It produced loud garbled speech, then shut down.

John pulled his wallet out of the back pocket of his black jeans and gave the waiter one of his credit cards. 'This should work.'

The waiter nodded to John and took the card away.

I glared at my phone as I restarted it. 'I am throwing this away and buying a new one in the mall downstairs right now.'

'Isn't it one of Gold's specials?' Simone said.

'I'll go back to something mundane.'

The waiter came back with John's card. 'Sorry, this one doesn't work either. Do you have cash? Please pay with cash.'

'I can go down to the ATM,' Simone said.

'I have a horrible feeling that your ATM card won't work either,' I said.

She dropped her voice. 'Oh, no.'

John concentrated, summoning Gold.

The phone spoke, sounding gravelly and rough. 'Information. Destroy. Gunung Rinjani. Can kill. You must come. The Demon King.' It fell out to static, then came back. 'We can win. Anak. Emma. Murasame. Lombok.'

'What?' John said.

'EMMA, COME!' the phone shrieked, and shut down.

Gold entered the restaurant and sat with us. He pulled out his wallet and handed the waiter a wad of five-hundred-dollar bills. 'Sorry about that.'

The waiter nodded to him and went back to the wait station.

John took my phone off the table and gave it to Gold. 'It just called Emma's name and said Gunung Rinjani Lombok. It's been screaming at Emma.'

'Really?' Gold said. 'Let me see.' His eyes unfocused as he studied it.

'We also need you to check our bank accounts because none of our credit cards work,' Simone said.

Gold snapped back from the phone and concentrated for a moment. His daughter BJ came into the restaurant and sat next to Simone. Gold passed the phone to BJ and both their eyes unfocused.

Gold hissed under his breath. 'All your bank accounts are gone.'

'All of them?' I said.

He nodded.

'Have we lost ownership of the properties? What about the Peak?' Simone said, distraught. 'Leo and Ge Ge are living there!'

'Accessing.' Gold went silent.

'Why is it taking you longer and longer to access information?' I said.

'The information on the network's growing exponentially as the humans add to the internet,' Gold said without moving his mouth. 'We're indexing it as fast as we can, but it'll take a while with most of us gone.'

'There are gaps in the phone's log. Interesting. How long has this been happening?' BJ asked me.

'On and off for a couple of weeks. It's been happening more and more often every day. It's yelled at me four times today, played music I don't own, and then it started saying things.'

Gold snapped back. 'It looks like you've been financially wiped out, my Lord. Lord Leo and Prince Ming will probably be evicted very soon.'

BJ shot to her feet with jubilation. 'It's Grandpa!'

'My stone? Where is it?' I said.

'Dad? Dad!' Gold said with delight.

'That's the southern Bastion. It's a trap,' John said.

'Gunung Rinjani is the name of the volcano on Lombok,' Gold said. 'It's the entrance to the southern Bastion.'

'It's a trap,' John repeated. 'The King needs Emma. That's why the message came to her phone.'

'The message is fake?' Simone said.

'It's genuine. It has Grandpa's digital signature on it. It's definitely from him,' BJ said.

'We must go and see,' Simone said. 'It says it has a way to defeat the Demon King.'

'It's still a trap,' John said. 'Don't go.'

'The stone's my Retainer and I have a duty as its Lady,' I said.

John opened his mouth, then closed it again and smiled wryly. 'Tomorrow. It's already dark.'

'First thing.'

'One of us has to go with you,' BJ said. 'You'll need a stone to find Grandpa if he's taken a small form.'

'You stay. I'll go,' Gold said. 'It's too dangerous.'

'You're the only one who can reinstate their bank accounts and property ownership, Dad,' BJ said. 'All the documents are encrypted in *your* lattice.'

'Damn,' Gold said.

'Take Zara,' John said.

Gold and BJ shared a look. He raised his eyebrows, and she shook her head.

He nodded and turned back to us. 'Best if it's a member of the family. Zara may not be able to identify Dad if he's really small.'

'I can do it,' BJ said. 'I'll be fine with Lady Emma.'

'I'll go too,' Simone said.

'No,' John and I said in unison.

'The King wants you,' I said. 'If we need you, we'll call you. I'll take Martin; he's close to you in power.'

'Just be careful, little guy,' Gold said to BJ.

'Girl,' BJ said.

The waiter returned with the folder and hovered over us. We took the hint, rose and left the restaurant together.

* * *

It was very late when I finally found him. He had conjured a bench and put it on top of the western wall, and was sitting with his feet up on the battlement, looking out over the peaks that surrounded the Mountain and the full moon high in the sky. I stopped when I saw him. His eyes were glittering with tears in the moonlight.

He wiped his hand over them and turned away. 'I'd prefer nobody saw me like this,' he said, his voice hoarse.

I sat next to him and leaned into him. 'I can't see you.'

'I haven't visited your sister, I can't face her,' he said. 'How is she?'

'Recovering. I haven't visited her either; my parents suggested that we stay away from her right now. She doesn't want to see either of us.'

He took a deep shuddering breath. 'I understand.'

'My parents want me to kill them if they're held hostage,' I said.

'I'm not surprised. You were nobility long before you met me.' He wiped one hand over his face again. 'They're helpless humans and completely innocent. All they did was make the mistake of ...' He didn't finish.

'Being my family,' I said. 'And I made the mistake of falling in love with you.'

He gasped once.

'We'll work something out,' I said. 'Whatever it takes to keep them out of his hands. I trust you.'

'I wished I trusted myself as much. Little Matthew's only three years old.'

'Is there any way we can take them completely clear of this entire conflict? Wipe their memories, change their faces, anything?'

'The answer to your question is: no. Whatever we do, the King will find them.'

'Damn.' I leaned on his shoulder again. He was so distraught that he was freezing through the thick cotton of his Mountain uniform. 'Cold.'

'Sorry.' He warmed up and put his arm around my shoulders. 'I doubt that you can talk our son into giving you back the Murasame, Emma, even if you manage to break into the centre of Hell.'

'That sword is the only weapon that can destroy the King. It's worth a shot.'

'I know.'

'And your opinion?'

'This King is so ancient and tempered that he can withstand either of the basic forces. Yang or yin, he can resist. So your only chance is the sword. And if it comes to that, the best chance is Seven Stars.'

I stiffened. 'No.'

'He would be gone for good, Emma. It is the best option.'

'If you destroy him, another Demon King will rise to try us again, and without your protection the Celestial will fall. If you sacrifice yourself by using Seven Stars, we might win now, but we will ultimately lose.'

'I may have to do it if the lives of innocents are threatened.'

'I won't let you!'

He pulled back to see me and smiled. 'Is that an order?'

'Yes!'

'But you're quite happy to throw me into a jade cage?'

'I've pulled you out of a cage once already. Doing it again will be easy.'

'That's a new definition of "easy" that I haven't encountered before.'

The humour in his voice cheered me, and I put my arm around his waist and sighed. Three more days, but at least I could touch him until the end, and give him whatever comfort I could.

'We're thinking of going after I've located my stone,' I said. 'It mentioned the Murasame. It may know where it is.'

'I don't like your chances.'

'Are they better than zero?'

'Not much.'

'Anything better than zero is worth a try.'

'I cannot come with you. My place is in the Heavens.'

'We know.'

'Let's go to bed.' He rose and rubbed his hands over his face, then reached down to help me up. 'First thing tomorrow morning I will teach you how to suicide with shen energy. Then I will watch you go south with my most talented son and a stone child that is far too young to be involved in this, and worry myself sick about you never coming back.'

'Deal.'

14

We topped out over the edge of the volcano's caldera and stepped off the cloud to stand together overlooking the steaming lake. A small new volcanic cone stuck out at one side of it. Lava flowed from a hole in the side of the inner mound, looking like a gaping wound. The sulphur fumes were strong enough to burn my lungs, and I pulled out the mask I'd brought and put it over my face. It didn't do much to filter the awful rotten-egg smell but at least my lungs weren't on fire any more.

BJ took her True Form, and lifted higher to see over the black ash-covered ground.

'Where's the entrance to the Bastion?' I said, my voice muffled by the mask.

'The hole there with lava coming out,' Martin said. 'You need to withstand the lava to enter.'

'I can't see him,' BJ said, and floated away. 'I'll have a look further down.'

'Jade Building Block,' I shouted.

'Emma, that was a bad idea —' Martin began, then stopped and cocked his head.

I heard it as well. The reply was thin and almost non-existent. 'Emma?'

'Grandpa?' BJ said.

Four humanoid guard demons emerged from the hole in the hill, shrugging the lava off themselves.

Martin drew the Silver Serpent and I summoned Dark Heavens.

'You're using Dad's sword?' Martin said, eyeing me. 'I would have thought a "strong woman" like you would have demanded her own weapon a long time ago.'

'I wish everybody would stop giving me grief about this,' I said as we moved into position ready to fight. 'The forge doesn't have time to make anything for me, and Dark Heavens still resonates.'

'Not good enough,' he said. 'Three on the right.'

'Far left,' I said, and moved left of Martin to give him room to take out the others.

The demons were a challenge: bigger than level fifty but not Mothers. The King must have specially bred them to be powerful guards.

I tried pulling the chi out of my demon and turning it into a bead, but it resisted me. It was too big. I loaded Dark Heavens with shen energy and launched it at the demon instead. It ducked to avoid the energy and I called the shen back in, cursing quietly to myself. I was still too new an Immortal to handle it accurately.

The demon took a swing at me with its nasty-looking halberd; it had a black serrated blade and what appeared to be a carbon-fibre shaft. I used Dark Heavens to push the halberd in the direction it was already going, then quickly released it to cut the demon off at the ankles. It blocked me and threw me back, then grinned to reveal the tusks in the corners of its mouth.

'You'll have to be faster than that, little girl.'

I parried the next blow it sent at my head.

'Calling me "little girl" isn't an insult, stupid. I've seen a "little girl" take out the whole throne room full of demons.'

The demon opened its mouth to argue with me and its expression filled with shock, then it exploded into black streamers. Martin had taken it out from behind after destroying the other three.

'You should have had no trouble at all dispatching that,' Martin said, putting the Silver Serpent away. 'What's the matter, Emma?'

'I was experimenting on it,' I said as I dismissed Dark Heavens. 'I wanted to see if I could turn it into a black bead, and when that didn't work I tried to shen it.'

'You were *playing* with it?'

I shrugged. 'Well, yeah.'

'We don't have long before they send more, and the next wave will probably be much larger,' Martin said, looking around. 'I suggest you hurry, Black Jade.'

There was no reply.

'BJ?' I called.

Again no reply.

'BJ!' I shouted, becoming concerned.

'Wonderful, now we've lost both of them,' Martin said. 'Gold will skin us alive.'

'Worse. The demons have kidnapped her before, and if they have her again it would destroy both of them. We must find her.'

I scrabbled down the glassy scree towards the lake. The edges of the stones were sharp and I cut my hands on them as I tried to slow my momentum.

'Stone?' I said. 'BJ?'

Martin lowered his head and closed his eyes, then his eyebrows creased. 'I can't sense anything.'

'Say something, stone,' I said.

There was no reply.

'BJ!' I shouted at the top of my voice.

Again there was no reply. They were lost. Both of them were lost, and the demons were probably holding poor BJ again. She still had nightmares about the first time it had happened, and she wouldn't cope if they had her again. I hated to think what she was going through.

'We have to find her,' I said, my voice shaking.

I looked around at the stone-covered ground. Any of the pebbles in the scree could be either of them.

'Bring another stone in,' Martin said. 'Supervise it carefully and make sure it doesn't wander off.' He raised his head. 'More guards are on their way. At least twenty of them.' He glanced down at me. 'Can you take out ten level fifty-fives?'

'I can take about five,' I said. 'Can you take down fifteen?'

He resummoned the Silver Serpent. 'I can try. I'm glad Father's taught you shen suicide.'

'Uh ...' I summoned Dark Heavens. 'He really didn't have time. He started to teach me and Er Lang called him away.'

'Wonderful,' he said softly. 'Stay in my line of vision. I do not want what happened to the stones happening to you as well.' He hefted the Silver Serpent. 'Here they come. Nice and big.'

The demons came out of the hole, ignoring the lava, and I wheezed with dismay. Martin lowered the Silver Serpent and raised it again. They were the black-armoured demons that had been transported on the *Liaoning*: more than two metres tall, and with disturbingly small faces on mounds that jutted from their shoulders instead of heads.

'BJ!' I shouted, then dropped my voice to speak to Martin. 'How many can you yin?'

'About half of them. Emma, we need to retreat. Dying to them will serve no purpose.'

'Stone, talk to me, for god's sake. Stone or BJ, say something!' I shouted as the demons headed up the hill towards us. They weren't carrying weapons, but their huge hands had long nail-like claws that would tear us to pieces.

'We need to leave,' Martin said. *Come back when they've gone inside again.*

'All *right*!' I shouted with frustration, and I turned and ran up the slope.

Martin summoned a cloud, lifted me onto it, and we took off over the edge of the large caldera and quickly gained altitude.

I collapsed onto my hands and knees on the cloud. Not only had we not found my stone, we'd lost BJ. I fell to sit and ran my hand over my face. The demons had her. Gold would be destroyed when I told him, and I wouldn't blame him. I was close to the edge myself. She wasn't yet fifteen and we'd handed her over to them. They would use her for their vile experiments. I turned around and looked back, but the demons were already too small to see.

'We'll return when they've gone back inside,' Martin said. He leaned down and put his hand on my shoulder. 'I'll make us invisible and we can slowly and carefully check all the stones there.'

'I'll ask Gold to come and help.'

'No, you're right, it would break him. We'll quietly go back and find your stone. It can help us find BJ.'

'I don't know what I'll do if the demons have her,' I said, my voice hoarse. 'The last time she was held by the demons, we rescued her just as Six was about to cut her up with a buzz-saw.'

He released my shoulder. 'I know.'

We hovered two kilometres away from the volcano, sitting cross-legged on the cloud for twenty minutes as we waited for the demons to leave. They patrolled the area a few times, then went back inside to report.

'They know it was us,' I said.

'I can hide us, but the stones won't be able to see us if I do. Do you know the Jade Building Block's chi signature, its spiritual essence?'

'It's difficult with a stone, their nature is so different,' I said. 'I can try.'

He nodded and stood. 'Let's go have a look.'

We returned to the crater and he made us invisible.

This is where we took off, he said.

I stepped off the cloud and put my hands out, feeling for the stone and finding nothing.

Stone? I said. *Jade Building Block?* I raised my mental voice and put all I had into it. *Jade Building Block!*

AUNTY EMMA! BJ shouted, sounding the way she had when she was a baby stone. *Where are you? I can't see you!*

I nearly collapsed with relief. *We're right here — Martin made us invisible. I'll knock two stones together, listen for the sound.*

I'm sorry, I'm sorry, I'm so sorry, she said. *Is everything okay? I thought you'd gone without me! Where are you? Are you here?* Her voice became desperate. *I can't see you! I can't hear anything!*

I bent down, picked up a stone and tapped it against another stone.

I heard that! she said, sounding thrilled. *I'm so glad you're here, I thought I'd lost you! I'm sorry I was gone, I wasn't expecting that to happen.*

What happened to you?

She sounded sheepish. *Dad told me lava was good, but he didn't tell me how good. It's bubbly and warm and soft and feels so delish ... knock the stones again?*

I tapped the stones. *You fell asleep in the lava?*

No. But I was kind of out of it. It felt so good that … what's the word? Euphoria. I was high! Her voice changed to regret again. *I'm so sorry, Aunty Emma, I didn't know that would happen.*

Not your fault, sweetheart, but I will have a stern talk with your father.

Me too, he should have warned me, she said. *There you are, I can see your heat signatures.* She appeared in front of us in tiny True Form, floating in the air. *Wow, Uncle Martin is really good at hiding people. I had no idea you were there until I was right on top of you. Did you find Grandpa?*

Not yet. Can you sense where he is?

Give me a minute.

Emma? Martin said.

I brought him up to date.

Good, he said. *Now find your stone and let's get out of here. Did you know about lava making them high?*

First time I've heard of it, he said with amusement.

Grandpa? Call it, Aunty Emma, BJ said.

Jade Building Block?

Help, the stone said.

Did you hear that, BJ?

Yes. Again, Grandpa!

BJ?

BJ zoomed through the air and stopped, then took human form. She crouched and picked up a tiny pebble. 'Grandpa?'

'Black Jade,' the stone said with relief. 'You're in danger here. Run.'

'They saw you — they're coming back,' Martin said.

'BJ, run!' the stone shouted.

Martin summoned a cloud and we jumped onto it. Twenty-five demon guards charged out of the hole as we topped over the edge of the crater and flew away.

'Is it him?' I said.

'I'm checking,' BJ said, holding the stone in her hand. 'Speak to me, Grandpa.'

'I want,' the stone said, then was silent.

'What do you want?' I said. 'To go home?'

'Flyers incoming. Hold on,' Martin said, and the cloud increased in speed until the air blew past us.

'Where am I?' the stone said.

'You're with Emma, me and Prince Ming, Grandpa,' BJ said. 'We're taking you home to the Northern Heavens.'

'Who?'

BJ dropped her head and concentrated. 'What did they do to you?'

'Who?'

'Grandpa's lattice has been damaged,' she said. 'Some of the personality centres and the memory storage have been destroyed. It's fused, like it's melted. He may not remember anything.'

'I remember,' the stone said.

'What?' I said.

'There's something really important I have to tell you.'

We waited.

'He probably doesn't remember what it is,' BJ said.

'Let's take him home,' I said.

'No,' BJ said. 'Isolate him. It's definitely Grandpa, no other stone looks like this, but I have no idea what they did to him and he could be ...'

'A plant,' I said.

'They've done sickening things with us before. I hate to think what they've done to him. He may not be himself.'

'How did he escape?' Martin said, without looking away from the direction we were going. 'There were plenty of guards. He was in a jade cage. Now he's free and doesn't remember what happened.'

'Too convenient,' I said grimly.

'I know,' BJ said.

'Where do we put him?' Martin said.

'Dad will know what to do with him,' BJ said, and she shoved the stone into her chest. She turned to face the direction we were going and sat cross-legged on the cloud. 'Might be best to give him to Grandma.'

'The Murasame,' the stone said from inside her, making her body vibrate.

'That feels weird,' she said.

'What about it?' I said.

'It can ...'

'What?' BJ said.

I sat cross-legged as well. 'It can destroy the Demon King.'

'I know where he is. How to break in,' the stone said. 'The child knows you. He'd give it to you. You can destroy the King with it.'

'You could destroy the Demon King with it?' BJ asked me.

'Yes.'

'Wow,' she said softly. 'If you could destroy the King, it would all be over. We'd all be safe.'

'Safe?' the stone said.

'Let's take you home to Dad. He'll know what to do,' BJ said.

'I have a dad?' the stone said.

'No, I'm talking about my dad. Your son, Gold.'

'My son is gold? What's his name?'

'Let's take him home,' BJ said softly.

* * *

Gold was waiting for us back at the Northern Heavens. BJ took my stone out of her chest and they stood together studying it as she held it.

Gold's expression was stricken. 'So much damage.'

'Ah, my *son* is Gold,' the stone said. 'Hello, Gold. Is everything okay? How are the little ones?'

'They're safe, Dad,' Gold said. He gestured to BJ. 'Bring him into my lab and we'll take a look.'

'My own child calling me a *him*,' the stone said. 'You have been spending far too much time human, Gold.'

Gold quirked a smile at BJ.

We all headed to Gold's IT lab. It was pristinely clean, with cupboards holding his vast array of equipment on a raised static-free floor. Gold wheeled a trolley from the side and BJ placed the stone on it. Gold changed to True Form and floated to lie next to my stone. He extended a long tendril to touch the stone.

'Is it possible that he backed up the information lost from his lattice, and we can retrieve it from somewhere?' I said.

BJ stared at me, eyes wide.

'What did I say?'

'That's about the greatest insult you can throw at a stone, Lady Emma,' Gold said, his tendril touching the stone in different places. 'Suggesting that we store such a small amount of information that any sort of backup is possible. One of us worked it out: it would require a contemporary computer system larger than the current universe to hold the information stored in the lattice of any stone more than a hundred years old.'

'So could a stone hold the information of the entire universe?'

'If it attained Enlightenment, yes, but any being that attains Enlightenment does,' Gold said. 'There's so much damage. How did he do this to you, Dad?'

'Who?'

'The Demon King, Grandpa,' BJ said. 'The Demon King did things to you —'

The stone screamed, a sound so high-pitched that it was like a glass blade through my head. The sound dropped until it rumbled through the floor, then snapped off. 'It *hurts* it *hurts* it *hurts* make it stop I'll do anything make it *stop* make it *stop* I'll tell you!'

'Oh, Dad,' Gold said, his voice thick.

'No! I won't tell you anything,' the stone said. 'Don't stop there, destroy me completely. You won't get *fuck* out of me. I am sworn to the Celestial and serve the Dark Lady.'

'You're home in the Heavens and safe now, Dad,' Gold said. 'You're with Lady Emma in the Northern Heavens.'

'Gold?'

Gold tapped the stone with his tendril. 'I'm right here, Dad.'

'Emma. Emma! I'm out? This is real?' It extended a tendril and touched Gold's. 'Holy shit, this is real. I'm out. I'm *free*!' Its voice went soft. 'What happened to me?'

'We're trying to work it out. You flashed back when we mentioned the Demon King.'

There was a long silence.

'Dad?' Gold said.

'I don't know what that device was,' the stone said, its voice even softer. 'I was disappearing. My knowledge, my personality centres, all of it was melting. I was dissolving. Nothing would be left, nothing of me. It was so ...' It stopped for a moment.

'The King said he would destroy me completely unless I pledged allegiance.'

Gold shifted away from the stone. 'Then what happened?'

'I woke up here.' Its voice became desperate. 'No. I wouldn't. I remember being tortured and told to pledge allegiance, and then I was free and back with you. No. I would never pledge allegiance to the Demon King. That's just not possible! I would not turn!'

'If you'd turned, you wouldn't be telling us about it,' Gold said.

'Yes, it would,' I said.

'Yes, I would,' the stone said at the same time. 'You need to put me in a holding cell and keep me well away from anything important.'

'No —' Gold began, but I interrupted him.

'The stone is right.'

'What about the Murasame?' BJ said.

'Emma,' the stone said. 'Thank the Heavens I found you. I know where your son is, and he has the Murasame. You must go in and take the sword back. It's the only thing that will kill the Demon King. You must go.'

'Where is he?'

'Bottom of Level Nine, other side of the Lake of Blood. He's in the cell complex that holds the previous Kings. All the old mad Kings. The Demon King's …' Its voice trailed off. 'Where am I? Gold, is that you? Gold! I'm free!'

'There has to be something we can do about this,' Gold said.

'The Jade Emperor restored my memory when something similar happened to me,' I said.

'You're organic, and so is the Celestial. Even though we're sworn to the Jade Emperor, our natures are incompatible,' Gold said.

'The Grandmother?' I said.

'The Grandmother could hold him inside her for a million years and I still don't think it would fix it.'

'Emma, is that you?'

'It's me, stone.'

'Emma, you have to go to Level Nine. Your son is being held in a cell there, you need to pull him out, the poor child is locked up! He has the Murasame. Ask him to give it to you. If you use it on the King, all of this will be over. You must go to Level Nine.'

'How did you escape Hell, stone?' I said.

'I asked to be kept near the child, to teach him and care for him,' the stone said. 'They agreed, probably hoping to use both of us as bait to trap you. When the guards moved the child to Level Nine, they took my box and one of the stupid demons dropped it and let me out. They don't even know I'm gone.'

'The Demon King has ordered you to take me to the Ninth Level of Hell,' I said.

'The Demon King can go fuck himself.' The stone's voice softened. 'But it would be a good idea for you to take the Dark Lord and his big sword and go to Level Nine and rescue that child. And if the child won't come, you need to retrieve the Murasame. It's the only thing that will take out the Demon King, except Seven Stars itself, and we all know what would happen if the Dark Lord used that.'

Well? I asked Gold. *Is it the truth?*

Yes, it is, Gold said. *But is it a truth that someone else put there?*

15

The next morning Martin, Leo and I went into the training room on the Peak.

'Leo hasn't learnt shen suicide yet, so I'll have to do it,' Martin said.

'I hate this,' Leo said, his voice rough. He knelt on the mats.

'I haven't learnt it either,' I said, and knelt as well.

Simone came to the door and held out a new canvas tarpaulin, still in its plastic bag. 'You forgot this. Dad will kill you if you put blood on the mats.'

'Again,' I said, rising.

'Forgot,' Leo said, and rose as well.

Martin unwrapped the tarpaulin, and we shifted the mats to the side of the room, next to the windows, so he could lay it on the bare concrete floor.

'You guys better come back because I'm not old enough to look after Buffy all the time,' Simone said.

'We will,' I said.

'And you owe me for cleaning up after you!'

'Dinner's on us when we come back,' I said.

She nodded and closed the door on us.

Martin went to the wall and chose one of the biggest axes. He tested the edge with his thumb, then turned back to us, holding it ready.

It hit me: Martin was about to slice into me with that axe and it would hurt like hell, and I would die. All my self-preservation reflexes screamed at me to run. I knelt in the middle of the room on the crinkly tarpaulin and put my head down, fighting the panic.

Leo knelt next to me, and took my hand in his.

'Does this become easier the more you do it?' I said.

'It's harder,' Leo said, his voice rough with emotion. 'For god's sake, Ming, make it a single blow. Please.'

Leo's hand was shaking as he held mine.

'Who's first?' Martin said, standing next to us.

Neither of us replied.

Martin grunted as he slammed the axe into Leo's neck. It hit him off-centre, taking half the bottom of his head with it, but it was clean. Leo's head hit the tarp, his hand went limp in mine and he toppled, then his body disappeared.

'I don't know how to take the body with me!' I said, panicking even more.

I half-rose, and Martin's axe hit me across the shoulders. My back and shoulders blossomed into agony. I fell face first onto the tarp, suffocating on blood, the taste of the plastic in my nose and mouth. Blood pooled under my face, sticky and hot.

'Sorry,' Martin said, and the second blow slammed into me, crushing my head flat.

* * *

'Holy shit, that was fucking awful,' I said, leaning on the wall of my cell.

'I am so sorry, Emma. I did it quickly so you wouldn't have time to think,' Martin said from his cell on the other side of the corridor.

'No, it was my fault, I shouldn't have stood up like that.' I put my hands either side of my aching head.

'You stood up?' Leo said from the cell next to mine. 'How many hits did it take?'

'Two,' Martin said.

'Ouch,' Leo said. 'You should have done her first.'

'I couldn't.'

'Why not?'

'Because he loves you,' I said. 'The minute I'm home, I am having John teach me shen suicide whether he likes it or not.' I shook my head. 'How come I have a headache? I'm in Hell now.'

'Residual nerve stress,' Martin said. 'Your brain thinks the wounds are still there. Clear your thoughts. Do a quick inventory that everything's still present, remind yourself that you're whole, and if the pain won't go away, block it.'

I did as he said, and when my head still pounded I blocked the pain. The panic was still with me, making me weak and shaky. I touched the earth, touched the sky, cleared my thoughts, and the trembling stopped. I wished I had the Murasame with me; when the sword was in my hand I felt unstoppable.

'Got it?' Martin said.

I nodded.

'Let's go,' Leo said.

'Here she comes,' Martin said.

The demon guard nodded to us, then opened the cells and released us without saying a word. We walked up the stairs onto the central island that was the Celestial side of Hell. The wind whistled across the deserted space; the lawns and gardens had been abandoned and were full of weeds where they weren't dying off. We headed past the destroyed Court Ten building and to the edge of the newly-dug hole that stopped the demons from crossing onto the island.

Katie was patrolling the area with a laser weapon slung over her shoulder. When she saw us she quickly turned and headed in the opposite direction.

I changed to snake and we floated across the water barrier between the island and the end of the causeway. Martin made us invisible, and we headed towards the entrance to Level Eight. We had to pass through Eight to reach Nine.

Frankie? I said.

The reply sounded like a sharp intake of breath.

I stopped. 'I have him. A moment.'

Leo and Martin halted beside me.

156

Don't block me, I said quickly. *It's me, Emma, the lady who played cars with you on the floor. Remember? And I showed you ponies and dogs. We had a lot of fun!*

Emma? he said, his voice bright with hope. *Are you coming back to play with me?*

Yes, I am! I'm bringing some friends, and we'll have a lot of fun.

That would be good. Mummy knows you're coming, right? Mummy said it's okay?

Your mother says that you should be with me, I said, trying to control the emotion.

Martin broke in. *Do you know where to go once we're in Level Nine?*

The stone gave me a rough idea. Hopefully we can sneak through and find him without being detected.

You ask much, he said.

I know how good you are at hiding things, I said.

We reached the end of the causeway; the brass-studded doors were closed. I changed back to human and we stood invisible in front of the doors to study the guards on either side.

We will have to take out both of them at the same time, Martin said. *Leo, how's your ching use? If we use ching and make them implode without leaving a trace —*

NO WAY, I said fiercely, and Leo's expression matched my own. I glared up into Martin's eyes and poked him in the chest. *I know what happens when you use ching and I do NOT want to see that.*

You could just look away ...

I am not doing that in public, Leo said.

We're invisible! Martin said.

Emma can see us! Leo shot back.

I changed to snake, went to the demon on the left, bit its head off and pulled the essence into me, making it implode. The other guard was only beginning to register what had happened when I took its head off and ate it as well.

There, I said. *Achieved exactly the same thing without ruining my pants.*

Conceded. I'm glad you had an alternative, Martin said.

He went to the doors and touched the ring hanging from the left one. It slid open towards us and we backed up. On the other side was a four-metre-wide corridor with rough stone walls. We drew our weapons and eased ourselves into the corridor, checking for sentries or eye demons. Nothing.

We crept for twenty metres to the end of the corridor and stopped. There were no doors but the corridor was blocked by a shimmering field of blackness, like a net over the opening.

Sealed, Martin said. *And by a real expert. This is a quality job.*

Can you break it without alerting the guards? I said.

No, Martin said. He looked back down the corridor. *Only way in.*

Is that what our seals look like to the demons? Leo said. *That thing is really disturbing.*

Similar, Martin said. *Ordinary seals are invisible; it has to be a really good seal to be visible like this. Ours appear white to them.* He shook out his shoulders. *It's possible that alarms will sound when I break it. Be ready.*

He charged two steps through the barrier. It opened for him and closed behind him. He turned to face it, and opened a cut in his palm. His face went serene as he traced blood around the doorway. The edges of the opening glowed blinding white, and the seal barrier disappeared.

Leo and I went through, and the three of us ran down the corridor towards the Lake of Blood. A couple of half-dormant guards were at the entrance to the lake room, and Leo and I worked together to destroy them without being noticed.

There was a commotion behind us: more guards searching for whoever had broken the seal.

The Lake of Blood, Level Eight's torture pit, stretched before us. Waxy lifeless body parts floated to the surface of the red liquid and disappeared again.

I headed around the lake to Level Nine on the other side. Leo followed me, but Martin hadn't moved. I turned to see him: his face was rigid with control and his eyes glittered as he stared at the lake. His throat quivered.

'Ming,' Leo said, touching Martin on the arm.

Martin ignored him.

'Ming, love. Martin?' He put his hand on Martin's cheek. 'Martin, I'm here. You're safe.'

Martin turned his face to Leo, but didn't appear to see him.

He was in that lake for six years, Leo said to me. *In fifteen pieces, paralysed and drowning in blood, for six years. If his head made it to the surface, he could see and hear and breathe just for a moment, then he'd go back under and drown again.*

'Ming Gui,' I said.

His only respite was when they'd fish him out, let him reform, and take him to the Nests for the Mothers to play with.

'Martin? We have to find Frankie and the Murasame,' I said. 'If they win, you'll go back in there.'

He turned towards me and his eyes were wide and unseeing. 'I can't,' he said, as if from a great distance. 'I've been trying to attain Enlightenment, detachment, so that it holds no fear for me, but I can't face it. If they win, not even death will save me from it.' His voice broke and he dropped his head into his hands. 'I can't go back.'

'This sword is our only chance to avoid that fate, Ming Gui,' I said, trying to sound like John. 'We must find the Murasame, otherwise all of us will end up in there. You, me, Leo, Simone —'

'Buffy,' he gasped and straightened. 'Let's go find that sword.'

We slipped around the lake and I tried to avoid looking at the dismembered body parts that occasionally surfaced. If someone's head came to the top, it would emit liquid-filled strangling gurgles until it submerged again. Martin winced every time the heads made a sound.

'We can do this,' he said grimly. 'We can.'

'We can, love,' Leo said.

Martin took Leo's hand and clutched it as we walked around the lake. Leo pulled him closer and they walked with their arms around each other's waists, Martin leaning into Leo.

The entrance to Level Nine was on the other side — the Pit of the Trees of Swords. White corpses hung on the metre-long blades that protruded from black pillars, their arms and legs cut off.

Martin clutched Leo as we skirted the black-walled edge of Level Nine. Cells were carved into the rock wall of the cave on the far side. The demons in them were in human form, naked and emaciated, covered in filth. They screamed silently at us as they reached through the bars.

'With anti-psychotics,' I said, 'anti-depressants, basic care and hygiene —'

'These are the past Demon Kings and they knew this would be their fate if they fell,' Martin said. 'Each of them has been responsible for the deaths of thousands.'

'Oh,' I said, and shook my head. 'Still. A captor this cruel has lowered himself to their …' I realised what I was saying. 'Never mind.'

'Someone may be merciful in future and destroy them,' Martin said. 'In the meantime, they are a warning to any who would attempt the top job.'

'Why don't they make any noise?' Leo said.

'They're making plenty of noise, it's just muted so nobody can hear it,' Martin said. 'Sometimes …' He gathered himself. 'Sometimes they'd pull our heads out of the lake, throw them into a big net, and bring us to listen. We made more noise than they did. The Demon King called it his "Chorus of Delight".'

'Try not to let it get to you,' I said.

'Way past that,' he said. 'So where?'

'The stone said there's an opening deeper into the cell complex.' I pointed at a rectangular doorway between two of the previous Kings' cells. 'That looks like what it was describing.'

We moved as quietly as we could down the tunnel, with the old Kings scrabbling at us through the bars of their cells and silently screaming. The tunnel opened into a cavern that was a hundred metres each side. It contained a single-storey village-type house with a pitched tiled roof and plain concrete walls.

There are no guards here, Martin said. *That means we're probably on camera. We don't have long.*

I know, I said. *But the three of us are a formidable force and the King will want to round up some really high-level guards to face us.*

All the biggest guards are here on Level Nine. The most senior Mothers are in a Nest on the other side of the Trees, he said. *We need to be quick.*

I may not be able to when I'm talking to — I said, and stopped

160

when Frankie opened the front door of the house and stood in the doorway watching us.

My baby. The living embodiment of everything John and I meant to each other, and the child I would destroy the world for — and he didn't even know who I was.

He saw Leo and Martin, turned and ran into the house.

We followed him through the front door and down the plain whitewashed hallway with the living room on one side and the bedroom on the other. He slipped into the bedroom, then hid in the gap between the bed and the wall.

'It's me, Emma,' I said without moving closer to him, both men behind me. 'I'm the lady who played with the cars with you. Remember?'

'He's a bad guy,' Frankie said from behind the bed.

'Goddamn television,' Leo grumbled under his breath.

'What?' Martin said.

'I'm black,' Leo said, 'and he's been watching television while his "mother's" away. Every black man on American TV is either a gangster or a thug. It's the stereotype. I have this problem in Hong Kong as well. Everyone assumes I'm a bad guy.'

'They can be police chiefs too,' I said, sitting on the bed to get closer to Frankie. 'And the production companies are attempting to subvert the thug stereotype in kids' shows by making the black kid the geek.'

'Still …' Leo began.

'We do not have time for that particular discussion,' Martin said. 'Guards will be here soon.'

'I know.' I leaned over the bed to speak to Frankie. 'It's okay. These are my other sons. They're like brothers to you, even though they're grown-up, and they love you as well. They want to play.'

Frankie didn't move, his terrified breathing echoing against the wall.

'Have you ever wanted a pet lion?' I asked him. 'I've brought you a tame *lion* to play with.'

'Tame,' Leo muttered.

'Hardly,' Martin said in the same low tone.

Frankie's breathing accelerated. Wrong move.

'If they go away, will you come out and talk to me?' I said.

There was no reply except for the sound of his head moving against the blankets.

'Quickly, Emma,' Martin said. 'We don't have much time.'

They went out.

'They're gone now,' I said.

Frankie crawled down the side of the bed and appeared at the end. He looked nearly ten years old, but his dark eyes held the innocence of his real age; he was just over a year and a half old. He stood up and looked around, then threw himself at me and buried his head in my chest.

'Hello! Thank you for coming back!' He pulled back and wiped his eyes, and I did as well. 'Mummy says I have to tell her if you come visit. Will she send you away?'

'Probably,' I said sadly. 'But you don't have to tell her right away. We can play for a little while first, and then you can tell her.'

'But she'll send you away,' he said.

'I'll come back.'

He thought about it for a moment, then nodded. His mid-brown hair needed a cut and his fringe flipped over his forehead and nearly into his eyes. His smile was so full of desperate yearning for affection that I pulled him in for another hug.

'It's okay. I love you, Frankie, and I want to look after you and make you happy.'

He trembled in my arms.

'I will never hurt you,' I whispered.

He clutched me. 'That's what the lady said. She said you were good, and to talk to you if you came to visit.'

I pulled back to see him. 'The Lady?'

He nodded.

'Is she wearing all white and really nice?'

'I don't know, I've never seen her. She just talks to me.'

'She's wonderful, isn't she?' I said, and he nodded. 'Listen to her because she's always right.'

'Don't tell anyone about her,' he said. 'I like talking to her and I don't want her to be in trouble. Promise you won't tell anyone? Promise!'

I hugged him again, he was close to tears. 'Of course I promise. I won't tell anyone you talk to the Lady.' I looked around. 'Would you like to play? Do you have any toys in this horrible little house? The other house was much nicer, this one is small and dark and awful. If *I* was looking after you, we'd be living in a lovely big house with a *garden* and dogs and cats and ponies and lots of friends and ...' I took a huge risk that he was our son in every way. 'A *big* room for practising martial arts, with a whole *wall* full of interesting weapons to learn.'

He inhaled sharply and pulled back, his eyes huge.

'You have a sister who would love to play with you and teach you to ride a pony, and the two men outside are like your grown-up brothers and would take you shopping and to theme parks,' I said.

'What's a theme park?'

'A place with fun rides and things to do. Do you like Batman?'

'Yeah! I saw him on the TV.'

'You could *meet* Batman.'

'Cool!'

'Would you like to go to one now?' I said. 'I can take you.'

He hesitated. 'Daddy wouldn't like that.'

'Your father thinks going with me is the best thing you could do.'

'You talk like my father is someone different,' he said, morose. 'Daddy doesn't like me.'

So young to be so perceptive.

'Maybe there's another daddy, your *real* daddy, out there who would be kind to you,' I said. 'Maybe there's another mummy out there who loves you and wants to be with you all the time. Maybe you should have a real mummy and daddy who would never, ever hurt you.'

He wrapped himself around me and gasped into my chest. He knew they were cruel to him.

'Would you like to come home with me?' I said.

'I can't. They'll punish me. I have to stay here.' He looked up into my eyes, his own full of tears. 'If I leave, they'll kill every servant in the house.'

'Are the servants kind to you?'

'They're really nice,' he said. 'Last time you came, they found out and they killed Three-Eighty.' His shoulders heaved. 'They *killed* her.'

Time, Emma, Leo said. *There's movement over at the lake.*

'I have to go,' I said. 'If they find me here, they'll destroy your servants.'

'I understand,' he said, looking up into my eyes. 'Please come back again.'

'I will, and I'll arrange a way for you and all your servants to come with me. But before I go,' I said, 'do you remember that sword I gave you? The mean black one?'

He nodded.

'Can I borrow it for a while? I promise I'll give it back to you.'

He shrugged. 'Sure.'

He took my hand to lead me into the living room. The Murasame was on a carved ebony stand that seemed even blacker from the sword's dark aura.

'Put your hand on the sword and say that I'm its master now, the same as I did for you,' I said.

'Okay,' Frankie said. He went to the sword, put his hand on it, and concentrated. He shook his head. 'It doesn't want to go with you, it wants to stay with me.'

'I don't blame it; I want to stay with you as well,' I said, and his little shoulders sagged. 'Tell it. Be the boss!'

His face screwed up with determination.

'I am so proud of you,' I said.

He glanced at me, grinning, then turned back to the sword. He growled under his breath. 'It really doesn't want to go with you.'

I put my hand on it as well and jerked it away at the pain. I bent to speak softly to the blade. 'Do as the child tells you, you black b—' I didn't finish it. 'He's your master, you lousy piece of scrap iron, and you damn well do what he says.'

Frankie giggled. 'It said a bad word!'

There were crashes and the sounds of conflict behind us and Frankie spun towards the door, his face filling with fear.

'The guards have come for me. I have to go,' I said.

Cold realisation went through me: if Leo and Martin were killed, there was only one way for me to escape — through Court Ten — and if I did, the child would see me die in front of him.

'One last chance, quickly,' I said, taking his hand and putting it on the sword, then flinching away at the contact. 'Tell it!'

He concentrated and shook his head. 'It's being really ...' He searched for the word.

'I know. Stubborn. It runs in the family.' I pulled him in for a quick hug. 'I'll go before you're in trouble. I love you, Frankie.' I released him and tousled his hair. 'You need a haircut. Stay here, stay away from the guards, and I promise I'll be back.'

I kissed him on the cheek. *I'll talk to you silently sometimes, how about that? We can chat.*

He stared at me, uncomprehending, and I had no choice. I turned and ran back to Leo and Martin so we could escape.

I slid to a halt when I saw them. It was the Demon King himself, with a couple of guards, and Martin and Leo were standing next to him, their eyes wide with effort but unrestrained otherwise.

'Emma, darling,' the King said.

He was in his small twenty-five-year-old male human form, the same height as me. He approached me, and I tried to step back but couldn't move. I was frozen as well.

His blood-coloured eyes looked deep into mine. 'I thought for a moment that this would be unpleasant,' he said. 'But you sneaked in here through Court Ten, didn't you? You *made the choice* to come to my side of Hell.' He stroked my cheek and I was unable to move away. 'You're in my dominion now, and I can do what I like with you. I can send all three of you for a grand tour of all the Pits.'

'Please don't hurt her, Uncle George,' Frankie said behind me, his voice small.

'What did she say to you, Frankie?' the Demon King said, still stroking my face.

'She just wanted to play!'

'She wants to take you away from your mother and lock you up,' the King said.

He's locked up now! I shouted at him, unable to speak.

'Go inside, Frankie. Your father is on his way and he's really mad with you for not telling him that Emma was here,' the King said, his voice sleek with menace. 'You were supposed to tell anybody if she came.'

'I was about to!' Frankie said, full of tears. 'Don't hurt her. I *like* her!'

'Oh, I like her too,' the Demon King crooned into my face. 'I'd love snake for dinner.'

He gestured towards one of the guards and the demon walked around me. I couldn't turn to see what it did to Frankie. Frankie made some loud sounds of protest, then the door closed behind us.

The King paced in front of me. 'Emma, Emma, Emma. Why can't you just wait? As soon as I control the Heavens you'll be spending all your time with Frankie, teaching him how to be a good Celestial. It's only a couple of days; why can't you learn some patience? Now I'll have to force you to stay away from the Murasame, and unfortunately that probably means I'll have to torture one of the lads here to make you do as you're told.'

'I have passage out for them,' I said. 'I have two black jade coins.'

The King studied me with interest. 'That you do. Very well.' He held his hand out, and released me so I could move.

I removed the black jade earrings and passed them to him. 'Now let them go.'

'I choose who goes and who stays, my love,' the King said. He turned away from me to Leo and Martin, who were also standing unmoving. His voice became businesslike. 'Pick a Pit, Ming Gui.'

'Don't send him to the Pits,' I said. 'This was my idea. Send me.'

'But you don't care about yourself, you're far too noble. Threatening you will achieve nothing. The only way to make you behave is to torture the ones you love.' He turned back to Martin. 'So where would you like to go? How about I toss you back into the lake, Turtle? You spent a great deal of time there, you should be used to it. Warm and comfortable, eh?'

Martin made soft sounds and his throat worked. He looked nauseous. Leo trembled as he fought the binding.

'I'll leave and won't return if you'll let me take both of them with me,' I said.

The King spun and spoke quickly. 'Promise you won't try for the sword again, and that you won't talk to Frankie without my permission. Promise you'll stay out of my dominion until I give you permission to return.'

I hesitated. If I relinquished the Murasame, I was handing the Heavens to him. I couldn't do it.

'Red Hot Grates. Nice change for him,' he said. 'I'll rotate him between the lake and the grates.' He put his hands on my arms. 'The sword wouldn't go with you, Emma, you're wasting your time. When I win, you can spend all your time with Frankie anyway. Face it, dear one, you've lost, so take your boys home where they are safe, and pack your bags ready to move down here and do your job as nanny when I take over.'

I couldn't look at Leo and Martin. 'I won't try for the sword again. I promise.'

'Good girl.' He turned back to Leo and Martin. 'Take her home and never again enter my dominion without my permission, or you will join the old mad Kings and I will raise your daughter as my own, as a sister for Frankie. He needs a sibling and Buffy is adorable.'

'Don't you touch Buffy!' Leo said.

The King nodded to him. 'Out.'

We landed on the Demonic side of Hell at the end of the causeway, outside the huge doors. Martin collapsed, curled up on the ground, and shook with gasping sobs. Leo sat cross-legged and took Martin into his lap, holding him like a child as he choked with fear and desperation. I sat on the pavers next to them and let Martin work it through.

* * *

'Crown Prince Xuan Ming Gui of the Northern Heavens. Lord Leo Alexander of the Northern Heavens. Lady Emma Donahoe of the Northern Heavens,' the guard said, and gestured for us to enter the Jade Emperor's small audience chamber.

We knelt and did the obeisances, then waited as the Emperor sat on his throne, which was two metres long with silk cushions.

'Before you say anything, the answer is no,' the Jade Emperor said.

'We're not here to ask you to let us marry,' Leo said.

'I know,' the Emperor said.

Martin bowed his head. 'This small Shen requests that you release him from the Heavens and reattach him to the Wheel.'

'You want to Fall?' the Emperor said. He rubbed his chin. 'This is new. Why would you *want* to Fall?'

Martin's face was full of struggle, and after an uncomfortable couple of minutes, Leo answered for him. 'He can't face being in the Pits again when we lose.'

'When we lose, eh? If that's your attitude, then we've lost already,' the Emperor said. 'You have a child, Prince Ming. You would leave her without a parent?'

'My husband Leo will take care of her.'

'And how will she react when she discovers that you've *chosen* to be destroyed, instead of staying to care for her when she loves you as a father?'

Martin didn't look up from the floor. He struggled to speak, coughed, then said, 'I hope that one day she will understand and forgive me.'

'Lord Leo Alexander,' the Emperor said.

Leo saluted the Jade Emperor. 'Majesty.'

'You are supporting your partner in this ridiculous request? You *want* to see him gone from your life forever?'

'I want to be with Prince Ming for the rest of eternity,' Leo said, his voice rough with emotion. 'But if he was returned to the Pits, it would destroy him. I love him too much to see him suffer like that.'

'Once an Immortal has Fallen there is no return,' the Emperor said. 'This life, all of these memories, would be lost. Even worse, Prince Ming, once Fallen you would retain an echo of what you were: fleeting moments where you would nearly remember, and they would tear you apart.'

'I'd rather that than return to the Pits,' Martin said.

Leo put his hand on Martin's shoulder and Martin nodded acknowledgement.

'Lady Emma Donahoe,' the Emperor said.

I saluted as well. 'Majesty.'

'You are actually supporting this insanity?'

'The Dark Lord Fell, but he is here in the Heavens now,' I said. 'If a spirit is Worthy, they will end up in the Heavens again. It's inevitable.'

'The Dark Lord was guided by a Buddha, Miss Donahoe, and it took him a thousand incarnations to return to us.'

'A thousand incarnations is tens of thousands of years,' Leo said. 'Lord Xuan's not more than five thousand years old, he says so himself. What aren't you telling us, Majesty?'

'Time is irrelevant when the soul is returned to the Earthly,' the Emperor said. 'More than one incarnation can exist at the same time. Isn't this obvious?'

'Oh,' Leo said. 'A *thousand* incarnations?'

'If he ever returns, it will take at least a thousand incarnations, and the man that rises again will not be the man you see now. The Wheel changes a spirit's essence.'

'I still request that you sentence me to Fall,' Martin said.

'This is a one-way trip,' the Emperor said. 'And I can only do it while I control the Heavens — which means I would have to do it before we face the demons. If we win on Saturday, I could have reattached you to the Wheel and destroyed your existence for no reason.'

'I request you do it anyway, Majesty,' Martin said.

'What does Simone say?' the Emperor said.

None of us replied.

'I see. Does Buffy know?'

Again none of us answered.

'What about the Dark Lord? Have you at least discussed this with your *father*?'

'His opinion is irrelevant. This is between me, my husband, and my child.'

'He is not your husband!' the Jade Emperor snapped. 'What about your stepmother?'

'She's just here to escort us past the guards.'

A Palace fairy appeared behind the Jade Emperor with an open scroll floating in front of her.

'The ruling with regard to Prince Xuan Ming Gui of the Northern Heavens is as follows,' the Jade Emperor said, and a brush appeared floating above the scroll. The Emperor stopped and leaned his elbow on the arm of the throne. 'Are you absolutely sure about this, Ming Gui?'

Martin's face was bright with hope, but his eyes glittered with tears. Leo made no attempt to brush the tears from his own face.

'I am sure, Majesty. Please, release me from this Immortal existence and reattach me to the Wheel.'

'The judgement is as follows,' the Emperor said. 'Request denied. Prince Ming is to assist in the defence of the Heavens. His skills are needed. If he makes this request again, his partner, Leo Alexander, will be executed.'

'What?' Martin said. 'You'll execute *Leo*?'

'Dismissed,' the Emperor said.

Martin stood and glared at the Emperor. 'You can't do this! You can't execute Leo for something that I do!'

'I am the Jade Emperor and I can do anything I want! If you are all not out of this room in thirty seconds, I'll execute *Princess Simone and Lord Xuan* as well as *all of you*. Out!'

'You'll execute *Simone*?' I cried, horrified.

'Ten seconds!' the Emperor said.

We hurried out.

16

I stood in the doorway of our bedroom in the Northern Heavens. It was smaller and less comfortable than our room on the Mountain — we only stayed in the Northern Palace when we had overnight administrative tasks or state dinners. The bed was a simple Western-style with a bedhead and side tables, unlike our lovely ebony four-poster on the Mountain.

John had buried himself under the black silk quilt, only his dark eyes and wild tangle of hair visible on the pillow. I crawled in next to him and nestled under his arm, nuzzling into his chest.

'This is probably our last chance for a long time,' he said.

'No. The Jade Emperor has to know something. We'll win.' I pulled myself closer. 'We have to trust him. This time tomorrow we'll be back on the Mountain and everything will be okay.'

'Tell me what you want,' he said. 'Anything you want, I will make it happen for you.'

I pulled back to see him. His eyes were full of sadness.

'No,' I said. 'Tell me what you want. How do you want to spend this night? If you just want to cuddle, let's do that. You're always the one who asks me what I want from you. This time, tell me what *you* want.'

'One condition,' he said.

'If it's too freaky I'll say no.'

He nodded, satisfied.

'Well?'

He hesitated, not sure where to start.

'My snake?' I said. 'You've been lusting after it forever. I've seen the way you look at me.'

He pulled himself up to sit against the bedhead. 'You have read my mind. But there are things that will happen if you say yes.'

'Ooh,' I said, acting entranced. 'I hope so.'

He smiled, then it disappeared. 'The Turtle will be present and separate.'

That stopped me. 'Doing what?'

He shrugged.

I failed to control the laughter. 'Okay. Is that all?'

'The bed's too small. We'll have to go to the living room.'

'Why not in here?'

'Not enough room. You saw the old Serpent Concubine Pavilion — we had a …' He searched for the word.

'You had a pit,' I said. 'Wow. A little snaky love nest. And I knocked it down.' I shook my head. 'I am such an idiot.'

'I would not take you in there anyway.' He hesitated. 'Are you sure about this?'

I climbed out of bed, moved to the middle of the bedroom floor, and transformed. I pictured his Serpent in my mind — all four sexy metres of it — and immediately generated the scent.

He made a deep moan of pleasure, his eyes glittering.

I writhed sinuously into the living room, then turned back to see him. He'd already changed and was following me like he was mesmerised.

The Turtle and Serpent separated. The Turtle changed to human form and sat cross-legged on the couch, its face intense. The Serpent came to me and raised its head so its eyes were level with mine. It flicked its tongue and generated its own scent. The aroma hit my tongue; I tasted it, and it sent me over the edge.

I grabbed him with my coils and pulled him down next to me. I tasted of *him*, the purest, wildest, most entrancing essence of him. I was driven even wilder when the cactuses came out, and we slid over each other, revelling in each other's scent and the touch of our scales.

'Emma,' the Turtle said, but I didn't really hear it. I was lost in the taste and the scent and the sensation.

'Emma!' he said more strongly, and the Serpent tapped the top of my head with its nose. 'Emma. Talk to me.' He lowered his voice. 'Please don't be all animal. I can't do it if you're all animal.'

'No, don't stop,' I said, breathless with need. 'Don't stop. Do it! I need this.' My voice went hoarse as I moved into position. 'Xuan Wu. I need you. Now!'

'If it hurts for even a second or feels wrong ...' he began, but didn't have a chance to finish because I grabbed him with my coils and shoved myself onto him. He roared with triumph, pulled me down, and thrust into me. It was divine — the sensation of his spines wasn't painful, it was like scratching a nagging itch, a filling, a completion.

'Are you still there?' he said into my serpent ear.

'So good.' He moved and I moaned. 'So good. So ...'

He moved again. He twined over me and we moved together in the scent, fresh and bright and clean and wonderful. He filled me from nose to tail with sensation and scales and movement and exhilarating aroma.

Then he pushed harder and we locked together and the pleasure hit new heights. Where we had been two we were now one. We twined around each other, our scales rubbing deliciously together, immersed in the sweet-smelling essence.

We lifted and the floor fell away and the stars spun around us. We lay on a mountaintop, two as one, and the stars rotated, brilliant in their cold beauty. The air was freezing but I felt no chill; I was lost in the sensation of being one with the Xuan Wu.

'Tell me when you're close,' he said into my ear, his voice soft and silken. 'It's not the same as mammals, but when you're near ...'

'Yes,' I said. 'Yes, now. So much.' I pushed against him, writhing with more than need. 'Now.'

He rotated inside me and the stars exploded. The Turtle was speaking with John's voice some distance away, but I didn't really hear it. The stars coalesced into a bright point of need within me, and then he pushed again and everything went away for a long time. The stars spun wildly around me and I was completely submerged in his scent, his exquisite black scales, and his love for me.

It was like coming down from an incredible high as we lay side by side in serpent form on the floor, still wrapped comfortably around each other.

'Heavens, that was wonderful,' he breathed.

'I've never felt anything like it.' I flicked my tongue; the scents were still around us. 'I could just lie like this forever, it was even better than the Turtle.' I raised my head. 'Oh. Sorry.'

'Nothing to apologise for,' the Turtle said from the sofa above us, its voice warm and satisfied. It was reclining in human form with an expression of contentment I'd never seen on John's face before, its head resting on its arm. It sat up. 'I haven't done that in ages. I'm glad we had this final chance.'

'I wish my snake form could accommodate both of you like my human form can,' I said, almost to myself.

The serpent made a deep hissing sound and its scent filled the air around us again.

I slid against him, making the scent stronger. 'More?'

He rubbed his head against mine. 'Yes, please.'

'Can you?'

'There's two of them, remember?'

The Turtle made a soft sound of pleasure and fell back on the sofa.

'You're not missing out?' I said to the Turtle.

'I'm right there with you,' the Turtle said. 'Like ...' The Serpent wrapped itself around me to hold me tight, and I squeaked with pleasure. 'This.'

* * *

We lay on the carpet in the living room, side by side. The Turtle reclined on the couch in human form, dozing as well. I was warm and comfortable and didn't want to move.

'We should have done this a long time ago,' I said. 'Wait. What the hell? I feel it! I could do it.'

'Are you okay?' he said. The Serpent touched its head to mine.

'John, I have everything while I'm snake. All my internal organs. *All* of them. And I could keep your seed and use it later to make ...' I took a deep breath. 'Wow. Little serpent babies.'

'You have to stay snake for the whole process to succeed,' he said. 'With a big snake Shen it can take up to a year.'

'Would the children be ... children? Would they be sentient? They wouldn't be animals, would they?'

'No. They're always serpent Shen.'

'I would lay the eggs and leave them.'

'That's what we do.' He grunted and shifted next to me. 'Let me up, I want to rejoin.'

I uncurled from around him. The Turtle stepped off the couch, changed to True Form, and the Serpent coiled around it. I changed back to human and sat on the floor next to him. He rubbed his snake head affectionately against me.

'It's gone,' I said.

'That's how it works.'

'You don't have a problem with me ...? I mean, we could have had more children.'

'It's your choice what you do with your body, Emma. Whatever form you take, it is your decision alone.'

I leaned my head against him. 'Maybe one day.'

His voice was warm and low. 'Maybe. When you're ready. But not for a long time now.'

'You're sure we'll lose?'

'Absolutely positive, love. We have no chance.'

I rubbed the back of my head against his smooth shell. 'How much time do we have left?'

'All the time in the world.' He changed to human form, stood, and reached down to me. 'Come to bed, my love, and hold me. Because it is our last time.'

I took his hand and he helped me up. I wrapped my arm around his waist and we walked into the bedroom. When we were in bed, we held each other tight, and spent the rest of the night making plans for a future we probably wouldn't have. Neither of us wanted to see the dawn.

* * *

In the morning I did a final patrol of the Mountain, checking the disposition of our defences. An awful sense of foreboding filled me. This was the last time I would be able to wander through our Mountain home and enjoy the sounds of the students and the fresh pine-filled air. If they won, the demons could finish the job they'd been trying to do for many years and destroy the Mountain completely. When they won. The sure knowledge filled me that they would attack and they would win; and it didn't matter how much we fought, we would lose.

I walked alongside a row of cherry and plum trees that framed the path for two hundred metres along the cliff edge. The compound's wall stood on the far side of the fifty-metre-wide chasm, with the remaining Disciples and Celestial Masters patrolling its top. The plum trees had finished; their dark red flowers bloomed at the end of the snow and peeked through the white as a promise of future warmth. The cherries were in full blossom and shedding a flurry of pink petals that covered the ground. I raised my hand to touch one as it fluttered past me, certain in the knowledge that these trees would not be gracing the Mountain with their beauty for much longer. The demons took great delight in destroying every lovely thing we created.

I wanted to be with John, but his first allegiance was to the Heavens and he stood with the army outside the Northern Palace. It was up to the Celestial Masters and me to lead the defence of the Mountain and my family. The remaining Disciples were young, undertrained, underdisciplined and terrified. In the last forty-eight hours, many of them had returned to their families on the Earthly and I didn't blame them. If the Northern Heavens fell, there was no way we could retain the Mountain. All the Heavens would fall.

My phone rang and I pulled it out of my pocket: my mother.

'Yes, Mum?'

'Sorry to call you again, but my nerves are just so on edge. Have you heard anything?'

'No. Nothing's happened.'

'We have less than an hour before they attack — are you far away?'

'Not far, I'm near the admin section, I can be there in a couple of minutes. Try not to worry too much.'

She was silent for a moment, then her voice came back very

faintly and full of biting sarcasm. 'She says try not to worry ...' she said as she ended the call.

Emma.

My heart leapt. *John.*

Where are you?

Can you look through my eyes?

He was silent a moment, then, *I suppose it makes no difference now.* His consciousness touched mine and we shared the beauty of the trees. *Thank you.*

We watched the trees silently together. I brushed my hand through the clouds of petals and John shared my appreciation for them.

The future does not look good, he said.

I know.

I would give anything to spend another hour with you before everything is destroyed.

Me too, I said. *And we both know that won't happen.*

You will be safe.

And for the rest of my long life, my safety will mean that you are in a cage in True Form being tortured by demons.

Worth it, he said. *Just promise that you'll keep Simone safe for me.*

I will.

We won't have a chance to say goodbye, he said. *But I want you to know: all of it was worth it. All of it will be worth it. Do not doubt for a second that I am glad to pay the price. And I am sure that our daughter will one day grow strong enough to surprise us all.*

I love you, John, and all of it was worth it for me as well.

I am sorry that I led you here.

I'm not. Remember that you vowed to marry me, even if the Heavens and the Earth —

I'm sorry, my love, but our time is finished.

I caught one of the petals between my fingers, slid it into the pocket of my Mountain uniform, and hurried back to Persimmon Tree.

I joined my parents in the living room. Greg had tuned the television to the camera mounted on the Northern Palace's wall that pointed at the field next to the lake. I ran my eye over the defensive features for the hundredth time.

The lake was on the left; any aquatic demon would need to exit the water to attack us and would lose its underwater advantage. The field was wide and flat and the ground was solid, but would eventually turn to mud once battle had commenced. Regardless of the surface, soldiers always ended up fighting in mud. The land to the right of the lake spread to low rolling hills, meaning that we couldn't hold the demon force in a small, narrow area and there was a chance they could flank us and cut us off. Defensive barriers had been placed fifty metres in front of our army; they were a metre and a half tall, sloped upwards and ended in spikes that would impale any attackers. We'd used the last of the steel and wood to build them, and placed razor wire in the gaps where we hadn't had enough raw materials to cover the entire area. The demons would have to work through them to reach us and fight hand-to-hand; the bottlenecks would throttle their movement.

'You should be with him,' my father said, nodding towards John's back.

He stood on a wooden raised platform overlooking the field. The army stood in ranks facing away from the camera, ready for the attack. Banners on pikes stood out as markers for the largest Immortals. The Four Winds were there, surrounded by their own remaining soldiers; and the Mountain's senior Disciples in their black livery stood under a black banner embossed in silver with the Seven Stars of the Big Dipper. The Thirty-Six and the remaining demons of the army stood in formation around them. So few to face so many.

John was deep in discussion with Er Lang; and Simone stood next to them in her Celestial Form, accompanied by her horse, Freddo. She looked tense and frightened. John turned and said something to Simone, and she glared at him and shook her head. He spoke to her again and she frowned, then she and Freddo disappeared.

'There are two possible outcomes,' I said, checking behind me that the boys couldn't hear from the bedroom where Yi Hao was keeping them busy. 'Either we win, or we lose. If we win, John will come back and we'll celebrate. If we lose, John will die, the Demon King will have him in the Pits, and it'll be up to me to defend you.'

'Are you *sure* you can negotiate something with them if you lose?' Amanda said.

I winced at her use of 'you'. I wasn't one of them any longer.

'I have an agreement with him already,' I said. 'You'll be safe.'

'Then why do you need to stay here and defend us?' my mother said.

I rose and paced from one end of the room to the other. 'To make sure he sticks to our agreement.'

'Wait,' my mother said. 'What agreement? What are you giving him?'

'Shut up, Mum,' Jennifer said.

'Are you giving yourself in return for our safety?' my father said.

I didn't reply. I just stood behind the couch with my arms crossed and watched the television.

'Emma!' my father said.

'Let it go, Dad,' Jennifer said.

On the TV, John and Er Lang nodded together and the message came through telepathically.

No demons sighted as yet. They will attack at noon. Stay close and safe.

'Emma, we spoke about this,' my father said.

I was silent, watching the screen.

'Emma,' he growled.

'None of us will be hurt if the Celestial loses,' I said. 'The King will use you as hostages —'

My mother moaned softly with dismay.

'— to ensure my good behaviour because he needs me to do something else. We'll all be safe.'

'How safe?' Jennifer said.

'Whatever happens, you'll be safe.'

'Are you sure?' Amanda said.

'I promise.'

'Why do I not believe you?' Jennifer said, looking away. 'The boys have already been captured and tortured because of you.'

'What does he need you to do?' my father said. 'If it's what I think it is —'

'No. He needs me to be a mother to his child. That's all.'

'You can't be a mother,' Amanda said. 'You —'

'Shut up, Amanda,' Jennifer said.

'Stop telling everybody to shut up!' Amanda snapped.

'Well, you stop asking stupid questions!' Jennifer snapped back. 'She's one of *them*. She can change into a snake, she can probably change into a demon, and she can probably lay disgusting eggs if she lets the Demon King *mate* with her.'

I looked away.

'Jennifer, that's enough,' my mother said, a sharp edge to her usually mild voice. 'I suggest you go make sure that little Matthew is okay. It sounds like Colin and Andrew are giving him a hard time.'

'He's fine,' Jennifer grunted, but she pulled herself up and went to the children anyway.

'Is she right?' my mother said after she'd gone.

'No. I can't have any more children.'

'Then what will you be a mother to? His child? He has hundreds of children. Why this one? Why you?'

'Wait — *more* children?' Amanda said.

My mother put it together straight away, and my father wasn't far behind.

'I never saw you pregnant,' my mother said.

'Jesus, Emma, he has your child?' my father said.

'It was when you were held by him in Europe, wasn't it?' Amanda said. 'You were gone for weeks, and the King had control over you.'

'You had a child with the Demon King?' my mother said.

'And John understands and has stayed with you,' my father said. 'He's a prince.'

'Emperor,' I said. 'I was already pregnant when the Demon King took me. The child is mine and John's.' I tried to keep control of my voice and failed. 'The Demon King ripped him out of me prematurely and kept the baby for himself. That's why I can't have any more.'

My mother blanched and fell to sit on the couch with her hand over her mouth.

'Oh, Emma,' Amanda said.

'His name is Frankie. Because of his ... unusual heritage, he's maturing much faster than a normal human child. He's about eighteen months old, but he looks like a ten year old.'

'The Demon King is holding him hostage to control you?' my mother said.

I watched the screen and decided to tell them the truth. 'As John's son, he can take the Jade Throne if the Demon King wins. The King's set him up to be a puppet Jade Emperor. He needs me to escort Frankie to Heaven when he takes the throne. Only his biological mother can do that.'

'Why haven't you tried to rescue him?' my father said.

'I have. Twice. You know how John is always saying "Going in to attempt a rescue in the centre of their power is a foolish waste of life"? It is. Leo and Martin nearly ended up ...'

I didn't say it. On the screen, the army stood silent and motionless, waiting for the attack. The camera's time stamp said 11:20; we had forty more minutes.

I took a deep breath and tried to ignore the pain in my chest that always appeared when I thought of Frankie. 'If the Demon King wins, he wants me to be Frankie's nanny. As his biological mother I have to be the one to protect him when the King brings him up to the Heavens to take the throne.'

'He wants you to be nanny to your own child? That's monstrous,' my mother said.

'I'd be with him, I suppose,' I said with forced cheerfulness.

On the screen, the sky was a brilliant Celestial blue with the occasional fluffy white cloud; a delightful day. The Celestial soldiers' robes and hair were lifted by the fresh spring breeze.

'He's a lovely boy,' I went on as I watched the soldiers. 'Sweet nature, big dark eyes from his father, tawny hair from me. He's curious and gentle and bright as a little button.' My throat filled and I swallowed it. 'He's not evil like they are, he's too caring, and they hate it. They want him completely obedient, so ...' It was very hard to speak. 'They broke his arm for no reason at all, just to keep him terrified and under their control.'

My mother rushed to wrap her arms around me. I let go into her shoulder, my throat strangling me and my chest hurting.

'If we win, I'll never see him again,' I said, choking on the words. 'And if we lose, I'll never see John again. The best I can hope for is that all of you are safe.'

'Why didn't you tell us?' Jennifer said from behind me.

'You need to share, honey,' my father said next to me. 'We're your family.'

'Another grandson,' my mother said into my hair.

Someone stroked my back; Jennifer. 'You should have told us, Em, that's awful. We could have helped.'

'Something's happening,' Amanda said, her voice sharp. 'Dragons!'

I pulled away from my mother, took some gasping breaths and wiped my eyes. Amanda was right: half-a-dozen dragons in True Form, all brilliant glittering colours in the Celestial sunshine, were gathered around John and Er Lang as John spoke to them.

'What's he saying?' my father said. 'I wish we could hear!'

I linked up with John and rested lightly on his consciousness. He felt me there and touched my mind, aware of my grief, and his warm caring eased my spirit as much as my family's support.

'He's sending them to be sentinels at the edge of the Heavens,' I said. 'We don't know where the demons will attack from, and the guards at the Gates aren't reporting anything. He's worried the demons will come in from somewhere else so he's sending dragons to patrol.'

'When are the demons supposed to be here?' my mother said.

'Pretty,' Matthew crowed from the doorway, and Colin picked him up and carried him, protesting, back into the room.

Colin reappeared in the doorway. 'What's happening?'

'They're supposed to be here at noon,' I said. The time stamp at the corner of the screen said 11:37. 'We should be able to see them by now. Where are they?'

'How do they know what time?' Jennifer said.

'The Jade Emperor told us,' I said, confused. 'He's always right about everything.'

I flopped to sit on the couch and watched the dragons take off with a visible blast of air beneath them, leaving just John and Er Lang discussing strategy on the platform.

'Even if the demons didn't come through the Gates,' I said, 'they should be close enough to see.'

I sat rigid with concern as the clock in the corner of the screen clicked over. John and Er Lang stopped talking together and stood silently on the dais, the breeze ruffling their long hair. The soldiers stood in orderly ranks, chatting to boost each other's morale.

The clock showed 11:44 and still no movement. John cocked his head, listening. Er Lang said something to him and he shook his head.

'What the hell is going on?' my father said.

'They're not coming?' Jennifer said with relief. 'No war?'

'It could be a ruse,' I said. 'The Jade Emperor's never wrong. Maybe the demons changed their minds at the last minute.'

The soldiers on the field readied themselves, lifting their weapons.

The clock clicked over to 11:49 and still no movement. I resisted the powerful urge to contact John telepathically and ask him what was happening. It was obvious they didn't know any more about it than we did.

'Is there anything we need to do?' my mother said. 'Should we hide in the bathroom or something?'

The clock showed 11:54.

'No,' I said. 'But if we lose, keep the boys still and quiet in their room so they don't attract unneeded attention.'

'My son is not going through that again,' Jennifer said, her voice low and fierce.

'I'm here,' Greg said, and took her hand. She clutched it.

It was 11:56 and still no movement. The soldiers in the field stood motionless. I checked to confirm that the camera feed hadn't frozen.

The time clicked over to 11:57.

'This is insane,' I said. 'We should be able to see them. What's going on?'

'We should have filled the bath with water in case the water's cut off,' my mother said, and started for the bathroom.

My father took her arm to stop her. 'Too late for that now. Stay here with us.'

The clock reached 11:59 and we all held our breath. Everything was completely still and quiet. The time sat on 11:59 for what seemed like five minutes, then it clicked over to 12:00.

Amanda made a tiny sobbing sound of terror.

John and Er Lang didn't move on their platform. The soldiers shifted, readying themselves. They looked around, wondering if the attack would be coming from a different direction. I gripped the arm of the couch so hard my fingernails dug into the leather, leaving marks. My mother took my father's hand and held it.

The clock ticked over to 12:01 and everybody jumped.

We all sat still and silent as we watched the army. The boys in the other room were playing a raucous game, thumping against the walls, but nobody stopped them. The clock ticked over again, and then again.

At 12:11, after an interminable wait, Er Lang said something to John, but John didn't reply.

At 12:15, Gold appeared next to John. John spoke to him, then Gold saluted and disappeared.

'John probably asked Gold to go to the Jade Emperor and see what's happening,' I said.

My phone rang and I checked the caller: Jade. I answered it.

'Emma, do you know what's happening? Has the demon attack been called off?'

The phone beeped: another call coming through.

'I don't know what's happening but they may still attack. Stay alert.'

'But the Jade Emperor said noon, didn't he?'

'I really don't know, and I have another call. Stay where you are and don't lower your guard.' I hung up on her before she could say anything and switched to the other call; it was Meredith.

'Emma?' she said. 'What's happening? Has it been called off?'

'Keep the Mountain on high alert,' I said. 'As far as we know they're still coming. We're checking with the Jade Emperor. I'll update you as soon as I know something.' My phone beeped again, then again. Two more calls. 'Tell everybody you know to sit tight and hold on; they may still be coming.'

Stand by, John said. *They may still attack. Stay alert.*

I answered the next call: Er Hao. On the television, Er Lang was also on the phone, turning on the spot as he spoke into it. John had the distracted look he wore when talking telepathically.

'So how long will we wait?' my father said. 'Before we know?'

'Yi Hao said they haven't attacked?' Er Hao said on the phone.

'Keep Buffy inside until we're sure,' I said. 'Is Leo there?'

'He won't move from the front door, ma'am.'

'Good. We still don't know what will happen.'

Gold reappeared next to John and I tapped into John to listen.

'My Lord,' Gold said, and hesitated.

'What did he say?' John said.

'Uh …' Gold looked around, then back at John. 'He said he doesn't know.'

'What?' Er Lang said.

'Did you ask him for more than that?' John said. 'Did you push him?'

'Push the Jade Emperor,' Gold said under his breath.

'Well?'

'My Lord, I did. I asked if he knew anything. Where they are. When they'll attack. What will happen!'

'And?'

'He told me he doesn't know anything and threw me out. He actually slammed the door in my face.'

'My turn,' Er Lang said grimly, and disappeared.

'What. The. Hell,' I said.

'What, Emma?' my father said.

'Gold asked the Jade Emperor, and the JE said he doesn't know what will happen.'

'But don't you kind of count on him knowing everything? Isn't he like the top god around here?' Amanda said. 'How can he not know?'

'He's supposed to know everything,' I said.

'So what happens now?' my mother said.

'We sit tight until we're absolutely sure that they won't attack. We'll stay on high alert with the army on the field for at least the next twenty-four hours.'

'And what do *we* do?' my mother said.

'Stay here and stay guarded until we're sure the attack isn't coming. Hopefully we'll have about twenty minutes' notice when they breach the entrance to the Heavens, but there's a chance they'll sneak in through one of the lesser-known gates. It's happened before. So we'll stay here and wait until we're sure we know what's happening.'

'I wish I'd brought a book now,' Amanda said ruefully. 'The last thing I expected was to be sitting here doing nothing.'

'Welcome to war,' I said with grim humour. 'You're either sitting bored out of your brain hoping something will happen, or terrified that you're about to be torn —' I saw their faces. 'Never mind. Sorry.'

'Sometimes I think you're around John far too much,' my mother said weakly. 'You sound just like him.'

Er Lang reappeared on the television screen and he and John had a short conversation. Er Lang was agitated, moving with jerky intensity. John nodded as he listened, then raised his hand to Er Lang who subsided, still obviously frustrated.

We will break for lunch, John broadcasted. *The army will rotate. After lunch we will reform and hold position until dark. Stay on high alert. We are still expecting to be attacked in the next twenty-four hours.*

'Twenty-four hours?' my mother said with dismay. 'We have to hang around waiting for twenty-four hours?'

'Even after that I won't feel safe,' my father said.

'You can fill the bath with water now if you like,' I said. 'But I think Jennifer will probably want to bath Matthew in it tonight.'

I went to the doorway to tell Yi Hao, and found her laughing under all the boys who had piled onto her like a mountain of puppies.

17

Two hours later I was doing a Tai Chi set in the courtyard outside Persimmon Tree when my mother opened the front door.

'Something's happening, love. You need to come and see.'

I followed her back inside. Every adult in the family was gathered around the television. Jennifer was clutching Greg's hand with tears running down her face, and everybody else's expressions were grim with dismay.

At first I thought there was something wrong with the screen; then I realised that the black blot on the horizon was the demon army. Tens of thousands of them, marching in step or slithering or flying.

John and Er Lang stood silently on the platform watching them. The soldiers in front of the platform were trembling.

The demon army stopped before the individual demons were clearly visible; a dark morphing horde that covered the ground as far as the eye could see. A small cluster came out of the group, one of them holding a white flag on a lance.

'I didn't know they used white flags here as well,' I mused as we watched them approach.

'We've been using them longer than the West has,' Greg said. 'The Dark Lord speculated that the Romans appropriated the symbology from us. Not that the Romans ever surrendered to anyone,' he added under his breath.

'They're surrendering?' Jennifer said, full of hope.

'No, it's a flag of truce for parley,' Greg said.

'Oh,' she said, the hope turning to disappointment.

It was the Demon King's Number One, Andy Ho, in human form and riding a big bay horse. He was flanked by a pair of bull's-head demon Dukes who were on foot; so tall that their heads were level with his shoulders. He stopped halfway between the armies and stood on the grass, waiting.

John nodded, and Er Lang summoned his horse and mounted it. His dog walked beside the horse through the quivering ranks of Celestial soldiers. It seemed to take forever for him to ride the hundred and fifty metres from the dais to meet the demons. He stopped in front of Andy, and the horses stood without moving.

Andy and Er Lang spoke for a couple of minutes, then Andy wheeled his horse and returned to the demon army at a canter, the Dukes running beside him and easily matching his speed.

Er Lang rode back and dismounted at the platform. His horse disappeared and he strode up the stairs onto the dais to stand next to John. He spoke to John for a moment, then disappeared again.

'What happened?' my mother said.

She turned to me, and everybody else gave me questioning looks too.

'I don't know,' I said.

Emma? Greg said.

'I really don't know. I'm staying out of his head to avoid distracting him. He needs to concentrate.'

The demon army parted on the other side of the plain and everybody on our side readied themselves.

A shiny new Land Rover with a white cloth attached to the antenna and towing a trailer drove between the demons and halted at the centre of the field. Five humanoids jumped out. They swiftly unpacked the trailer and assembled a small garden marquee like those used in street markets on the Earthly: closed on three sides and open towards us. They erected a plastic folding table inside the tent, then four folding chairs. They covered the table and chairs with crisp white linen covers, and brought out a pitcher of water on a silver tray with four glasses. One of the demons placed a leather portfolio and an expensive fountain pen onto the table with a flourish, then they all returned to the Land Rover and drove back behind their lines.

'They're having a wedding?' my mother said, bewildered.

'I've seen something like that before,' my father said. 'Oh. I remember. France.'

'I didn't see anything like that in France,' my mother said.

'You didn't come on the tour, you went to Reims Cathedral,' my father said.

My mother sagged with dismay. 'The Museum of Surrender.'

My father nodded.

'My guess is that the demons offered us a chance to surrender, and Er Lang's gone to talk to the Jade Emperor to see what he wants to do,' I said.

My mother made a soft sound of dismay.

Er Lang reappeared next to John and spoke to him. John stood silently, unmoving. Er Lang became agitated, waving one hand towards the demon army. John grew even more still.

'Don't do it,' Jennifer whispered.

Er Lang finished talking and glared at John, who stared down at him, impassive. There was a long moment while they faced off, then John shook his head.

Er Lang stomped around in a circle with his head down, nearly treading on his dog, who quickly backed away. Then he planted his feet, put his hands on his hips, and looked directly into the camera.

Emma, come and talk some fucking sense into him.

I jumped, and everybody looked at me.

Greg went very still, then nodded and put his hand out towards me.

'No,' I said. 'The Dark Lord knows what he's doing.'

'We don't doubt that, Xiaoyizi,' Greg said, using my family relationship title, 'wife's little sister'. 'But he's taking orders from the Jade Emperor, who doesn't.'

'What?' my mother said, looking from me to Greg. 'What did he say?'

'He's the *Jade Emperor*,' I said. 'He's so powerful they don't even put statues of him in the temples.'

'Even so. Go and talk to the Dark Lord. Something's wrong. The Jade Emperor should be there for us, and he's hiding away in his Palace, refusing to answer our calls.' He nodded towards the screen, where John was stubbornly standing with his arms crossed over his chest, glaring at Er Lang. 'Your humanity is sorely needed right now.'

He put his hand out towards me again.

'If my humanity is needed, then we are in really, really deep shit,' I said as I took his hand and the room disappeared around me.

We landed next to John and Er Lang on the platform. The acrid scent of the soldiers' fear filled the air around us.

'Talk to him,' Er Lang said, and strode off the dais to meet with the section leaders.

Greg disappeared, and it was just me and John on the platform. I opened my mouth to speak to John but he spoke first.

'If we surrender it's all over. The demons will have control over every place a human can live. No human will be safe. He'll use the ones we most love as toys.'

The Demon King appeared on the platform next to us. He raised his hands holding a white handkerchief and grinned. 'Truce,' he said, but couldn't say more than that because Er Lang yelled with fury, ran up the stairs, and stood panting with the blade of his halberd at the Demon King's throat.

'This is very bad manners, and no way to treat an adversary under a flag of truce,' the King said without moving, his voice mild. 'Back off, Number Two. You know it wouldn't work anyway.'

'Stand down,' John said.

Er Lang backed off, glowering.

The Demon King gestured with his head towards the marquee. 'Save everybody a great deal of anguish and do it, Ah Wu. I'm waiting for you.'

He disappeared and reappeared in the marquee.

'He's meeting you halfway!' Er Lang shouted at John. 'Take the smart gweipoh with you, make the right decision, and do the same.'

'I advised the Jade Emperor to surrender three weeks ago,' John grumbled as he took full huge ugly Celestial Form and stepped down off the dais. 'We've said all that needs to be said. There are no more words. The Jade Emperor has not ordered surrender, so we must fight.'

'Go with him and talk some sense into him,' Er Lang said to me as John walked away.

'You go with him,' I said. 'You're Second Heavenly General and I'm just a smart gweipoh.'

'He'll listen to you. He isn't listening to me. Go,' Er Lang said.

I reluctantly followed John through the ranks of soldiers. Pao was right: this was not my place. Er Lang was vastly more experienced at this than I was and should have been the one beside John.

'Do you think he has something up his sleeve?' I said as I caught up with John, who had slowed his pace for me.

'Who, the Demon King or the Jade Emperor?' he said without looking at me.

'Oh, I'm damn sure the King has something up his sleeve. What about the JE?'

'I wish I knew,' John said.

It took all my courage to walk across the open ground with the armies in front of and behind me. Something inside me, left over from being merged with John, resonated with joy at the thought of battle. The rest of me — the real me — felt nauseous and terrified.

'Lady Emma, Xuan Tian,' the Demon King said as we approached. 'Thank you for coming. I would speak to the two of you.'

'Speak to the Dark Lord,' I said. 'I have nothing to say to you.'

'I understand that,' the King said. 'But there are things I need to say to *you*. Truce. I just want to talk.' He gestured towards the table and chairs inside the marquee. 'Nobody else can hear what we say here. We can be completely open. And this has gone quite far enough.'

'So you'll call your army off?' I said, waiting two metres away to see if he tried anything.

John shrank to human form and sat at the table. 'You have multiple agreements with all of us. What do you want to talk about now? I don't think there's anything left to say.'

'If nations were willing to talk even when there's nothing left to say, there'd be many fewer wars,' the King said. 'Sit, Emma, this is legitimate.' He gestured towards John. 'He's always been willing to negotiate anything to avoid war.'

I sat next to John and shot him a questioning look. He shrugged.

'Very well,' the King said, sitting on the other side of the table. 'You've seen the size of my army. You said you'd talk to the Jade Emperor. What the hell, Ah Wu? How many do you have — four, five thousand? Don't throw them to their deaths. There has to be a better way.'

'I don't have a choice,' John said, staring at the water carafe on the table.

'The Jade Emperor's completely lost it,' the King said. 'This is madness. If you stop it now we can salvage something out of this. I don't want to kill these poor terrified humans, there is no honour in it. It will be a massacre.'

'I still have no choice.'

'Do the sensible thing: surrender and renounce your allegiance. You won't have to obey this madman any longer, and every life on the field will be saved.'

John was silent.

'You'll kill them anyway,' I said.

'Not if you turn and take responsibility for them,' the King said to John. 'Call it off now, pledge allegiance to me, and I won't put you in a jade cage. Instead, I will give you your Mountain and your Northern Heavens to rule independently. They will be untouched and they will be yours.'

John's head snapped up and he looked into the Demon King's blood-coloured eyes.

'You will have complete jurisdiction over your North and your Mountain. You can run the places as you see fit. Make them into refuges for the remaining Celestials if you want. We have to do *something* to avoid this bloodbath. I don't want to be held responsible for this. My newly conquered subjects will hate me.' The King pushed the portfolio towards John and placed the pen on top. 'Please, Ah Wu, do the right thing by your friends, your family and your subjects: surrender the Heavens and swear allegiance to me now. I don't want to kill every single terrified soldier out there for no good reason.'

'I am sworn to the Jade Emperor,' John said.

'You've changed allegiance before! Do it now, to protect the humans.'

'Changing allegiance would not be protecting them,' John said. 'If I swear allegiance to you and join your corrupt administration, I will betray them to demons who relish making humans suffer. The humans come first. They always come first.'

'Throwing them to their deaths is not putting them first!' the King said, sweeping one hand towards our army. 'When I defeat you in battle and occupy the Heavens, I'll be forced to use terror to subdue the population. If you capitulate now, they will follow your lead and the result will be a peaceful change of administration. Please.' He placed his hand on the portfolio. 'Save your subjects this suffering, swallow your damn stubborn pride, and admit that I've won.' He rounded on me. 'Tell him, Emma, for fuck's sake. Stop this madness now.'

'John,' I said, without looking away from the Demon King.

'Yes, Emma?'

'Has the Jade Emperor ever made a mistake in his leadership that has led to a Celestial defeat?'

John hesitated for a long moment, then said, 'Yes, he has.'

I tried not to let my shock show. That wasn't the answer I'd been expecting.

The Demon King's face filled with triumph. 'He made exceptionally bad decisions a dozen times during the Shang/Zhou. And he's been leading you towards this defeat for more than twenty years. If he'd permitted you to live with Michelle on the Earthly and provided you with the resources to defend her adequately, none of this would have happened. You wouldn't have been forced to set up such a small, exposed and understaffed residence that put all of you at risk. It's his fault we're all here right now.'

'Is that correct?' I said, remembering how John had used Leo, a mortal human, as guard when all the Celestial Masters were available to him. 'The Jade Emperor wouldn't permit you the resources to guard Michelle properly?'

John hesitated, then nodded without looking at me.

'I'd like to discuss this silently with him,' I said.

'Go right ahead,' the King said, obviously relieved. 'Talk some goddamn sense into him.'

If you surrender, what will the Jade Emperor do? Can he still force the army to fight? I said.

No. The army is mine, as First Heavenly General. If I turn, the Jade Emperor will have no choice but to throw open the gates of the Celestial Palace and surrender the Heavens.

Do you believe what he says about the Mountain and the North? That he'll let us stay there and look after the refugees?

You've never asked me, Emma, he said, *if it was true when he said he was a human child with her feet bound. China has been binding the feet of its women for a thousand years. This King is obviously much, much older than that.*

I assumed it was true, I said, dark realisation blossoming within me. John was right: the King and Yue Gui had been demon lovers in Hell long before the practice started. The Demon King couldn't possibly have been a human woman with her feet bound. *It was a lie?*

Of course it was a lie. He pinpoints your greatest weaknesses and tells you what you want to hear, confirming your existing beliefs. One of your weaknesses is your need to fight the oppression of women. He played on that.

It was all a lie? He was never a child with her feet bound?

It's possible that it is the truth — foot binding has been around for a very long time — but the chance is vanishingly small. He's been female in the past, all of the biggest ones have, but lying is like breathing for demons. They must be cunning and deceitful simply to survive.

And now he's offering you the thing you want most in the world, I said, *your Mountain and Heavens safe, and your subjects protected. Is that a lie too?*

Are we willing to risk finding out? If I turn and pledge allegiance to him, I will be compelled to obey every cruel order he gives me.

But if we fight, we'll lose.

Unless the Jade Emperor has, as you said, something up his sleeve.

My spirit crashed like a great rock. *This all comes down to whether or not you trust the Jade Emperor. His silence could be a test of your trust.*

No. He would not do that to me. If he had a secret weapon, he would share it with me. My guess is that he has some wildly improbable solution that will no longer exist if he as much as whispers it to any of us.

Tears filled my eyes and I wiped them away. 'This is impossible.'

'I know,' the Demon King said, his voice full of pain. 'How many soldiers are lined up there?'

'Five thousand, one hundred and three,' John said.

'How many are mortal?'

'Four thousand, eight hundred and sixty-five,' John said. 'Two thousand, two hundred and thirty-four have families: spouses and children. Three thousand, eight hundred and sixty-nine have living parents or siblings. More than twelve thousand people will have their lives destroyed when these last remaining fighters are lost.'

'They'll hate you,' the King said. 'They'll hate me. We can stop this. The daylight's fading. Decide.'

'History will judge us,' I said.

'So make the right fucking decision,' the King said, his voice a low growl.

John rose and bowed to the Demon King. 'I will see you on the field. Remember our agreement. I will enter a cage in True Form if you will keep my family safe.'

He put his hand on my shoulder and teleported me back to Persimmon Tree, left me there and returned to the platform.

He drew his sword and raised it. 'Prepare for attack!'

'What happened? What did you say? What did they say?' my family asked me all at once.

'Turn the television off,' I said. 'You don't want to see what happens next.'

'No,' my mother said. 'We trust John. He and the Jade Emperor will protect us. Everything will be fine.'

'You can't see the future, Mum,' I said, moving to turn the television off. 'It's all bad.'

My father took my wrist to stop me. 'She's right. We have to trust the Jade Emperor. John beat the demons before. They can do it.'

'Oh god,' Jennifer said, and I turned to see.

The demons were approaching at a run and thundered through the barricades. The vanguard were trapped on the razor wire, and the rest of the demons climbed over their bodies to reach our forces.

The Celestial army charged to meet them.

I was glad for the lack of sound. The clash of metal from the initial contact, and the ensuing screams from the soldiers in the front lines who died in the first minutes of battle, always broke my heart.

The ground shook and I staggered, then looked around, bewildered.

'What was that?' my mother said.

'Earthquake?' Greg said.

'What's *that*?' Amanda shouted, pointing at the screen.

The platform that John and Er Lang had been standing on was gone, crushed under a massive scaled … thing. It looked like a grey snake's coils but must have been ten metres across. The camera showed nothing but the wide body of the reptile; the head wasn't in view.

'They created a giant Snake Mother,' Greg said with dismay. 'I cannot believe this.'

A roar shook the earth again, and we all held onto the couch as the ground shifted beneath us.

'That thing is *huge*,' my mother said. 'We can hear it all the way from here? It must be fifty kilometres away!'

'Demons,' said a voice as big as the Earth itself, and the remaining pockets of fighting stopped. Soldiers from both sides ran from the Snake Mother in panic.

John, is that a huge Snake Mother? I said.

No, he said, his voice full of wonder. *It is Nu Wa.*

'Oh lord, it's Nu Wa,' I said.

'She's enormous!' Greg said.

Nu Wa lowered her head to speak and it became visible on the screen. She had the face of a beautiful woman, but no other human features.

'Demons,' she said again, and we heard it from the Mountain. 'These are my children and you will not hurt them. Be gone!'

The demon soldiers stood frozen, watching her. Then they must have been given the order because they attacked the Celestial army again. Some of our soldiers were still staring at Nu Wa and were taken by surprise, killed before they knew what was happening.

'You will not touch my children!' Nu Wa roared.

She slammed the length of her snake body onto the ground, her face hitting the grass, and the earth shook so violently that the remote controls in front of us bounced off the coffee table. The Celestial soldiers were untouched, but the demons exploded as one, turning into black dust that quickly disappeared.

We sat stunned for a long moment.

'Holy shit,' Greg whispered. 'She destroyed them all.'

'What happened?' my mother said.

Greg was shaking his head with wonder.

'Emma?' my father said.

Nu Wa raised her coils again, and the Celestial army stood and looked around, bewildered.

John, what happened? I said.

Nu Wa destroyed the entire demon army. Every demon on the field is gone.

I jumped up. 'Yi Hao, are you okay?'

'Yes, ma'am,' Yi Hao said from the doorway. 'Has it started?'

'I think we just won,' I said with wonder.

18

'We won!' Jennifer yelled, throwing her arms into the air. She embraced Greg and kissed him hard, then leapt up and ran into the boys' room. 'We won! We're safe!'

My parents hugged each other, and Amanda and Alan touched foreheads. Greg had a huge grin on his face.

I watched the screen: the Celestial army were celebrating, jumping with joy and embracing each other. Nu Wa had changed to her small matronly human form and John was holding her hands and speaking earnestly to her, with Er Lang on one knee next to them.

I fell to sit on the couch, feeling as if a huge weight had lifted off me. My premonitions had been wrong, because Nu Wa was too primal and ancient to be predicted. It was over and we could start living our lives without the threat of the demons. My dream of sharing a peaceful family life with John on the Mountain had come true.

Greg came to me and put his hand out, and I took it. He teleported me to the battlefield, and I knelt in front of Nu Wa.

The army had broken ranks and were yelling, some of them still jumping up and down. Many were on their phones talking to loved ones with tears streaming down their faces. The noise was immense.

'The destruction of the platform was a small price to pay,' John was saying to Nu Wa. 'Immensely preferable to the destruction of the Heavens.'

'I suppose you're right,' Nu Wa said. 'And here she is, the Turtle's Folly. So young and small to be so wise.'

'We serpent women are exceptional, my Lady,' I said.

'That we are,' she said with amusement, tapping my head. 'Up you get, dear, and you too, Er Lang. Now where's that old fool who likes to think he runs things?'

The Jade Emperor appeared next to us, and everybody except Nu Wa fell to one knee again.

'Thank you for coming,' he said. 'I knew you couldn't sit by and let the Heavens fall.'

'You shouldn't have relied on me,' she said. 'It was a terrible decision. There was a good chance that you'd all be at their mercy right now. But I suppose I should thank you for giving me the opportunity to atone.'

'All the Heavens are in your debt, Goddess,' he said. 'Rise, everyone, and thank the Mother.'

'The Demon King and his most senior lieutenants escaped before I destroyed them,' she said as we all stood. 'Don't waste any time meeting with them to negotiate a new treaty with Hell. They'll be plotting again straight away.'

'Xuan Tian,' the Jade Emperor said.

'Majesty,' John said. 'And we need to clear the demons from the Earthly. We still have a great deal of work to do.'

'Will you stay, Lady?' the Jade Emperor said. 'I'm sure the citizens of the Heavens would like to show their gratitude.' He nodded to John. 'Ah Wu, if you don't mind hosting the banquet for the families who have not been made homeless? The ones who have lost everything should be shown the greatest support, and I will provide them with a celebration at the Celestial Palace.'

'We would be honoured, Majesty,' John said.

Jade, did you get that? I said.

How many demons can I take food shopping on the Earthly? she said.

Take as many as you need.

Budget?

If you don't go completely overboard with the spending I will be very disappointed.

She was silent for a moment, then said, *I need to work out what to save for the wedding. Some dancers at this one, but we won't use martial arts demonstrations —*

Jade, I said, *I have things to do.*

Red and gold for the colour scheme of course, but — She stopped talking mid-sentence.

'I need to contact the Demon King and start the treaty negotiations now,' John said.

'Go,' the Jade Emperor said.

John took my hands. *I'll be back directly. Wait for me.* I fell into his dark eyes, full of quiet joy at our victory. *No displays of affection in front of the Mother. We will have to celebrate privately later.*

I raised his hands to my face and kissed them anyway. *We have all the time in the world.*

'You two must marry immediately,' Nu Wa said.

'I agree,' the Jade Emperor said.

'We can marry now?' I said, and looked back to see the Jade Emperor beaming at us. I turned back to John. He was gazing down at me with the same intensity that I felt.

'Of course,' the Emperor said. 'But do not hurry to wed; take your time to organise it. We want this to be the grandest and most lavish wedding the Heavens have ever seen.'

'No,' John and I moaned quietly, and touched foreheads.

Nu Wa chuckled.

'It will happen, so deal with it,' the Jade Emperor said. 'Ah Wu, chase down the Demon King and begin negotiations immediately.'

'Majesty.' John kissed the top of my head and disappeared.

The Jade Emperor smiled down at Nu Wa. 'Lady? My wife awaits us at the Celestial Palace. She has come down from the Peach Garden to see you and says it has been far too long since you last talked. Tea?'

'I would be delighted,' she said.

'Lady Emma, dismissed. Call upon Er Lang and the Four Winds to assist you in re-establishing our administration.'

'Majesty,' I said.

The Jade Emperor's head shot up and his expression went blank. 'What is that? That should not be there.'

He turned to look. The Demon King and a few of his most senior commanders stood at the other end of the field.

Nu Wa studied them as well. 'They have returned,' she said.

John reappeared. 'The Demon King is here.'

'Good. We can use his marquee to negotiate *his* surrender,' I said.

A hammering roar became audible at the edge of hearing, from the other side of the field where the Demon King stood.

'Helicopters?' I said. 'Who brought helicopters?'

Five helicopter gunships appeared over the horizon. A convoy of armoured personnel carriers, at least twenty of them, drove beneath them, lifting a cloud of dust. They stopped on the far side of the field, three hundred metres away, and the helicopters landed behind them, blowing more dust into the air. A battalion of European human mercenaries, fully equipped in modern battledress, some armed with automatic rifles and some with handheld rocket launchers, scrambled out of the personnel carriers. A couple of big trucks drove up and disgorged more soldiers.

'Reform the lines!' Er Lang shouted, running down to the army. 'Reform! We will be attacked!'

Our soldiers quickly ran to retake their positions. Some scrabbled around on the ground, looking for their weapons.

'Humans,' John said with dismay. 'He has humans fighting for him.'

Nu Wa's expression was infinitely sad. 'I cannot help you with this. I will not harm my children. Any of my children. All humans are sacred,' she said, and disappeared.

More soldiers appeared through the dust. The Demon King had thousands of them.

'The Heavens have never fought modern Earthly forces before,' John said.

'And we never will,' the Jade Emperor said. 'Disable them without harming them. We protect humans, we do not kill them.'

'Celestials kill humans all the time,' I said. 'This is no different. They're attacking us. We have the right to defend ourselves.'

Er Lang returned to us. 'Ready for your order, Majesty. I suggest we fill the sky with dragons to fight the helicopters, and focus on destroying the ground troops with our most powerful Immortals.'

'We will disable them and prevent them from harming us, but we will not harm them,' the Jade Emperor said again. 'The Celestial protects humans.'

'The Celestial harms humans all the time!' I yelled, frustrated.

'Madam, remember your place. You are young and new to the Celestial,' he said. 'Individual Immortals sometimes behave in an immoral manner and are punished for it. But We are the Celestial and We protect the mortal residents of the Earthly.'

'That's right, I'm new. I was one of those mortals last year,' I said. 'If an army attacked my home, I would not hesitate to defend it with everything I had.'

'And now you are Immortal and better than that. Stop arguing with me or I will order you silent.' He turned to Er Lang. 'Defend as you have suggested, but *no humans are to be harmed.* Understood?'

'It's the twenty-first century meeting the sixteenth, Majesty,' John said. 'We may not be able to stop them without harming them.'

'We must,' the Jade Emperor said.

'Reconsider, Majesty,' John said, his voice strained. 'Modern weapons are more destructive than you have ever seen, and we must defend ourselves.'

'We do not harm humans,' the Jade Emperor said, and disappeared. He reappeared on top of the wall above us.

'Can you use mind control on the human soldiers?' I asked John.

'The Demon King is already well established in their heads. If we attempt to break his hold it will destroy their minds.'

'And that counts as harm.' I dropped my voice. 'He's attacking us at our greatest weakness.'

'I know,' John said. He looked around. 'We need someone to move you to safety.'

'I'll stay and help fight. It's all or nothing now.'

'I don't think I have a choice; there's nobody to carry you,' John said as the human mercenaries formed ranks and marched towards us.

The Celestial soldiers took up their weapons again.

'This is guns against swords,' I said. 'Even with our abilities —'

'I know,' he said, took Celestial Form and drew Seven Stars.

I summoned Dark Heavens and matched his motion, growing to my own battle form as well. 'Fight well, Dark Lord. I will see you on the other side.'

'Dark Lady, you honour me.'

'The honour is all mine,' I said, and both of us moved to the front lines.

The Tiger and a few of his children stood their ground next to us. When the humans were within range, the soldiers dropped to one knee to fire at us and the cats stopped the bullets.

John and I shared a look. Ranged weapons were not best used in the open like this; the soldiers should have had some sort of cover. The human mercenaries must have known that — further proof that the King was in their heads, using them as disposable battle fodder.

Great rocks emerged from the earth in front of us, giving us the cover we needed, and our fighters moved behind them. I silently thanked the Jade Emperor while at the same time despairing at the small numbers we had left. Many of our soldiers had already been killed in the battle with the demons.

Four helicopters lifted off and flew towards us. They released rockets, and Celestials — John, Er Lang, the Phoenix and the Dragon — flew up to intercept them.

John and the Dragon weren't damaged by the blasts; but the Phoenix couldn't fly well after donating her tail to the infirmary, and she exploded into a cloud of red feathers as the missile she caught blew up. The Dragon attempted to grab one of the helicopters, but they fired a rocket at him from inside and he fell, dead.

The helicopters sent more rockets at us. Er Lang caught one, and so did John, but another two hit our forces and killed more than fifty soldiers in a wide crater of carnage.

The soldiers with handheld launchers concentrated on destroying the Jade Emperor's barricades, taking all the soldiers behind them as well; and he was obviously having difficulty replacing them as they were blown up.

The soldiers on foot marched towards us, took aim and fired. The Tiger and his children caught most of the bullets, but more of our soldiers fell.

The Tiger roared and launched himself at the human soldiers.

Stand down and do not harm the humans, the Jade Emperor said from the top of the wall.

The Tiger roared again with frustration and obeyed the order, returning to the front of the lines. One of the mercenaries shot him between the eyes and he fell.

Fall back, the Jade Emperor said.

Fall back, John said, and the Celestial army retreated, most still facing the enemy, until we were clustered around the Northern Palace's wall and the remains of the platform.

I stood close to the wall near the gates, ready to escort our soldiers inside if it came to a siege.

A rock wall appeared before the gates of the Northern Heavens, defending them; and the Jade Emperor appeared at the centre of our forces. He raised his arms and concentrated on the human army approaching us, his will streaming towards them. The soldiers hesitated, and some of them backed up. The Jade Emperor yanked off his hat and threw it on the ground next to him. Sweat beaded on his forehead. John stood beside him on one side and Er Lang on the other, guarding him as the Jade Emperor forced the humans back step by step. It was a battle of wills: the Emperor against the Demon King.

A shot rang out. John jumped in front of the Jade Emperor and blocked it with Seven Stars. Three more shots rang out at the same time and John and Er Lang blocked them.

There was silence for a moment, then a single shot rang out from the other side of the field, three hundred metres away, and the side of the Jade Emperor's head exploded into bloody fragments at the same time. He toppled, dead, and the barrier in front of the gates fell.

The human army charged towards us. They outnumbered us by at least five to one, and sprayed us with bullets as they ran. The helicopters had flown back behind their lines to re-arm but they would be returning soon.

The Demon King had the Jade Emperor in Hell. It was all over.

'Quickly, before the aircraft return,' Er Lang said.

Open the gates, John said.

The gates of the Northern Heavens opened, swinging outwards.

Retreat into the city, John said, but it was too late.

Our forces turned and ran, and the humans fired on them as they tried to escape. At least a third of our troops fell. The human army didn't stop firing, picking them off as they retreated.

The human soldiers charged through our people and stopped on the other side under the gates. Half of them stayed in position there, and the other half moved out to take over the Northern Heavens. The refugees screamed and ran from the invaders.

The human soldiers on the field formed a ring around our remaining troops, taking them down while our soldiers were still forced to obey the order not to attack.

Cease fire! John roared above the sound of the carnage. *We surrender.*

The human soldiers stopped shooting at us and stood absolutely still and unmoving. The screams of the refugees inside the Northern Heavens echoed off the walls as they continued to run.

You surrender? the Demon King said.

We concede, John said.

Do. It. Right, the Demon King said with vicious satisfaction.

Lay down your weapons, John said, and the remaining Celestial soldiers placed their weapons on the ground in front of them. Some of them collapsed onto their knees, sobbing.

The human mercenaries stood around them, their faces blank.

John unhitched Dark Heavens from his back and drew the sword, holding the scabbard in his left hand with the black and silver leather harness hanging from it.

He turned and looked into my eyes. *Goodbye, my love. Care for our children and tell them that I loved them.*

You vowed to marry me, and that can only happen when we win back the Heavens, I said. *It will happen.*

It may take an eternity, he said. *Do not wait for me. You have waited enough.*

'Never,' I said as he strode through the tattered remains of the Celestial army, not appearing to see any of them as they parted to allow him through.

He picked his way through the bodies of our soldiers. My heart broke; one of them was Kenny. He'd returned from helping the orphans to die on the battlefield.

The Demon King took his largest warrior form on the other side of the field: smaller than John, with a wild mane of blood-coloured hair that stood straight up and went down his back. His scaled armour was red and gold.

Kenny's body lit up and John turned.

'Yes,' I whispered.

Kenny became blindingly white and floated above the field, his expression beatific. John knelt and lowered his head as Kenny lifted into the air, then exploded into a cloud of golden particles. He'd been Raised.

Then the awful realisation hit me: Kenny would spend the rest of his Immortal existence in the Pits, as a plaything for our new demon masters.

John stood and walked across the grass, which withered and died in a trail behind him. He stopped at the marquee, towering over it, and it blackened and collapsed.

The Demon King was slower than him and arrived at the remains of the marquee a moment later. They stood facing each other, and the King's pale, beautiful face lit up into a smile that only just touched his lips.

John remained expressionless as he held Seven Stars out in front of him horizontally, then slid it into its scabbard. He knelt and placed the sword on the ground.

The Demon King picked up John's sword. John moved to stand, but the King stopped him with his hand on top of John's head and pushed him back down onto his knees. He stood with his hand on John's head, then bent and spoke into John's ear.

'Suck my dick,' he whispered, and I heard it through my link with John. 'Right here, right now. Do it willingly and I'll pack up my toys and go home.'

The King straightened, his expression full of triumph.

John knelt silent and unmoving with the King's hand on his head for a long time.

'No,' I whispered.

John nodded without looking up.

'Oh god no,' I moaned, but couldn't turn away.

The King obviously decided the Heavens were worth more than completely humiliating Xuan Wu. He pulled Seven Stars from its scabbard, swung one-handed and took John's head off with his own sword. John's body fell sideways.

'Open the gates of the Celestial Palace,' the King said, and we could all hear it. 'You can't hurt my soldiers, so let's do this the easy way. Show no resistance and you will be spared.'

He wiped Seven Stars on John's back, put it away, and stalked back to his army.

I glanced over the remaining Celestial army and couldn't find a single Immortal still alive. The Four Winds, the Thirty-Six and Er Lang were all dead.

I turned and looked up at the camera. *Greg, come and get me. I need to be in Persimmon Tree right now to protect the family!*

Simone appeared next to me, took my hand, and the world disappeared.

19

We reappeared in the living room of Persimmon Tree, and my family clustered around us.

'I don't have time to mess around,' Simone said. 'I found three seats on a plane to the UK.' She raised her head and concentrated and Freddo appeared at one side of the room. 'There are soldiers coming. You need to be quick.'

Greg raced into the bedroom and came back holding Matthew, with Andrew and Mark — the boys who'd been held and tortured by demons in the past — following. Colin held back, but Amanda's youngest, David, followed. Greg gently put Matthew onto Freddo's back, then lifted David to sit behind him.

'That's too many,' Simone said. 'They're too young to go without their mothers. I can only take two boys and one mother.'

Jennifer and Amanda shared a look.

'You go with Matthew,' Amanda said. 'He's the youngest.'

'I can't leave Colin and Andrew,' Jennifer said. 'I won't leave my boys!'

'Take Andrew too,' Colin said. 'I'll be fine, Mum. I'm nearly eighteen, and I've been trained. I can handle myself.'

'No, I'm staying with Mark,' Andrew said, putting his hand on his cousin's shoulder. 'I'm not leaving him after all we went through together.' He gestured towards Amanda. 'Take both our mums and Matthew. He's the littlest.'

'I don't want to go anywhere! I want to stay here with Mummy and Daddy!' Matthew howled.

'Hurry up and make a decision,' Simone said. 'We don't have much time!'

Greg made the decision for them. 'If their mothers aren't here, the boys can't be taken from the Heavens.' He pulled Andrew off Freddo's back, grabbed Jen and Amanda and pushed them next to the horse. 'Go, Simone.'

'No!' Jennifer yelled, but it was too late. Simone and Freddo disappeared, together with my sisters and Matthew.

Andrew and Mark took each other's hand and collapsed onto the couch. My parents held them as they wept. David broke down, and sat on the floor with his back to the wall. Colin went to him.

I stood in the middle of the room next to Greg, hovering with indecision about who to comfort first.

Three European soldiers kicked open the door and charged into the room, their weapons held ready but not pointed at us. We all shot to our feet and raised our hands.

One of the soldiers looked around, then focused on Greg. 'Are you the head of the household?'

Greg nodded. 'We surrender. We have weapons but they're only decorative and we'll happily hand them over.'

'Do you speak English?' the soldier said.

'Emma? I don't know what language I'm speaking,' Greg said. 'I could be speaking Chinese. The language charm may be failing.'

'We will be happy to surrender any training weapons we have,' I said. 'This is a martial arts academy, but we have no desire to fight with you.'

The soldier said something in another language.

'What?' I said. 'I'm speaking English!'

'Don't have enough Arabic,' the soldier said. 'Jerry?'

Another soldier spoke to me in Arabic. I just looked blankly at him, horrified that the charm was fading. When he switched to another language, I shook my head. This should not be happening. Greg and I were Immortals and able to communicate in any language.

209

'I don't know what language these people speak, but it isn't anything common around here,' the soldier said. 'Maybe some dialect? The captain said we were in a remote area. Kurdish or something?'

'I speak English,' I said, forming the words clearly in my head.

'Look at you all, covered in veils even inside in this heat,' one of the soldiers said. 'You don't need to be frightened any more. You're free.' He looked back at the other two. 'We need one of the girls to search these women. They could be male terrorists under all those sheets.'

'I'll find Tiff,' one of them said, and went out.

'They're not seeing or hearing reality,' my father said with dismay.

'Don't worry, Grandfather, everything will be fine,' one of the soldiers said to my father. 'Now I'll just search you ...' He slung his gun over his shoulder and moved towards my father with his hands out. 'Don't move.'

'Stay away from my grandfather!' Colin shouted. My mother grabbed his arm to stop him from running to my father. 'Don't touch him!' he shouted, freeing himself from my mother and jumping between the soldier and my father.

The soldier swung his gun around and pointed it at Colin. 'Back off, sister.'

'Colin!' I shouted, but everybody else was shouting as well.

'Back off, Colin!' Greg yelled.

'Move and let him do it, Colin,' my father said.

'Move!' the soldier shouted at Colin, waving the weapon threateningly in his face.

'Colin!' Andrew wailed.

'Everybody shut up!' Colin roared.

He changed into a three-metre-long black snake, and my mother screamed. Colin charged the soldier and knocked him to the other side of the room. The second soldier fired at him and everybody ducked. A short blast of bullets went through Colin's serpent body and into the ceiling behind me.

Colin fell, limp. His neck was shredded. He writhed a few times and went still. Red blood pooled around him.

Andrew and Mark were both screaming now, and my mother

held Andrew back from running to his brother. My father stood in front of them to protect them, and Greg stood next to him. The youngest, David, huddled in the corner, hugging himself.

The soldiers stared at Colin's snake body with disbelief, ignoring my family's reaction.

'Jesus fucking Christ, did you see that?' one of them said. 'Where did it come from? What a *monster*!'

'That was my *brother*!' Andrew roared, still struggling.

'Yeah, I'd be hysterical too if I found that in my living room,' another soldier said with humour.

'Andrew,' Greg said into his ear. 'Son, take control. If you don't calm down, they'll shoot the rest of us.'

'I don't care!' Andrew screamed. 'They killed my brother!'

'We have to move this thing outside and take a photo of it for Facebook,' the soldier said. 'Shit, I didn't know they even grew that big.'

'That's my brother, not a fucking *trophy*!' Andrew shouted.

I moved in front of my family as they held a still struggling Andrew, and raised my hands. 'Please, leave us. Go away. You've done enough.'

The soldiers ignored us, discussing who'd carry the head and who'd carry the tail outside. One of them pulled out a phone and took some quick photos of Colin, grinning broadly.

'Might even make some extra cash out of this,' he said. 'Never seen anything like it.'

Your soldiers just murdered one of my nephews, I said to the Demon King, hoping my telepathy worked.

Andrew fell to sit on the couch and my mother held him. Andrew looked catatonic. Mark and David had collapsed in the corner and my father was talking to them.

WHAT? the Demon King said.

Colin changed and they killed him.

He changed to snake?

Yes. He's dead. I rubbed it in. *They want to take him outside and photograph him for Facebook.*

FUCK FUCK FUCK … His voice disappeared.

My mother was sobbing as she tried to rouse Andrew. The soldiers didn't seem to notice my family's grief; they were prising

Colin's mouth open with the ends of their rifles and discussing how they'd remove his fangs and skin to sell.

'Greg!' Andrew looked up at his stepfather, his face twisted with grief. 'Go down there and find him. You can go. You're one of them. Go and bring him out!'

'It doesn't work like that,' Greg said gently.

'Emma, he's your nephew. Go!' my mother said.

'Greg's right, Mum, it doesn't work like that.'

'Why not?' Andrew demanded. 'You're famous for breaking the rules. Do it!'

The Demon King stormed in, accompanied by a couple of big black-armoured demons. He stopped when he saw the soldiers examining Colin.

Mark made a high-pitched sound of terror, and my mother rose to stand in front of him and Andrew.

'You *fuckers*!' the King roared, and waved one hand at the soldiers.

The armoured demons grabbed them and lifted them by their throats, their legs dangling as they choked. The demons pulled their guns off them, one of them yanking so hard that the soldier's arm audibly cracked and he screamed.

Greg stood in front of my family, and I faced the King.

'What were you thinking, working with humans?' I said. 'What a stupid thing to do! You know how much this is stressing my family — it was inevitable!'

'I never ordered this,' he said. He looked around. 'Are the other boys okay?'

'They'll be fine as long as you *leave them alone*. Don't go near them. They remember what you did to them,' I said as I waved one hand at my hysterical family.

'All right. Leave this with me. These human shits will *suffer*,' the King said, and moved to leave.

'Bring him back!' Andrew yelled, and the King turned to look at him. Andrew was standing, rigid with fury, and glaring at the King. 'Go to that place — Hell. Go to Hell and bring him *back*. I know you can do it.' He swiped one hand through the air. 'Trade me for him. Anything. I'll do anything for you. Just bring. Him. Back!'

'If you change as well, I might think about it,' the King said. He nodded to the demons. 'Bring them.'

Andrew gave a wordless scream of anguish and lunged at the door. Greg held him and Andrew punched him. He only stopped struggling when three more armoured demons entered. One took Colin's body out, and the other two stationed themselves on either side of the door.

'Don't let them take him,' Andrew said, forlorn. 'That's my brother. Don't let them take him!'

'We don't have a choice,' Greg said, and pulled him down onto the couch next to him.

Send the guards outside and let us mourn our dead, I said to the King. *The sight of them standing there might make one of the other boys change.*

There was no reply.

I sighed and moved to sit on the couch across from my family and put my head in my hands. I heard movement behind me, and turned to see the two guards leaving.

'They're stationed outside the door,' Greg said.

'What do we do?' my mother moaned. 'What do we do, what do we do?'

'We survive,' my father said into her hair as he held her. 'And we care for the family we have left.' He raised his head. 'Andrew?'

'Andrew needs some time,' Greg said. He put his arm around Andrew, who was unresponsive again. 'Come on, son, I'll take you to your room.'

Simone appeared next to me.

'I'll take you two at a time,' she said, and looked around. 'Where's Colin?'

'Run, Simone. The Demon King was just here, and he'll be looking for you,' my mother said.

'Go. Take Emma,' Greg said. 'I'll change to Emma's form and stay with them.'

'I'll take the rest of you,' Simone said. 'I can hide you somewhere.'

'You can't take the boys without their mothers, so we're all staying here,' my mother said. 'We talked about this, Simone, so do what we planned. You're our last hope.'

'Go,' my father said.

'Are you sure, Poppy? I can take —'

'Just go!' my mother said.

Simone grabbed my shoulder and everything disappeared. We reappeared in front of the Peak apartment block.

'Take me back, my family need me,' I said. 'Colin —'

'Leo and Buffy are under attack,' Simone said. 'We'll go up the stairs and ambush them.' She saw me hesitate. 'Leo's down and they'll take Buffy. Come *on*!'

I summoned Dark Heavens and we went up the stairs, dodging the buckets of household rubbish. We charged out of the stairwell on the top floor into the backs of half-a-dozen big humanoids. Leo was down, slumped in the doorway, but still fending them off with his blade. The humanoids were clustered around him, attempting to break through into the apartment.

Simone threw shen into three of them, I took the head off one, and she finished the final two with her blades. Leo dropped his sword and panted, his face ashen.

'Simone,' I said, but she ignored me. She knelt next to Leo and put her hand on his face, then her eyes widened.

'How long have you been fighting them?' she said.

'Seems like a day,' he said, still panting, 'but probably less than half an hour.' He looked up at her. 'What happened? Did we win?'

'Simone, take me back,' I said.

'Emma, help me,' she said, taking one of Leo's arms.

I shook my head, then took his other arm and we helped him onto the couch in the apartment.

'Don't put me here. I'll bleed on the upholstery,' he said.

'Wouldn't be the first time,' Simone said. 'Is it mortal?'

'No. I've lost a lot of blood, but I'll be fine. It's mostly exhaustion and lacerations from their blades.' He gazed up at her, desperate. 'Where's Ming? Did we win?'

'The Heavens have fallen,' I said, and Leo slumped on the sofa and wiped his hand over his face. 'We need to get out of here, more will be coming. Simone, take me back.'

'Don't worry about your family, the soldiers won't hurt them.'

'They already killed Colin!' I said.

Her expression went blank. 'What?'

'He changed into a big snake and they killed him. Colin's dead.'

She put her hand over her mouth and turned away. Her shoulders shuddered as she fought the emotion.

'So what happens now?' Leo said.

'Now you and Buffy go into hiding while the Demon King's occupied with his new conquest,' I said. 'You bought the plane tickets, didn't you?'

'I didn't believe you,' he moaned. 'I trusted the Jade Emperor. I was so sure we'd win.' He looked around. 'Where's my goddamn wheelchair?'

'Simone, can you take them onto an airplane and change their faces as well?' I said.

'I can't leave you here,' she said.

'Take me back to Persimmon Tree, then take Leo and Buffy to America.'

'No,' Leo said. 'Take Buffy. She'll be fine with my sister. I have to stay here and help.'

'Leo, we *lost*,' I said. 'The King will be after you. He's after all of us. You have to run!'

'Martin needs me. He's in Hell alone and it will break him.'

'He's not in Hell, he's in the Northern Heavens and still alive,' Simone said. 'He'll never forgive you if you leave Buffy alone. I'll never forgive you either. Stay with her.'

'Er Hao!' I called, and she came out of the hallway.

'Is it finished?' she said. 'We won?'

'Pack for Buffy and yourself,' I said. 'She's staying at her aunt's house in America.'

'No!' Buffy shouted, and ran around Er Hao to her father. 'I don't want to go. Aunty Elise is mean.'

'Buffy, honey,' Leo said, taking her hands and gazing into her eyes, 'it's not safe here any more. You saw all those bad people at the doorway?'

'Demons,' she said. 'You killed them. We're fine now.'

'More are coming,' I said. 'Lots more. More than all of us can fight. Stay with Aunty Elise while we kill them, then you can come back.'

'I'll help,' she said, determined.

'You can help by staying with Aunty Elise for a while,' Leo said. 'Er Hao, pack bags for all of us. We're all going.'

'Good.' I rose and put my hand out. 'Quickly, Simone, take me back to the Mountain.'

'No,' Simone said. 'Go to America with Leo, Buffy and Er Hao.'

'Don't be ridiculous. I need to be with my family to protect them. Take me up, Simone.'

'Er Hao, pack for them while I guard the door,' Simone said, then rose and turned to face the front door.

'Er Hao, where's my wheelchair?' Leo said.

'I'll find it for you, sir,' Er Hao said. 'I'll be right back.'

'Simone, I need to be up at Persimmon Tree *right now*!' I shouted at her back. 'The Demon King will torture my family!'

'Here's your wheelchair, sir,' Er Hao said.

Leo pulled himself into it, wincing from the pain of his injuries. 'Simone, bring Emma's family down. They can come too.'

'I already did,' Simone said. 'I put Matthew and Aunty Jen and Aunty Amanda on a plane to London.'

'Take me back up,' I said. 'The rest of my family need me. The whole Mountain needs me.'

'I can't,' she said. She resummoned her blades. 'I promised Pop that I'd take you out if we lost and keep you somewhere safe.'

'I'm not a thing to be kept safe. I'm a human being and I need to protect my family.'

'I gave my word, Emma,' she said, her voice mild.

'You promised to leave them there?' I said, horrified.

She pulled her phone out of her jeans' pocket, speed-dialled, and looked at the screen. My father appeared on it.

'Talk to her, she's being stupid,' she said, and handed the phone to me.

'Did anything happen?' I asked him.

'No. The Demon King hasn't come back and the guards haven't moved. From what we're hearing, he's busy in the Celestial Palace, putting human soldiers everywhere, rounding up the population, and executing every Immortal he finds.'

'Has he found Martin?' Leo said.

My father hesitated, then said, 'I'm sorry, Leo.'

'No,' Leo said, and wheeled himself away.

'It'll be a while before he bothers with us. He's busy consolidating his control and killing all the Immortals,' my father said. 'The Mountain students are too junior for him to worry about.'

'I must be there when the King discovers that Jen and Amanda are gone,' I said.

'You *are* here,' he said. 'Well, you were. Greg made himself look like you, and a demon with a really weird face came through, took Greg, and they cut his head off. The King thinks you're in Hell, so stay away and start organising the Resistance. Don't you dare go down without a fight. Gather as many people as you can and start harassing the Demon King so we can win the Heavens back.'

'Fight him, Emma,' my mother said from behind my father. 'There aren't many Immortals left who are free agents, and you and Simone are two of them.'

Mark came up behind her and nodded into the screen.

'So use your brains and Simone's muscles and start working on a way to win this back for us,' my mother finished.

'I have an agreement with the King —'

My father cut me off. 'I don't care if he owns your soul. He won't kill us; he wants us for our genetic material. He won't torture us if we cooperate. He thinks you're in Hell; and he's stuck here consolidating his rule in Heaven, so he won't know for a while that it's really Greg. So stay away and start looking for ways to fight back. You were somehow mentally joined with John, so use his experience and *start fighting back.*'

'We love you, sweetheart,' my mother said. 'Now go and fight that bastard and win the Heavens back.'

'Get him,' David growled, and the screen cut off.

Leo wheeled himself into the room with a duffel bag on his lap. Er Hao stood next to him, holding Buffy's hand.

Simone took her phone back and quickly flipped through it. She studied a variety of things for nearly five minutes and I grew impatient.

'What —'

'I'm not checking my Facebook, if that's what you think,' she said. 'Found one.' She looked up at Leo. 'I'll be right back.' She disappeared.

'Oh, she's finding a flight for you,' I said, and summoned Dark Heavens. I turned to the door to defend it.

'Ma'am,' Er Hao said quietly as she came up behind me.

'Did you pack for yourself? It will be cold in Chicago,' I said.

'I cannot go. It is too far from my Centre,' she said. 'I am too small, so leave me here and I will slow them down.'

'Not happening,' I said.

'Please.' She lowered her voice. 'I cannot go with the family. I beg you, destroy me now so that they will not find me.'

'We'll hide you somewhere else,' I said.

'Ma'am,' she began, but Simone's reappearance cut her off.

'All three of you to the centre of the room,' Simone said. Freddo appeared next to the windows. 'Buffy on Freddo, and Leo and Er Hao with me.'

'I cannot go, Princess,' Er Hao said. 'It is too far from my Centre.' She closed her eyes. 'Destroy me now so they cannot take me.'

'Come back and take Er Hao somewhere else,' Freddo said. He tossed his head. 'More demons coming, Simmony.'

Er Hao faced the door. 'I will hold them off. You go.'

Simone took my shoulder and the Peak apartment disappeared.

* * *

We reappeared on the second floor of a mouldy deserted concrete building with the wind whistling through it. The ceiling had fallen in, and a dead dog lay on a rotting couch nearby, its corpse so desiccated it no longer smelled. Large smashed windows overlooked a dry overgrown swimming pool and a tennis court, then a narrow beach and the flat ocean on the other side of a high chain-link fence.

'Sea Ranch?' I said.

'I'll be right back.' She disappeared.

I picked my way through the fallen masonry to sit on the ground next to the broken windows, wrapping my hands around my knees.

Only accessible by boat from the rest of Hong Kong, Sea Ranch had been an attempt to build a millionaires' enclave, with a luxurious clubhouse and low-rise buildings with spacious apartments facing the ocean. But the project had died, and most of the apartments were now used for weekend rentals to kids who came to play mah jongg, make barbecues on the beach and indulge in the rare chance to have sex in privacy. During the week the mouldering development was deserted, except for a few diehard original investors who refused to leave their expensive tumbledown condominiums.

I pulled my phone out and checked my messages. None.

I opened my social media pages and everybody was sharing questions about the status of the Heavens, until a post by Gold that read:

Gold McGolderson: Everybody go dark. Get off social media and throw away your phones. You can be tracked through your posts, and even if your GPS is off, your location is easily triangulated through the cellular network. They're breaking into my Celestial network as well. I'm trying to keep them out but it's only a matter of time. Every post you put up here will be a marker to where you are. Once they're into the network they'll be able to hack into your phone's GPS and find you. If you're free, throw your phone away, disconnect all your electronics, and stay very quiet.

The social media pages after that were deserted.

I hesitated, looking at my phone, then placed it on the ground next to me and blasted it with energy. When the heat hit the battery it exploded, producing a cloud of foul-smelling smoke.

Simone reappeared and sat on the ground next to me. 'Leo and Buffy will be in America tomorrow.' She saw the remains of my phone. 'What did you do?'

'Blew my phone up. Gold says we can be tracked by them and we need to get rid of them.'

'Even his specials?'

'They're taking over his network,' I said.

Simone pulled her phone out and stared at it. 'How will we contact each other in an emergency?' she said as she put it on the carpet.

'Telepathy.'

'Yours isn't terribly reliable.'

She blasted the phone with shen energy and it burst into a blinding white flame.

'What did you do about Er Hao?' I said. 'Is she safe?'

'I parked her in one of the tunnels in Western, where Martin hid me all that time ago. She's dormant. I don't think anyone except me and Martin know where they are.'

'Thank you,' I said with relief. 'Now what do we do?'

'Do you have any ideas?'

'Take me back to the Mountain,' I said.

'I can't. I promised. We need to find a place here on the Earthly to set up a centre of operations and do what your family said — start the Resistance. So where can we go? Do you have any ideas?'

'The Mountain,' I said.

'Emma, I *promised*.'

I turned away to look out the window.

'We can't stay here. If they tracked our phones, this was our last location,' Simone said. She rose. 'I'll go find a deserted village. We can start from there.'

'It won't be sealed,' I said. 'The Earthly is infested with demons and they'll be able to come straight in. We need to find somewhere sealed so we can sleep at night.'

'Do you know how to seal buildings?' she said. 'I don't.'

'No, I'm too small.'

'If only Ronnie —' She raised her head. 'I'll be right back.' She disappeared.

John? I said.

There was no reply.

20

Simone returned five minutes later and crouched next to me. I didn't look up.

'Don't you dare give up now,' she said fiercely. 'I've found us somewhere they won't think to look — Ronnie's old flat. They obviously can't break in, because it's never been touched. It's sealed up tight. Emma!'

I looked up from my knees.

'Let's go set ourselves up and start contacting everybody who escaped. The Demon King will be too busy to look for us — he probably doesn't have any demons left after what Nu Wa did — so let's take advantage of the breathing space and move.'

'I promised the Demon King I'd take Frankie to Heaven for him,' I said. 'If he asks me to do it, I have to go.'

'He won't risk Frankie until the Heavens are secure. He'll need to hatch a new demon army to do that — the Heavens are too large to hold with that human force. We have a while before he sees Greg in Hell and realises he isn't you. Let's take advantage of the opportunity.' She patted my shoulder. 'Up you get. You can't stop now, Dark Lady, the Heavens still need you. Get to work.'

I sighed, wiped my eyes, and rose, dusting my hands on the pants of my Mountain uniform. 'Are Buffy and Leo okay?'

'They'll be in the US tomorrow.'

She held her hand out to me and I took it. We landed across the road from the concrete apartment building. The block was from the fifties: five storeys high, stained with exhaust fumes, and with narrow windows overlooking the street. The three-metre-wide ground floor was taken up by Ronnie's shop, with a small metal gated entrance at one side.

I looked up and down the street while Simone concentrated, checking inside the building. Its walls glowed in shafts of sunlight that streamed across the road, bringing the bare ugly concrete into bright contrast.

'What the hell,' I said, and looked up. There wasn't a cloud in the sky — and it was blue. 'The sky's *clear*. No pollution. I haven't seen it like that in years.'

Simone glanced up. 'Oh, so that's what's different. I was wondering.' We went across the road to the building. 'The King's taken all the demons to occupy Heaven. There's hardly any left here except for the executive copies.'

She stood in front of Ronnie's shop and studied it. The roller door was closed and plastered with movie posters in a layer that was five centimetres thick and peeling at the corners. No 'For Sale' or 'To Let' signs though. Ronnie had owned the shop and the flat above it.

'Everything's still inside the shop,' Simone said. We went to the barred steel gate that led to the stairs to the flats. 'They really can't get in.'

'Or they just didn't bother,' I said.

Six letterboxes sat on a piece of wood next to the door, with buttons for the apartment intercoms, which were black with dirt. Simone concentrated and the door unlocked. I pulled it open and we carefully walked up the stairs, both of us alert.

We reached the first floor and stopped at Ronnie's flat. Simone unlocked the gate and the door inside. Just as we were about to enter, a family came up the stairs and stopped on the landing: a couple, with a boy of about five and a two-year-old girl.

Human, Simone said.

'Call Aunty-la,' the woman said, seeing me, a European.

'Aunty,' the children said loudly in unison.

222

'Hello,' I said. I gestured with my head towards Ronnie's flat. 'We're friends of Ronnie's.'

'Wah, your Cantonese is very good,' the man said. 'We haven't seen Ronnie in a while.'

'He's in China visiting his family,' Simone said. 'He said we could use his flat. We're his relatives from Canada.'

I glanced at her and she shrugged.

'I know Ronnie has family in Canada,' the man said. 'It's good you're looking after it for him. We were worried.'

'He's caring for his sick mother, we don't know how long he'll be,' I said.

'Tell him we hope she's better soon,' the woman said. 'We have his mail up at 5A. Come and collect it any time.'

'Thank you,' I said.

The man hefted the little girl in his arms. 'Charlotte, Ricky, time to go.'

'Goodbye, Aunty,' the children said in unison, and the whole family cheerfully waved and went up the next flight of stairs. I watched the little girl cling to her father's shoulder as he carried her, their blissful normality making my heart ache.

'Canada?' I said as we went into the flat.

'Always a fifty-fifty bet that anyone who's lived overseas has been in Canada,' Simone said.

'The other fifty-fifty is Australia.'

'Yeah,' she said. She saw the state of the apartment, untouched for months. 'Oh, dear.'

Everything was covered in a thick layer of greasy dust. I ran one finger over the top of the television and it came away black.

'No demons to clean up after you, Simone, we'll have to do this ourselves,' I said.

'I'm no stranger to cleaning,' she huffed. 'I helped out at Sweetie Peachy in Spring Garden Lane, remember?' Her voice went wistful. 'God, I hope all the workers at Eighty-Eight are okay.'

'We can sneak in and check on them later.'

I went into the tiny kitchen, only two metres long and a metre wide, and looked around. The stove had a gas bottle under the ledge and I felt it — still nearly full. I went back into the living room, opened the fridge and instantly regretted it.

223

'Can you yin this?' I said.

'I won't yin anything unless it's life or death,' she said, wrinkling her nose at the smell. 'Wow, science experiment — some of that stuff is completely unrecognisable. Wait, is that a pig's head?' She choked. 'Yin's too dangerous to use on a whim. We have to do this the old-fashioned way.'

I went into the main bedroom. Ronnie had a double bed jammed against the wall with very little space around it. There was no bed linen. The other bedroom was even smaller, not even enough room for a double bed, and was piled to the ceiling with stock from the shop below: Hell money, incense, and paper offerings.

'If the people upstairs knew all this death-related stuff was in here they'd have a fit,' Simone said, picking up a plastic-wrapped wad of gold-painted paper that would be folded at a funeral into gold bars. 'So much bad luck.' She tossed it back onto the pile. 'Is there any cleaning stuff anywhere?'

I opened the accordion door to the bathroom, which was a metre and a half long and less than a metre wide. A cheap pink plastic showerhead hung on a string over the toilet. The ugly green tiles were black with dirt and mould.

'There's bleach and things stacked in the corner here,' I said, 'but we might need some heavy-duty stuff. I saw a supermarket down the street — I'll go and buy some.'

'No, you won't,' she said over my shoulder. 'You'll stay here where it's safe and I'll steal them. It's too dangerous for you to go alone. And besides, we don't have any money.'

I opened my mouth to argue and closed it again.

'Ronnie's seals were the best anywhere. You're safe here,' she said. 'Yell if anything happens. I'll be right back.' She disappeared.

I went into the living room and sat on the tired black leather couch facing the television. We didn't have any extra clothes, and Ronnie obviously did his laundry somewhere else.

I put my head in my hands. I couldn't even talk to John. I had no idea what to do next, beyond cleaning the flat and making it liveable for Simone. I only had a short time before the Demon King demanded I honour my vow to him. I considered turning myself in to avoid any retaliation against my family, and decided that once

Simone was settled, I'd sneak out, walk into a police station and surrender to the Superintendent Cheung copy.

Emma, Michael's here. Let him in.

My head shot up and I raced to the door to open it.

Michael's white-haired head appeared on the stairs. He smiled when he saw me, gave me a quick hug, and pushed me into the apartment, closing the door behind us.

'I can't stay long, they're on to me,' he said. 'It's only a matter of time before they hunt me down.'

'You're Number One Son —'

'Yeah, that doesn't work any more,' he said, interrupting me. 'Dad's fallen. I'm back to being just me, not Number anything. I'm powerful, but they're stronger — really weird-looking demons with tiny faces that are impossible to fight.'

'What about Clarissa?'

'Can she stay with you?'

'Of course she can! Where is she?'

'She's hiding on top of Tai Mo Shan. I just told Simone where she is so she can pick her up. Simone says you're out of cash.' He looked around. 'We need to find something quickly.'

'I have just the thing,' I said, and showed him into the second bedroom.

'Heh,' he said, lifting one of the packets of paper clothing that would be burnt for relatives in Heaven, 'this works.'

He put the clothes down and picked up a stack of Hell money in its plastic wrapper. He opened it and separated out a wad of notes a centimetre thick, then ripped it in half crosswise to make a square. He passed the rest to me, and I held them as he concentrated and changed the square to a bar of gold.

He tossed it onto the bed. 'Unfortunately I can't do a hallmark on it, so it's blank. A small family jeweller will buy it without asking too many questions, particularly if you offer it for less than the market price.'

'Wait,' I said as he reached for the rest of the notes. 'If that's the case, make it into a melted lump of gold that looks like it was in a house fire. Simone can take the form of an old lady and pretend it was all the jewellery she kept in a shoebox under her bed, and it was caught in the fire.'

'Perfect.' He picked up the bar he'd just made, softened it, and pulled at it like play-doh until it appeared to have melted. He made a few more and placed them on the bed. 'That should keep you going for a while.'

He put his arm around my shoulders and landed a quick kiss on my cheek. 'Thanks for looking after Clarissa.' He raised his head. 'They're close. I'll lead them away.'

He disappeared.

Simone opened the apartment door and came in holding a couple of shopping bags. 'Here's all the cleaning stuff we need. Don't do it all before I'm back with Clarissa.' She went out again, closing both doors behind her.

I took a plastic garbage bag and a pair of rubber gloves out of one of the shopping bags, ready to tackle the fridge.

A couple of minutes later Simone returned with Clarissa, who'd obviously been crying; her eyes were red and swollen. I went to her and embraced her, and she sobbed into my shoulder. I didn't join in her tears. Something inside me was blank and empty. Instead of grief I felt … nothing.

'So what's the plan now, Emma?' Clarissa said when she'd calmed down. 'What will you do?'

'Settle in, then decide. I never thought we'd end up like this.' I looked around. 'Simone?' She was gone.

'I hope she can find more people who escaped,' Clarissa said. She sat on the couch. 'I feel so guilty. Everybody else is held in the Heavens and I'm here.'

'Don't feel guilty,' I said. 'You can help us. We need to find everybody who escaped and start a network.'

Simone reappeared fifteen minutes later with my carry-on suitcase. 'Smally put together some clothes for you.'

'You went back up there?' I said. 'How are they? What happened? Is everybody okay?'

'Not much has happened,' she said. 'The Demon King's establishing his control. All the Immortals have been executed, and since the Heavens belong to the demons, our side of Hell does as well.' She nodded to Clarissa. 'You're not supposed to know about any of this.'

'Too late,' Clarissa said.

'Anyway, all the Immortals have been executed and they're in cells in Hell. The mortals are under curfew inside their homes while the King consolidates control. Anyone found out of doors without a really good reason is taken to the main square of the Celestial Palace and executed in front of a CCTV system that's feeding through the entire Heavens.'

'He's executing *mortals*?' I said, horrified. 'I have to go back up and stop it!'

'You'll just be executed too,' Simone said. 'He's using Hell as a prisoner-of-war camp for the Immortals — none of them can escape the cells.'

'John can,' I said.

'Daddy ...' Her voice broke. 'He and the Jade Emperor are in cells at the bottom of Level Nine where they keep the mad Kings. They can't escape.'

'How are my family holding up?' I said.

'Our family,' Simone said. 'The King hasn't had time to do anything with them. He's much too busy allocating living accommodation for his human soldiers in the Celestial Palace and arranging the guard rotations on the other Palaces. It'll be a while before he's secure enough to start experimenting again. We have time.'

I leaned on the wall next to the fridge and stared out the window, feeling blank inside.

Clarissa turned on the television.

'After the coup, the new regime is consolidating its hold,' the reporter said.

'What?' I said, and moved around to see.

'The general in charge has called for calm, but pockets of protest against the takeover are still occurring. The military is using tear gas and rubber bullets to subdue the crowds —'

'That's happening in three or four Asian countries right now,' Simone said. 'Reflections on the Earthly of what's happening in the Celestial. Demons are in control.'

'Will it happen in China?' Clarissa said.

'It happened a long time ago,' Simone said. 'So what now?'

'I don't know,' I said. 'I need time to think.'

'Get in touch with your inner Xuan Wu,' she said.

I rested my head in my hands. 'I'd rather be in touch with the outside one.'

Clarissa came to me and put her arm around my shoulders. 'I know how you feel, Emma. I'm lost without Michael.'

'Pathetic,' Simone said with scorn from the other side of the room. 'Your man isn't around so you shut down.'

Both Clarissa and I stared at her, dumbfounded, then something snapped inside my head and everything came into cold focus.

'All right,' I said, turning the television off with the remote. 'Here's what we'll do. For now, we'll find all the free Celestials and make a refuge for them somewhere remote on the Earthly. After that, we'll start playing the long game — we're all Immortal after all.' I paced the tiny living room. 'When the Manchu invaded the Ming, they were set on conquest and brutally subjugated the population. But five hundred years later they were almost indistinguishable in culture and philosophy from the Hans they'd conquered.'

'These conquerors aren't Manchurians, they're *demons*,' Simone said.

'So was your father,' I said. 'So was your sister. So am I. We will work like water, slowly and softly, shaping them in our image.'

'You're a demon?' Clarissa asked me.

'All of us are,' Simone said. 'That's the point. Demons can turn to the Celestial. So that's Emma's ...' Her voice trailed off as she realised. 'You'll be Frankie's nanny. You'll teach Frankie when he takes the throne.'

'You work from the outside while I work from the inside,' I said.

'I'm lost,' Clarissa said. 'Ming and Qing? I never studied that.' She went into the kitchen and collected the rubber gloves. 'So you do your political stuff while I clean out the fridge.'

* * *

It was a quiet and morose meal. We sat around a folding table, covered in a thin disposable cloth, and ate a simple meal of soup noodles with disposable chopsticks from plastic bowls that Simone had picked up at the wet market. There was hardly any crockery in the kitchen — Ronnie's diet had obviously been far from human.

The light outside the windows grew dim, and the neon from the dried seafood shops across the road lit up, filling the flat with an eerie pink and purple glow. I sat and looked at my noodles, then mechanically ate them. They didn't taste of anything. Nothing felt of anything.

'I need a shopping list for tomorrow,' Simone said.

I didn't reply.

'Do you shower in the morning or evening?' Simone asked Clarissa.

'How much hot water do we have?'

'It's a flow-through one,' Simone said. 'Unlimited but the pressure is terrible.'

'I'll go first,' I said, and rose without waiting for a reply.

I went into the bedroom and grabbed a change of clothes from the bag Smally had packed for me. She'd put in all new clothes and hadn't included any of my old tatty ones. I appreciated that she was trying to make me dress better, but what she'd given me wasn't nearly as comforting as my old T-shirts. I didn't have a single item of clothing that had been near John.

I closed the thin accordion door separating the bathroom from the living room — it didn't provide much in the way of privacy — and hung my clothes on hooks on the wall. I pulled off my Mountain uniform and the cherry blossom petal fell out of the pocket onto the floor. I picked it up and held it in the palm of my hand, and it broke me. Its soft silken touch was agony. The edges were already going brown and by the next day it would be gone.

I slid down the wall to sit on the green tiles and let the misery out as quietly as I could so the others wouldn't hear me. I shook with great gasping sobs that wanted to tear my throat out and collapse my chest. I put my hands over my face, and the pain and despair flooded out of me and onto the ugly green tiles.

I would never see those trees bloom again in the Mountain's regal beauty. The ancient forge with its mismatched bricks had survived the first attack, and now it would be destroyed. I remembered the barracks, with the *Turtle's Folly* sign proudly over the entrance. The Golden Temple on top of the highest of the seven peaks, glowing in the afternoon sun to remind everybody of the true nature of the Master of Wudang. The three halls edging the main court — True Way, Yuzhengong — that had been destroyed before and which I had carefully rebuilt. Dragon Tiger, with its ancient bronze Buddha statue. Purple Mist, with its beautiful carvings in the ceiling overseeing each student's pledge of allegiance to the Dark Lord.

John, in human form, his long hair swinging around him as he performed an exhibition set on the main court; the students watching, enthralled by his deadly grace.

The Demon King would destroy our Mountain as soon as he had the means to raze it to the ground; it was only a matter of time.

The Golden Temple had much greater value than the cladding on its walls and roof, but it was gold, and he would tear the temple down and destroy John's statue to take the metal, ripping out John's heart at the same time.

And the students — the real heart of Wudang: so many dead, so many severely injured, so many broken trying to protect their home.

My family were in the King's hands. He could do what he liked to them — and he wanted to cut them up.

Colin, who'd had so much potential, was dead.

John was trapped in Hell.

My son was at the mercy of sadistic monsters that he thought were his parents.

All my friends, all my family, all the people I loved, were suffering and I had no way to protect them. This tiny fragile piece of vegetation was all that remained of the beauty that had surrounded me, and very soon even it would be gone as well. I clutched the little pink petal in my hand and mourned everything we had lost.

Simone came in and I tried to push her away, but she crouched next to me on the tiles and held me as I shook. Clarissa watched me from the living room with a compassion that made my anguish even greater.

* * *

I was lying awake next to Clarissa in the double bed when I heard Simone moving around in the living room. I went out and found her looking out through the blinds at the street below. I stood next to her and looked out as well.

A group of men in business suits were standing under the neon signs of the dried seafood shop across the road, the blue lights making them appear ghostly.

Time, Emma, the Demon King said.

I went back into the bedroom and pulled on some jeans and a T-shirt. The bedside clock said 2 a.m. Clarissa didn't wake, probably exhausted from the emotional turmoil.

Simone followed me to the front door, and I turned to stop her with a hand on her chest. She didn't say anything, she just threw her arms around my neck and held me close.

I embraced her and patted her back. *Stay here*, I said. *You're needed.*

You need me too.

Stay free so you can sneak in and visit me, okay?

She nodded into my shoulder and released me. Then she pulled me in again for another fierce hug, and turned away so I couldn't see the tears running down her face.

Goodbye, I said, and she shook her head and went back to the windows.

I went down the stairs, out of the building and across the deserted street to the Demon King and the four Dukes escorting him.

'Such a shame,' he said, studying the building. 'His seals were astounding. Best anywhere. I was hoping he'd finally grow sick of me trying to kill him and come back to me. I wanted to promote him to prince after his punishment was finished. His spawn would be as outstanding as he was.' He turned to me. 'I'm not ready yet for you to bring Frankie up.'

I turned and ran back across the road.

I'm giving you a chance to say goodbye, he said, and I stopped in the middle of the street. *I'm putting him in the cage tomorrow. Your family are untouched, and you will be as well. I do have a heart, Emma, and once he's in that cage he won't be talking to you ever again. So come and say goodbye.*

A taxi drove around me, blaring its horn. I walked back to the King.

231

'Bring Simone,' he said. 'Let her say goodbye to her father.'

'You'll try to imprison her.'

'I won't. I give you my word.'

I heard that, Simone said. *Do we trust him?*

Of course not. Stay there. He wants you.

'I won't imprison her,' he said. 'I mean it. I don't want her to come to me against her will.'

'That's the only way it will happen,' I said. 'So let's go.'

He gestured for me to approach and put his hand out. I took it. His skin was silky smooth, but as cold as a dead thing's. The world disappeared around us.

21

We landed in the residential part of the Northern Heavens Imperial Palace. It was dark and quiet; everybody was sleeping. I looked around and recognised the courtyard between the Imperial Residence and the Crown Prince's Pavilion. The Ancient Dragon Tree was visible through the moon gate on my right. This used to be my own front yard. The tents were still present in the courtyard, but there were no signs of life.

Andy Ho walked out of the Imperial Residence and stopped at the moon gate, wrapping a black silk robe — one of John's — around himself.

'You never cease to amaze me, Dad,' he said. 'How'd you do it?'

'If you ever experience love, you'll understand,' the King said.

Andy shook his head, bewildered. He pushed his feet harder into his cheap plastic slippers, nodded to the King, and led us to the Crown Prince's Pavilion.

We walked through another silent courtyard, past an alert American guard armed with a rifle who nodded to the King and Andy.

'What do they see?' I said.

'American officers,' the King said. 'They think they're in the Middle East fighting to liberate a democratic republic from radical insurgents, and freeing the local population from religious oppression and ethnic cleansing.'

'Priceless,' Andy said.

He opened the door to the Crown Prince's Pavilion and the scent of Martin's favourite incense and Leo's cologne filled the air, making my throat ache.

The living room held a modern European-style leather couch flanked by antique Qing rosewood chairs, and a Ming-style coffee table inlaid with mother-of-pearl. Their little dining area had a round rosewood table with comfortable Western chairs. The floor was polished wood, and the house was traditional courtyard style with all the rooms looking into a central garden. Three cardboard boxes were stacked next to the wall in the dining room; they'd been furnishing a room for Buffy for when she was big enough to come up.

Smally was waiting for me in Leo and Martin's bedroom, next to their custom-made leather-trimmed waterbed. She stood silently, rigid with terror.

I rounded on the King. 'What did you do to her?'

He raised his hands. 'I found your maid, had her put some stuff together for you, and brought her here. I want you to be comfortable, Emma.' He dropped his hands. 'Settle down.'

I turned back to Smally. 'Did he hurt you?'

She opened and closed her mouth but was too scared to make a sound.

'Go back to sleep and we'll come for you tomorrow morning,' the King said. 'Big day tomorrow, caging the reptile. Should be fun.'

He patted Andy on the shoulder as he went out.

Andy untied his robe and opened it to reveal his nakedness. Smally gasped with horror and crouched to bury her face into the side of the bed.

Andy ignored her, proudly displaying his golden skin, tight over his muscular chest and abs. 'Like the new human form? It cost me a fortune.'

He winked and thrust his pelvis towards me, showing off his oversized genitalia. His erection grew to an inhuman size, well past where his navel would be if he was human.

234

'Lord Xuan usually keeps his genitals small so they're out of the way when he's training,' I said.

'Wait.' His mouth flopped open. 'Did you just say that the First Heavenly General has a *small dick*?'

'Depends on the circumstances, but most of the time, yes. And he's the best lover I've ever had, because he knows exactly what to do with it. That,' I pointed at him, 'would just be painful. Not appealing at all.'

'You are incredibly boring.' He retied the robe. 'Don't try to leave this building without permission; the soldier will shoot you. You'd be stuck in the Pits while we put the Turtle in the cage, and you wouldn't have a chance to say goodbye. Call me if you want to come out — you're welcome to visit me. The number's next to the phone there.'

I didn't reply.

'Early night, Emma,' he said, yawned and sauntered towards the door. 'Call me and pay me a visit. It would piss Dad right off, and he wouldn't be able to do a damn thing about it.'

Smally scurried to me when he'd gone out. 'Are you all right, ma'am?'

'I'm fine, Smally. Did they really not hurt you?'

'They really didn't.' She looked around. 'I'm sorry, but I put all your best clothes in that bag for Princess Simone. These are old ones. I will find you some bed clothes. You need to sleep. A lot has happened.'

'I think sleep is the last thing I'll be able to do,' I said.

* * *

At dawn I gave up, went into the kitchen and raided Martin's hoard of sweet American breakfast food, then made a huge cup of coffee using Leo's coffee maker. I wasn't hungry but I needed the energy. I felt stupidly fatigued from lack of sleep and needed to regain my edge.

The King entered without warning, and leaned on the kitchen counter. He wrinkled his nose. 'Coffee's vile stuff. Could never understand the attraction.'

I took a sip, revelling in the caffeine kick. 'There's tea here as well.'

'Offering me your hospitality? That's what I like to hear.'

'You are a guest in my son's home,' I said, but he either pretended not to or genuinely didn't hear the sarcasm.

'You will be in your other son's home very soon,' he said. 'When we go out, there will be a camera crew waiting with cue cards for you. You will say what's on them as if you mean it.'

'What's on them?' I said, putting the coffee down.

'Political bullshit to calm the populace. Nothing that will call your loyalty into question.'

'And if I don't read them?' I said, already knowing the answer.

Smally screamed from the bedroom: a high-pitched wail of agony that dissolved into gasping sobs. I jumped; I hadn't expected a demonstration.

The King quirked a small smile. 'You had to ask, didn't you?'

I ran into the bedroom and held Smally where she was curled up on the floor.

'Stop hurting her!' I shouted. 'Let her go!'

'I did stop,' the King said. 'It's a bad case of PTSD, she's having flashbacks. Was she one of Simon's? If she was, you should destroy her. Put her out of her misery.'

'Please, ma'am, destroy me,' Smally said, her voice a whimper. 'I can't do this.'

'I'll do it,' the King said, and put his hand out towards her.

I stood in front of her. 'No!'

'Seriously?' he said with amusement. 'Come on, she's worthless. Let me find you one that isn't broken.'

'Do it, do it,' Smally moaned. 'Please. Let me go.'

'She wants it,' the King said.

'Don't hurt her.' I turned back to Smally and pulled her up. She resisted me, wanting to stay in a ball on the floor. 'Smally, I need you to help me here. You can't give up now.' I winced at the echo of Simone's words to me. 'I need you!'

She nodded and rose, still trembling. She tried to speak, but the words didn't come out.

The King gestured with his head. 'Come on, hurry up and get dressed. The television cameras await. You'll be a star.'

236

The camera crew were waiting outside the pavilion. Someone shone a reflective light sheet at me. A demon stood behind the camera holding large handwritten cue cards. I took a deep breath.

'To preserve your safety,' I read aloud, 'remain in your homes until the new administration is established. Nobody will be hurt if you obey them.'

The demon changed the cards around.

'Later today the Dark Lord will be incarcerated into a cage that he chose to enter himself. You will be able to watch him ...' The next card said *Say this with emphasis,* and I knew better than to provoke the Demon King by reading the stage directions aloud. '... *enter the cage of his own free will.* He has been given ample opportunity and plenty of options to avoid this, but it is his choice. As a show of good faith, his cage will remain in the Hall of Supreme Harmony and he will not be harmed. I will not be harmed, and none of the Celestial's loyal subjects will be harmed, provided they comply with the new administration. The Celestial Regent ...' I hesitated as I realised that I was referring to the Demon King. He wasn't just King of the Demons any more. '... doesn't want to mistreat us. He wants us to be content and work together to achieve an age of prosperity in this grand new Imperial dynasty.'

I waited for the card to change, but it didn't. The light flicked off.

'I'm disappointed, Emma,' Andy said from behind the camera. He'd been leaning on the wall behind the light, not visible to me. 'I thought you'd try to send a message to your family, or Simone. I had your punishment ready and everything.'

'That's why I didn't,' I said.

'Back inside,' the King said. 'The Turtle goes into the cage at noon. Get some rest; you look terrible.'

* * *

'I'm hoping you can talk some sense into him,' the Demon King said after we'd landed in the forecourt of the Hall of Supreme Harmony. He led me across the square, escorted by his Dukes.

The tent city had been removed and the square was eerily quiet, just the warm late spring breeze whistling across it. There was a time when flowering trees and shrubs in pots had decorated the square, and phoenixes had wandered between them, their colourful feathers ablaze. The water in the fung shui moat had held splashing playing dragons. Now it was all gone, and the sky was the brown haze of demonic occupation.

'Talk some sense into who?' I said.

'If he pledges to me, I'll still give him the Northern Heavens. I've promised it to Andy, but he'll make a mess of it,' the King said. 'For Andy, it's all challenges and politics. He's a good Number One, but has no idea about running a government. Ah Wu could be my public face, reassuring the Celestial populace that someone they trust is in charge.'

'The Dark Lord is honour-bound to keep his word,' I said. 'If he pledges to you, he will obey every order you give him.'

'I know. That's why I'm asking him to do it.'

'And that's why he won't.'

'You won't talk to him?'

I shook my head. 'Will you still let me say goodbye?'

He stopped at the entrance to the Hall of Supreme Harmony, the Jade Emperor's main audience hall, and put his hands on his hips. 'I said I would, didn't I? I've rigged another feed through to the Celestial communications network to reinforce the message that I am fair and compassionate and will rule the Heavens justly.' He smiled, looking up at the windows above the hall's gold-tiled curving roof. 'I love saying that more and more every time. As soon as we've settled the new administration, you can bring darling Frankie up and we'll have the coronation of a lifetime. Simone will love it.' He nodded. 'Let's get this unpleasant task out of the way and go back to our lives.'

A pair of the armoured demons with the tiny faces opened the doors for us, and we went in. Human soldiers guarded the exits, their expressions blank.

A jade cage larger than the one that had held the Serpent in Hell stood on the dais at the other side of the hall. The red carpet leading to the dais was still there, together with the gold silk lanterns flanking it. The Jade Emperor's throne, golden rosewood carved with six-toed dragons, stood on the dais next to the cage. A digital camera on a tripod was set up facing the dais, with a cable running to a computer. Twelve carved Ming-style chairs stood in two rows facing the throne, and a collection of Mothers and Dukes in human form knelt on one knee in front of them — an audience being rewarded for particularly good service to the King. He nodded to them, and they rose and sat to watch the show, their faces full of vicious delight.

'This is becoming extremely tedious,' the King said. 'I am so tired of having that reptile hanging around in his box criticising everything I do. Make him take the offer, Emma.'

Four demon guards came in, escorting John. He was in human form, in his plain black Mountain uniform. He appeared unharmed, but he looked tired and his hair had come completely out and fell over his shoulder. He smiled when our eyes met — he was glad to see me. It broke my heart.

'No talking silently. Say it all out loud or your chance is gone,' the King said.

He walked to John — in human form, he was a head shorter — and looked up at him. 'Take the Northern Heavens in my name and you can live there with Emma and Simone. I will leave you to manage it independently. Pledge allegiance and I won't do this to you.' His voice filled with exasperation. 'Stop being so stubborn and take the offer. It's a good one!'

'I will not give you control of a super-weapon that is capable of destroying all life on the planet,' John said.

'Don't be ridiculous. I can't use Seven Stars to destroy anything,' the King said.

'Not the sword. Me,' John said.

The King hesitated, then nodded with grim amusement. 'Fair point. Very well, a quick goodbye. I have wasted enough time on you two already.' He turned to me. 'Remember that the entire population of the Heavens is watching you, so don't embarrass yourselves.' He waved at the cameraman. 'Go.'

'I want you to vow again that my family will remain unharmed,' John said.

'I promise. All of them. Emma's family too. You're worth it,' the King said. He lowered his voice. 'But you're worth more running the North for me.'

'Emma,' John said, and turned towards the dais. He went to it and hopped up to sit on it, and I joined him. He glared at the demon guards, and they checked with the Demon King, who nodded. They backed away, giving us some privacy.

John turned to speak to me. 'I chose this.'

'I know,' I said. I put my hand on the side of his face, and his eyes were full of such anguish that my heart ached. 'You will be alive. I will be alive. One day we will be together again.' I made no effort to stop the tears from flowing. I sniffled, and smiled at the irony. Our final farewell, in front of thousands, and I needed to blow my nose.

He cupped my face in his hand, rubbing his thumb over the tears. 'You have been closest to me in all my millennia. You have shared with me, you were one with me, you have seen deep into my dark heart and still you love me.' He touched his forehead to mine. 'I thank you, Dark Lady. Your love has given me great joy.'

'You have Raised me and you promised to marry me,' I said. 'It will happen, even if Heaven and Earth must be moved. I will wait for you. I will be here, with your children and our son, and one day, however long it takes, we will be a family.'

'Time's up,' the Demon King said. 'I have places to be.'

John slipped his hand around the back of my neck and pulled me in for a final kiss. I couldn't hold him as closely as I wanted while we sat side by side, but I tried my best. We shared everything we felt for each other, concentrating on the fierce unity that joined our souls. I drank of him, and tasted him, and tried to capture his cool dark essence and stamp it into my memory to ease my spirit in the long lonely years to come.

I pulled back, then threw my arms around his neck, shoving my face into the side of his throat, choking through breaths full of the freshness of the ocean.

One of the Mothers clapped softly and slowly. Another joined her, then the applause petered out.

'I will be here,' he said into my ear. 'I will be thinking of you. And you and your family will be safe.'

'I love you, Xuan Wu, and I will be waiting for you.'

'Time!' the King snapped. 'The girls want to see you go into the cage. Hurry it up.'

We pulled back and gazed into each other's eyes, wanting the moment to last forever.

'Now,' the Demon King said. 'Or the deal is off.'

John closed his eyes and nodded. We jumped down off the dais and I moved back to give him room to transform.

He changed to True Form; the cold-eyed Serpent writhing above the Turtle, merging into it where they touched. I went to him and touched the side of the Turtle's face, and he rubbed his cheek on my hand with his eyes closed. The Serpent touched its nose to the top of my head at the same time.

'I love you, Emma Donahoe,' he said in his normal human voice. 'I wish we could have had more time together.'

'We will.'

'No, you won't,' the Demon King said. 'In.'

The Turtle and Serpent both nodded their heads. Xuan Wu turned and stomped up the stairs onto the dais with the Demon King following him closely. The Serpent looked back at me, then he walked into the cage. The Demon King closed the door gently and pushed the latch into place. John's presence disappeared. I had no sense of him; not even the touch of his energy. He was right in front of me and I felt horribly alone.

'He won't try to escape,' I said.

'I know that,' the Demon King said.

'So show him the courtesy of keeping the cage clean. The one in Hell was filthy.'

The Demon King waved one hand at the camera. 'Off.' He took a step closer to me and crossed his arms over his chest. 'In about two hundred years, you'll be a strong enough Immortal to regrow your uterus. How about you two make a brother or sister for Frankie? I'll let you have conjugal visits if you do that for me.'

'Not happening, Ah Mo,' John said from inside the cage.

The King waved one hand at him without looking away from me. 'You shut up or I'll knock you out again.'

John's Turtle opened its mouth and I glared at him; I didn't want to see him punished. He subsided.

'Just keep the cage clean,' I said to the King.

'You know what?' he said. 'No. I've been far too lenient with you, and given you too much, and you've taken advantage of me.

It's time for you to pay. Come to work as Frankie's nanny and I won't harm your family.'

I nodded to the King, wiping the tears blurring my eyes so I had a last chance to see my Xuan Wu. 'I will always love you.'

'You are my heart, Dark Lady,' John said.

'You were warned,' the King said.

'Worth it,' John said.

'You bring this on yourself, Turtle.' The Demon King put his hand on my shoulder. 'Now that's over and out of the way, I can get things *done*.'

* * *

The hall disappeared and we were beside the Trees of Swords on Level Nine. The King took me past the old mad Kings and I stopped. One of the cells held the Jade Emperor. He wore simple white prisoner's garb, and sat in a corner with his face in his knees and his arms wrapped around them. The Demon King pushed me along before I had a chance to speak to him.

At Frankie's house, he opened the door for me and gestured for me to go into the little living room. Frankie was sitting on the floor, playing dominos with a young woman who was impossibly small. She appeared to be a teenager, but was the same height as Frankie — about the same as a ten year old.

She looked up from the game and her face lit up. She ran to me and bowed. 'It's you! The lady who saved me.' Her smile disappeared. 'You were *with* the lady who saved me.' She bowed again, her hands clasped in front of her. 'Thank you. Thank you! I am alive because of you.' She moved closer. 'I know I tried to bite you when you were saving me, but I've learnt better now. I will not harm you, I will protect you. I promise.' She quickly bowed again.

'What the hell are you talking about, Edu?' the Demon King said.

'When I was hatched,' Edu said, 'my Mother was about to bite my head off, and this snake lady and the awesome snake woman with her saved me and took me to the nursery. I am alive because of them.'

'Oh,' I said, remembering the time Simone and I had travelled into Hell to rescue BJ from Demon Prince Six. We'd had to pass through the Nests of the biggest Mothers and had helped hatch one of the Mother's clutches; one of the surviving babies had been, uniquely, in human form. Now she smiled up at me with menace. Her name — Vicious — was stunningly accurate.

'Your mother was about to *eat* you?' Frankie said, horrified.

'Of course,' Edu said. 'That's what Mothers do.'

Frankie's eyes were wide as he digested this.

The Demon King studied me. 'You saved Edu from her Mother? I thought it was just that blue bastard in the Nest messing around with my breeding stock.' He smiled. 'You did me a huge favour. Edu is a unique hybrid that I think will grow to be human-sized and absolutely indistinguishable from humans by *any* Celestial. Smart too, and outstandingly strong. She has a great deal of potential.'

'Thank you, Father,' Edu said.

The Demon King pulled me to one side. 'Listen to me. The reptile will be fed regularly and not tortured as long as he keeps quiet.' He scowled. 'I expected some gratitude.'

I remained silent.

'I will be watching you. Do not try to subvert Frankie or Edu. Teach them the ways of the Celestial and what they'll need to rule the Heavens and the Earthly, but further than that and I will take the reptile and bury him in a very deep hole. Is that understood?'

'You'll bury him alive?' I said.

'Cage and all.'

'He'll just die. I fail to see the point.'

'He's so big that it will take him years to suffocate. He will land in Hell and do a full tour of the Pits, five years in each one. As soon as he's out I will dig up the cage, put him back into it and *do it all again*. Do you understand?'

'Yes,' I said, my voice weak.

'So do as I ask and he will stay in Supreme Harmony. You will be able to see him, and if you're very good I may even let you speak to him. If I bury him and send him to Hell, you will not see him for a long time.'

He waited.

'I understand,' I said.

'Once again I was expecting gratitude and you're too ill-mannered to provide it,' he said. 'I'll have other children come to learn from you as well. You're too valuable a resource to waste.'

'I won't teach martial arts.'

'You don't have to,' he said with a fierce grin. 'Your Wudang Masters refuse to teach too, but about twenty-odd *extremely* well-trained humans showed up all over the world recently with only a vague idea of where they'd been for the past twelve months. Your rejects were all I needed. And when Frankie takes the throne, you'll obey him. You'll have no choice.' He pointed at Edu and Frankie. 'Get to work.'

22

Late that night I was lying awake on the kitchen floor when I realised with a shock that I wasn't alone. Someone — two people — were just outside the window. I could sense them: they were Shen, not demons, and glowed as small floating balls in my Inner Eye.

I stood up and opened the window a crack. 'Come in and be quiet,' I whispered.

Gold and BJ came into the kitchen and changed to human form.

'You shouldn't be here,' I hissed. 'You know they can control stones.'

'We have to be quick,' Gold said. 'BJ.'

'I'll be your comms,' BJ said.

'I'm underground. You won't be able to communicate with anyone.'

'We're doing it now while we're free,' Gold said. 'They have to move the child eventually, and you can link up then.'

'I'll bury myself in your nervous system,' BJ said. 'The same way the demons had stones controlling Leo and Yue Gui. I'll sit in the back of your neck and link to your spinal cord, and then go as small as I can so they can't see me.'

'One: that sounds incredibly painful; and two: are you sure they won't see you?' I said.

She nodded. 'And you're an Immortal. Just block the pain.'

I hesitated. 'Exactly how much of my thought processes will you see if you link into my nervous system?'

She didn't reply but her face said it all.

'Gold, you're putting *Black Jade* where she can see everything I think and do. You know how much black jade I've been presented with over the years, don't you? This is a terrible idea.'

BJ's face went strange. 'I know the prophecy —'

'It's a *prophecy* now?' I said with disbelief.

'That you'll be replaced, and the Dark Lord will marry someone else,' she finished.

'It's beside the point, because even if he does marry someone else, he can still marry you as well,' Gold said.

'Is divorce allowed on the Celestial Plane? Same-sex marriage isn't.'

Gold snorted with derision. 'We're Immortal. Of course it is.'

'When the wedding date is set, we'll lock me up so there's no chance of either of us being compromised,' BJ said. 'Right now it's more important that you have assistance, data and comms on the ground with you.'

'Can't my stone — the Jade Building Block — do this? It's been put inside me before.'

'You can trust me,' BJ said.

'I'd really prefer the Building Block. Where is it? You didn't leave it alone, did you?'

Gold and BJ shared a look.

'What?' I said, and went ice-cold. 'No.'

BJ looked away.

'We went back to my lab to sabotage the Celestial network. We wanted to stop the demons from using it,' Gold said. 'The stone wasn't there, and there were a bunch of guard demons waiting for us.'

'Dad destroyed all the demons and we escaped,' BJ said with pride. 'He took down three level thirties with physical. Do you want to see my recording? It was *awesome*.'

'People keep forgetting that I've been serving the Dark Lord for more than twenty years, and he's trained me since the day I arrived in the household,' Gold said. 'He enjoyed teaching me.

He only had to show me the moves once and I perfected them immediately. The only disadvantage is the lag between the stone giving the order and the body carrying it out — it can be up to half a second.'

'What about the Jade Building Block?' I said.

'We have no idea where it is,' BJ said. 'We call and it doesn't answer.'

'Did you tell Nu Wa? The stone is one of her creations. She must know where it is.'

'Nu Wa's retreated to her mountaintop in Kunlun,' Gold said. 'There's no way to communicate with her.'

I wiped my eyes and took a deep shaking breath. 'Okay, BJ, put yourself into my spine and let's go to work. Do you have a backup plan if they find you?'

'I'll think of something,' BJ said.

'Gold, go,' I told him. 'Every second you're here you're in more danger.'

'I have to open you up to put BJ in. Lie on your stomach.'

'Can the demons see us? We're probably being monitored.'

'Not with my abilities.' He gave me a gentle push. 'Stomach, Emma.'

I lay my stomach on the floor, put my head on the rolled-up blanket and closed my eyes. Searing pain tore into the back of my neck and I blocked the meridians. There was pressure and movement as Gold worked on me, opening me up and putting BJ inside.

Testing. Say something silently, BJ said.

Can you hear me?

Now speak to me, Gold said.

I'm sorry about your parent.

We will find him, even if we have to go to the top of the Kunlun mountains. BJ?

I'm good. Go.

More pressure as Gold pushed my neck from side to side as he worked.

'Move your fingers and toes,' he said.

I wriggled them and felt a bolt of concern. 'They are moving, aren't they?'

'Yes. Can you feel this?' He touched my hands and feet.

'Yes,' I said.

'Good. No nerve damage. Try healing that up.'

I concentrated my healing energy and closed the wound.

Can you hear me, Emma? BJ said.

Yes. Gold?

Good to go. I'll leave you to it, Gold said. *Stay safe, Emma.*

Are my family okay?

They haven't been touched. They're under guard in Persimmon Tree Pavilion on the Mountain. They're all safe.

How is the Dark Lord?

They haven't tortured him. He's in the cage and being minimally cared for — food and water. They're busy preparing the Celestial Palace for the coronation. Simone has disappeared. Leo and Buffy are safe in the United States, and your sisters and nephew are in the Dark Lord's house in London for a few days while they find somewhere to live.

Amy?

She's in the North with the rest of the residents under house arrest. I will return to her as soon as we're done here.

Thank you. Go.

Gold changed to True Form and slipped out of the room.

I have a list of calls and messages for you, BJ said. *But nothing so urgent you need to do it right now. Get some sleep.*

I haven't slept since the Heavens fell. I've been lying here for hours wondering what I can do — and what I could have done — to avoid this situation. I'm worried about my family and about Simone, and you, and Chang and the orphans, and my students and —

Lady Emma, BJ said, a formal edge to her voice. *Shut up and go to sleep.*

Like I said, I can't — I began, but never finished it.

* * *

The grey sky brightened and I gave up trying to go back to sleep. The thoughts spun through my head. What could I have done differently? What could I do now? How was Simone coping? Were my family safe?

It was pointless lying there beating myself up. I needed to move.

You there, BJ?

I'm here. It's really early, Aunty Emma, go back to sleep.

Yeah, I've been trying for a while and it's not happening. Can you give me the messages while I find some breakfast?

Okay.

I folded up my blanket, then made a cup of tea. I looked around for bread and peanut butter, but when I found it I couldn't face making toast and eating it. I wanted to change into clean clothes, but the King hadn't provided any. I should have slept nude, wrapped in the blanket, and washed my clothes during the night, but then I'd have to wear them damp.

The King will have to provide you with more clothes, BJ said.

Yeah, I know. You said you had messages for me?

Most of the messages from yesterday are people checking up on you. You don't need to answer. I told everybody the situation before we came down here. Brother Chang has been calling me non-stop and he sounds desperate.

Did you tell him there's nothing I can do?

They're out on the street.

What?

Listen.

'*Emma!*' Chang did sound desperate. '*Emma, I need some cash right now. The hotel's not owned by the Tiger any more and the new management have thrown us out. They claim that we owe them thousands of dollars! Can you send someone to pick us up? We're all sitting in the street in front of the hotel and I'm worried Child Services will come. The police have already stopped by twice to warn us to move on.*'

There was a click, then a buzz. *Next one*, BJ said.

'*Please help us, Emma,*' Chang said. '*The police keep cruising past. You have to help me! The police are here again — oh no, they have a wagon, they're taking us in. Help!*'

That's all, BJ said.

I went through the dark living room and opened the front door. The King hadn't stationed an armoured demon there. Instead, there was a big Duke, to keep Mothers away rather than stop me from escaping.

'What's your number?' I asked him.

'Forty-One. Or Hak Yu if you like. I have a human name.'

'I need to see the King right now. Immediately. It's very important.'

'Did something happen to the kids?' he said as his eyes unfocused.

'Just find him,' I said.

'He's in the Celestial Palace fucking a couple of senior Mothers, and that's always tricky. If he doesn't finish up carefully he'll kill them. He wants to know what the huge problem is.'

'How long will he be?'

The Duke nodded, obviously listening to the King. 'Show me first. The King has the Heavens to run. Is one of the kids sick?'

I pulled back inside, leaving the door open to speak to the Duke. 'I'll wait for him.'

'No, tell me. If something happens to either of those kids on my watch, my head is gone.'

'There's no problem with the kids. This is to do with something else entirely unrelated and I can wait for him. It's urgent, but not that urgent.'

The Duke shrugged. 'Suit yourself.'

I closed the door and went back to the kitchen. I should have asked the Duke how long it usually took to 'finish up' a couple of Mothers but I really didn't want to know.

An hour later I was in the bathroom arguing with Frankie.

'You're too little,' I said. 'It will go everywhere.'

'Then they clean it up. It's what they're here for.'

I opened my mouth to tell him that wasn't what they were there for and realised that in the case of these demon servants it was true.

'When we're in the Heavens you'll treat your staff like human beings or ...' I heard what I was saying. 'You'll treat everybody with respect. And clean up after yourself.'

'But I don't know how!'

'I'll teach you — that's what I'm here for. Now you sit down here,' I picked him up and sat him on the toilet seat, 'and do your business without making a mess.'

'I'll fall in,' he said.

'I know it's hard, but I'll find you a toddler toilet seat and that will make it much easier for you.'

The King came in. 'So what's so important you had to drag me away from a couple of my girls who haven't seen me in weeks?'

'Chang's orphans,' I said. 'They've been thrown out of the hotel in Australia. Do you have contacts there to retrieve them?'

'No,' the King said, and moved to go out. 'I thought it was important.'

'It is important!' I said, helping Frankie pull his little pants up. 'Those kids will be homeless again. We have to bring them —'

'Oh, we have to, do we? No, we don't. The Australian authorities will deal with them. They'll find them a shelter or something.'

'If they think those kids are illegal immigrants, they'll put them in one of those awful detention camps!'

'So?' he said, leaning on the door frame. 'They'll be fine. They'll have food and water and a roof over their heads, and nothing more than that. Good motivation to make something of themselves — get a job and an education and do something with their lives.'

'There's no job or education in the refugee camps!'

He shrugged and turned away. 'Not my problem. Don't call me unless it's something to do with *my* kids, okay?'

'Please. The children,' I began, but he'd disappeared.

'Can we play now?' Frankie said.

'Sure,' I said absently as I tried to think of a way to find the orphans and re-home them. 'Let's pull some Lego out.'

If we had a phone, I said to BJ as I sat on the living room floor with Frankie and the Lego.

We don't, BJ said. *There's no phone network, no wireless and no cables in this place. He's way ahead of us.*

Is there any way we can contact Simone to help them?

Only if she comes down here to see you.

There has to be something I can do!

Lady Emma, BJ said, *I'm sorry. There isn't.*

'Emma?' Edu said, and slapped my shoulder. I realised she'd been speaking to me for a while.

'Sorry, Edu. Yes?'

'She asked you what a pony is,' Frankie said. 'Remember you showed me?'

'I can't show you,' I said. 'I need a computer to do it and your dad won't let me have one.'

'Why not?' Frankie said. 'That was fun.'

'I'll see if I can find some DVDs for you,' I said.

'What's a DVD?' they asked in unison.

* * *

'What's this?' Frankie said, looking at the peanut butter sandwiches I'd placed in front of them.

'Human food?' Edu said.

I explained about sandwiches, and watched as they tried peanut butter for the first time and, like most demons, were instantly appreciative.

The front door opened and the King came in, accompanied by three silent wide-eyed children. My heart plummeted. It was Gold's kids, Jade and Richie, and my nephew Matthew.

Oh god, no! BJ wailed in my head.

'Where's Amy and my sister?' I said.

'Who?' the King said.

'Their mothers!' I shouted, pointing at the children, who didn't move. He must have been controlling them, otherwise they'd be distressed.

'I sent them home,' the King said. 'I have no use for them.' He pushed the children forward. 'Go to Aunty Emma, she'll look after you.' He turned and opened the door to go out.

'These children can't be here,' I said to the King. 'They don't belong. Take them back to their parents.'

'These are friends for Frankie,' he said. 'Better still, these are relatives. Well, except the stone's ones, but I want Frankie to be happy and these children can play with him.'

'They can't be here, they're human, and not dea ...' I didn't finish the word. 'This is not the place for them.'

He shrugged. 'All the rules are being rewritten.'

'There isn't space for them all,' I said.

'There will be plenty when we move them up. How much space do they need?'

'They need their own rooms, so send them home to their parents.'

'No, Frankie needs playmates. Be ready, I'm letting them go.'

The three children all took a deep breath together and their eyes widened.

I crouched to speak to them, touching their shoulders to reassure them. 'You're safe, kids, nobody will hurt you.'

'Where's my mummy, Aunty Emma?' Matthew said.

'You know how you're a lion?' I said, and he nodded. 'Well, right now I need you to be a lion. I'll look after you here for a little while, and then you can go home.'

'Okay.'

I rose. 'Send them home. They can be playmates when Frankie moves up to the Heavens.'

The King moved closer to me. 'They're insurance right now.'

'I won't try to escape. I'm doing the job to the best of my ability. You don't need to take these children away from their mothers!'

'When it comes to you, having insurance is always a good idea. They stay.'

'Then I need clothes for them, and clothes for me too. I need a DVD player and an online ordering account.' I gestured towards Frankie and Edu in the living room, who were still eating the peanut butter sandwiches and watching us with wide eyes. 'They need to *see* what I'm talking about. If you won't give me a computer with internet, at least allow me to show them videos.'

'Draw pictures,' he said.

'Not good enough! They've been stuck inside for *weeks*. They need to go outside into the fresh air and sunshine. I have to take them to the surface ...' I realised what I was saying and that the children could hear me. 'They need to see the sun!'

'You're a fucking pain in the ass, you know that?' he said, and stormed out.

'Good,' I said as he slammed the door. I crouched to speak to the three little ones. 'Come and have a sandwich.'

Matthew looked around, then his face went red and tears ran down his cheeks. 'I don't think I can be a lion, Aunty Emma.'

'Oh, darling,' I said, and crushed him to me.

His crying set the other two off and the three of them wailed. Frankie's eyes were wide with concern, but Edu watched with an expression of cruel pleasure.

23

The King entered without knocking, accompanied by a Duke carrying a large cardboard box. He stopped in the living room when he saw me reading to the children.

'That's what I like to see.'

'Is that a DVD player or a computer?' I said.

'It's more clothes for all of you.' He frowned. 'Humans are disgusting.'

'I need to shop for DVDs and I need access to the internet,' I said. 'I need more books than this. You have to give me shopping rights because there's a bunch of stuff I need to buy for them.'

'You need, you need — that's all I hear from you. So needy. I brought you the clothes you asked for, isn't that enough?' He waved one hand over his shoulder towards the guard Duke standing behind him in human form. 'Bring her.'

'Where are you —' I began, but couldn't finish it.

The Duke took three swift steps towards me and put his hand on my shoulder. We teleported to the middle of a soccer pitch in a factory compound somewhere in China. Ten five-storey blocks of ugly residential monoliths stood in a row, with hard-faced uniformed guards on every corner. Nets were strung between the buildings to thwart workers' suicide attempts. A three-metre-high wall stood on the other side, with a few stunted trees attempting to screen it.

BJ, contact them!

Processing, BJ said.

The air was bitingly cold, and the sky was brown with a pollution haze that obscured everything on the other side of the wall.

The King led me away from the residential buildings towards the blank windowless factory buildings.

'Where are we?' I said. *BJ?*

Can't talk and download at the same time. Wait.

'Not important. You need to see this, it's fascinating.' He grinned over his shoulder at me. 'Francis is in Europe showing his scientists, so you're the only one around here who has the brains to appreciate this. It's a breakthrough.'

'How are my family? I need to talk to them.' *BJ? My family?*

I'm doing a big data download from Dad. Big dump. Bear with me. Any messages for anyone?

'There we are again with the needy,' the King said.

The entrance to the factory building had more guards on either side. They had the same faces as the ones in the residential section: demon duplicates.

The Demon King noticed my distraction. 'Are you talking to anyone? I thought your telepathy was intermittent.'

'It is. I'm trying to contact Simone.'

'Good! Tell her to come in — all is forgiven. She can stay with your family.'

Tell them that I love them, and that I'm trying to send Little Jade and Richie back to your dad and Amy.

I am. I'm talking to Dad.

'She's not replying,' I said.

'Shame.'

I glanced at the guards as we went through the door. 'Do you have human workers? The identical copy guards must freak them out.'

'I'm in their heads. They don't see anything.'

'They still try to kill themselves though.'

'I can't be in their heads all the time. I don't know why they jump. They come from villages where they had nothing. I give them jobs and income, and within weeks they forget to be grateful. They start asking for ridiculous things like days off. Stupid.'

The reception area was clean and modern, all white with a black granite counter. A pretty young woman sat at the desk in a blue mock-military uniform, under a huge logo on the wall that said *Franskit Industries* in English and *Kwok Ho Fan See* — a phonetic version — in characters.

The receptionist quickly rose and bowed to the Demon King. 'Good morning, Mr Kwok.'

The King patted her shoulder. 'Good morning, Stella. It's good to see you again.'

She flushed and looked down. 'It's always a great pleasure to see you, sir.' She looked up into his eyes. 'If there's anything at all you need, please don't hesitate to contact me.' She swept one hand towards her empty desk. 'I am always here for you.'

'That's what I like to hear,' he said, moving closer. His smile widened. 'Would you like to come have dinner with me later? Just you and me?'

She gasped, then opened and closed her mouth like a goldfish, the blush spreading to her neck. She trembled.

'Good girl,' he said, and turned away. He nodded to one of my guards. 'Bring her later.'

I opened my mouth to tell her the truth but didn't get a chance. The door in front of us clicked open and the guard shoved me through.

'Don't you dare eat her!' I shouted at the Demon King before the door closed.

'Heh,' he said as he led us into a lift lobby with three lifts in it. 'Don't be stupid. She's useful, and she's human — I'm just having fun with her. She thinks she has a chance. She's a virgin though, and her blood is *choice*.'

The Duke made a low sound of appreciation as he pressed the button for the lift.

'How can virginity make a woman taste different? It makes no sense,' I said.

'It doesn't taste different.' He shrugged. 'It's just the concept. Precious. A virgin's never been used by any other man.'

'*Used?*' I said. 'Like a *thing*? I thought you were a woman yourself.'

He didn't reply.

The download's done, BJ said. *Everybody's safe. I have pictures and messages for you — I'll show them to you later. Simone hasn't responded yet, I'm still trying to contact her. Dad and Amy say thank you for looking after my little brother and sister.*

Thanks, BJ. Are my sisters okay?

Yes.

Even Jennifer?

Lady Jennifer ... didn't talk much, but she did ask after Matthew.

Tell her he's fine.

I already did, she said.

Have you contacted Simone?

Simone's not replying. She's left Ronnie's apartment in Hong Kong — it's deserted.

What about the orphans? I said. *Has Chang found a place for them?*

The lift doors opened. I followed the King out, with the Duke behind me.

They're being held by the Australian authorities. I'm trying to break into the Australian records system remotely but it seems to be stone-proof. They know about our abilities. I'm working on it.

'Now I know for sure that you're talking to someone,' the King said.

'What did you do to my stone?' I said.

'Nothing,' he said, and his voice had the ring of truth. Great, now I couldn't tell when he was lying. 'I never had your stone. Are you talking to it? Tell it to come in as well, I'll be merciful. You need it.'

'Never mind,' I said.

'Look,' he stopped and turned to speak to me, 'I'm not a monster. I want the Heavens to prosper. I don't want to watch my back all the time. I am prepared to be merciful to all who pledge allegiance. Tell them to come in and all is forgiven. Simone can have the Crown Prince's Residence. If Leo returns from the US and surrenders, I'll free Martin from the Pits and they can stay in the Peak apartment with the little black girl.' He spread his hands. 'I want peace and prosperity.'

Should I tell Leo that? BJ said.

Go right ahead, but it'd be a waste of time.

'I'll keep that in mind,' I said. 'So where are we going?'

'This way.'

He took me to the end of the plain concrete corridor and opened a door on the right. We entered a lab, with benches, sinks and microscopes. A stainless-steel table stood in the middle of the room holding a half-dissected three-metre-long snake corpse packed in ice. Its white flesh glistened where the skin had been peeled away.

'Oh god,' I said, and put my hand over my mouth, which suddenly tasted of sour peanut butter. 'Is that my nephew?'

The King pointed at six decorative octagonal fish tanks, each half a metre high and the same across, that stood on pedestals at the other end of the room, bubbling with grey liquid. Each of them held a floating black snake, forty centimetres long.

'Your nephew lives,' the King said.

I was rooted to the spot with horror. 'Colin?'

'Was that his name? Oh, that's right, the oldest one. These are clones. A masterpiece. A breakthrough.' He put his hands in his pockets. 'I am so proud of this.'

'You carved up his corpse!'

'Well, of course I did.' He shook his head. 'Better than carving him up while he was alive, eh? There are twenty more clones growing in eggs in the next room. We ran out of eggs and put the leftovers in tanks, but these ones aren't doing as well.' He studied me appraisingly. 'As soon as we have more eggs to put them in, I'll take some tissue samples off your snake form and make clones of you. You'll finally have all the children you've dreamed of.'

'Not happening,' I said.

He shrugged. 'Makes no difference. Once Frankie's on the throne, everybody will have no choice. You'll have to obey him.' He nodded towards Colin's corpse. 'This one's good, but you'll be way better.'

'He was my nephew.' I went to the table and touched Colin's shining black scales. The little bully who'd made Simone's life miserable in London had grown into a noble young man, and could have been great with more training. I dropped my head as my eyes filled with tears. I hadn't been able to protect him. 'I am so sorry, Colin.' I turned back to the King. 'You killed him. He needs to be returned to his family so they can bury him.'

'He's not dead!' the King said. 'We have more than twenty of him here. I'll give one to your family as payment for his death, and do some work on the others to make them even more powerful and obedient. They'll have their child back.'

I stepped back, full of nausea. Twenty of these things. 'This is not Colin.'

'Of course it is! The DNA is identical. It's him!'

'At best his twin brother.' I turned away. 'Do me a favour, George, and don't let my family see them. It would break my sister's heart.'

'But I'm bringing her son back. What mother wouldn't want to see her baby again?'

'It's not her son. It's a copy.'

'Close enough. I don't understand you. This is a huge breakthrough in cloning. I don't need the other boys now I have this. I'm giving you your nephew back alive, and instead of being happy about it you look sick. What the hell is wrong with you?'

'I don't think you'd ever understand, George.'

Has Simone replied yet, BJ?

No, Aunty Emma, she's disappeared completely.

I don't know whether that's a good or a bad thing.

I said out loud, 'While we're here on the Earthly, take me shopping to buy stuff for the kids. They need educational enrichment.'

His face grew cunning. 'Agree to training the clones when they hatch, and I will.'

'It looks like your son will not be reaching his full potential then.'

'He's your son too, sweetheart. And the others are your little nephew and the children of your stone Retainer. You have a duty as their Lady to provide them with the best of care. Agree to teach the clones as well and I'll let you go shopping with an unlimited credit card.'

I hesitated, looking into his blood-coloured eyes, then sagged with defeat.

'Good,' he said.

'Send Colin's body home to his family so they can give him a proper goodbye,' I said.

'No need, because he's *not dead*!' the King said. He slapped one hand on the autopsy table, making Colin's white flesh jiggle. 'If these clones work out, there's an unlimited supply of them from the original corpse.'

I wiped my hand over my eyes and tried to control my voice. 'Give him back to his family.'

'I need material to work on. Would you rather I used the other boys? *Alive?*'

I shook my head, speechless with dismay.

'You really are incredibly ungrateful,' the King said. 'As bad as the workers in the factory. None of you understand the lengths I go to to keep you happy.' He turned to the Duke. 'Take her shopping wherever she likes. If she gives you any trouble, call me.'

'What if she tries to escape?' the Duke said. His expression grew hungry. 'How hard can I punish her?'

'Heh. She won't. She gave her word, and I have her child.'

The Duke bowed to the King, obviously disappointed. 'Majesty.' He put his hand on my shoulder. 'Where to?'

'The big Kinokuniya on Orchard Road in Singapore,' I said, and the lab disappeared.

* * *

The Duke watched with disbelief as I added the last DVD to the pile on the counter. 'This is nearly five hundred dollars' worth!'

'Check with your father that it's okay,' I said.

'No need.' He handed the credit card to the smiling assistant.

'Thanks,' I said to her. 'You've been a terrific help.'

'My pleasure,' she said, and added it up. 'He's right. Five hundred and twelve, twenty.'

'Crazy,' the Duke said as he put the PIN number in.

The assistant put the books and DVDs into three big bags and turned them around so the handles were facing me. 'I hope you come back when next term starts. It's so encouraging to see a teacher like you who buys art supplies for creative work as well as books for spelling and maths.'

'Thank you,' I said, and reached to take the bags.

'No,' the Duke said, and shoved my hand away. He turned to the assistant. 'Hold them for me. I'll come and collect them later.'

'What?' I said. 'No, I want to take them back now.'

'Please don't argue with me,' he said, menacingly polite. 'I will return with them later today. They're too heavy for you to carry on the train.'

I opened my mouth and closed it again.

He turned back to the assistant. 'Put them under the counter under the name of Miss Kwok, and I will collect them later.'

'I understand, sir,' she said, writing a note to attach to the bags. 'I'll hold them for you.'

'Miss Black,' the demon said, gesturing for me to go.

I clutched at the opportunity for some normal human interaction, not wanting to leave. 'Thanks again,' I said to the assistant.

'See you next term!' she said cheerfully as she placed the bags under the counter.

'Miss Black. Now.' The guard was a threatening presence behind me as I walked to the door.

When we were through the door, I rounded on him. 'What's the point of buying all that stuff if you won't let me give it to the kids? There's no need to clear it. You saw for yourself what I bought.'

He put his hand on my shoulder and the world disappeared. We landed in the living room, where the Demon King in his Kitty Kwok form was sitting with the children, who were all crying. Frankie sat in the King's lap with his face buried in her chest. The room reeked of burning plastic, but there was no smoke.

I ran to Little Jade and Richie to hold them but Little Jade pushed me away.

'Why'd you break everything?' she said.

'I didn't break anything,' I said, bewildered.

'Look!' the King said, and pointed the remote control at the television.

A grainy black-and-white image of the living room appeared. It was night. I walked onto the screen, went up to the children's toy box and pulled out the dollhouse I'd been using to teach them about human lives. The image of me on the screen smashed it into pieces.

The children wailed louder.

I watched with horror as the copy of me took everything out of the toy box and destroyed it. She tore all the books apart, shredding them, then smashed every other toy. She broke all the pencils and crushed the crayons under her heel. She couldn't break the Lego, so she took it into the kitchen.

'Why'd you do that?' Richie cried.

'That was so mean,' Frankie said.

'You went into the toy box and broke every single toy they own,' the Demon King said over the top of Frankie's head. 'Then you melted the Lego on the stove. Why would you do such a thing?'

Frankie's sobs grew louder and she held him closer.

'I didn't —' I started.

'You did!' Frankie wailed. 'We can see you!'

I opened and closed my mouth, lost for words. Eventually I managed to squeak out, 'Why?'

'You tell us!' Little Jade shouted, and ran out of the room into the bedroom. Her brother followed her.

BJ …

I'll talk to them when they let you touch them. What will you do about Frankie? I can't talk to him, he can't know I'm here.

There's nothing I can do.

'Frankie, I'm sorry. I've just bought you books and videos,' I said.

He turned to see me. 'What? What did you buy? Where are they?'

'She's lying again,' the King said. 'Look.' She gestured, and the Duke came in holding the shopping bags. 'Look what I bought you, my darling. All these wonderful things for you.'

Frankie stopped crying and went to the bags to look through my purchases. 'Ponies!' He held up a picture book of farm animals. 'So many new things!'

'Don't you dare damage any of these new gifts,' the King said to me. 'You can teach the children without being mean to them. You're a monster!'

'I won't be mean. I'll never be mean. I love them. I love Frankie,' I said.

'You say that now, but we've all seen the video of you destroying the toys. You can't be trusted,' the King said. She crouched to speak

262

to Frankie as he went through the books. 'Is this good enough? Do you need more?'

Frankie looked up at her, and a swift expression of fear swept across his face. 'No, thank you, Mummy, this is more than I could ever want. I don't need more than this. Can I share them with my friends?'

'Of course you can, my darling. And I'll make sure that Emma can't break anything again. I'll keep a guard on her room to stop her from doing it. I was silly to trust her. She's a mean person, not sweet and nice at all.'

Frankie glowered at me from under his long fringe. 'Thanks, Mummy.'

'A most productive day, I think,' the King said, rising. 'Well done, Emma, you helped enormously. Next time think about how close you are growing to *my* son.' She bent and hugged Frankie. 'I'll be back later to have dinner with you.'

'Really?' he said, gazing up into her eyes with adoration.

She kissed him on the cheek. 'This time, really, I will. I need to see what toys were broken so I can replace them.'

He kissed her back. 'Thank you, Mummy. I love you very much.'

'I love you too, sweetheart,' she said, rose and went out.

I fell to sit in a chair, dumbfounded, trying to work out a way to tell Frankie the truth. The Duke was standing next to the door, enjoying my discomfort. I shook my head and wiped my eyes. There was no way I could tell him when the evidence was right in front of him.

The Duke went out. I sidled to sit next to Frankie and he went rigid beside me.

When I reached for one of the books to read it to him, his little face screwed up. 'Don't break them!'

I drew my hand back. 'Okay, Frankie.'

'Jade and Richie have no more toys to play with and it's all your fault,' he grumbled while he went through the contents of the bag. He raised the coloured pencils and looked at them with wonder. He tried to open the box and failed. I reached to help him and he snatched them away. 'Don't touch anything!'

'I'll open the box for you. I won't break them. I promise.'

He eyed me suspiciously.

'I keep my promises,' I said. I dropped my voice. 'We have a secret and I've never told anybody.'

He watched me for a long moment.

'I promise,' I said.

He hesitated again, then handed the box to me. I smiled with relief and opened it. 'There's drawing paper in there as well. How about we draw some animals?'

'I want to see what's in the rest of the bags,' he said. He snapped his chin up. 'Bring my friends in here, I want to show them.'

'You don't order me around,' I said.

'Mummy says that when I sit on the throne, everybody will have to do what I tell them. So start now,' he said.

'Mummy's not teaching you right,' I muttered as I pulled myself to my feet to go and find Jade and Richie.

* * *

Later that evening, I tucked Frankie into bed. He'd started to forgive me, but the King was obviously holding back on replacing all the broken toys to make his point.

When I opened the book of farm animals, he took it from me. 'I'll look at it myself. You go out.'

'Are you sure?' I said. 'I can read it to you.'

'You'll break it. Go out. I'll read it myself for a little while.'

'I won't break anything, I promise.'

He shook his head and turned away.

'All right. I'll come back in five minutes and turn the light off.'

'Go away and let me read!'

I gave up and went into the living room. The other children were already asleep — I'd saved the pleasure of putting Frankie to bed for last — and the house was quiet. The guard demon was a dark presence outside the front door.

I proceeded to put the toys away and heard a soft voice in Frankie's bedroom. I raised my head and listened; again a soft voice. I sent out my awareness and didn't sense anything. The realisation hit me: I didn't sense anything — not even Frankie. I rushed into his bedroom. He was sitting alone, reading his book.

He glanced up at me. 'Let me read some more.'

I concentrated, sending my senses out, and everything seemed normal. He glowed like a small dark star in front of me.

'Are you all right?' I asked him.

'Go away, Emma,' he said, turning back to the book.

'Was someone in here?' I dropped my voice. 'Was the Lady here?'

'Don't be silly,' he said loudly. 'Nobody can come in.' He wiggled on the bed so he was turned away from me. 'Leave me alone.' He turned back and glared at me. 'And Mummy's watching you. If you break anything else you'll be in big trouble.' He waved the book at me. 'Go. Away!'

'Five more minutes until I turn your light out,' I said.

He didn't reply, making a show of studying the book, and I went out, defeated.

* * *

It was 11 pm before the kitchen was clean enough to satisfy the King's exacting standards. I curled up in my thin blanket on the kitchen floor and propped myself against the cupboards.

Okay, BJ, I said.

Only you can see this, she said.

The projection was like a small television screen in front of me. My mother was on the screen, but she wasn't in Persimmon Tree any more; the family had been moved to the Mountain's student barracks. The barracks were full of people — there were mattresses on the floor between the beds and in the aisles as well. The place held four times the number of people it had been designed for.

'Okay, go,' Gold said. He was taking the recording.

'The King brought Mandy and Jen back, love,' my mother said softly. 'Jen's not talking to anyone, and there are no Immortal staff here to help her out. Andrew's looking after her, but he's as wrecked as she is. She's lost her husband and two of her sons. She's destroyed.'

I told her that Matthew's okay, BJ said.

My mother continued. 'Mandy's okay, I suppose. Mark isn't doing well — the whole demon thing is pushing him into flashbacks again.' She smiled sadly. 'We thought he'd finally recovered from it and it's all come out again. He can't sleep, and when he does he wakes up screaming, worse since David was taken.'

David was taken? I asked BJ.

'Your father and David were taken away, along with all able-bodied men and strong women,' my mother said. 'Gold tells us that they haven't been hurt, they're just working on a project for the Demon ...' She looked around. 'For the Celestial Regent.'

The Western Palace is being rebuilt, BJ said.

Jade's daughter, Jackie, came to my mother. She sat next to her on the bed and took her hand.

'Lady Emma, I haven't heard from my mother. They took her ...' She choked, then recovered. 'They took her with the other Immortals. Lord Gold tells us that you're ... you're in Hell. Have you seen my mother? You're there too. If you see her ...' She turned away and wiped her eyes, then turned back to Gold. 'Please tell her I love her, and I really miss her. I'm ...' She lost her voice again. 'I'm all alone.'

'I'm here for you, love,' my mother said, and Jackie leaned her head on my mother's shoulder. My mother put her arm around her and squeezed her tight.

'Guards are coming,' Gold said. 'I have to go.'

'Tell Emma that we love her, and that we're counting on her to free all of us,' my mother said. She spoke more quickly. 'And find Simone!'

The little television screen disappeared.

So my father and David are being used as slave labour. My mother's looking after my sisters, who have broken down with good reason. Mark's broken as well, and Andrew's having night terrors, I said.

None of this is your responsibility, BJ said.

My family is destroyed, in pieces all over the Planes. I pulled my knees up and wrapped my arms around them. *I failed them all.*

Not your fault —

They are my family and my Retainers. All have suffered because I have failed. I buried my head in my knees. *I will find a way to make this right.*

I'm here with you, BJ said.

I nodded into my knees. *Thanks, BJ. And thank your father.* I heaved a deep sigh. *Where the hell is Simone?*

BJ didn't reply.

24

Frankie stood against the door frame in the kitchen, his chin up. I marked the frame level with the top of his head, and he turned to see it. 'I'm taller than Richie!'

'You grow so fast,' I said, studying the marks. 'You've grown ten centimetres in two months.'

'I grow faster than Jade and Richie,' Frankie said. 'Mummy said it's because I'm better than them.'

Nobody is better than anybody else, I said. *Being better comes from treating other people better — that's what's important.*

He shook his head. 'Talk to me out loud or Daddy will be angry.'

'Okay.'

There was a squeal from the living room: Little Jade again. I stormed in and grabbed Edu by the scruff of her neck to pull her off the smaller girl.

'Let me go!' Edu shouted, kicking me.

I held her tight and glared into her face. 'We talked about you hitting people.'

She swung her little fist and punched me on the face, a stinging blow.

I shook her in reply. 'Into your room for time out. Now!'

'You can't make me!' she yelled. 'I'll be *Empress* one day and then I'll skin you alive!'

I lifted her, took her to the bedroom she shared with the human children, pushed her inside and closed the door on her. She knew better than to come straight back out, but she kicked the door furiously, screaming and cursing me on the other side.

She suddenly went silent.

'Mummy's here,' Frankie said.

The children scattered, hiding in the kitchen and bedrooms. Frankie stood in the middle of the living room to wait for the King. I held his shoulder and stood next to him.

The King opened the door in Kitty Kwok form. 'Hello, Frankie darling.'

'Mummy!' Frankie yelled, and raced to her.

She put her arms out and he threw himself into them, and they had a long embrace.

'It's time for the rehearsal,' she said. 'Are you ready?'

He appeared confused. 'What rehearsal?'

She glared at me. 'You were supposed to be coaching him for the rehearsal.'

'I don't know anything about any rehearsal,' I said.

Her expression darkened. 'I told you at least three times that the rehearsal for Frankie's coronation would be today. You're so forgetful. I don't know why I have someone as stupid as you minding these children. I should find someone with half a brain.'

I shook my head. The King had never mentioned any rehearsal to me.

'I want you to look after me all the time, Mummy!' Frankie shouted.

The King crouched to speak to him. 'I want to be with you, my darling, but I have other things to do. Now.' She rose. 'Emma, take Frankie's hand and don't let it go.' She clapped her hands with excitement. 'You're going to *Heaven*, Frankie, and you'll see your new throne.'

'Yay!' Frankie shouted with enthusiasm. 'Come and hold my hand, Emma, I'm going to see my throne!'

The King gazed into my eyes as she put her hand on Frankie's shoulder. 'Try anything and these three will suffer the consequences.'

'I understand,' I said. 'It's worth it for him to be in the sunshine. Can we take the other children as well?'

'I already told you I can't. Why do you never listen to me?'

I opened my mouth to say, 'No, you didn't,' but Hell disappeared from around me.

* * *

I put my hand on my thumping forehead and struggled to sit up and look around. I was in the Hall of Supreme Harmony, on the floor against the back wall, facing the rear of the dais. Voices were echoing through the room, booming through my head and making it hurt even more, but I couldn't make out what they were saying.

The dais ... John.

I struggled to my feet, leaning against the wall, and used it as a support as I worked my way to the corner of the room, then along the next wall until I could see what was happening on the dais. There were no chairs in the hall, and I wasn't capable of moving without help, so I just braced my back against the wall and watched. John wasn't on the dais; just the Demon King, Frankie and a small group of demon Dukes. A sound engineer sat with her equipment at the back of the room, and a park bench stood on the dais in place of the Jade Throne.

BJ, where's the Dark Lord?

He was removed a week ago and nobody knows where he is, Aunty Emma.

Before you do the info transfer ... my family?

Everybody's okay.

I sagged with relief against the wall. The King was keeping his word.

'Look who's up and around,' the King said to me. 'Just in time to take Frankie home.' She turned to Frankie. 'Don't worry if you don't remember what to do; I will help you.' She held her arms out to him. 'Hop down and we'll take you home to your little friends.'

'Can we go outside for a while, Mummy?' Frankie said as she helped him down off the bench. 'I want to see the sky.'

'Of course, darling,' she said with pleasure. 'All my lovely children can see the sky now. Everybody adores me.' She took his hand and led him out of the hall.

I leaned against the wall and breathed, trying to regain my energy. Protecting Frankie on the trip to Heaven had wiped me out.

John?

No reply.

Simone?

Again no reply.

Dad says that neither of them have been heard from in a while, BJ said. *I downloaded some pictures for you while you were unconscious.* She quickly flipped through the photos my family had sent, projecting them inside my head. *Everybody's okay.*

My family look awful, I said. *They're all so thin and pale.*

It's taking a while to rebuild the food distribution network, and there are still many people without homes. The King has Dad working twenty-four hours a day on the logistics.

Put me through to your dad? I want to thank him.

Lady Emma, Gold said. *Welcome back. Are you home for good? We need you here. Morale is very low and the Dark Lord has been taken away.*

I'm here for a coronation rehearsal. I think they'll be heading back to Hell soon. BJ just told me what you're doing. Thanks for taking care of everyone.

We're rebuilding, but the corruption is hurting everybody.

Corruption?

Demons have been put in positions of power on the Celestial, and if you want anything done you have to bribe them. They're taking the pick of the resources — food and housing — and the ordinary residents of the Heavens are given what's left over. I'm doing my best but it's difficult. BJ tells me that my kids are okay. They're not too unhappy, are they?

The King hasn't hurt them, they're playmates for Frankie. They're doing well and I'm caring for them. They're missing you and Amy and the sunshine, but when Frankie's crowned they'll move up here and live in the Palace with him and you'll be able to see them.

One good thing to come out of this misery. We'll be able to see more of our kids, and you'll be able to see more of your family.

I hope so.

We're also hoping that when Frankie's crowned Emperor, he can stop them from eating us, Gold said.

What? I said, horrified.

People keep disappearing, whole families. They disappear during the night. The Demon King is having senior demons executed, but it hasn't stopped.

Dear Lord, be careful, Gold.

We are.

The King returned, holding Frankie's hand. 'Emma, over here. Time for us to go home.'

'When is the coronation?' I said as I staggered to them, the room spinning around me. I stopped and took a deep breath, then made it the rest of the way.

'Hurry up! You are so slow,' she said. 'I already told you: it's in a week. We're consulting a fung shui master to find a dynasty name for him. I think we may call him the Serpent Emperor. What do you think?'

I put my hand on Frankie's shoulder. 'Serpents are wise healers. That's perfect.'

I came around on the couch in the living room of the little house.

'About time,' the King said from a chair across the room.

The children were playing with their new Lego on the floor. As usual, Edu had created her own hoard of it in front of her.

The King came and bent over me with menace. 'The coronation is in one week. Do you hear me? *Seven days.*'

'I hear you,' I said.

'It's traditional for the new Emperor to give a speech outlining his policies for the realm. You write it, I don't have time. Write the usual bull—' She looked back at the children. '— the usual stuff to keep everybody happy. About five minutes' worth. Frankie can parrot it when he's enthroned.'

'What do you want me to write? What are your plans for the realm?'

'Wealth and prosperity,' she said expansively. 'For the right people, of course. My people. Everybody else can go to Hell.

And in many cases, that's exactly what will happen. So focus on economic growth, everyone having more money, employment for all, that sort of nonsense. Whatever politicians on the Earthly say when they're elected. Understand?'

I nodded.

'Once Frankie's on the throne and settled, we won't need you any more. I'll reward you for your good service by letting you choose where you go. You can go to the Peach Garden as Dowager Mother, or you can become a Buddhist nun. You don't have to make the decision now. Let me know what you want after Frankie's reign is established.'

'What's in the Peach Garden?' I said, aware that the Jade Empress spent most of her time there.

'Peach trees,' the King snapped. 'I don't know. Something to do with time. Sounds boring.' She straightened and turned to speak to Frankie. 'I'm going now, my darling. Give me another hug.'

Frankie ran to her with his arms out.

She embraced him warmly, tousled his hair, and kissed the top of his head. 'I love you.'

'I love you too, Mummy. I hope I get it right on Wednesday.'

'You will. You'll love your new house, and I can be close to you all the time.'

He held her closer. 'Thank you, Mummy.'

'I'm so glad one of you knows when to be grateful,' she said. 'Now let me go, I have things I need to do.'

He released her and stepped back. 'Goodbye, Mummy. I love you.'

She touched the side of his face. 'I love you too.'

She went out.

* * *

Two days later the King brought Mr Li to fit us for robes for the coronation. He had a couple of demon staff to assist, and was sombre and businesslike as he measured Frankie.

'Are the refugees who were in your factory all right?' I whispered as I held my arms out for him to measure.

'They are now in the Western Heavens,' he replied in the same low tones. 'They are assisting in the construction of the Demon King's ... the Celestial Regent's new Summer Palace.'

'And are you okay, Mr Li?'

He smiled wanly, but didn't reply.

He finished taking notes and returned to the Demon King. 'Gold silk for the Prince?'

'Yes. And for me.'

Mr Li stared at the King. 'Imperial gold is reserved for the Emperor.'

'We're rewriting the rules. The robe isn't to be Qing style; I want it more flowing and old-fashioned, like on the wuxia movies. Something to make him look glamorous and handsome.'

Mr Li bobbed his head. 'And Miss Donahoe?'

'Buddhist nun's robes. Brown. All brown. She must be as plain as possible. When she's done caring for Frankie she'll become a nun.'

I opened my mouth and closed it again. Being a Buddhist nun didn't sound so bad, but I wouldn't take the vows as long as there was any chance of me and John being together.

'We'll shave her head just before the ceremony,' the King continued. 'Nobody is to notice her at all.'

He watched me, obviously waiting for my reaction. I shrugged. Wouldn't be the first time I'd been bald, and the only real discomfort would be the stupid itching as my hair grew back. It was mid-summer and my head wouldn't be cold, so really no issue.

'When can you have the samples?' the King asked Mr Li.

'Tomorrow, my Lord. I will bring them for the young Emperor to try.'

'Good,' the King said, and waved him away.

Mr Li smiled consolingly at me, then he and his assistants were teleported out by a couple of large Dukes.

'How's that speech coming?' the King asked me.

'Mostly done.'

'Email me a copy and I'll take a look.'

'I don't have email,' I said. 'Give me a computer and I'll be able to send it.'

'Oh, yeah. Give it to your guard to pass to me.' He knelt to speak to Frankie. 'I have to go now, sweetie, but your mother will be by tomorrow to see your fancy new clothes.'

Frankie nodded. 'Thank you, Uncle George.'

'Be good for Emma,' the King said, and went out, followed by his Duke bodyguards.

* * *

Later that evening I was woken by soft voices. I opened my eyes and saw nothing. I opened my inner sight and still saw nothing. The whisper of a woman's voice echoed nearby, but it was difficult to place where it was coming from.

I rose and went into the living room. There were no moon or stars in Hell, just a blank grey sky on the other side of the house windows, so I turned on the light to see. I headed to Frankie's room to see if Kwan Yin was visiting him again.

Something slammed hard against the front door and I jumped back with alarm.

The door flew open and I stepped back again. A demon Prince, at least level ninety, stood in the doorway. He looked like a small fifty-year-old balding man with a wrinkled leathery face. The Duke that guarded the door was gone; the Prince had taken it down.

The Prince grinned. 'Two for one.'

Without a weapon I couldn't destroy it. I tried to summon Dark Heavens but it wouldn't come. I needed help, and with everybody imprisoned only the King himself could take out something this big.

There's a Prince here to kidnap your son, I said to the King, hoping he was contactable. *Don't draw attention to yourself*, I added to BJ.

The Prince raised his hands, still grinning. 'I'm sure you'd like to escape. Come with me and we'll go to a lovely estate a long way away from the King, where he'll never find you.'

'Okay, anything to be out of here,' I said. 'Can I pack a bag first?'

'Of course. And one for the little one as well.' He came to the middle of the room. 'Quickly, we don't have much time.'

'All right,' I said, and went into Frankie's room.

Frankie's eyes were bright over the top of his quilt in the racing-car bed. The noise had woken him. I pulled out the expensive Japanese case the King had bought for Frankie's move up to Heaven, and tossed some clothes into it.

'Out of bed, love, we're going on a trip,' I said.

'Where to?' Frankie said, throwing the covers off.

'Somewhere safe.'

'I'm safe here,' Frankie said, unsure. 'You're running away! Daddy said he'd kill my friends if we ever run away.'

'Your mummy sent someone to collect us, it's okay,' I said, closing the case. I wrapped his little robe around him and tied the belt.

There was a roar like a large animal in the living room, and Frankie backed up, terrified.

'Stay here,' I said, and crept to the door.

A Duke was facing off against the Demon Prince. The Prince was a big lizard-type and his head scraped the ceiling. The Duke had taken full True Form, two metres tall with a bull's head, but he was no match for the unarmed Prince even with a halberd. The Duke was trained, however, and managed to dodge the Prince's blows and even make a few slices at the Prince himself.

The Demon King stormed through the front door in True Form — like a Snake Mother, but blood-red where they were black. The Duke moved back to guard me and Frankie. The King and the Prince swung at each other, each landing some good blows. The Prince grabbed the King in his mouth and shook him.

The door to the bedroom next to Frankie's opened and the other children poked their heads out, then stood in the doorway watching the demons fighting. Edu grinned with excitement, but the human children looked terrified.

'Stay there,' I said. 'Go back into your room.'

'Emma!' Little Jade yelled, and ran across the living room to me.

The Duke scooped her up and brought her to me, then collected the other children in his massive arms and carried them to me as well. I pushed them inside Frankie's room.

'Stay in here where it's safe,' I said, and stood guard in the doorway.

The Duke took position in front of me, his massive back blocking my view so I was forced to peer around him.

The Prince backed up and concentrated with his hands out to attack the King with energy. He was trying for Kingship.

'Stupid bastard,' the Duke said under his breath.

I jumped when I felt something next to me. The children had crept up beside me and were watching with fascinated horror.

The King caught the energy and slammed it into the Prince so fast the Prince staggered backwards. The King pressed the attack, moving forward on his coils and grabbing the Prince's head with one hand and his shoulder with the other. He ripped the Prince's head off and ate it, opening his jaws wide to fit it in. He crunched the head, then tore the Prince's left arm off and ate that as well.

I ushered all the children into the room, closing the door behind us. I knelt to speak to them. 'It won't hurt you. It was protecting you.'

'It ate the other one,' Frankie said, his voice hollow.

'They will never hurt you.'

'They're like the big scary black ones with snake tails, but they're bigger and scarier. It *ate* the other one!' Frankie said again.

I pulled him into an embrace. 'I will protect you, darling, they'll never hurt you.'

'Promise?' he said into my shoulder.

'Always.'

'Really?' Matthew said.

I pulled him in as well. 'Really. They won't hurt you.'

'I'm scared, Emma,' Little Jade said.

The door opened and we all turned to see. It was the King in Kitty Kwok form.

'About time you grew some brains,' she said to me. She knelt and held her arms out. 'Are you all right, my darling?'

Frankie didn't run to the King; he sidled up to her then nestled against her, his face still stricken with fear. 'There were monsters.'

'No monster will ever come in here again,' she said. 'And I've decided. Tomorrow we'll move you to your new home. You'll never have to be afraid of them again.' She nodded to me. 'Pack the rest of his clothes and toys. I don't want to risk another Prince taking a stupid chance. We're moving him up tomorrow.'

277

'What about us?' Little Jade said.

'You too. Go back to bed, the monsters are gone. I'll protect you,' the King said. 'Leave us, Emma. I want to tuck my son in and explain that he's in no danger.'

I took the other kids into the living room. I restored the sofa, which had been knocked over, but there were no other signs of the battle that had taken place. The Duke stood next to the front door, still in True Form, his bull's face expressionless.

I took the children into their bedroom, and they crawled back into bed.

'Can you stay a while, Emma?' Matthew said.

'I'll stay while you go to sleep.'

'You're all scared,' Edu said with scorn. 'We don't have to worry while Father is in charge. Nobody's been able to defeat him in more than a thousand years.'

'They were monsters,' Little Jade said as she snuggled under the covers, then threw them over her head.

'I'll stay here,' I said. 'You're perfectly safe. Now go to sleep; we're going somewhere really nice tomorrow.'

None of them replied. Too traumatised.

Why didn't you go with the Prince? It was a chance to escape, BJ said.

A demon Prince has good reason to kill Frankie. If it was just me I might think about it, but I won't jeopardise my little boy.

The King came in. 'I helped him sleep. Do you want me to do the same for them?'

I looked around at the terrified children. 'Yes.'

I moved aside as she put her hand on each child's head in turn, sending them to sleep. She gestured for me to join her in the living room and I followed her out.

She linked her hands behind her back. 'Well done. I'll give you your own room in the Celestial Palace as a reward; you won't have to sleep in the kitchen.'

I suppressed the thrill of joy and gratitude at the King's kindness and generosity. My own room; what a treasure. I stopped and realised: great, Stockholm syndrome after only nine weeks of incarceration.

It's not a surprising reaction, Aunty Emma, but I'll remind you if you start to fall.

'Thank you,' I said.

'Continue to serve the children this well and I may find other ways to reward you,' she said. 'You could go shopping again. Or spend a few hours with the Turtle.' She gazed into my eyes. 'If you bring Simone in for me, I will reward you *handsomely*.'

'If you hear about her, let me know,' I said. 'I'm seriously worried about her. I've been trying to contact her for ages and she's not responding.'

'I will,' she said. She pointed at the kitchen door. 'Go back to bed. You'll need an early start to have everything packed for the move. Do you want me to knock you out as well?'

I backed away towards the kitchen, my skin crawling at the idea of touching her. 'No, it's fine. I'll see you tomorrow.'

'I'll put two Dukes on the door for tonight,' she said, and turned to the bull's head, taking male human form to speak to him. 'Now for you.'

The Duke fell to one knee and lowered his head.

'You jumped in to defend a woman and a child when a demon senior to you — a Prince — attacked them. You had no orders to guard them and no reason to help. That is conduct most unbecoming for a demon of your seniority.'

'The child is your adopted son and there could be a considerable reward for protecting it,' the Duke said. 'It was a gamble.'

'And then you *stayed* to guard when I took over, again without orders to do so. Do you have a death wish?'

The Duke dropped his bull's head. 'I think there may be something wrong with me, Father. Was my mother part-human?'

'Stand up,' the King said.

The Duke rose to his feet and towered over us.

The King generated black energy, glowing above his hands.

The Duke raised his muzzle, ready to die.

'That's black chi,' I said. 'You *can* generate it.'

'Of course I can, I'm the only one,' the King said, and threw it at the Duke.

'No!' I shouted, then stopped, confused.

The Duke changed from a bull's-head demon to a big brown humanoid. It looked at its clawed hands, one and then the other, then fell to one knee and saluted the Demon King. 'I will not betray your trust, Majesty.'

'I don't know what number that one was, but you can have his number and his Nest. Kill everything in it or you'll share his fate.'

'My pleasure, Majesty,' the Duke said, and disappeared.

'Wait,' I said. 'Black chi promotes them?'

'Of course it does. Or demotes them, depending how I use it. It can be very destructive if I use too much, but just the right amount and I can turn a thrall into a Mother, or a Duke into a Prince.'

'And if a Prince takes it from you, they become King,' I said, understanding. 'What if you do it to a lesser demon?'

He shrugged. 'Depends on the demon.' He glanced sharply at me. 'Have you seen black chi before? Only the King has it.'

I didn't reply.

'The Turtle can generate it? I often wondered if he was a King in exile.'

'I think it's part of him as Dark Lord,' I said.

'All the more reason.' He went out into the living room. 'Go to sleep. Big day tomorrow.'

'All the more reason for what?' I said, but he closed the kitchen door on me.

I sat on the floor, tried to generate black chi and failed.

You used to be a Demon King? BJ said with awe.

No, it was residual effects from being merged with Xuan Wu, who, apparently, really is a King in exile.

I wrapped myself in my thin blanket on the floor and tried to work out a way that the Xuan Wu's nature could be used as a strategic advantage. As long as he was in the cage we were safe, but we would never be free.

25

The next day the King came early in Kitty form, with a few thralls to carry the boxes and bags. I had packed for everybody and our suitcases were in the living room. All the children sat on the couch, waiting for transport.

'Oh, you stupid woman, why did you pack up the other kids?' the King said. 'I never said they were coming. They'll come later when I bring their mothers down to take them.' She glared at the children. 'Take their bags into their rooms and unpack. They're coming later.'

Didn't the King say the other kids were coming? I asked BJ.

Processing ... yes. But she didn't say when. She's trying to make you distrust your memory. She's brainwashing you, Aunty Emma, be careful.

The small demons picked up the other kids' bags. One of them grabbed my striped canvas bag and I stopped it.

'That's mine.'

'Nothing's yours,' the demon said, and backhanded me away, but left the bag.

'All right, Frankie, are you ready?' the King said, her hands clasped in front of her with forced delight.

'I want my friends,' Frankie said, unsure. 'I don't want to leave them here if it's dangerous.'

'They'll be fine,' the King said. 'They're coming along in a couple of days, after I have their room fixed up. The Dukes will guard them.' She put her hand out to Frankie. 'So let's go, eh? Come and see your house in Heaven.'

Frankie went to her and took her hand.

'Emma,' the King said, and gestured with her head. I put my hand on Frankie's shoulder and everything disappeared.

* * *

I woke and had a moment of disorientation. There were no black and silver silk swags on the bed above me, it was bare ceiling. I was still on the Celestial Plane though, so I was either in our Northern Heavens Residence or the apartments in the Celestial Palace ... I looked left and saw a plain wall. John wasn't there. I was on a small hard bed in a single room. Infirmary? Had I been injured?

John?

The bed filled the room from one end to the other, jammed against the wall, with a window above it. I reached up and opened the wooden venetian blind, to see the courtyard where John and I had spoken with Er Lang and the Jade Emperor all that time ago. I was in the Jade Emperor's own Residence in the Celestial Palace ... It all rushed back to me and I bent with pain, then took some deep breaths to calm myself.

I couldn't open the window — it was sealed shut — so I pushed my battered bag to the side to give me enough space to put my feet on the floor. I went out of the room into the kitchen. The surfaces were dull and some of the metal was rusted; the Celestial Palace's fairies were obviously not present.

I took another deep breath of the almost dizzyingly pure air and watched dust motes dancing in the beams of sunshine coming in through the window. I reached across the sink to open the window. A peach tree swayed on the other side, green against the impossibly blue sky with its fluffy white clouds. The Celestial breeze brushed me again and I inhaled deeply, then staggered back into my room, fell face-first on the bed and wept with joy and misery into my pillow.

Aunty Emma, BJ said five minutes later. *Aunty Emma, are you okay? You've been crying …*

I know, I said. *It was too much.*

I sat up and looked around. A small thin towel lay on the end of the bed and I used it to wipe my face.

I'm fine.

I rose and went back into the kitchen. It was devoid of food; I'd need to make a shopping list for the demons. The refrigerator wasn't working — it had a block of ice in a plastic bin on the top shelf to keep it cold — and there were gas camping lanterns on the benchtops. With no Palace fairies present, there was obviously no electricity. I would have to do everything the old-fashioned way.

I went out of the kitchen into the dining room, which contained a six-seater rosewood table and a display unit that had housed vases from all dynasties but was now empty. I went through the living room and stopped at a sliding wooden door fitted with paper screens between the decorative red slats.

It was a courtyard house, with a small garden containing a fish pond in the middle. I hesitated, then carefully slid my foot outside the door and onto the raised veranda that bordered the garden.

Nothing happened, so I walked out onto it and leaned against the railing. The sunlight hit me and I raised my face to its warmth. I couldn't help myself: tears ran down my cheeks, cool where the Celestial breeze touched them. It was nearly three months since I'd last felt the sun's warmth.

The air was fresh with the scent of grass and trees, and birds sang nearby. A fish splashed in the pond, and the sound of the water filled my heart with joy and pain.

John?

No reply.

Simone?

No reply.

BJ, can you contact —

Hello, Emma, Gold said. *Give us a moment.*

Dad and I are arranging a time for you to talk to your family, BJ said. *It will have to be later this evening when you aren't being watched.*

I bent my head to my hands and wiped my eyes, then ran my hand through my hair and retied my ponytail. *Thank you.*

It feels good, doesn't it? BJ said.

You should come out now. You don't need to be in my neck any more.

I had a moment of disorientation, the floor swerving away from me, then everything righted itself.

I think I do, BJ said. *Turn around.*

The Demon King was standing in the dining room in male form.

'Don't try to go out the front door,' he said. 'The guards will stop you.' He gestured to my left, where the wing of the house had three doors opening onto the veranda. 'The first room is mine. Don't go in there either, unless you want a faceful of me doing a couple of Mothers.'

He came to me, took me by the elbow and walked me along the veranda. Two Dukes were stationed outside each door, and they nodded to the King.

'The second door is Frankie's room. He's in there taking a nap right now; he's had too many trips up and down and it's wearing him out. The third door will be for his friends when I bring them up.'

'I understand,' I said.

He released me and walked to the room at the far end of the veranda. This was the Jade Emperor's small hearing room, again stripped of everything valuable. Only the three rosewood couches and the coffee tables between them remained.

'Where's the screen?' I said, gesturing towards the centre couch.

'It was too … bright,' the King said. 'I'm having something more suitable made.'

He walked through the hearing room to the entry hall, where another pair of Dukes stood on either side of the double front doors. The Murasame stood next to the wall on its ebony stand. A pale rectangular patch on the wall showed where one of the Jade Emperor's ink paintings had been removed.

'Don't go out,' the King repeated.

'I understand.'

'Is that the only thing you can say?'

'Can I go into the courtyard?' I said.

'You can't go out of the house, I just told you that!' he snapped.

'No.' I waved one hand towards the fish pond. 'I mean this courtyard. The grass here.'

'Of course you can; what a stupid question. I said you can't go *out*, and that's *in*.'

'Thank you,' I said. 'You need someone to buy food. The house is empty.'

'I know that, stupid. I'll have a couple of servants stationed here.' He lit up with a cruel smile. 'How would you like your little demons back?'

My heart leapt. I hoped that Er Hao was still hidden away, but I had no idea about the other two, and I'd been concerned for them. 'Yi Hao and Smally?'

'Whatever their names are. Do you want them?'

'Yes, please,' I said, trying to hide my delight.

'Yes, please, *Your Majesty*. Say it and they're yours.'

'Yes, please, Your Majesty.'

'Kneel and say it.'

I stared at him. 'You said —'

'Kneel!'

I hesitated, but if I brought my demon staff here, they would be safe and protected. I fell to one knee.

'Both! Head on the floor!' he said with vicious glee.

I hesitated again.

'Do it and I'll give them to you. Or don't, and I'll bring them here and destroy them in front of you. Your choice.'

I pulled my other leg down and kowtowed to him. 'Please, Your Majesty.'

'Suck my dick while you're down there and I'll give you time with the Turtle.'

I didn't reply.

'Whatever.' He turned away. 'Give the guards a shopping list. Make sure all of Frankie's favourite food is on it, and include a couple of hearts for me.'

I pulled myself to my feet, thrilled at the thought of my demons being stationed with me. 'I will.'

'Yes, Majesty.'

I didn't reply.

'Say it!'

'Yes, Majesty,' I said with defeat.

His expression was full of satisfaction. 'Now we're getting somewhere.' He pointed at the living room. 'Frankie's toys are in the boxes. Sort them out and have them ready for him when he wakes.'

'Yes, Majesty.'

'See, that wasn't so hard, was it? Continue to behave and I might even give you access to the bathroom and you can have a shower.'

I tried to control my expression as the shock of pure joy ran through me. Washing with a washcloth in the kitchen sink had been adequate, but a shower with hot water would be *wonderful*.

I had a better idea. 'If I continue to behave, will you give me my stone back?'

'I don't have your stone.'

'I know you do. You have to. You have everything in the Heavens.'

'As soon as Frankie's on the throne, he can order the stone to go to you. It's sworn to the Celestial, isn't it?'

'Yes.'

'There you are. Continue to show sufficient respect and I'll give it back to you. You are doing very well. Now start work on those toys,' he said, and went out the front doors, the Dukes saluting him as he passed.

I headed to the living room to sort out the boxes.

Stockholm syndrome, BJ said.

Shower syndrome, I replied with amusement. *Don't worry.*

You don't hate him, Aunty Emma. You don't seem to feel much at all. I'm concerned that his manipulation is working.

I'm working from the inside while Simone works from the outside, I said. *Just keep reminding me that I'm not actually on his side.*

See? Not time for me to leave you yet.

Thanks for being here.

She sounded amused. *No problem at all.*

After I'd read Frankie a bedtime story, I turned the light off and went out of his room, through the large kitchen and into my servant's room. I sat on the bed.

Okay, BJ, put my dad through.

Hello, love.

I bent with agony and tried to stop my eyes from filling. I gave up and wiped them on the thin towel. *Hi, Dad.*

Are you okay?

As well as can be expected, I suppose, I said, his compassion breaking me even more. *You're all safe, right? He hasn't done anything to you?*

No, we're fine. All good. We have enough to eat and a roof over our heads, which is better than many. There's talk that the schools may reopen, and David can leave the worksite and go to school.

I wiped my eyes again. *That's good to hear. They have you working?*

We're building a new palace here in the West. I'm one of the lucky ones — I'm wiring it up. Other people are lifting rocks, and I'm taking it easy putting in light fittings. It's a god-awful ugly building. People are saying something about a palace built by someone called Cixi.

Empress Cixi, I said. *She ruled through her son, a puppet Emperor.*

Another one, he said. *And you're with the Emperor? When are you coming to see us?*

Yes, I'm looking after him. I'm not allowed out of the Imperial Residence, but I hope I may be able to visit you eventually.

Can you talk to your mother? he said.

I don't know. BJ?

Not right now, she says she's with a lot of people. Maybe later.

Thanks, love, my father said. *If you do contact her, tell her that I miss her, and that when this work is done I hope we can be together again. And ask her how all the kids are. Jen was in a bad way when I was taken from them.* His voice became urgent. *And keep fighting, Emma! They're coming, I have to stop. I love you!*

26

'So raise your hands like this,' I said, demonstrating. 'Then lower them gently, like they're on strings.'

Frankie's little face filled with concentration. He did the move, then his expression went strange and he went straight into Holding the Ball, then did the next four moves flawlessly.

'Oh,' I said. 'You've been learning already. Who's been teaching you?'

He dropped his hands. 'Nobody. It just … came.'

'Not really surprising,' I said. 'Okay. Let's do those four moves —'

'Why isn't he learning with the training sword?' the King said from the dining room.

'Because he's not ready yet,' I said, showing Frankie how to do Grasping the Bird's Tail.

He had it first try.

'He's tall enough now, isn't he?' the King said. 'He looks about twelve!'

'He's tall enough, but he doesn't have good enough coordination. He needs to learn the moves slowly without a weapon before he learns them fast with one.'

'You have to teach him everything,' the King said suspiciously.

'The way he's learning, in six months he'll be teaching me,' I said. 'He is very much his father's son.'

'Superior to the girl in every way,' the King said softly.

'I wouldn't say that. Simone has her strengths.'

'Not with this,' the King said, gesturing towards Frankie, who had moved into Brush Knee and Twist without being shown.

'His mother's a practitioner,' I said. 'Hers wasn't.' I nodded to Frankie. 'Let's go through them again.'

We performed the moves together; he had already learnt as much as I had in my first four lessons with John.

'You really are exceptional, Frankie.'

'I want to use the sword,' he said, his eyes unseeing as he concentrated.

'It won't be long before you're ready for it.' I spoke to the King without looking away from Frankie. 'Where are my demons? I could use their assistance in caring for five children, particularly when one of them continually bullies the other four.'

'You didn't tell me the littlest one could drive a bulldozer!' the King said, pulling a chair from the dining table and putting it on the veranda so he could sit and watch us. 'You can have her as soon as she's finished in the Summer Palace. Why the hell were you using her as a handmaid when she could operate heavy machinery?'

'She helped rebuild the Mountain, but she didn't enjoy driving,' I said. 'Too much noise and vibration. She was happier in the Imperial household. It made her feel special to be working directly with the Imperial family.'

'No wonder you lost the war, throwing away valuable skills like that.' He crossed his legs, relaxed, as he watched us. 'I'm looking for the other two, but they don't believe me and they're hiding. Maybe make a video and put it on YouTube saying to come in?'

'I don't have internet access,' I said. 'Give me a computer and I'll do it. Push your foot further to the side, Frankie. Good.'

'Good try,' he said. 'If they won't come in, I'll give you a couple of thralls. The kitchen is disgusting.'

'I'd rather have my own demons.'

'Not your demons any more. Mine. Everything is mine. I'll bring them when I find them. They can't hide forever.'

He rose and went out.

Late that evening I'd put Frankie to bed and was cleaning the kitchen again, when the King called my name from the living room. I went in to see him. He had Amy hanging limply off one arm and he was holding Little Jade's hand with the other. He released Little Jade and she stood silent and terrified.

'Look after her,' he said and disappeared, taking Amy with him.

I went to Little Jade and hugged her. 'Hello, darling.'

She looked around. 'Where's Mummy? Mummy was here. Is she okay?' She sniffled, then wailed, 'Mummy!'

The King reappeared with Amy and Richie. He released Richie and pushed him towards me, then rotated a still unconscious Amy and dropped her onto the couch. 'Look after them.' He disappeared.

'Mummy!' Jade screamed, and she and Richie ran to Amy.

She was lying half-off the sofa, so I made her more comfortable, then put my hand on her forehead to check her. Drained, but she would be okay. Little Jade and Richie climbed up on the sofa with her.

'Mummy. Mummy!' Little Jade shouted, lifting Amy's hand to her own cheek.

'Is she dead?' Richie said, his voice full of tears.

'She's fine,' I said. 'She's just drained from the trip up here. Sit carefully next to her and look after her, and she'll wake up soon.'

'Are you sure?'

'Absolutely positive.'

Little Jade lay next to Amy, still holding her hand. 'Please be okay, Mummy.'

The King reappeared on the other side of the room holding my sister Jennifer and Matthew. Jennifer collapsed, and the King dragged her to the other sofa and dropped her.

Matthew hugged her where she lay. 'Mummy! Mummy! Wake up!'

'So much noise,' the King said with distaste. 'Shut them up, Emma.'

I went to Matthew and took his hand. 'Mummy's fine, Mattie. She just needs to sleep for a little while. She'll wake up soon.'

Amy started to come around.

'Mummy!' Little Jade shrieked, and wriggled off her.

Amy sat up, bleary-eyed and confused. She saw Little Jade and Richie and pulled them into a huge hug. 'My babies. My babies!'

Jennifer came around shortly after, grabbed Matthew and held him tight against her chest. She saw me, and turned away.

'Frankie, your friends are here,' the King called without looking away from us.

Frankie came in, saw the children, and lit up. 'You're back!'

Everybody ignored him.

'You should greet your Emperor,' the King said, but again the children ignored him. 'All right, time to say goodbye to your mothers, because they can't stay here.'

The children howled.

'Don't send their mothers away, they need them!' I said.

'You said they didn't need their mothers, that they'd be fine with you, and you'd provide better care anyway,' the King said.

'Don't be ridiculous, Emma would never say anything like that,' Amy said.

'Beside the point. Say goodbye.'

'I'm not going,' Amy said. 'These are my children and they need me.'

'They have Emma,' the King said.

'Matthew's only a baby!' Jennifer said.

'Time for you to go.'

'What can I do to stay?' Jennifer said. 'Do you need someone else to look after them? This is a big house, does Emma need help with the housework? Let me help. I'll do anything!'

'Me too,' Amy said. 'I'll do anything to stay here.'

'Nothing here for you except distracting my son's playmates. Go home.'

The King waved to one of the Dukes guarding the door. The Duke went to Amy, took her shoulder and disappeared.

'Mummy!' Jade screeched.

Jen stood up to shout at the King. 'You already killed one of my sons. The other one's working for you. Leave one for me! Just one!' She pulled Matthew into her and her voice was hoarse with tears. 'Let me have one baby. I have no children left.' She turned to me. 'Emma, don't just stand there, stop them! Do something!'

The Duke reappeared, pushed Matthew away from his mother, and disappeared with her. Matthew and Richie wailed, then dissolved into racking sobs.

'What a racket!' the King said. 'Shut them up, Emma!'

'You just took their mothers away,' I said. 'There's no way I can make them calm unless you bring their mothers back.'

'I told you that their mothers would be a distraction from their real job of playing with Frankie,' the King said. He gestured towards the children. 'Stop them.'

The Western King entered. 'What is this damn noise? I'll sort it out.' He stood over the children. 'Shut the hell up right now or you'll get the belt!'

They ran from him and huddled together in the corner of the sofa, still crying.

'All right,' the Western King said with grim satisfaction. 'You asked for it.' He summoned a leather belt and folded it over his hand. 'I'll enjoy this. You little shits deserve it.'

The children screamed, ducking their heads and putting their hands over them.

He swung the belt at them but I moved faster. I put myself between him and the children and took the blow on my back. I bent over the children where they cringed on the sofa, taking the blows for them, and they clutched at me.

The end of the belt missed me and hit them, making them shriek with pain.

'Stop it, you're scaring them even more,' I shouted, but the blows didn't subside.

'Daddy, Daddy, please stop,' Frankie said, his voice soft and terrified.

'Francis, stop, you're not achieving anything,' the King said.

'I'll achieve peace of mind,' the Western King grunted, swinging again.

The buckle hit Matthew and he screamed through his sobs.

'Stop and we can discuss this,' I said. 'All you need to do is talk —'

'Talk!' he bellowed, and swung the belt again. The buckle slapped the back of my head. He continued hitting us in time to his words. 'They don't need talk, they need discipline. A good solid beating now and then never hurt anyone. Spoilt brats.'

'Daddy,' Frankie said from the side of the room. 'Don't hit my friends. Stop hitting them.' His voice rose in pitch. 'Stop!'

The Western King rounded on him. 'Shut up or you'll be next. It's been a while since you had a good thrashing!'

Frankie cringed away and hid behind the Eastern King.

The Western King reached down and dragged me off the children. He threw me to the other side of the room with strength I couldn't fight. 'Get the fuck out of my way. These pathetic runts need to learn a lesson.'

The Eastern King put his hand on his arm. 'Darling, stop. You'll make little Frankie hate you even more.'

'Good!' the Western King said. 'You spoil the child. Look at him — he'll grow up weak and indulged. By the time I was his age, I'd already killed twenty nest mates.'

'You have what you wanted,' I said, and pointed at the children who were huddled in the corner of the couch, wide-eyed and silent. 'They're quiet now.'

The Western King stormed back to the children and prepared to hit them again.

'No, Francis, not in front of Frankie,' the Eastern King said.

The Western King slapped Matthew's shoulder and he started to cry again. The other two children jumped off the couch to run away, and the King grabbed them and threw them back on.

The Eastern King took True Form: blood-red and skinless, with a snake tail. He towered over everybody, his head nearly touching the ceiling. The children shrieked with terror.

'Francis, stop this now or I will make you stop!' he roared, his voice deep and resonating.

The Western King hesitated, his face a mask of rage, then he cuffed Little Jade on the side of the head and charged out.

The Eastern King shrank back down to human form. 'I will be so glad when Frankie's finally on that damn throne and we can start rewriting the rules,' he said, his voice mild. 'The first thing we'll do is order everybody to love him and be happy to obey his every wish.' He nodded to me. 'Sort them out, but leave the best bed for Edu, I'm bringing her tomorrow. Come on, Frankie, bedtime.'

'Okay, Uncle George,' Frankie said, his huge glazed eyes speaking volumes about how the Western King had been treating him. As the King led him out, Frankie looked back at me, his eyes still unfocused.

I sat on the floor with my back to the couch and wiped my hands over my eyes. I turned to put my hand on Little Jade's face; she was all right. Matthew had a couple of scratches where the belt buckle had broken the skin, and I healed them for him.

'Can you bring Mummy back now, Aunty Emma?' Matthew said. 'Can we go find her?'

'Oh, darling,' I said. 'I need to explain some stuff for you.'

* * *

Matthew, Little Jade and Richie took a long time to fall asleep in the room next to Frankie's. Once they'd settled, I left them in their bunks and went next door to check on Frankie. The King was gone, and Frankie was sitting up in bed looking at one of his picture books.

He closed the book. 'Are they okay?'

'They miss their mummies. They'll be sad for a while,' I said.

'I understand. Mummy says that when I'm Emperor, she'll bring friends for me who are more fun.' He looked away. 'But I like these friends. They're nicer.' He dropped his voice to a whisper. 'Edu's mean. I don't want Mummy to bring her tomorrow.'

'I don't either,' I said, my voice low.

'Would the other children still be my friends if I brought their mummies back?' he said.

'They would love you forever, I think,' I said. 'They've been having fun playing with you when they're not sad about their mummies. If they could be with their mothers, I think they'd still come and play with you. They like you.'

'Mummy says that when I'm Emperor, people will have to do what I tell them, and I can *make* them love me.'

'Yes. I hope you won't hurt people.'

'I don't want to make people love me. I don't want to hurt people. I want everybody to be happy,' he said. He sighed with misery. 'But it seems whatever I do, people are hurt.'

'So young to be so wise,' I said. 'I can help you. Advise you.'

'That's what the ... she ... I thought,' he said.

'The Lady said that?' I said softly.

He nodded, then looked around. 'Be careful.'

'I will.' I put my arm around him. 'You will have to be very careful as well. When you're Emperor, if you want something to happen, it will happen.'

He watched me silently, obviously not understanding the full import of my words.

'If you want it to rain, it will rain. If you want the children to love you, they will love you. If you want someone to die, they will die.'

'I could make people die?' His breath caught. 'What if I'm mad with someone?' He clutched me. 'I don't want this!'

'Wise,' I said. 'I will help you to control your power. Learning to use your sword is a good start.' I gave him a squeeze. 'You and me together, we can do our best to make everybody happy.'

'Thanks, Emma,' he said, his voice small. He brightened. 'Can I stop Daddy from hitting my friends?'

'No. You'll only be able to order people from this part of the world. He's not from here.'

'Well, poop,' he said, and we chuckled together.

I kissed him on the forehead. 'You are a very special little boy and I love you with all my heart.'

'I love you too.' He nestled down under the silk quilt. 'Can you stay while I go to sleep?'

I brushed my hand over his forehead. 'I will be here for you forever. You are my whole world.'

My heart ached. That was the first time he'd said that to me. I felt a small moment of triumph, then resolved to make sure that the Demon King never took him away from me. Frankie and I would have to be careful not to be too affectionate in front of him.

* * *

Late the next morning the Zhu sisters — Bo Niang and Bei Niang, two of the Generals from the Thirty-Six — came in the front door accompanied by a Duke. They were both in their mid-teens female forms and wearing the black-and-white of servants, the same as me.

'You're kidding,' I said. 'He said he'd give me *demon* servants.'

'Things are all topsy-turvy, Emma,' Bo said. 'The humans are servants, and the demons are masters.'

'New servants?' Frankie said, watching us.

'This is Comet,' I said, gesturing towards Bo, 'and Esteem,' I indicated Bei. 'Or Bo and Bei. They're strong and smart and really cool.'

'You're here to help Emma?' Frankie asked them.

Bei went to him and knelt before him. 'And you must be Frankie.'

Frankie nodded.

'Where are Gold's kids?' Bo asked me.

I gestured with my head. 'Watching television.'

We all went into the living room. Edu had once again taken the entire couch and forced the other children to sit on the floor.

'Aunty Bei! Aunty Bo!' Little Jade shouted, and ran to them. 'Where's your cool armour?'

'Hello, little dragon,' Bei said. 'And little Richie. Hello, Matthew. Who's this?'

'This is Edu. Human spawn of the Demon King himself,' I said.

'I'm a Demon Prince and I'll be *Empress*,' Edu said. 'And when I am, I'll kill —'

'Don't even think about finishing that sentence,' I said.

'I'm terrible with kids, but it looks like you do need help,' Bo said to me.

'I don't mind helping out with the kids,' Bei said. 'Bo can help out around the house.'

'You're Celestial Generals,' I said, exasperated. 'You shouldn't be doing housework!'

'Caring for the next generation is the highest honour anyone can attain,' Bei said with dignity. 'Now show Bo where the laundry is. She's good with machines and stuff.'

Bo nodded. 'Leave the kids with Bei, and show me what needs to be done.'

I hesitated, then said, 'I really appreciate it, guys.'

'When the Little Emperor is crowned and the Celestial Palace returns, we'll probably be back to laying bricks in the new Western Palace,' Bo said as I guided her to the overflowing laundry. Five kids generated more dirty clothes than I could keep up with, particularly when I couldn't go outside to hang them to dry. She saw the pile. 'Oh, my. Go look after the little ones, Emma, let me handle this.'

'I really appreciate it, Bo.'

'The Demon King's an idiot,' Bo said. 'I'm terrible with children. I have no affinity for them and I've never wanted any of my own. Marshal Xiao adores kids — he'd be a much better choice — but the Demon King brought us purely because we're women.' She lowered her voice. 'That's Lord Xuan's son? And yours?'

'Yes. But I'm not allowed to tell him.'

'I know, I was told that too.' She smiled and patted my arm. 'He seems a nice kid. I look forward to telling him stories about some of the crazy shit the thirty-seven of us pulled together.'

'I can't wait to hear them too,' I said.

She gave me a gentle push. 'Go look after the kids. It'll be fine.'

* * *

Later that day the King came in male human form, with a Duke holding a digital tablet.

'Take the children outside,' he said, and I rose. 'Not you, Emma,' he said. 'Here.'

He gestured towards the dining table for me to join him. The Duke passed him the tablet.

The King gestured dismissively towards Bei. 'Take them outside. I want to talk to Emma without any of them present.'

'As you wish,' Bei said. 'Mei Mei!'

'Coming,' Bo said. She came to the kitchen doorway, saw the Demon King and scowled.

'Take the children out,' the King said again. He saw Bo's face. 'Do as you're told!'

She sneered. 'Majesty.'

She and Bei took the children out the front doors with a Duke accompanying them. The children yelled with delight as they took off running. I winced. They didn't spend enough time outside.

'Right,' the King said, all business. 'I need your advice here.'

He flipped through the tablet until he came to a photograph of a blonde fourteen-year-old girl. She had strong cheekbones and a light dusting of freckles under her mischievous blue eyes.

I took the tablet from him, trying to remember where I knew her from, and then it clicked. 'Kimberley.'

'Yes. Your dead friend's daughter. What was her name?' He checked the tablet. 'Louise. One of the Tiger's wives. This is Princess Kimberley, daughter of the Bai Hu, a mortal human. She's also the daughter of your dead friend, so you'll want to look after her.' He looked up at me. 'What do you think?'

'What do I think about what?'

He sighed with exasperation. 'For Frankie!'

'For Frankie *what*?'

'Are you completely stupid? I told you about this before. He needs a wife from each of the Bastions to seal his reign. If he marries a daughter from each Bastion, and has Edu as his Empress, nobody will ever stand against him. So what do you think — Kimberley from the West?' He cocked his head to study her photo. 'A bit white for me, but pretty enough.'

'You can't be finding wives for him — he's two years old.'

'I know, it should have been done before he was born. Okay, no objections to Kimberley; what about Eva?' He showed me a photo of the Phoenix's half-human daughter Evangeline, whose African-American father had given her a glowing dark complexion, rich brown eyes and afro hair. 'Nice counterpoint to the white one. Eva can work energy and fire, and there's talk she may be able to manipulate yang. She's a sweet girl as well, and I think she's already friends with Simone.'

'Frankie doesn't need wives, George.'

'But he does. This is politics. We need to seal the empire, and if he fathers grandchildren for the Four Winds they'll never rebel against him. You've obviously no problem with Eva either. How about this one?' He showed me a photo of Jackie. 'Granddaughter of the Dragon King, daughter of the Blue Dragon, so royal dragon both ways. Lovely pure-Asian girl. No attachments; both of her parents are Immortals held in the cells in Hell, and both her nest mates are dead.'

'I know who Jackie is — her mother is the Jade Girl. She's part of the family,' I said.

'Even better.' He flipped through more photos on the tablet. 'Now I need your help to find the last wife.'

'He'll marry *all* of them?' I said, incredulous.

'One from the North,' he said. 'I'm doing you a favour here, allowing you to care for your friends' children when he takes them as wives. So do something for me.'

'I don't know anyone suitable in the North that Frankie isn't related to on his father's side,' I said.

'Yeah, the only one is the black kid, Buffy, but she's fully human and adopted. Might as well be a servant. So the first choice is Simone.'

All the breath left me in a long gasp. 'She's his *sister*!'

'I know. I checked the genetics and it turns out they're too closely related. You and Simone's mother had a great deal of genetic heritage in common.' He sighed with feeling. 'Such a shame, she'd be perfect. If they were pure demon it wouldn't be an issue, but humans are trouble. So I need you to contact Simone and bring her in for me.'

'She can't marry him, so you don't need her.'

'That's exactly why I do need her. Her half-demon daughter would be good enough.' He smiled. 'They'd be perfect. One of my spawn for the fifth wife and we have the complete set. Like a winning hand of cards.'

I jumped to my feet. 'I will not bring Simone here for you to rape her.'

'I'm not into rape, you know that. She'll be perfectly willing once Frankie takes the throne and is giving the orders.'

BJ, tell Simone. Tell her to run from the East right now.

'Good. You're talking to her. Now tell me where she is,' he said.

I'm sorry, Aunty Emma, she doesn't answer, BJ said. *Nobody in the stone network has seen her.*

'She doesn't answer me. I have no idea where she is.'

He studied me.

'I'm telling the truth,' I said.

'Fine.' He stood. 'As soon as Frankie's enthroned and has control, he'll order her to come in and we can start the procedures anyway.'

For god's sake, BJ, tell Simone to run!

I am, BJ said with misery. *But she's still not answering.*

The King handed the tablet to the guard Duke. 'Those children were thrilled to be allowed outside,' he said to me. 'You need to take them out more.'

'I can't. I'm not allowed out of the house.'

'Yes, you are,' he said. 'Take them out every day.'

'You ordered me to stay inside.'

'Well, now I'm ordering you to take the children outside!' he said loudly. 'There! Does nobody listen when I give orders?' He went to the door. 'Try to run away and I will make these children suffer.'

'You don't need to worry, I'll never leave my ... Frankie,' I said.

'Good,' he said, and went out.

I moved to follow him through the front doors, but the Duke blocked my way.

'You heard him,' I said. 'Let me out!'

The Duke hesitated, then opened the doors for me.

'Assign me a guard,' I said to the King. 'A Celestial may take exception to the fact that I'm working for you.'

'Good point,' the King said, and gestured for one of the other Dukes to escort me. 'And it's Celestial Regent.'

The guard escorted me through the front doors and along an alley with three-metre-high red walls on either side. It was a defensive feature to protect the Jade Emperor in case the Celestial Palace was assaulted — which hadn't worked. The Northern Imperial apartments were on the other side of that wall, and I remembered the courtyard where John and I had sat on the grass all that time ago, enjoying the sunshine together. I wondered if the demons had taken down the *Xuan Tian Shang Di* sign that hung on the wall over John's desk; a gift from the Jade Emperor in his own hand. Probably destroyed.

I made a mental note to have a calligraphy teacher assigned to Frankie the minute his characters were fluent. At present they were the clumsy attempts of a young child, but he was learning quickly.

The wall opened to a moon gate to our left: the entrance to the staff quarters. A large grassy court was on the other side of the wall, with a couple of wide shady mulberry trees; natural ones, not Shen. This was the relaxation garden for the human and Shen staff when their employers visited the Palace. The quarters were deserted, and the children were running and shouting on the grass, sharing a game with Bo and Bei.

I sat on a stone bench to watch them, and the Duke stationed himself next to the moon gate. The children saw me and waved, but didn't stop running. It was probably the first time they'd had a chance since they'd been taken to Hell.

I breathed deeply of the Celestial fresh air and enjoyed the peace. The coronation was in two days, and then everything would change.

27

On the day of the coronation, the Demon King came in Kitty Kwok form wearing a many-layered robe of Imperial gold embroidered with six-toed dragons. The sleeves were long and sheer, and her hair was done in a complex style and decorated with golden phoenixes. She brought our robes in cardboard boxes, and laid them on the couch.

'These are your Emperor's clothes, Frankie. Come and get dressed.' She opened a second box and pulled out the brown nun's robe and tossed it to me. 'Shave your head and put this on, and be quick about it.'

It was still too early for Bo and Bei to arrive, so I shaved my head myself in my little room. It took a while and made a mess on the floor, particularly since my razor was blunt from overuse. I pulled the brown robe on and tied the sash, then found a dustpan and broom, swept up the hair and threw it away.

When I emerged, Frankie giggled. 'You look like a man! I can't tell whether you're a man or a lady!'

I made my voice low and gruff. 'That's because I'm awesome.'

He dissolved into cackles of laughter, and the King tutted at him as she tied the belt of his robe. 'Emma isn't a man or a lady. She can't have babies, so she's a nothing.'

'That's sad, Emma,' Frankie said.

'Keep your mouth shut,' the King told me before I could say anything.

'We match, Mummy,' Frankie said, holding his sleeve against her robe. 'We're the same.'

She kissed the top of his head. 'We will always be the same.'

'Why don't my friends have fun costumes?' he said.

'They're all somewhere else. Today is just you,' she said, and rose. 'Turn around, let me see.' He spun for her and she patted his head. 'You are the cutest little Emperor ever.'

'No, you are the cutest, Mummy,' he said.

The Western King came in from the bedroom wearing a European white dress uniform with full regalia: peaked cap, gold-fringed epaulettes, crimson sash across his chest, multiple star-shaped medals, and a sword hanging from his side.

'You look awesome too, Father,' Frankie said. 'You're so handsome. I think your clothes are better than ours.'

'You think the clothes your mother made aren't good enough?' the Western King said.

'No, no, of course not,' Frankie said, his voice going up with panic. 'You look so handsome, but those clothes would only ...' He hesitated, then gathered himself. 'I don't think I'm good enough to wear something like that.'

The Western King put his hands on his belt and his sword. 'That's right. You aren't.' He nodded to the Eastern King. 'You look spectacular, my love. But are you sure you don't want to wear a uniform too? You know how much I like it when you wear one.'

'Once we're established,' the Eastern King said.

The Western King shrugged. 'Won't be long before we have full control, if it works like you say it will.'

'It will.' She grinned at him. 'I'll wear a uniform later if you like.'

'You read my mind.'

'Time to go,' she said to Frankie. 'There's a special carriage out there; you'll be pulled by *dragons*.'

'Ooh, cool,' he said with delight.

'Follow, Emma,' the King said, and we went out the front door.

We walked the hundred metres down the alley to the end, where it opened into a paved court with a dragon fountain in the centre.

A cheering crowd had gathered there, held back by demon guards. The people were all wearing new brightly coloured T-shirts and waving small coloured flags — obviously props given to them by the King. The Palace buildings were draped in silk swags of Imperial gold that matched the roof tiles, and gold and red banners flew from flagpoles around the buildings.

An open carriage, Western-style, stood in the middle of the court, with a dozen Dukes on demon horses stationed around it. Six smaller demons stood holding gold silk umbrellas. Jade and another green dragon I didn't recognise were in the carriage's traces. Both of them looked tired, and their scales were dull with infirmity.

Are you all right, Jade? I said as I followed the directions of the guards to the rear of the carriage, so I could walk beside it.

The two Kings climbed in, and sat with Frankie between them.

Emma! Jade said. *Where's Jackie? She wasn't here when I was brought up to pull the carriage. She was taken two days ago. Do you know where she is? Did they hurt her? She wasn't eaten, was she? So many people have disappeared —*

Don't be concerned, I said. *Jackie hasn't been harmed; she's being cared for.*

But why?

I hesitated, then decided to tell her the truth. *She'll be groomed to marry the young Emperor.*

But the demons ... She hesitated. *Will the Little Emperor hurt her?*

No, he's a caring and compassionate child, and he may send her back to you when he discovers the marriage plans. Even if he doesn't reject her, the marriage won't happen for a long time. In the meantime, she won't be harmed; I'll make sure of it.

Oh, thank the Heavens.

'Go,' the Eastern King said, and the dragons pushed into the traces.

Jade made a soft sound of pain as the carriage started to move. *Please care for her.*

I will. After the coronation she'll be moved into the consort's residence.

I could hear Jade grunting with effort in my head. The traces fitted her poorly and she wasn't built to pull a load.

Will there be other consorts? she said.

The King plans to have four concubines, one from each of the Winds' houses — Jackie will be the East — and a demon Empress.

Thank you! she said, relieved. *So that's what happened to the girls. They all disappeared on the same day. I will tell their parents; they will be so happy to hear that they're alive and not eaten. Thank you, Emma, thank you so much.*

We turned onto the main thoroughfare through the Celestial Palace, travelling along its wide boulevard with border plantings of peach trees. The crowd on either side of the road, all underweight and desperate-looking, cheered and waved their little flags in a sea of bright colours. Stony-faced demon sentries flanked the route, and obvious plain-clothes guards stalked among the crowds, alert for trouble.

Don't thank me, I said to Jade. *This is a catastrophe for them. Their lives will be ruined.*

They will have lives, and they are not in the Pits.

That should not be something to celebrate.

We arrived in the square. The entire area, three hundred metres across, was completely empty except for demon guards in human form stationed at regular intervals around its edge. The Hall of Supreme Harmony stood on the square's northern side.

The Eastern King took Frankie's hand and guided him out of the carriage and led him to a sedan chair carried by four horse-head Dukes. I followed in the entourage, giving Jade a friendly pat on her scales as I went past.

I will care for her, I said. *I'll talk to Frankie about letting her see you.*

Thank you, Emma.

I followed the sedan chair as the Dukes carried it over the centre bridge that spanned the fung shui waterway, and then onto the carpet through the empty square up to the Hall of Supreme Harmony, the riders and parasol carriers flanking us.

At the hall, the Dukes carried the chair over the marble ramp and up to the huge double doors five metres above the stone pavers of the square. The doors opened and they carried the chair inside, then stopped. The riders and attendants remained on the platform outside.

The hall was full of silent demons: Mothers and Dukes, with a few smiling human copies from the Earthly. They stood on either side of the carpeted aisle, their faces glowing with triumph.

The Dukes carefully lowered the sedan chair, and Frankie and the Demon Kings stepped out. The Eastern King's expression was bright with pleasure as she walked Frankie up the aisle to the dais, the demons silent around them. I followed, and nobody stopped me.

They climbed the stairs onto the dais and I followed them there too. I was flooded with memories from this place. John had knelt on that carpet many times in his majestic Celestial Form. I'd stood on the dais as First Heavenly General, guarding the Jade Emperor. Simone had made a wildly stupid oath here that would limit her choices for love in the future. All was gone, and the throne was empty.

Stand at the back of the dais and keep your damn head down and your hands together like a nun, the King said, and I obeyed.

The King put her hand on Frankie's shoulder and stood at his right, facing the crowd. 'Demonkind,' she said, and the hall went even more silent. 'We won. The Heavens are ours. One of our own will take the Jade Throne and a bright new dynasty will arise for all of us. We will recover from the shame of being driven from the Earth by the Xuan Wu, and be stronger than we ever were. We are the rightful rulers of the Three Platforms and the Nine Heavens.' She looked around at them. 'I have fulfilled my promise, my children. Welcome to life in the sunshine.'

The demons went wild, cheering so loudly that the clerestory windows above us rattled.

The Demon King raised her hand. 'Let's see if this works, shall we?' She looked down to speak to Frankie. 'Time to take your throne, Little Emperor.'

She took his hand and guided him to the Jade Throne that was carved with six-toed dragons. He stepped up onto a footstool, turned with his face full of concentration and sat on the gold silk cushions. As one, the hall went silent. Everyone except the Western King fell to one knee.

'Wen sui, wen sui, wen wen sui,' we all said in unison.

The sun broke through the windows above us, shining rays of light that shifted across the dais. Frankie's expression went blank, then filled with a new level of heightened awareness. His robes changed to fit him better and he sat with more confidence. Two Palace fairies in silvery robes materialised on either side of the throne.

'It worked,' the Eastern King said, breathless. 'Tell us to rise, darling.'

'Rise,' Frankie said, and everybody stood up. 'Wow,' he added under his breath.

'Now to test if you really do have full control,' the King said. 'A girl has been hiding from you since you came up here; she doesn't want to come and play. I think you should tell her to. Order Princess Simone of the Northern Heavens to present, Frankie.'

The silence in the hall deepened as the demons held their breath expectantly.

'Um ...' Frankie raised his voice. 'Princess Simone of the Northern Heavens is to present!'

Simone appeared in front him wearing her robes and armour. She fell to one knee. 'Wen sui, wen sui, wen wen sui.'

The demons erupted again in cheers and celebration.

The Eastern King's face was full of joy. 'It worked. It worked!'

The Western King grabbed her, lifted her and spun her around. 'You are the best!'

She kissed him hard. 'So are you.'

He released her and she took Frankie's hands. 'Oh, my darling, things are about to become very, very good for us. I love you so much.' She rested her cheek on the top of his head. 'Everything will be all right now.'

The demons were raucously celebrating. A few fights broke out at the back of the hall. The guards dealt with them quickly, destroying all the demons involved and any nearby as well.

'Tell her: "Go to the Northern Heavens Celestial Palace Residence and stay there",' the Eastern King said.

'Go to the Northern Heavens Celestial Palace Residence,' Frankie said.

'And stay there!' the Western King shouted.

'And stay there,' Frankie added, his voice small.

Simone disappeared without rising.

'Now the last part, then we can have a really nice lunch,' the King said.

She guided Frankie off the throne, back down the stairs and along the carpet to the exit. I followed them out through the double doors to the platform that overlooked the great court. The white marble balustrade was carved with cloud patterns representing the heavenly clouds that surrounded the entire Celestial Palace complex. The wind whistled across the empty space below.

A pair of Dukes in black armour that mimicked the Imperial Elite uniforms stood on either side of us. One pushed me back so I was standing behind and to the right of Frankie.

'Say, "All the Celestial Shen are ordered to kowtow to the First Serpent Emperor",' the Eastern King told Frankie.

'All Celestial Shen are ordered to kowtow to the First Serpent Emperor,' Frankie said. 'That's me!'

There was a rush of wind across the square and the Celestials appeared in neat rows covering its area. The Four Winds were at the front, with the Generals in ranks on the other side of the carpet. Behind them stood all the Celestials I knew: the senior children of the Four Winds, and the Taoist Immortals. All the Shen of Heaven were there, except for John and the Jade Emperor, who were unable to leave their prisons.

'Down!' one of the Dukes roared, and everybody in the square fell to their knees.

'One kowtow,' the Duke said, and everybody bowed low over their knees, touching their foreheads to the paving.

'Two kowtow. Three kowtow. Up!'

The Shen all stood.

'Down!'

Two more times the Shen kowtowed three times to Frankie, a total of nine Imperial obeisances. When the nine were done, the Shen stood in orderly ranks. They didn't make a sound. I checked through the crowd for family members, my heart breaking as I saw them. Leo and Martin were there, the first time I'd seen them in months. Michael knelt behind his father. Some of them gazed desperately into my eyes and I was unable to say anything to them.

'Tell them they're ordered to love you,' the King said. 'No, wait. Order every resident of the Celestial to love you.'

'Yay,' Frankie said under his breath, then raised his voice. 'You are all ordered to love me! You have to love me.' He hesitated, then said, 'Cheer for me if you love me!'

The Shen broke into cheering as loud as the demons had cheered inside the hall. My throat filled at the sight of the Winds and all the senior Celestials forced to worship my son, and I realised I was cheering as well. We had all lost our wills.

'Silence in the name of the Emperor!' the Duke shouted, and we immediately stopped cheering. The quiet was eerie.

The King held her hand out to one of the Dukes, who passed her my speech. 'Repeat what I say to you, Frankie, then you can go play with your friends.'

'Okay, Mummy,' Frankie said.

'Here we go,' the King said. 'As the first Serpent Jade Emperor of this Dark Reptile Dynasty, I will provide the people of the Celestial ...'

Frankie carefully repeated the words of the speech, concentrating to get it right.

Simone? I said.

Don't talk to me, Emma.

The King wants to father a child on you. Can you run? Run now. Run!

I said don't talk to me. She cut off communication.

Frankie finished the speech and looked up at the Demon King, expectant.

'Now order everybody to obey me,' the Demon King said.

'Why you, Mummy?'

'Because it will make things easier.'

'But *I'm* the Emperor.'

'Yes, you are, my sweet little boy, but you can't be here all the time, so I'll run things for you when you can't.'

'Okay, Mummy,' Frankie said, unsure. 'You all have to obey my mummy when she tells you things, and that's an order!'

I opened my mouth to order the Kings arrested and the Celestials freed, but didn't have the chance. The Western King took three huge strides to me and slapped me so hard I was knocked down.

'No, Daddy, *why*?' Frankie wailed. 'Don't hurt my Emma!'

'Say another word and the child will suffer,' the Western King said into my face. He grabbed me by the arm and hauled me to my feet, then shook me. I opened my mouth again and he backhanded me. 'You were ordered to shut *up*.' He clamped his hand over my face to stop me from speaking, holding me so tight I couldn't breathe. 'Hurry up and fix this, George!'

'You said it wrong, my darling,' the Eastern King said to Frankie. 'You were supposed to say "All Celestials are ordered to obey the Celestial Regent, not my mother".'

'But that's the same thing,' Frankie said, confused. He glanced back at me, his expression blank, then turned back to the crowd.

I tried to breathe through the Western King's hand but only a sliver of air was entering. My chest pumped with the effort. If he didn't release me soon, I'd pass out.

'You are ordered to obey the Celestial Regent, not my mummy,' Frankie said loudly. 'I don't know how that's different,' he added under his breath.

The Western King released me and I fell to my knees, gasping. He went to Frankie and raised his hand to hit him. Frankie quailed, still on the throne.

'Not here, my love,' the Eastern King said, and the Western King subsided. 'Now, Frankie, last one. Say "The Celestial Regent has freedom of will and does not have to obey me".'

'Is that you, Mummy?' Frankie said.

'That's right.'

'Okay. The Celestial Regent has …' He looked up at her. He'd forgotten.

'Freedom of will and does not have to obey me,' she finished.

Frankie recited the rest of the words.

'I think that's enough for today,' the Eastern King said. 'He's tired and making mistakes.'

'Excuses,' the Western King said.

'Let's go home and have the best lunch ever,' the Eastern King said with forced brightness to Frankie. 'You're really the Emperor now, my darling, and they love you as much as I do!'

'Did you see them, Emma?' Frankie called to me as I struggled to my feet. 'Did you see them all bow to me?' He smiled up at the Eastern King. 'Let's go have something to eat. I'm *hungry*.'

28

The Residence was glowing with Celestial radiance when we returned. A small waterfall in the fishpond ran over the decorative stones, and the water was clearer already. The fridge rattled; the electricity was back. A fairy waited for us in the living room.

'Disappear,' the Eastern King said, and the fairy faded away. The Eastern King turned to the Western King. 'How long will you be gone?'

'Just until tomorrow. I need to father a bunch of new high levels to replace those useless human soldiers.' The Western King smiled. 'So do you.'

'Ah, the things we do for our little children,' the Eastern King said. 'Come back when you're done and we'll have some real fun.'

'Uniform?'

'Just for you, my love.'

They shared a long passionate kiss.

'Ew,' Frankie said under his breath, and shot a quick smile at me.

The Western King disappeared.

'Now, to work,' the Eastern King said. She nodded to the guards. 'Bring Simone in. Emma, order the Palace fairies to make us some lunch.'

'What about the other children?' I said.

'They're with the servants. They'll be back later today. Food!' she snapped.

I went into the kitchen and spoke to the empty air. 'Lunch for the Emperor, please.'

A couple of fairies appeared, bowed to me, and stood in the middle of the kitchen as the food prepared itself — a sliced raw cow's heart for the King, and peanut butter sandwiches for Frankie.

'Peanut butter sandwiches when he's just been crowned Emperor of everything?' I said.

The fairies ignored me, so I went out to the dining room, which was already set for two.

The guards returned with Simone.

She saw me and scowled. 'Traitor.'

'What?' the King said.

'She's in your pocket,' she said to him. 'She was following your orders even before my brother was controlling everybody.' She sneered at me. 'You had the chance to fix everything and you let them control you. You're so weak. You should have given the order no matter how much they hurt you! Coward.'

Simone, please tell me what you're planning here …

'I said don't talk to me!' she shouted.

I subsided. Whatever she had planned, it didn't include me. I only hoped that it worked.

'Simone, drop the act,' the King said, patient. 'She's loved you like a mother since you were a tiny girl. I don't know why you're pretending like this.'

'She'll do anything for *him*,' Simone said, pointing at Frankie. 'She loves him more than me. She's thrown her life away for him. Frankie gave her the chance to free the Celestial and she didn't make a single move to stop you!' She turned back to Frankie and her expression softened. 'I'm not mad with you, Frankie. You're my brother and I love you. But Emma stopped caring for me the minute you showed up.'

'I'm your brother?' Frankie said, his voice small.

'Frankie, make her love me,' the King said. 'Order her to love me.'

Frankie silently stared at Simone.

'Yes, you're my brother,' she said. 'Hello, Frankie, I'm your big sister, Simone. We have the same daddy but different mummies. Would you like to play with me? I'd love to spend time with you.'

'Quiet, Simone,' the King said.

'You're my sister?' Frankie said.

'Yes, I'm your sister,' she said.

'Order her to love me, Frankie. I need her,' the King said.

Frankie hesitated, then asked the King, 'Why?'

'Because I want you to.'

'Why do you want her to love *you*? She's my sister. I want her to love *me*. Why do you want her here?'

'I don't,' the King said. 'I need her —'

'Need her for what?' Frankie said. 'Why do you need her? You have me!'

'So she won't hurt you!' the King said.

'I would never hurt my little brother,' Simone said.

'She can't hurt me, I'm the *Emperor*,' Frankie said. 'Why do you want my sister when you already have me? Daddy is always saying I'm a bad son; is she better than me?' His voice thickened and he turned away to bury his face in the back of the couch. 'Don't send me away, Mummy, I love you!'

'It's all right, Frankie,' Simone said. 'Your mother's mean.'

I went to Frankie to comfort him, but he pushed me away. 'You love her more than me as well!' He turned back to the King. 'Send her away! I don't want her here!' He spun and shouted at Simone. 'Go *away*!'

She disappeared.

'Your father will hear about this,' the King said, rigid with rage. 'When I tell you to do something, you *do* it. I don't love her, I *need* her. She has a job to do. Now order her back.'

Frankie ran out of the room, around the veranda and into his bedroom, slamming the door behind him. The King stormed after him, and stood shouting at him through the door.

Simone?

How many times do I have to tell you? Do not talk to me!

She cut off communication. I fell to sit on the couch while the King continued to yell and bang on Frankie's bedroom door.

She doesn't mean it, Aunty Emma, BJ said.

She's made it quite clear that she does mean it. Can you explain to her that she needs to run?

She won't talk to me either.

The fairies floated into the room carrying the dishes, and placed them on the dining table. One gestured to me. I watched the King banging fruitlessly on Frankie's door, then followed the fairy into the kitchen. She'd prepared a small meal of vegetarian noodles for me; they sat on a table that hadn't been there before.

I nodded my thanks to her, then sat in front of the food and looked at it.

You need to eat, Aunty Emma, you haven't eaten anything in days.

I'm —

Even as an Immortal, you still need to eat.

I picked up the spoon and chopsticks and mechanically ate.

Simone was right. I'd been standing around helpless while all this was happening. I could have toppled the Kings in those five seconds of power ...

Is having you in my spinal column affecting my reflexes, BJ? I said.

No?

I should have been able to defend myself against the Western King. He was through me without any trouble whatsoever. I couldn't even block him. I'm not that out of practice. Is it because of you?

I don't think so, she said, but she sounded unsure.

Can you remove yourself without help?

No, I need someone to open you up before I can come out.

Can you ask your dad for me?

You want me out?

I hesitated, then said, *I think it would be a good idea.*

I hadn't been myself since Gold had put BJ inside me. I had a horrible thought: what if she wasn't BJ at all? She'd disappeared for at least twenty minutes when we were at the Southern Bastion — what if she'd been replaced? It would explain why Simone wouldn't talk to me, and why I'd stood there obediently while the King was ruling the Heavens without making any attempt to stop him ...

I'm not an agent of the Demon King, Emma, BJ said. *If I was, he'd have used me to control you. He doesn't know I'm here.*

No, BJ wasn't controlled by the King. But Andy, the Demon King's Number One, had used a stone to block the King's view when he made a pact with me in the past. If this BJ was a copy, created by Andy, then I had done the stupidest thing possible and put an agent for Andy right into my head.

I had a moment of disorientation and stared at the food.

You need to eat, Aunty Emma, you haven't eaten anything in days, BJ said.

I'm —

Even as an Immortal, you still need to eat.

I picked up the spoon and chopsticks and mechanically ate.

Simone was right. I'd been standing around helpless while all this was happening. I could have toppled the Kings in those five seconds of power ...

You're working from the inside, remember? BJ said.

I just feel so worthless. I had the chance and I blew it.

The European King is faster and stronger than you — I saw that, Aunty Emma. You didn't have a chance.

I sighed. As I ate, I realised that the noodles were exceptional. I'd been eating demon-contaminated and stale food for so many weeks that the fresh Celestial taste was wonderful.

I nodded to the fairy again. 'Thank you so much, this is delicious.'

The fairy nodded back.

'Is there any way you can talk to me?' I asked her. 'The spirit of the city in Europe had a human form to interact with us.'

The fairy changed to an old man, then to a child.

'You're too young?' I said.

The fairy returned to her normal form and nodded.

'Do you understand what I'm doing?'

She patted me on the shoulder and disappeared.

She's right, Aunty Emma, BJ said. *You're doing your best.*

* * *

An hour later Frankie was still refusing to come out, and the King couldn't break down the door no matter how hard she tried.

Eventually she was forced to leave him and go to the Imperial State Offices to begin passing Edicts that cemented the administration.

Ten minutes after she'd gone, Frankie ran out of his room and into the bathroom, then came to me. 'I won't bring Simone back.'

'I won't make you,' I said. 'What would you like to do?'

'I'm hungry. Then I want to talk to my friends.' He went to the dining room and saw his sandwiches. 'Yes!' He sat and tucked into them. 'These are the best.'

'I don't know how to ask the other children to come here,' I said.

'It's okay, Bo and Bei will bring them when I'm done.' He snapped his chin up. 'Read me a story while I eat.'

Bound to do as he said, I jumped to my feet and hurried to the living room to find a book for him. I read to him while he ate his sandwiches, and the fairy took the plate away when he was done.

He stood in the middle of the living room, facing the door. Bo and Bei came in escorting the children, and when they saw Frankie they all stopped and knelt.

'Wen sui, wen sui, wen wen sui,' they said in unison.

'Rise,' Frankie said, and the children stood, obviously confused.

'That was strange, why did we do that?' Little Jade said.

'I'm the Son of Heaven now,' Frankie said. 'I'm the Emperor.'

'I hope you listen to Emma and become a fair and just ruler,' Bei said.

'I will. And the first thing I'll do is send them back to their mummies,' Frankie said.

'What?' Richie said.

'Yay!' Little Jade yelled, and ran to hug Frankie. 'Can we still come and visit and play with you?'

Matthew burst into tears.

'If you like,' Frankie said, suddenly shy. 'I'd like that. But right now, go and be with your mummies and daddies. I'm with mine, you should be with yours.'

Well done, Emma, Bo said.

He did it himself. We spoke about it earlier, but this is all him, I said. *I'm not sure it's a good idea. He'll be in trouble with the Western King later, and he's already in serious trouble with the Eastern King.*

I hope you can defuse the situation. He's learning a valuable lesson about helping others; don't stop him.

I'm not. I agree with you. I'll try to protect him.

'We'll bring the children —'

'My *friends*,' Frankie said.

'We're his friends!' Little Jade said.

'We'll bring them back in a couple of days to play with you. Is that acceptable, Majesty?' Bei said.

'Quite acceptable,' Frankie said, clasping his hands behind his back in the image of John. 'Let them spend time with their parents, and then they can come back and play with me.'

'Thank you!' Little Jade shouted, jumping up and down. 'Thank you, Frankie!'

She jumped around the room, and the two boys joined her. They ran in circles, screaming with delight. Little Jade hugged Frankie again, and the two boys patted him on the back.

He grinned. 'Go on, before my mummy comes back.'

The three children raced out of the Residence and the Zhu sisters had to run to keep up.

Frankie watched them go. 'Can I go out too? I want to go out and see more. I want to see *everything*.'

'How much can you see? You should have …' I tried to put it into words. 'You should be able to see more of the world; it should all be there for you.'

'The Palace says I'm too young to com … com …'

'Comprehend?'

'Yes, that. I can see little bits in my head, but I want to see more!'

'All right, but we'll have to arrange it with your mummy,' I said. 'You'll need guards.'

'Okay,' he said. 'I understand.'

I shot him a look. His face was completely blank and innocent.

* * *

It was late in the evening when the Eastern King returned, obviously exhausted.

Frankie ran to her when she entered and hugged her. 'Hello, Mummy!'

'My darling.' She hugged him back. She opened her mouth, probably to discuss Simone again, then obviously changed her mind. 'It's very quiet. Are your friends asleep already? Where are they?'

'Come and sit,' Frankie said. He took her hand and guided her into the hearing room, and sat her on the couch. He sat next to her. 'Are you hungry? I can have the Palace make you something.'

'I don't need to eat as much as you do, my sweet.' She stroked his cheek. 'I'm not angry with you. There was no need to hide in your bedroom. Can we talk about it?'

'I want to talk about the children,' Frankie said. 'I love you very much, Mummy, and thank you for finding them, but I don't want them around all the time. They're too noisy, so I sent them home. I'll have them here to play every couple of days, but I think they're too young for me. Can you find me older friends?'

'How about Simone?' she said, full of hope.

'No. Not her, she's *mean.*'

'I can bring Edu back from her training if you want.'

'No, she's too young. Can you find me some older girls to play with? I want to play with big girls.'

She hesitated, then lit up with a huge smile. 'I know just who you need.' She sized him up. 'Yes. You have grown, and if you were truly one of us you'd be active already. It's time for you to meet them.'

He hugged her. 'Thank you, Mummy.' He kissed her on the cheek then smiled up at her. 'Go to bed. You look really tired.'

'I am,' she said. 'And I still have some jobs to do before your father comes back tomorrow.' She rose and hugged him again. 'We'll talk about Simone tomorrow as well. Goodnight, Frankie.'

'Goodnight, Mummy.'

The King nodded to me. 'Make sure he goes to bed early. He's had a big day.'

'I will, Majesty,' I said.

She went into her room and closed the door.

I sat next to Frankie on the couch and put my arm around him. 'That was very clever of you, Frankie. How did you know your mummy has older friends for you?'

He didn't reply.

'You did the right thing letting the other children go. I'm so proud of you,' I said.

'Thanks, Emma. I'm glad you're still here, otherwise I'd be all alone.'

'I will never leave you.'

He cuddled into me and we sat holding each other until he fell asleep in my arms. I took him into his bedroom, and slipped him out of his clothes and into his bed without him waking up.

I thought about my words as I settled to sleep in my little servant's room. I'd said that to Simone as well, and now I had left her for Frankie. She wasn't really jealous of him, was she?

Of course not, Aunty Emma, don't be silly. Don't let this situation make you doubt yourself. Be strong.

Thanks, BJ.

* * *

Something touched my face and I jerked awake, disoriented for a moment. Frankie was crouched in front of me.

'Why aren't you in a proper bed?' he said.

Still half-asleep, I answered without thinking. 'This is my bed.'

'But there's a big spare room where the other children were. Why ...' His expression cleared. 'Oh.'

'I'm okay, Frankie,' I said. 'Go back to bed.'

He crawled under the blanket next to me and I put my arm around him. 'It's too quiet with all my friends gone. I miss them. I'm all alone.'

'I'm here,' I said, holding him close.

'I came to find you,' he said. 'I hoped you'd still be in the house.' He shrugged in my arms. 'It was too quiet.'

'You were lonely?' I said, my heart breaking.

'The Palace is nice, but I needed someone to talk to.' He leaned his head into me. 'The Palace says you can have a bed in my room, if you like.' He straightened. 'Or we can make this room better for you. Tell the Palace what you want in here, and it will set the room up for you just the way you like it.'

A memory of our comfortable bedroom on the Mountain, with John in his black silk robe sitting on one of the armchairs next to the fireplace reading the student reports, made my heart ache.

'Thank you, sweetheart, but I think you're in enough trouble already.'

'Okay,' he said, and climbed out of bed. 'I'll tell the Palace to make it look smaller during the day. Mummy will never know.'

The room grew larger, and the furniture changed to a proper double bed and full-sized wardrobe. As the bed changed, I sank into the soft mattress, now covered in fine sheets. A silk rug appeared on the floor. Another door opened on the far side of the room.

'That's your bathroom,' he said.

I got out of bed and walked in to look. The bathroom wasn't luxurious, but it was clean and serviceable and, even better, it had a bath. I eyed the showerhead with what I hoped wasn't too obvious avarice.

I hugged him. 'Thank you, sweetheart.'

He hugged me back. 'Can you come and sit with me while I fall asleep?'

'Of course,' I said, and allowed him to lead me back to his bedroom. The guard Dukes nodded to us as we went in. He climbed into bed and I pulled the covers over him.

'I'm glad you have somewhere nice to sleep now.' He snuggled down into his pillow and sighed. 'I love you, Emma.'

I brushed my hand over his forehead. 'I love you too.'

I went back to the kitchen when he was asleep and stood for a long time looking at the bathroom he'd made for me. It was tempting, but I didn't want to risk it. I didn't know how much the King, in his role as Celestial Regent, knew about the Palace.

'If the Celestial Regent finds out about this, Frankie will be beaten again,' I said softly. 'Make it disappear, please.'

The room changed back to the small bedroom and the bathroom disappeared.

'Thank you.'

I crawled back into my small hard bed to sleep.

29

The next morning Frankie and I accompanied the King, in his male human form, to the Jade Emperor's private administrative offices. They were in a pavilion in the northwest corner of the Palace complex, near the wall and surrounded by a carefully tended ornamental garden. I'd never been in this building before.

We went in together, and the King stopped us in the secretarial anteroom, where the desk was covered with a large pile of Imperial Edicts.

'Frankie, sit here,' he said, indicating the desk. 'I'll have someone help you to sign the Edicts, and chop them for you.'

'He has a seal already?' I said.

'It appeared the minute he took the throne.' The King smiled at Frankie. 'Would you like to see your seal, Frankie?'

Frankie nodded, and the King took him into the Jade Emperor's office. I followed. It looked like a perfectly normal office. The desk was golden-brown rosewood, satin smooth from centuries of use and care. Matching timber cabinets along the side of the room held scrolls and modern binders. A large pale rectangle on the wall showed where another artwork had been removed.

The King pointed at the seal on its ink pad on a side table. 'That's yours.'

The fifteen-centimetre-high square seal was made of black jade, transparent at the edges but disappearing into opaqueness at its heart. It was carved into the shape of a twining snake holding a ball in its mouth, and the scales glistened with opalescent colours. I tried to control my reaction. It was almost identical to the seal that the staff of the Northern Heavens had made for me when I was regent, but mine had been plain black.

Frankie's eyes were wide. 'That's mine.' It wasn't a question.

'Your assistant will do the seal for you; you just write your name on the papers, okay?' the King said.

The door opened and a Shen entered: a dragon woman in human form. It was Toi, the Shen who had worked with the King to breed Simone's horse Freddo as an agent for him. She smiled smugly when she saw me, then fell to one knee in front of Frankie.

'Wen sui, wen sui, wen wen sui,' she said.

'Rise,' Frankie said.

She stood, then saluted and bowed to Frankie. 'Majesty, I am Madam Toi.' She nodded to the Demon King. 'Celestial Regent.'

The King gestured towards the anteroom. 'There's a pile of Edicts on the desk there for Frankie to sign. Show him how to do it and help him out with the chop, will you?'

She bowed to him. 'Majesty.' She smiled down at Frankie. 'Come on, little Majesty, let's practise writing your name. Won't this be fun?'

'What do you need me to do?' I said.

'Just sit in the corner and be quiet,' the King said.

'If I'm not needed, can I return to the Residence and tidy his toys?' I asked, thinking I may have the chance to sneak in and collapse on one of the children's beds to catch up on some much-needed sleep.

The King grunted. 'You stay where I can see you. Tamed is one thing, but trusting is something else. The minute you're out of my sight you'll try something, and you know it.'

* * *

I was woken from a doze on the floor in the corner of the office by the King's Number One entering in male human form.

Frankie rose to speak to him. 'Hello, Uncle Andy.'

'Hello, Frankie. Are you being good for your Uncle George?'

'I am, sir.'

'Good.' He grinned at Toi. 'And who are you, lovely lady?'

Toi blushed and bowed to him. 'I am the Shen who assisted the King in creating the horses, sire.'

'Horses, eh?' Andy said. 'I must come and see your animals.'

'You are most welcome, Highness. I would love to see you mounting something of mine.'

'I like that idea.' Andy looked around. 'Where's the Celestial Regent? He summoned me.'

The office door opened to reveal the King sitting behind the Jade Emperor's desk. 'One.'

Andy knelt. 'Loathsome Majesty. Celestial Regent.' He grinned up at the King. 'Dad.'

The King gestured to Andy. 'In.' He raised his head and spoke to the air. 'Something suitable for Number One.'

Andy sat in a visitors' chair, and a fairy appeared holding a tray containing two glasses and what looked like a carafe of blood. The door closed and I couldn't hear what they were saying.

BJ, can you eavesdrop? He has a computer in there.

Hold on …

BJ was silent.

BJ?

Give me a moment.

He has a computer in there, BJ, you must be able to listen in?

I'm having trouble.

Why? You're right next door, and it should be on the Celestial network. Is there something wrong?

This was strange. BJ shouldn't have any issues —

Yes, let her hear, Andy said. *She might work out a way to delay this. I'm not ready.*

I had a moment of disorientation, probably still half-asleep. Where was I? I looked around and remembered: the King was talking to Andy and I needed BJ to eavesdrop for me.

BJ?

Sorry, it took me a while but I'm in, BJ said.

'This is the only way,' the King said.

'Don't leave me alone! I can't do it,' Andy said.

'Of course you can. Do as I order you — sign an oath in blood that you'll obey Francis; and after I'm gone, you can take female form, kill Edu and marry Frankie. Be the Empress and rule everything.' The King grunted with amusement. 'You must be the first Number One in history who hasn't plotted to stab me in the back, and that's why you'll make an excellent successor.'

'And obey Francis?'

'He wants the best for the entire region.'

'He's not from here!' Andy dropped his voice. 'You're letting the Westerners conquer us *again*. Colonialism *again*. You're helping him to build an empire. We should be autonomous.'

'Then I won't give you the throne of Hell. I'll pass it to Edu.'

'She's just a child.'

'At least she does as she's told.'

'Let me find another way. There has to be another way!'

'There isn't. Two Princes have tried to release him in the last three days, and I kept his location a *secret*. It's only a matter of time before one of them makes it through and lets him out.'

'Just send him to the cells on Level Nine.'

'They'll try to release him from there too. As long as he lives, he's a threat. He must be *eliminated*.'

I realised with horror exactly what the King was planning. He knew. He knew, and he would sacrifice himself to see Xuan Wu destroyed for good. I dropped my head in my hands.

'Are you okay, Emma?' Frankie said. 'Did something happen?'

I looked up and saw Toi watching me.

'No, Frankie, everything's fine,' I said weakly.

* * *

When Frankie had signed all the Edicts, we returned to the Residence and sat in the courtyard on a rug next to the pond. The fish poked their eyes out of the water, watching us as we painted and cut out pictures of people doing ordinary things like shopping and sports.

The King stayed in his bedroom for two hours entertaining a series of Mothers.

324

I kept turning it over in my head. There had to be a way to avoid this. I didn't know how long I had. If we were lucky, the Eastern King wouldn't rush to sacrifice himself; he'd wait until the Heavens were fully under his control, Frankie had married his five wives, and everything was secure. Simone was the wildcard. He couldn't do anything until he'd brought her in as well. As long as Simone was free, I had time. I just needed to think of something.

The King came out of his bedroom in male human form, wearing a uniform similar to the Western King's — overdone decorations and everything. He stood in the living room waiting. The Western King entered, accompanied by two of the black-armoured demons, and stopped when he saw the Eastern King. He didn't speak, he just grabbed the Eastern King's hand and dragged him into the bedroom.

'Emma,' Frankie said softly after the door had closed. 'Be careful around Uncle George, okay?'

'I am,' I said.

He bent to speak conspiratorially to me. 'Uncle George is my mummy. In a different form. Be *really careful* around him.'

'I know,' I said.

He nodded, satisfied, then pointed at the next sheet of paper. 'What's this little boy doing?'

'Playing soccer. Next time we're in the garden with the other kids, I'll show you how to play this game. It's really fun.'

'I want to go shopping. It looks like fun too.'

'As soon as Uncle George — your mummy — and Daddy come out, I'll talk to them about it,' I said. 'I'd love to take you.'

'They've been so busy,' he said. 'They haven't had time for me.' He didn't look upset about it. 'I *won't* make Simone come back.'

'Did your mummy ask you to?'

'I won't. I don't care what my daddy does. I *won't*.'

'You're doing the right thing. Don't tell Simone to come back. I'll protect you.'

He nudged me affectionately with his shoulder, then sat straighter to paint the soccer player.

An hour later we were reading a book together when the Kings started shouting — loudly enough for us to hear them through the bedroom door. There were bangs inside, and Frankie blanched. The splintering crashes became so loud that the house shook. They were destroying the furniture. The Eastern King had told the Western King that he was going to sacrifice himself to destroy John.

'Come with me,' I said, and took Frankie out of the Residence. We walked quickly down the alley to the staff garden.

'Can you find us a ball to play with, please?' I said to the air.

When we went through the moon gate, a number of different balls — from tennis to basket balls — were on the grass.

'Thank you!' I said.

'Can I have a pony?' Frankie said.

A grey Welsh mountain pony, just the right size for him and complete with tack, appeared on the grass.

'Wow, this is great. Can I ask for anything?' he said.

I didn't answer the question. 'Is this a Shen or a natural pony?'

'I want a car!' Frankie said.

A child's electric car appeared on the grass next to the pony.

'You say "please",' I said.

'Cake!' Frankie said.

A small table appeared with a fruit gateau on it.

'Damn,' I said softly. 'Frankie, stop. *Stop!*'

'This is so fun!' he shouted, running to the pony. 'Help me on!'

A fairy appeared and lifted him onto the pony.

'Is that a natural animal?' I asked the fairy. 'It's not a Shen, is it?'

The fairy shook her head.

'How do I make it go? Make it go!' Frankie yelled, shaking the reins and tugging on them. The pony shifted with discomfort.

'Now hold on just a minute, young man!' I said, and went to him to hold his arm. 'Listen to me. This is a living creature and you are hurting ...' I looked under the pony. 'Her. Be kind to her, okay?'

Frankie stopped moving. 'I'm hurting her?'

'Those reins are attached to a big piece of metal in this poor animal's mouth. How would you feel if someone started jerking that around on *you*?'

'Take me off,' he said. 'I don't want to hurt her.'

'You're not now. Provided you're gentle you won't hurt her, and she'll be happy to carry you. Okay?'

'Okay,' he said, sobering.

'Do you want to learn to ride her?'

'Yes!'

'Yes, *please*. I say it, and you should too.' He opened his mouth. 'Emperor or not.'

'Yes, please, Emma,' he said.

'Okay then. A helmet for the Emperor, and a lunge rein, please.' The lunging equipment appeared on the pony, and the helmet on Frankie's head. 'Thank you. Clear the area, please.' The car, balls and cake disappeared. 'Good. Now let's see how sore we can make your bum before the end of the day.'

He giggled. 'You said a bad word.'

'You might want to say some too, when we're finished. Now let go of the reins and hold the saddle. Yes, like that.'

I bound up the reins out of the way, then waved the lunging whip at the pony's rump without touching it. She moved obediently into a circle.

'Hold on tight,' I said, 'because it's about to get *bouncy*.'

Thirty minutes later the Eastern King stormed into the garden in female form, her face a mask of fury. She stopped when she saw Frankie trotting around on the pony with a huge grin on his face.

'Look at me, Mummy,' he shouted. 'I'm riding!'

Her expression softened, and she turned and left.

* * *

Emma?

I shot upright. My awareness flooded with the sense of John through our spiritual link. He was present and alive somewhere on the Celestial, and my heart ached at the sensation; something I'd taken so much for granted in the past.

It was deep in the night, and crickets chirped outside my window.

John? I said.

Another demon Prince is here to let me out. He wants me to destroy the King; he's unhappy that the Western King is taking over. He spoke with force. *Wait, I'm talking to Emma, she's right there! Emma. The Prince says that the Murasame is in the Imperial Residence. Is it?*

Yes. It's in the entry hall. I inhaled sharply. *You can use it to destroy the Kings!*

Yes. This is the first time that both of them have been in the same place as the sword. It's the best opportunity I've had so far. I'm not sure I should risk it though.

You must. The Eastern King is planning to sacrifice himself to destroy you.

He knows?

Yes, I said. *He'll make Frankie order you to do it. You have to destroy them now with the Murasame — it's our only chance.*

Then I have no choice, he said, and his voice went tight with effort. He was leaving the cage. *Go to our son and keep him out of this. If Frankie orders me to stop, I must obey him.*

I levered myself off the bed. *May fate walk on our side and keep us safe from the Pits, Xuan Wu.*

For the Heavens, he said, and went silent.

I didn't bother with a robe; I could move more easily in my pyjamas. I crept out of my room, through the kitchen, and into the living room. The bedrooms were on the right, all opening onto the raised veranda that bordered the central garden. I went out of the living room onto the veranda and crept quietly along it.

I passed the first door; its two guards waved me past to Frankie's room. Frankie's door also had two big Dukes guarding it, and they allowed me through and into his room.

I gently closed the red wooden door behind me, and moved as quietly as I could across the hardwood floor to Frankie's four-poster. He was a tiny shape curled up in the middle of the bed; he'd thrown off the silk quilts in the warmth. His tawny hair lay across his forehead, and his face was angelic in sleep.

I hope Frankie will forgive us for what we're about to do, I said to BJ, then raised my head. John was nearby: I could feel his cold dark essence. He was on the roof.

Good luck, Aunty Emma, BJ said.

John moved silently, his presence drifting across the roof towards the entry hall where the sword was kept. There were a couple of quiet crunches, almost at the edge of hearing: he was disposing of guards. I watched with my Inner Eye. He was in the entry hall. His essence was mirrored by the Murasame's aura, and it flared to dark life as he took the sword in his hand. The sword screamed; a terrified sound that cut through the air.

Frankie shot upright in his bed. 'What's happening?'

There were shouts outside and guards ran along the veranda.

I sat on the bed to put my arm around Frankie. 'I don't know what's happening. Let's stay here and the guards will handle it.'

There were more crashes and screams. Someone rang a bell nearby, and guards ran past. The door slammed open, making both of us jump.

Frankie clutched me. 'Is there another monster here?' he said, his voice quivering.

Two Dukes came in and took position inside the door, facing away from us.

'What's happening?' Frankie said. 'Hey!' he shouted at the guards. 'What's going on?'

'We think there's a Celestial here,' one of the Dukes said.

The Demon King charged into the room in her Kitty Kwok form. 'Your boyfriend will never make it here, Emma. Tell him to give up now and I'll put him back in the cage.'

John stormed in behind her, and the guards closed ranks. He ran the Murasame through each of them in turn before they could move. He was in Celestial Form and his ugly face was full of grim pleasure at the mayhem.

The Demon King grabbed Frankie and stood with him in front of her as a shield. 'Take me and you take the child.'

'Go to Emma, Frankie,' John said.

'Tell him to put the sword down and go back to his cage, Frankie,' the Demon King said.

Frankie didn't reply to either of them; he just hung wide-eyed and silent in the King's grasp.

I reached out to pull him away from the King, and she hit me one-handed with a ball of black energy that knocked me backwards into the frame of Frankie's bed, winding me.

'You can't kill me without killing your son, Turtle,' the King said with malice. 'Drop the sword. That's an order from the Celestial Regent.'

John didn't move. 'I only obey the Jade Emperor.'

'Frankie, tell him to drop the sword!' the King shouted.

Frankie didn't speak, frozen with fear.

'Dammit! Drop the sword or I'll send Emma to the Pits,' the King said, desperate. 'You kill me, you kill the kid!'

'Frankie, go to Emma!' John said again.

The Demon King tightened her grip on Frankie and he squeaked with pain. 'You promised to stay in the cage, Turtle. I don't think I've ever seen you break your word before.'

'I didn't promise to stay in the cage. I promised to *go* into the cage,' John said. 'I'm not stupid enough to promise to stay in it. I haven't broken my word.'

'Excuses. You can't be trusted to stay put. Frankie, tell him to drop the sword *now* or I will call your father.'

John hefted the Murasame, disappeared and reappeared behind the King. He raised the sword to take the King's head off without harming Frankie.

Frankie shrieked and John stopped mid-swing.

The Murasame disappeared from John's hand and reappeared spearing him through the head, in the front and out the back. The sword grew until its blade was twenty centimetres tall. John's eyes widened, then he fell onto his back like a dead tree and disappeared.

The Murasame returned to its normal size, and reappeared floating in front of me with its tip a centimetre from my chest.

'Are you all right, George?' the Western King said from the doorway.

'Yes. We handled it,' the Eastern King said. 'Frankie, say "Xuan Wu is ordered to return to the jade cage".'

Frankie clutched her and whimpered.

The Western King strode over and slapped Frankie on the side of the head. 'Do as you're told!'

'Xuan Wu return to …' Frankie said. 'What's next?' He ducked when the Western King raised his hand again.

'The jade cage!' I said. 'Don't hit him.'

'The jade cage,' Frankie moaned.

The Eastern King lowered Frankie and concentrated, listening.

The Western King linked his hands behind his back. 'George

330

won't hold back on punishing either of you for this,' he said to me. 'I think I will enjoy this very much.'

'It worked. He's back in the cage on Level Nine,' the Eastern King said. She focused on me. 'Now what do I do with you, Emma? You must pay for putting my darling son's life at risk, but sending you to the Red-Hot Grates in Level Seven would break your mind. I want you fully aware of everything that's happening to you.'

'Break her mind anyway,' the Western King said with malice.

A Duke appeared on the other side of the room and fell to one knee. 'Majesty.'

'Take her to Level Eight,' the King said. 'Put her in the lake.'

'Yes,' the Western King hissed under his breath.

'No!' Frankie said, clutching the Eastern King's legs. 'Don't send her away!'

'She was working with the big dark man,' the Eastern King said. 'They were about to kill us.'

'I want her *here*, Mummy.'

'Thank you,' I breathed.

Frankie glanced at me, his face unmoving, then back at the Eastern King. 'I like her looking after me.' He gazed up into her eyes. 'You're the best mummy in the world. You're so strong, nobody can beat you. I love you.'

Her expression softened. 'I love you too, little Francis.'

Frankie hugged her. 'Leave Emma here with me? Please?' He pitched his voice higher, wheedling. 'She can't do anything while the sword is here, look at it. Leave her here. *Please?*'

'Repeat after me and I'll let you keep her,' the King said, and tousled his hair. 'Xuan Wu is ordered to stay in the jade cage.'

'Spoilt brat,' the Western King said, and went out.

'Xuan Wu is ordered to stay in the jade cage,' Frankie said.

'Good boy.' The King glared at me. 'Try anything like that again and Frankie will not be able to talk me out of punishing you. You lose your bedroom. You're sleeping on the kitchen floor again.'

'I understand,' I said. I nodded towards the Murasame where it floated in front of me, its point a centimetre from my breastbone. 'Can you call off the sword, sweetheart?'

Frankie's face was rigid with restraint, his mouth a firm line.

'Are you controlling it, darling?' the King said. 'I'm so glad it's protecting you, but you can send it back to its stand now.'

'Promise to start teaching me the sword tomorrow,' Frankie said to me. 'I want to learn to use it and defend myself.' He glanced up at the King. 'And my mummy.'

'I will. I promise,' I said.

'You're the best little boy in the whole world,' the King breathed.

The sword disappeared, and a dark flare in the entry hall indicated that it had returned to its stand.

'It was never this powerful when anyone else had it,' the King said with pride. 'You really are exceptional, Frankie.'

Frankie didn't reply. His head nodded with exhaustion.

'Sleep time,' the King said, and helped him to climb back into bed. She spoke to me without looking away from him. 'Go to the kitchen and meditate on your crimes.'

I bowed to her and went out, propping myself against the wall as I made my way back to the kitchen. I'd suspected for a while that Frankie was more aware of the situation than he seemed, but now I was sure of it. I pulled some blankets onto the kitchen floor and curled up in a corner next to the cupboards. I wondered exactly how aware he was.

30

Early the next morning I went to the entry hall and crouched next to the Murasame where it sat on its stand. The King had lied about there being a matching wakizashi for the dark katana; the Murasame was one of a kind.

'Thank you for looking after Frankie,' I said to it.

Its aura was completely blank. It seemed a lifeless piece of metal.

'I would never let anyone hurt him either,' I said. 'I'm glad you're there to help me protect him.' I put my hand over it without touching it. 'Can you talk to me? If we can talk, we can work together.'

I received nothing from it.

'Do I need to touch you to communicate? Is that okay?' I smiled. 'We shared a great deal of blood and mayhem together, Destroyer. I hope they were good times for you too. We have a bond that nobody else can match. Talk to me.'

I placed my hand on the handle and jerked it back as the pain flashed through it. I turned my hand over: the sword had cut a large shallow slice in my palm without moving. Fortunately it wasn't deep enough to take out any tendons.

I concentrated and healed the wound. 'I guess that answers that. When Frankie said that you bite, he wasn't wrong.'

The sword still seemed a completely lifeless hunk of metal; even its dark aura was gone.

'Well,' I said, 'if ever you feel the need to work with me to protect Frankie, just scream again like a thousand tortured souls. That was horrifying.'

The sword didn't respond.

I rose to return to the kitchen, but stopped when Frankie shouted. He was in his room and in pain. I took a step back, then jumped the ten metres across the courtyard and skidded to a halt outside his door. The Western King was shouting angrily and unintelligibly inside. Frankie wailed in return, and the Eastern King spoke, placating both of them. The Western King shouted loudly again, there were crashes and Frankie screamed.

When he screamed again, I took three steps back to shoulder charge the door. I ran into it just as they opened it and hit the edge of the door, stunning myself.

The Eastern King was in Kitty Kwok form. She grabbed me by the shoulder as I fell and pushed me away. 'This is none of your business. Go back to the kitchen.'

'Stop hurting my —' I began, but the Eastern King punched me in the face.

'Shut up!'

Frankie started wailing again. The Western King slapped him and he dissolved into sobs.

'Stop hurting him, I'm here!' Simone shouted from inside Frankie's room.

Simone, I said. *Run. Run now. They'll destroy —*

Don't talk to me! she shouted into my head.

They're going to destroy your father! I said, but she didn't hear me. She'd shut off communication.

'All right, if you must do this stupid thing, let's do it,' the Western King said. He added under his breath, 'If I didn't love you more than my life, I would kill you myself.'

The Eastern King went into Frankie's room and pulled Simone out by the upper arm.

'Simone, run!' I said. 'They'll use Frankie —'

'Do not talk to me!' she shouted.

'Both of you shut up or the boy gets it again,' the Western King growled.

'Don't hurt him. I'll do anything you say,' Simone said. 'Emma, shut *up*.'

'Where's your Number One?' the Western King said.

'Andy will meet us there,' the Eastern King said. She smiled at Frankie, and spoke with forced cheer. 'Be a good boy now, because we're going to your new capital. You have your own house there too. Won't this be fun?'

The Western King dragged Frankie out of the room. Frankie stumbled beside him, trying to wipe the tears from his face. The side of his eye was swollen; he was already developing a black eye. When I saw the blood on his chin, I ran to him and knelt in front of him.

'He's bleeding!'

'Just a scratch,' the Western King said, and pushed me away. 'He's fine.'

'Let me heal him,' I said.

'That would defeat the purpose of the punishment,' the Western King said. He nodded towards the Eastern King. 'Go to Kitty.'

I hesitated.

'Come to me now!' the Eastern King said.

Forced to obey, I went to her. She took my shoulder, still holding Simone with her other hand. 'We should have done this a long time ago, Francis.'

Simone, if you won't listen to me then listen to them, I said. *They're going to destroy —*

She sent the mental equivalent of loud feedback into my head and I bent double with pain.

'I agree with Andy. I'd prefer we didn't do it at all,' the Western King said.

'After what happened last night we really don't have a choice, my love.'

I wrenched myself upright, gasping. 'Don't do it,' I said. 'It's not worth it. Xuan Wu will never renounce his allegiance; he will obey Frankie. All you have to do —'

'You shut *up*,' the Eastern King said, and I was silenced.

The Kings teleported us and we landed on a gravel road as wide as a four-lane highway, with construction equipment — piles of bricks and a bulldozer — to one side. A mound of glittering gravel and a stack of cement bags were on the other side. A hundred metres in front of us, a palace was being built of golden sandstone. The building was Western-style, rectangular, with double-height arched windows on the ground floor, and square windows for two more storeys above that. Statues decorated the edges of the pitched roof, and a tiled courtyard stood in front of the entry.

I saw the mountains in the distance and realised — this was where the Western Palace had been. The glittering pile of gravel was ground-up glass; they'd lifted the heat-fused ground and crushed it to make gravel. The earth around us was the red soil of the Western Palace, bare of any vegetation. A group of people were digging holes and planting shrubs a hundred metres away in the other direction. They were creating a decorative garden that was twenty metres across in front of the two-hundred-metre-wide building.

The shape of the buildings resonated with me; I'd seen something like it before but couldn't place it.

'Versailles?' Simone said with disbelief. 'You're duplicating *Versailles*? You do know what happened to the despotic kings who lived there, right?'

'Frankie won't live in there, he has his own house,' the Western King said, pointing at an incomplete double-storey mansion to one side. 'And the French kings didn't have the same sort of control we do. Nobody can ever rebel against us.'

'My father did last night,' she said viciously. 'I only wish that he'd finished you off.'

'She will make a *fine* mother for your children, George, darling,' the Western King said. 'We should have collected more, just to make sure it will take.'

'No, thanks, I'm still sore,' the Eastern King said with amusement.

Simone generated yin and threw it at the Eastern King, but it did nothing. It went right through both Kings and into the ground, leaving an ice-covered black hole a metre across.

'Wait, she tried to kill us,' the Western King said. 'You don't have control of her?'

'She's Prince level,' the Eastern King said. 'I've been trying to make her my Queen, but she insists on fighting me. It's a good thing she's sworn to the Celestial, otherwise we'd have no control over her at all. If she and her father both renounced their Celestial alignment, we'd be in serious trouble.'

'I see your point about doing this now,' the Western King said. 'It's necessary. Are you sure you have control?'

'Slap Frankie and find out,' the Eastern King said.

Simone tried to pull herself free. 'No! Don't hurt him. I'll do anything you say.'

'Frankie, tell her to kneel,' the Eastern King said.

'Kneel, Simone,' Frankie said, his voice flat.

Simone fell to her knees on the gravel, but her eyes didn't shift from the Eastern King. 'I *will* kill you one day.'

'We just had that gravel raked,' the Western King said, pointing at the hole Simone had made. 'You will go to the Pits the minute this is done.'

'When what's done?' she said.

I opened my mouth to tell her to run, but nothing came out. I was silenced.

BJ, tell her!

She won't listen to me. I'm trying to talk to her but it's not getting through.

'I have a better idea for punishment,' the Eastern King said. 'After this is done, send her straight to the Mountain and make her destroy the whole thing and everyone in it.'

'No!' Simone shouted. 'My family are there!'

I struggled to speak. *Simone, run! Do something! You mustn't obey them!*

She ignored me.

'We're only doing this because your father tried to kill the Jade Emperor last night,' the Eastern King said. 'His own son. Remember that this is *his* fault.'

'What is?' she said with frustration.

'You'll see.' The Eastern King crouched to talk to Frankie. 'Do you want to see your new house here, my darling?'

'I like the other house. The Celestial Palace is nice. I don't want to move,' Frankie said.

The Western King took a swift step towards him.

'No, I don't mind moving!' Frankie said, his voice high-pitched with fear. 'I'll go anywhere you say, Daddy!'

Simone jumped to her feet. 'Leave him alone!'

The Eastern King rose. 'You have full control of both of them, Francis. When Andy signs the oath, you can take it all.'

'What are you doing?' Simone said.

'Frankie,' the Eastern King said.

'Yes, Mummy?' His voice was small.

'Say "Simone and Emma, follow us and remain silent".'

'Simone and Emma, follow us and remain silent,' Frankie repeated without emotion.

'In the main hall,' the Western King said. 'They're waiting for us.'

'Is it finished?' the Eastern King said.

'Just. It was delayed while we collected the gold for the statues and chandeliers. We finally forced the Tiger to cooperate and he made it for us.'

Simone and I followed them as they walked to the grand gilt double doors of the Palace entrance.

'How did you make him comply?' the Eastern King said. 'Last I heard you had him in the Red-Hot Grates.'

'I threatened to put his children in the Red-Hot Grates. You were right, my love. Torture them and they brush it off: but threaten their families and they'll do anything you ask of them.'

'Hopefully Frankie will become emotionally attached to the wives we give him, and you'll just have to threaten them to keep him compliant,' the Eastern King said.

'Yeah, it may be a good thing after all that the boy's too soft. What about Simone?'

'Just threaten her brother and she'll do anything you say. She's as soft as he is,' the Eastern King said.

We entered a lobby with a ceiling as high as the roof — four storeys tall. Marble and gilt twin curved staircases led to landings on the second floor, then more stairs to the higher levels. Portraits of each of the Demon Kings, painted in oils in Western style, hung at the top of the stairs in front of us. They were each three metres tall and two wide, and showed the Kings in male form wearing their Western military uniforms.

Simone and I followed the Kings and Frankie through the entry hall and into another hall that occupied the entire side of the building, facing the gardens at the rear. It was two storeys high, twenty metres wide and two hundred metres long and resembled Versailles' Hall of Mirrors, with glass along one side, mirrors along the other, and enormous chandeliers hanging from the ceiling. Demons stood in orderly ranks facing the raised dais at the end of the hall, which held a Western-style gold-painted throne with red velvet cushions. The effect was obviously intended to be luxurious, but the crystal, gold and marble combined to give an impression of overdone decoration. The gardens outside were still under construction, and hundreds of people were working with spades and picks to clear the ground.

'This will truly be magnificent when it's finished,' the Eastern King said. She grinned at the Western King. 'What a shame I'll never see it.'

'You can always change your mind, love,' the Western King said sadly.

We went through the crowd to the dais and followed the Kings onto it. The Eastern King helped Frankie to sit on the throne, and she and the Western King stood either side of him.

'Order Emma and Simone to the back of the platform,' the Eastern King told Frankie. 'And tell them to stay still and quiet.'

Frankie repeated the order, and Simone and I moved. The windows behind us showed more construction work: open gashes in the ground and piles of rubble.

'It's time, Number One,' the Eastern King said.

Andy appeared at the front of the demons below us. He fell to one knee on the polished white marble floor. 'Loathsome Majesties.'

The Eastern King swept her hand to the side and a coffee table appeared on the dais. 'Come up and claim your inheritance, Number One. I think this is the first time in history that there has been a peaceful handover.' She smiled. 'The beginning of a grand era of peace and prosperity for all demonkind.'

Andy walked up the stairs onto the dais and stood next to the table. He looked down at the scroll, then up at the Eastern King. 'This is a terrible idea.'

'Faithful to the last,' the Eastern King said. 'Andy, swear allegiance in blood to Francis.'

'Reconsider, Dad,' Andy said. 'What if he's been steering you to this point all along?' He gestured towards the Western King, who stood with his hand on his sword. 'You're giving him everything you've built!'

'Do as you're told, Number One,' the Eastern King said. 'Sign the scroll.'

'I'm not ready for this!'

'Do it.'

'I should kill you now,' Andy said.

Instead, he picked up the small knife from the table, slashed his wrist, and pumped his hand a few times to make the blood flow. He picked up a brush, swiped it over the wound, then signed the scroll with a single horizontal stroke. He concentrated and the wound healed. The scroll was covered in script but it was too small to see what it said.

'Now in words.'

'I pledge my allegiance —'

'On your knees!' the Eastern King said.

'I'm not ready for this!' he said again, but fell to one knee. 'I pledge allegiance to you, Francis, King of Demonkind. Protect me, I am yours. I will obey you as long as you live.'

The Eastern King's expression went beatific and she made a soft sound of pleasure. Her eyes unfocused, and she panted a few times. She reached for the Western King and he held her as she shook with jerking tremors. She straightened, her face full of satisfaction.

A few demons in the hall cheered and she waved without looking at them.

Simone made some quiet sounds of disgust in her throat, but we were still restricted from saying anything.

Frankie sat silent on the throne, his expression dull and uninterested. He seemed a million miles away.

'All right, let's do it,' the Eastern King said. She took the Western King's hand and gazed into his eyes. 'My last gift to you. All the Heavens, the Earthly, and Hell itself. Once I am gone you will have half the world, and you will quickly conquer the other half. I only wish I could be around to see it.'

'You can still change your mind, my love.'

'Not as long as he lives.' She turned to face the audience. 'Bring him.'

The Dukes guarding the base of the dais pushed the crowd back. Five Dukes appeared in the space they'd made, each of them with one hand on the Celestial Jade cage containing John. He lay on the bottom of the cage in True Form, covered in still-bleeding cuts.

I looked desperately at Simone, but she was standing blank and emotionless, staring at the cage.

'Frankie,' the Eastern King said.

'Yes, Mummy?'

'Repeat my orders *exactly*.'

Frankie's voice was small. 'Yes, Mummy.'

'I'm not ready for this!' Andy growled under his breath.

'Xuan Wu, take human form and present yourself on your knees in front of me,' the Eastern King said.

Frankie repeated the order.

The Dukes gingerly opened the cage.

John took human form in his black Mountain uniform, his hair a mess and his feet bare, and stepped out of the cage. His face was expressionless, but his dark eyes glittered as he walked up the stairs onto the dais and knelt in front of Frankie.

He looked up at Frankie and said, 'George, if you love him, don't make him do this.' His voice was full of pain. 'When he understands what he has done, it will break him.'

'He's already broken,' the Western King said with relish.

'Andy, stand behind the throne until it's time for you to move up,' the Eastern King said.

'Majesty,' Andy said, and moved into position. He glared at John. 'You had to force this, didn't you? I'm not ready!'

'This will backfire on you in ways that you cannot begin to comprehend,' John said.

'Frankie, silence,' the Eastern King said.

'Silence!' Frankie repeated.

John looked me in the eyes. *I will be profoundly changed by this. Once it has happened, let me be dead to you. Do not love the thing that I become.*

I will always love you, whatever you become, I said.

John focused on Simone and they concentrated on each other.

'They're talking, shut them up,' the Western King said.

'Frankie!' the Eastern King barked. 'No one is to speak silently in my presence!'

Frankie repeated the order and John and Simone looked away from each other. John's face became even more stony and he knelt silent and unmoving.

The Eastern King held her arms out to the Western one. 'Francis.'

His control broke and he embraced her, burying his face in her neck. 'There has to be another way.'

'There isn't. This is what needs to happen,' the Eastern King said. She pulled the Western King tighter. 'We made it. We won. We've freed our children. But if they're to be safe, we must do this.' She pulled back and smiled, then brushed away the Western King's tears. 'No tears, my love. Joy for the freedom of our children.'

The Western King kissed her, a lingering kiss full of love, then wiped his eyes and turned away.

'Now,' the Eastern King said. She knelt in front of Frankie. 'You know how that big dark man tried to kill us last night?'

'I know,' Frankie said. 'He was scary.'

I was only peripherally aware of them talking. I focused on John, willing him to love me enough not to be changed by this; sure in the knowledge that when it happened, he would be gone.

'His name is Xuan Wu. This is him here,' the Eastern King said, pointing at John. 'In a different form.'

Frankie inhaled sharply and stared at John, his eyes wide. John lowered his head, full of grief. His own son was terrified of him, and with good reason.

'So we have to make sure he never hurts us again,' the Eastern King said. 'I know it sounds strange, but to make him go away forever you have to order Xuan Wu to destroy *me* with his sword, Seven Stars. Tell him to hit me with the loaded Seven Stars.'

I couldn't stop the tiny sound of pain that escaped me. John glanced at me, full of despair, but couldn't speak. We were still ordered to silence.

'He has to kill you?' Frankie said. He looked up at Simone, who was still staring at him, expressionless. He turned back to the Eastern King. 'I don't want you to die, Mummy.' He threw his arms around her. 'What will I do without you?'

'Don't worry, it's not real, little love,' the Eastern King said. 'I'll be gone for a while, then I'll be back. You'll be just fine. Daddy and Number One will advise you until I return. But make sure you do what Daddy tells you while I'm gone, okay?'

'I can't do it,' Frankie moaned.

'You have to,' the Eastern King said, rising. 'He needs to be destroyed. As long as he exists, all of us are in danger. He'll keep trying to kill us and won't ever give up.' She raised her head, her expression beatific. 'Order him, Frankie. If you love me, you'll do this for me. And remember, it's not forever. I'll be back with you before you know it.'

Frankie sat silently on the throne. He glanced at Simone, then at all of us in turn.

'Do it, Frankie,' the Western King growled, and Frankie flinched. 'Say it right now or you'll be punished. I mean it. Do it!'

'Thank you, my love,' the Eastern King said.

'I will never love anyone the way I love you,' the Western King said.

'For our children,' the Eastern King said.

'What do you want me to say again, Mummy?' Frankie said.

'Good boy,' the Western King said, full of approval, and Frankie lit up. 'Well done.'

'You say "Xuan Wu, kill the Celestial Regent with loaded Seven Stars",' the Eastern King said.

Frankie mechanically repeated the words. 'Xuan Wu. Kill the Celestial Regent with loaded Seven Stars.'

John didn't move, quivering with effort as he fought it. I had a wild moment of hope: maybe he was powerful enough to disobey Frankie. Maybe he had renounced his Celestial allegiance.

'That's an order,' Frankie said. He turned to Simone. 'Kill her with the …' He hesitated, then gathered himself. He pointed at the Eastern King. 'Kill her with the loaded blades!'

John turned like an automaton and took Celestial Form.

The Demon King raised her arms and lowered her head, ready to die.

Simone took Celestial Form, summoned her twin blades, Bo and Bei, and moved faster than the eye could see. She ran to the Eastern King and buried the points of the blades in her abdomen.

The King stared at her, dumbfounded, then changed to his bigger male form and grinned. 'That's not enough to take me out.' He concentrated, and the blades slid halfway out of him.

Simone grunted, put more effort into it and pushed the blades back in. 'You thought I'm weaker because I'm a girl.'

Her muscles bulged as she buried the blades deeper into the Demon King. His face went rigid as he put his hands on the hilts and fought her.

'You thought he'd be stronger than me because his mother's a snake and mine was just a human.' She glared into the King's eyes, and he smiled back at her, defiant. 'Well, you know what, stupid? I'm a girl, and I'm stronger than my brother.' She punctuated her next words by loading the indentations in the swords with her chakras, and his eyes went wide. 'And. My. Mother. Was. A. Serpent. Too!'

She ripped the blades across him, and he screamed as he dissolved into a blizzard of black demon essence that hit her like a tidal wave, forcing her back. She disappeared into the essence and it overwhelmed her. She was a dark shape within it, forced down by it.

'Simone!' Frankie yelled, and jumped off the throne, reaching for her.

John moved faster than any of us. He ran to her first, grabbed her, and both of them disappeared, taking all the demon essence with them.

The Eastern King was gone.

'George,' the Western King said. He fell to his knees and put his head in his hands. 'No. My George. My Kitty. I don't believe it.' He stood again. 'Frankie, listen to me. We have to —'

'Bring Simone back!' Frankie yelled, his face twisted with loathing.

'You'll do what I tell you!' the Western King said. 'You stupid little shit. George is gone for *nothing* because of you. What the hell is wrong with you? Do as I say!'

'Where's my Simone? You killed my Simone!'

'No, I didn't, you stupid little fuck,' the Western King said, his voice full of venom. '*You* did by letting them manipulate you. You let them destroy the love of my life and we lost *everything*.' He took two quick steps to Frankie and raised his hand to strike him.

I rushed to Frankie's side to defend him but I was too slow.

The Western King stopped and his face went blank with shock. Frankie had his right hand out, and the Murasame was lodged through the Western King without Frankie touching it.

The King looked down at the blade through him, then up at Frankie. 'You'll need more than that to stop me, you little shit.'

He grabbed the Murasame's handle and screamed with agony as he pulled the blade out.

'No,' the Murasame shouted with fury. 'You'll never hit this child again!'

It shrieked with triumph and darkened. Mist appeared around it, and I felt the cold two metres away. The Western King was covered in ice, spreading from the sword. He crystallised, as if he'd been dropped in liquid nitrogen, and became bright, hard and brittle.

'This is for every time you hurt this child!' the Murasame shouted in a thousand screaming voices, and it grew three times higher and thicker.

The Western King shattered from the inside out, exploding into chunks of demon essence that shot out in all directions, then stopped and hung suspended in the air. The frozen demon pieces contracted and tumbled back to be absorbed by the blade, hissing as they hit the dark metal. When they were all gone, the sword returned to its normal shape and size, floating in front of Frankie's face.

'Delicious,' it said with a voice of ice and darkness. 'Unlike anything I've ever tasted before.'

'Thanks, Muri,' Frankie said, his voice small.

'You are welcome, little one,' the sword said. 'Thank you for giving me to this child, Emma. His destructive potential is greater than your own and he is truly a worthy wielder of me. I look forward to enhancing his abilities as he grows.'

'I'm not sure that's a good idea, but we will discuss it later,' I said.

'I look forward to it,' the sword said, and disappeared.

I knelt in front of Frankie. 'Are you okay, love?'

'I *told* him I wasn't ready!' Andy said, and disappeared.

'Where's Simone? I want Simone!' Frankie said.

We have an agreement, One, I said to Andy. *Or should I say Loathsome Majesty? Don't go far; we need to meet and sign the treaty. And order these demons out of the Heavens before the Xuan Wu returns and removes them himself.*

I'll agree to anything you ask, just keep those fucking scary kids away from me, Andy said. *I wasn't ready for this, dammit. Dad spoilt everything.*

The demons disappeared from the hall, and the sky grew brighter.

'Where's Simone, Emma?' Frankie said. 'Is Simone dead too?' He shook with tears and put his arm over his eyes.

I pulled him into a huge hug. 'I'll always be here for you.'

He clutched me, still crying. 'Everybody's dead!'

31

John appeared next to me.

Frankie saw him and cowered against the throne. 'You killed my Simone!'

'Simone's fine, I would never hurt her,' John said. 'She's stuck where she is, she can't come up here any more, but you can go visit her any time. She's not hurt.'

'Really?' Frankie said, full of desperate hope.

Really, I'm fine, Simone said. *Just sort of stuck down here.*

'I need you to help me, Simone,' he said. 'Where are you? I want to be with you.'

You have to abdicate first, Simone said.

'I have to what?' Frankie sobbed quietly, the tears streaming down his face. 'Where's Simone?'

'Oh, Frankie,' I said, and gathered him into another huge hug. He clutched me. 'We'll go to her as soon as you abdicate,' I said into his shoulder. 'Everything will be okay.'

Do what they tell you, Simone said. *Listen to Dad, he's good at this sort of rubbish.*

'Dad?' Frankie said, suddenly fearful. 'You tried to *kill* me!'

'I will never hurt you,' John said.

'He won't hurt you, Frankie, I won't let him,' I said.

John shot me a look and I shrugged.

Say the words and come visit me, squirt, Simone said.

'What words do I have to say?' Frankie said.

'Say, "I abdicate the Jade Throne",' John said. 'Say, "The Qilin Jade Emperor is restored".'

Frankie said the words. When he'd finished, the Jade Emperor appeared in a flash of light next to the throne, smiling kindly.

The sky cleared to a brighter purer blue, and the sunlight intensified. The air sweetened and the feeling of oppression — which I hadn't even been aware of — lifted. The people working in the garden outside the window stopped and dropped their tools. They spoke to each other, obviously confused and asking what had happened.

The Demon Kings are destroyed and the Heavens are free, the Jade Emperor said. *The Jade Throne commends Princess Simone of the Northern Heavens for her courage and intelligence. Celebrate, Celestial residents, because the demons are expelled and order is restored.*

The people stared at each other with disbelief, then started hugging and laughing. Some ran off, probably to find family members, and others stood still and shocked. A few people fell to sit on the ground, weeping with joy. Some picked up their tools and continued to work, not believing that the Heavens were really free.

'Well done, House of the North. Princess Simone is to be particularly commended. Her sacrifice is honoured,' the Jade Emperor said.

Can you take the demon essence out so I can come back? Simone said.

'Sorry, Princess, you must find your own way.'

Not fair!

'Speak to the Lady, Simone, she will explain. Now.' The Jade Emperor rubbed his hands together. 'I appreciate that the House of the North needs to catch up, but there is a great deal of restoration to do, and a new treaty must be ratified with demonkind. Northern Heavens, I delegate all of this to you.'

'What? Give me a break! Can't Er Lang —' John began, but the Jade Emperor raised one hand.

'Dismissed.'

'At least let us —' John said, but the Jade Emperor disappeared.

The air cleared even more and felt fresher and purer. The world became brighter and more serene. Then it was as if a great silent bell rang through the Heavens and everything around us slotted into its rightful place. The Jade Emperor had returned to the Celestial Palace and order was restored.

The people outside who had taken up their tools dropped them again and stood stunned, looking at each other.

'I don't care what the Jade Emperor says, we're taking Frankie to see Simone right now,' I said.

'Yes, please,' Frankie said, his voice small.

I'm sending my horse. Hop on and he'll bring you to me, Simone said.

Freddo appeared in front of the dais and Frankie cowered.

Freddo knelt on his forelegs in front of Frankie. 'Good day, Prince Francis. I'm Simone's magical flying horse. Hop on and I'll take you to see her.'

Frankie straightened and his face filled with wonder. 'A magical flying horse?'

'Yes,' Freddo said with amusement.

'She told me about you. Where are your wings?'

'I'm working on it. So will you come with me to see Simone?'

Hurry up and hop on, silly! Simone said.

Frankie walked off the dais to Freddo's side, but was too small to climb on. John moved to lift him, but Frankie ran away from him, nearly colliding with the windows. 'Stay away!'

John flinched as if he'd been struck, then moved back.

'It's okay, Frankie, I'll do it,' I said.

He came to me, and I picked him up under his arms and lifted him to sit on Freddo, then held him as Freddo carefully stood upright again.

'Hold on to my mane,' Freddo said.

Frankie's expression filled with delight as he grabbed Freddo's mane and held it. 'I'm up so high! Walk around for me!'

Freddo carefully walked in a circle and I held Frankie as he crowed with delight. My throat thickened to see him so happy.

'Take him carefully,' John said.

'He won't feel the movement,' Freddo said. 'Lady Emma, if you will.'

I put my hand on Frankie's shoulder, and the hall disappeared around us. We landed next to the swimming pool that Simone had built for the Peak apartment building.

'Simone!' Frankie shouted. He slid down off Freddo's back and ran to her with his arms out. 'Thank you, Simone.' She crouched to hug him and he kissed her on the cheek. 'Thank you. I wouldn't have made it without you. I love you so much.' He threw his arms around her neck and buried his face in her shoulder. 'Thank you, Simone.'

'We're free now, Di Di, nobody will ever hurt us again,' she said, as tearful as he was. 'Can I tell them now?'

'Yes!' he said. 'Tell them everything!'

'I've been talking to him since he was ...' Simone pulled back to see his face, and brushed his hair out of his eyes. 'Three months old?'

'Younger than that,' he said, and embraced her again. They held each other tight, their eyes bright with tears. 'I was riding a flyer. There was a fight. You saw me and said hello, and then you were hurt and went away.' He gazed into her eyes. 'That was a long time ago.'

'Why didn't you tell us?' I said.

'He made me promise not to tell anyone,' Simone said. 'He was worried he'd be in trouble for talking to me.'

'I see.'

She rubbed his back. 'I'm sorry we couldn't bring you out sooner, but I wanted to be sure you'd be okay when I'd gone.'

'Oh lord, you thought it would destroy you,' I said.

'It nearly did,' John said. 'For a moment I feared I wasn't fast enough.'

'Worth it,' she said.

'You freed the Heavens, Simone,' I said. 'The demons are gone and the Jade Emperor is restored, all because of you. Do you have any idea how awesome you are?'

'Yeah!' Frankie said, gazing up at her with adoration.

'Oh, not you too,' she said. 'Daddy already gave me the "you're so awesome" talk — you don't need to. I just did what I had to do!'

'You put us all to shame. I should hand you my throne,' John said.

'Don't you dare,' she said fiercely. 'I want nothing to do with any of that bull—' She looked down at Frankie. '—dust.'

'It was worth a try,' John said.

'There's one more thing I have to do,' she said. 'Be brave, Frankie, it's about to get really freaky. Don't be scared.'

She concentrated on John. He changed to True Form and the two animals separated. The Serpent grabbed me and wrapped itself around me, pulling me to the ground. It flipped me over, still held in its coils, so I was on my stomach.

'Don't hurt my Emma!' Frankie shouted. 'Simone, stop them! Stop them!'

'No, Frankie, stay put,' Simone said, and grunted with effort. 'No, Frankie!'

'John?' I said.

'Hold still,' the Turtle said, and ripped the back of my neck open.

Frankie shrieked and I screamed with pain as the Turtle's beak scissored through me. BJ disappeared from my neck, and the Turtle's beak snapped.

'Damn, missed it,' John said. 'Frankie, let me go, I didn't hurt her. She's fine. Are you sure it was there, Simone? I didn't see anything.'

'It was there,' Simone said. 'Ask Emma.'

My mind cleared. It was like taking sunglasses off: the world around me became brighter and more colourful. The Serpent's cold healing energy moved through my neck and closed the wound.

'It's okay, Frankie, it's *okay*,' Simone said. 'Get off him! He didn't hurt her, she's *fine*!'

'Are you all right, love?' the Serpent said in John's female voice.

'That stone was controlling me and I had no idea!' I said.

'We know,' Simone said.

John released me and I turned around to sit up. Frankie was leaning on the Turtle, smacking its shell, and Simone was attempting to prise him off it.

'It's okay, Frankie,' she said, and wrenched him away.

John combined and returned to human form.

'What *was* that?' I said. 'It felt like BJ, it had her energy signature, it was definitely a Shen. I could have sworn it was her.'

'I knew something was up when she wouldn't talk to me,' Simone said. 'It was in your neck and you didn't seem yourself. It was like all the fight had gone out of you. It didn't look like a copy, it felt like BJ to me too — was she a demonic agent all along?'

'I couldn't even see it, I never knew it was there,' John said.

'Are you okay, Emma?' Frankie said.

'It's all right, love, he didn't hurt me,' I said, going to him. 'I had something bad in the back of my neck and they took it out.' He was still watching John with a mixture of suspicion and fear. 'It's really okay. Ask Simone.'

'You're very brave, Frankie,' John said gently. 'Most children run when I take my True Form.'

Frankie flinched, and John lowered his head and wiped his eyes.

'He will never hurt you,' Simone said. She bent to look Frankie in the eyes. 'Are you really okay, squirt? A lot's happened.'

He shook his head, silent. Tears ran down his cheeks and he gasped with a single sob.

'Don't be scared, Frankie,' she said, pulling him tight. 'You're safe now. Don't be afraid of the snakes, they will never hurt you. Emma and I are snakes, and you're not frightened of us.'

'You're snakes?' Frankie said, choking through his tears.

She nodded into the top of his head.

'When did you realise your mother was one of the serpent people?' John said Simone.

'When we met Mabel Defaiote and she said her name meant "white",' Simone said. 'I thought, wow, that's a coincidence, her name in Irish is the same as my mother's surname in French — and then I realised, there's no such thing as a coincidence. I put it all together. Mummy was French-Canadian, a Gallic Celt, one of the serpent people.' She shook her head. 'You should have told me; it would have made my True Form much easier to deal with.'

'You have a True Form?' John said.

Simone and I shared a look.

'And Emma knew all along,' John said with patient exasperation.

I sent him a mental image of what she looked like in True Form and he nodded. 'I see.'

'Actually I lost the arms when I stopped fighting it,' Simone said. 'It's pure snake now. We're all a big ugly reptile family.' She smiled down at Frankie. 'You have another grown-up brother and sister, but they're in Hell. We have to release everybody — they'll be so happy to see us. Oh.' She sagged with disappointment. 'I can't do anything, I'm stuck on the Earthly.'

'Simone, do you have a bunch of people stashed away somewhere?' I said. 'Celestials and loyal demons have been disappearing from the Heavens for weeks. There were rumours they were being eaten.'

'The tunnels in Western, and the Underground City in Beijing,' she said. 'We overflowed into the old fallout shelters in Beijing as well. I have about two hundred people and a hundred demons in hiding.'

'Do you have Yi Hao and Er Hao?'

'Yes.'

I sagged with relief.

'The timed lock on the door won't open for a couple of hours so I'd better go release them,' Simone said.

'No, Simone, don't leave me!' Frankie shouted. He dropped his voice. 'What happens to me now? My mummy and daddy are both dead. Can I go back to the Palace, please, Emma? Simone, can you come and live with me there?'

'Your mummy and daddy aren't dead, because they're right here,' Simone said. 'Remember I told you that you had real loving parents? Emma's your real mummy, and Xuan Wu's your real daddy.'

'Emma's my real mother?' Frankie turned and studied me appraisingly. 'Why didn't you tell me that?'

'They ordered me not to. I couldn't.'

'You should have told me, Emma,' he said.

'She didn't have a choice, Frankie,' John said.

'And you're my real father?'

John nodded.

'You tried to *kill* me.'

'I would not have hurt you. I could destroy the demon without touching you.' He saw Frankie's face. 'Believe me, Frankie. I promise I will never harm you.'

Frankie turned away from us and hugged Simone. 'Let's go back to the Palace, Simone.' He glanced at me under her arm. 'You can come too, Emma, but the man can't.'

'I can't go, squirt,' she said, squeezing him. 'I'm stuck on the Earthly now. You should be with your real parents.'

'I want to stay with you, Simone.'

'We understand, Frankie, don't worry,' I said. 'We know you want to stay with her and we'll work something out.'

'I want to go back to uni, and he can't come to the dorms with me,' Simone said. 'Frankie, you should go and live with them in Heaven.'

'I want to stay with *you*,' he said.

'How about I take the apartment one floor down from Martin and Leo's?' she said. 'We still have ownership of the Peak building, I sneaked the deeds out of the safe deposit box and kept them. I'll just fly over to Japan for classes. They already have Buffy, I'm sure they won't mind having you during the day as well.'

'I'll move down here and look after him,' I said. 'I promised both of you I would never leave you, and I meant it.' I turned to John. 'I'm sorry, John, but —'

'I'll move here too,' he said. 'I can travel and take True Form; it won't be a major issue.'

'That sounds wonderful,' I said. 'We can live as a family on the Earthly again. But that's a hell of a commute for both of you.'

'Worth it to be with our children,' John said. 'Simone? We could take a place in Tokyo to be closer to your studies.'

'No, Leo and Ge Ge are here with Buffy — Frankie should be with the family,' she said. 'It will be easy to come over from Japan, it'll take me less than half an hour.'

'It's settled then,' John said.

'The Jade Emperor will go ballistic when he hears,' I said.

'He doesn't have a choice,' John said. 'If he tries to stop me, I'll just tell him to —'

'Go to Hell,' we said in unison, and stopped.

He grinned at me, I grinned back, and then we were in each other's arms and kissing with all the fervour of the months we'd spent apart.

'Ew!' Frankie and Simone said loudly.

'So *gross*!' Frankie said.

'Totally,' Simone said.

We pulled back from one another, then quickly hugged again.

'Heavens come first,' he said into my ear, and gave me a squeeze. 'We need to free our people in Hell, and meet with the new Demon King to work out a treaty.' He turned to Simone. 'Can you take Frankie with you when you release the people you have hidden?'

'Of course, Dad,' Simone said. 'He'll be fine with me. Hurry up and free those people from the Pits.'

'Let's go, John,' I said. 'There are a great many people in Hell who will be extremely glad to see us.'

'The Jade Emperor is a slave driver,' John said. 'It'll be weeks before either of us can stop and enjoy the fact that our family is finally safe and we won.'

'And then we have a really huge wedding to organise!' Simone said, delighted.

John and I moaned in unison and headed to Hell.

32

We went straight to the Mountain after releasing the Celestials from Hell.

Wudang hadn't been damaged, and the Masters were busy shuttling the students home from the Western Palace construction site, and helping them to move tables out of the mess and onto the main square for an impromptu street party.

'It's fine, they love you,' John said, rubbing my back as we walked to Persimmon Tree Pavilion.

The door opened and there was my mother.

'Emma!' she shouted, and threw her arms around me. She held me so tight I couldn't breathe. 'Thank god!' She pulled back, released me, and took John's hand. 'John. You did it. You both did it.' She looked at us, her eyes brimming with tears. 'Where's Simone? Oh, that's right —'

What she said next was lost in the babble of voices as my sisters joined us.

'Where's everybody else?' I said. 'The family's okay, right?'

'Greg's rounding —' my mother began, and Greg appeared on the other side of the room with my father and Andrew.

My father ran to my mother and clutched her, burying his face in the side of her neck, and Andrew hugged Jennifer.

'Be right back,' Greg said, and disappeared.

'Me too,' John said, and disappeared as well.

My father squeezed my mother again, and smiled at me as he held her. 'Well done, Emma, you did it.'

'Simone did it,' I said.

'Not surprising, she's always been special,' Jennifer said, holding Andrew tight.

'Where's Mattie?' Andrew said.

Greg reappeared with Alan, and John appeared with Mark and David. Amanda squealed and ran to them.

'Mum?' Andrew said. 'Please tell me Matthew's okay.'

Matthew came out of the bedroom, half-asleep. He saw everybody and yelled with delight. 'Andrew!' He ran to him and they shared a huge hug.

'Matthew, little Mattie,' Andrew said.

'Are we really okay?' Matthew said. 'Emma, where's Frankie? Is he all right?'

'Frankie's fine, he's with Simone,' I said.

Jen pushed through the crush and hugged me. Alan patted my shoulder. Greg stood at the back, towering over everybody with a huge grin.

'Tell us it's all over, Em,' Amanda said. 'We heard the Jade Emperor, but we want to hear it from you.'

'Both Demon Kings are dead,' I said.

'The Jade Emperor is restored. We're free,' John said.

'Really?' Amanda said. 'No more occupation?'

'No more. The new Demon King has returned to Hell with all the demons. They're gone. We're safe and free.'

Jennifer whooped and hugged Greg.

'I'm sorry about Colin,' I said to Jennifer.

'He wasn't the only one lost,' she said. 'He died protecting the family.' She glanced up at Greg. 'Are we all really safe now?'

'Truly,' he said. 'It's over.'

'So what happens to us now?' my mother said.

John leaned against the wall. 'You don't have to squeeze into this tiny house any more. All of the Heavens and Earthly are yours. You can choose where you want to live, and the Celestial will support you.'

My mother and father sat on the couch, holding hands. Greg leaned on the back of the other couch, where Jennifer sat with Andrew and Matthew. Amanda and Alan sat next to her, and their boys, Mark and David, stood behind them next to Greg.

'You have plenty of time to decide. And until you make up your minds, you can stay in the Imperial Residence and the Crown Prince's Residence in the Northern Heavens,' I said. 'There's room for everybody.'

'Once everything's back to normal, tell us what sort of house you'd like and where, and we'll arrange it for you,' John said. 'Mountain or Northern Heavens, townhouse or farm — whatever you like, I can provide it.'

'Farm?' my mother said. She glanced at my father.

'We were thinking of an acreage near Brisbane,' my father said.

'What about Toi's place?' I asked John. 'Isn't that still empty after we confiscated it?'

John nodded. 'That's the stud where Freddo was bred. It's been empty with a skeleton staff of demon servants for a while now. It's a few hundred li —'

'A horse stud?' my mother said. 'Here in Heaven?'

'It's lovely,' I said. 'It has a mansion, stables, yards and beautiful green paddocks. You don't have to breed horses; you could do anything with it.'

My parents grinned at each other, then back at us.

'Is there enough room for all the grandkids?' my mother said. 'Can everyone come visit us?'

'Of course,' John said.

'Space for the whole family,' I said. 'You could move in right now.'

My mother squeezed my father's hand with delight.

'We'd love that,' my father said. 'Acreage in Heaven. Ponies for the boys.'

'It sounds *wonderful*,' my mother said.

'Can Jen and I stay with you until the West is rebuilt?' Greg asked my parents.

'Of course you can,' my mother said. 'You're returning to the West?'

'Dad's Number One quit,' Greg said. 'Michael left. I'm moving up to Number Three to help Dad's new Number One.'

'Rohan's been promoted to Number One?' I said.

'Rohan and I refused the position of Number One,' he said. 'Katie's better than both of us. Dad's finally promoted the best person for the job, and about time.'

'Congratulate Katie for us,' I said. 'Amanda? Alan? What do you want to do?'

'I want to ask you something, John,' Amanda said.

'Anything you want,' he said.

'A young man was helping us while we were locked up here. He worked hard to protect us all. His name is Justin.'

'The demon master,' I said.

'His job is managing all the demons on the Mountain,' Amanda said. 'He looks after them, and makes sure they do their jobs and they're cared for.'

'That's right,' John said.

'He doesn't want to do it, but he told me what's involved, and I think I'd enjoy it.'

'Are you sure?' John asked her.

'Yes. He's explained the job to me and I want to do it. I was working side by side with the demons during the occupation, and I like them.' She smiled wryly. 'As far as I understand, the job harms whoever does it, but I might be different.'

'Our unusual nature may mean she can do it without harm,' I said.

'That's what I was thinking,' Amanda said.

'Alan,' John said, 'have you two talked about this? We don't need an insurance assessor on the Celestial Plane.'

'Yes, we have. I'm not sure I want to return to that after being away from it for so long. I'd like to take some time and decide what I want to do.' He smiled at Amanda. 'If she wants to pursue this, I'll support her all the way.'

'We'll arrange it,' John said. 'Stay here in Persimmon Tree if you want.'

They may not want to; Colin died here, I said to John.

'Or anywhere else on the Mountain you please,' John said, nodding to acknowledge me. 'We have a couple of residences free here.'

Amanda squeezed Alan's hand. 'Thank you. Somewhere else would be better.'

'I'll arrange it,' John said.

'Can we see the farm?' my mother said, excited. 'You said there was a core staff of demons. How big is it in acres?'

'I'll take them to see it,' Greg said. 'Just show me where it is.'

'Can I see it too?' Matthew said.

'I'd like to see it as well,' Amanda said.

John bowed to them. 'I live to serve my Lady's family.'

My mother went to John and took his hand. 'Your family as well now.'

He smiled down at her. 'Thank you.'

* * *

We stayed at the farm for a while, then all returned to the Mountain to join the party, which was well underway in the main square. John and I shared in the celebrations; then, as dusk fell, we walked around the Mountain, ensuring that the Celestial weapons were safe in the armoury and the residents were secure.

Amy met us at the entrance to the Imperial Residence. 'Have you found Gold and BJ?' she said.

'BJ was working with the demons; she may have been controlled by them,' I said. 'We'll ask the Jade Emperor for his help in tracking them down. He's the element of stone; he should know where they are.'

'I'm so worried about them,' she said. 'None of them are answering. All three of them are missing now.'

'We will find them,' John said. He put his hand on her shoulder. 'Go home and be with your children. We will speak to the Jade Emperor first thing tomorrow.'

She nodded, obviously still concerned, and turned away.

We entered the Mountain's Imperial Residence. The furniture was still there, but the Xuan Wu statue in the courtyard was gone, and they'd removed all our paintings.

Smally and Yi Hao were in the kitchen. Smally was washing the floor, Yi Hao was wiping the cabinets, and they were arguing loudly.

'What's the matter?' I said.

'Ma'am!' they shouted, and ran to me.

Smally flopped to kneel on the floor in front of me and burst into tears. 'You're alive!'

Yi Hao clutched me. 'You're all right.' She pulled back. 'This house is a *wreck*.'

'Not my fault!' Smally said.

John went to the stove and filled the kettle.

Smally jumped to her feet and pushed him away from it. 'That is entirely unfitting, Highness!'

'Tell us what you want and we will make it for you,' Yi Hao said.

'Tea, tikuanyin, and bring it to the living room, please,' I said.

'Ma'am.'

They proceeded to argue over who would make the tea, so John and I left them to it and went into the living room together. We held each other on the couch, enjoying the closeness.

Both Yi Hao and Smally came in with the tea and cups.

'I have important work for both of you,' I said as they put the tea things on the table.

They straightened, attentive.

'Smally, you'll manage our Celestial Residences. Go to our Imperial apartments in the Northern Heavens and in the Celestial Palace and list what restoration work needs to be done. You'll be in charge of it,' I said. 'Yi Hao, head down to the Peak where Er Hao is, and help Princess Simone to set up our new Earthly Residence. You'll be my assistant on the Earthly.'

'Ma'am,' they said in unison, and disappeared.

'Artfully done,' John said, pouring the tea.

'What's next?' I said.

'We don't need to check the Northern Heavens; Ming and Yue are handling that, and there's another party happening. Drafting the treaty, let me see.' He concentrated. 'The new Demon King will meet us at 10 a.m. on the Earthly tomorrow. The Jade Emperor will provide us with the terms; we'll just have to negotiate the agreement.'

'Where will we stay tonight?' I said. 'I'd prefer to go down to Frankie now — I need to explain his new situation to him. He needs to understand that he's no longer Jade Emperor.'

'Of course. That's very important. No, wait. Simone and Frankie are way ahead of us. They're out shopping for furniture, and they'll meet us for dinner at Leo and Martin's apartment on the Peak.' He concentrated. 'We can sleep in one of the spare rooms there tonight. Zara says that Celestials are moving back home, the phoenixes are returning to the volcano …' He threw himself backwards and put his hands behind his head. 'Dinner with the family in about an hour, and nothing else until our appointment with the Demon King tomorrow. We can check the apartment below Martin and Leo's and see what else we need in there before we move in.'

'Let's go to our room and pack some stuff to take,' I said. 'It's hard enough having three households. Having another one on the Earthly will be a pain.'

'We must remove the demon essence from Simone,' he said.

There were explosions outside and both of us jumped to our feet.

John relaxed. 'Fireworks. There's a big celebration happening.'

'We should go and join them,' I said.

'Actually …' He turned to gaze into my eyes. 'How about a small celebration right here?'

'There's something I need to do first.'

'It must be important.'

'Absolutely vital. I need the longest hottest shower ever.'

'That's the best idea you've ever had. It's been *weeks*.' He studied me intensely. 'May I join you?'

I put my hand on his cheek. 'You don't need time in the sea or the Grotto?'

He took my hand and turned to go up the stairs. 'I need time with you more.'

* * *

'It will be strange being in the Peak with you again,' I said as we walked naked from the bathroom into our bedroom, warm and surrounded by the clean scent of soap. 'We never lived there together.'

We stopped and studied our Mountain bedroom: the fireplace, the comfortable chairs, and our ebony bed with its silver and black silken hangings.

362

'Just one thing missing,' I said softly.

'I was thinking the same thing,' he said, and we were on the bed together, skin to skin.

'It's been a long time,' he said into my ear. 'Months. Months without you.' He ran his hand down my side. 'I missed you so much.'

I kissed his throat. 'When you were in the cage, I couldn't sense you. I love this ...' I pulled myself closer. 'Being wrapped up in you, surrounded by you.'

He nuzzled into me. 'I feel the same way.' He made soft sounds of pleasure as he explored me. 'Take Celestial Form.'

'I don't really ...' I began, and stopped pretending I didn't have one.

I took my larger battle form, and he joined me in Celestial Form; his smallest one, to match my size. The bed creaked under our weight.

His beard tickled me as he spoke into the side of my throat. 'The Tiger has a special bed. Bigger.' He slid on top of me, his mahogany-brown skin glowing against my white. 'Focus on your ching. Your essence.'

I concentrated on the essence, deep and low, and it sprang to life. He closed his eyes, touched his forehead to mine, and I felt his ching as well. We were in contact down the lengths of our bodies and the red ching flared between us.

'Keep it under control, try not to let it —'

But it was too late. It escaped me and merged with his and I screamed and bucked under him. He was swept away with me and we were lost in a wild flood of energy that surged between us.

I came around with him lying next to me, studying my face.

'My fault,' he said, stroking my cheek. 'I overestimated your energy ability, particularly after several months of incarceration.'

'We didn't even ...' I shook my head. 'We hadn't even started!' I lifted my head and dropped it. 'Wow. I ache all over. That nearly killed me.'

'I know. Your heart stopped for a couple of minutes. I was about to do CPR.'

'I'll be sore as anything tomorrow. I think every muscle went into spasm.'

'I'll give you a hot bath with bubbles and a full-body massage with shen energy if you are.'

I turned to smile into his face. 'You just made nearly dying worthwhile.'

'I'm sorry, love, it was my mistake. I've never tried that with anyone before,' he said, rueful.

'But I bet you've wanted to try it for a long time.'

He nodded.

'Excellent practice for me,' I said with enthusiasm. 'I think I will very much enjoy mastering this particular energy work.' I raised my head. 'Why is the bed wonky? Oh shit, we broke the bed again, didn't we?'

He nodded again.

'I think we should ask the Tiger to make one out of metal for us.'

'Never,' he said, and cuddled closer to me. 'I will not give that damn cat the satisfaction. He'd tell everybody. The Dragon will do one for us out of stronger wood and keep it quiet. Oh.' He smiled and lifted my hair. 'Look.'

My hair had grown back long and black. I concentrated and changed it to brown. I ran my hands down the smooth muscles of his back to cup his behind, then drifted them up again, and he shivered with pleasure.

I moved closer to breathe into his ear. 'Again? Let's take our time. Dinner won't be for a while.'

He ran his fingertips up and down my back. 'You're not too drained?'

'Absolutely not. I'm fine. But I don't think I can deal with anything more than vanilla right now. That was intense.'

'I think there's some ice-cream in the freezer. I can bring it.'

'That's not what I meant, and we're having dinner with the family, remember?'

'Then we'll find some time for the vanilla afterwards,' he said, and pulled me tighter.

* * *

The early evening lights were coming on across the harbour when we returned to the Peak. The pollution was so reduced that the evening was as clear as it had been when I'd first arrived to live there as a nanny — a spectacular show of colourful lights.

We landed in the lift lobby outside the apartment door, and John concentrated.

Martin opened the door. 'My Lord, my Lady, welcome home.'

We went in and removed our shoes.

'In the dining room,' Martin said.

All the family was sitting around the table: Leo, Buffy, Simone and Frankie. Both of us saluted when we saw that Kwan Yin had joined us as well.

I ran to her and she stood to give me a hug.

'I am so glad it is all over,' she said. 'Well done, all of you.'

'Holy Bodhisattva Kwan Yin.' John bowed to her. 'I present to you my son, Prince Franklin —'

Simone squeaked.

'Prince Xuan Si Shu Franklin, my first human son.'

'"Memory of Mercy" — I am honoured,' she said.

'My name's Francis, not Franklin,' Frankie said.

'It's Franklin now,' Simone said. 'Francis was the name of that horrible man who pretended to be your father. Franklin was one of the nicest people *ever*.'

'It makes no difference,' I said. 'People will still call you Frankie, sweetheart.'

'Oh, okay,' he said, and returned to his food.

'Are you starving?' I asked him.

He ignored me, he was too busy eating.

'Sit. Eat. Catch up,' Kwan Yin said. She nodded to Martin. 'If you have need of me, just call.'

He bowed to her. 'Thank you for your help, my Lady.'

She disappeared.

'She was really nice,' Frankie said, but didn't stop shovelling food into his mouth.

'Slow down, you'll be sick,' Simone said.

'But it's so *yummy*,' he said.

John and I sat. I picked some vegetables off the plate in the centre of the table and put them in his bowl while he served us rice.

'Is everything good? You have clothes and furniture and things?' I said.

'Yeah, all organised,' Simone said. 'The furniture's already here. We found a Shen who owns a furniture shop — she sent it straight up and I brought it through the windows, easy.'

She concentrated and a glowing floor plan of the Peak apartment appeared suspended in the air in front of her, showing the four bedrooms, the training room, and the two student rooms on the end.

'Daddy and Emma,' she said, and John's old room glowed. 'Frankie.' The room next to the master bedroom. 'Me.' The next one after that. 'The other bedroom's free, but we'll probably need two offices, one for each of you —'

'No, wait, that's this apartment,' John said. 'We'll take the three-bedroom one on the next floor down. Ming and Leo don't have to move out.'

'We already did,' Leo said. 'You need the training room, my Lord, and both you and Emma will be administering the Heavens from here so you'll need offices.'

Simone marked the fourth bedroom with my name and the office with John's. She raised one finger and drew two little stick figures shouting across the hallway, complete with random symbols to indicate that we were swearing at each other.

'And you'll want to have students here to give them live-in martial arts training,' she said. The training room and two student rooms glowed. 'All fixed.'

'We do not want you to move out; you live here,' I said to Leo.

'Too late, we already did,' Martin said. 'The three of us don't need all this space, and you do.'

'We'll be up and down the stairs all the time anyway,' Leo said. 'And you can give us private training here, so it's all good. We'll probably eat like this most nights.'

John hesitated with his chopsticks halfway to his mouth, then smiled and shook his head. 'Family dinners? That sounds —'

'Fantastic,' I said, and picked up some more vegetables.

'We already moved all our stuff downstairs, we just shifted it directly,' Leo said.

'I bought you some furniture for your bedroom, Daddy,' Simone said, 'it's similar to what you had before. Go and check it, and if you don't like it you can change it. The Shen said any time until 10 p.m., and for you probably later.'

'Is it black?' I said.

'Of course,' she said.

I shrugged. 'Then he likes it.'

John opened his mouth to say something, and closed it again.

* * *

After dinner we went to check the furniture Simone had purchased for us. John went to the door of the master bedroom, stopped and smiled at me, then opened the door. I followed him into the familiar bedroom that I had dreamed about sneaking into so many times.

'Do me a favour?' I said.

'Hmm?' he said, poking his head into the bathroom to check it.

'Lie on that.' I pointed at the bed.

He shrugged and lay on top of the quilt. He banged his head on the pillow and turned to look at me. 'Are you tired?'

'No,' I said, and crawled onto the bed beside him. I wrapped my arms around him and held him close, something I'd dreamed of doing every night when we'd lived there. He slid his arms around me and kissed my forehead and I couldn't help myself: I burst into tears and clutched him.

'Emma, Emma,' he said, holding me. 'What's the matter? What's wrong?'

'We. Made. It,' I gasped through the sobs. All my joy flooded out in a wash of tears. 'We're here. In this room. Together. You're whole again. We have a child of our own next door, and Simone is safe here too. Leo is here and content. We're all safe. The Heavens are safe. The Mountain is safe. I love you. I'm so happy.'

'Oh,' he said, and held me as I wept.

Ten minutes later I'd stopped crying and we lay holding each other, enjoying the closeness. I sniffled, feeling the after effects of the rush of emotion.

'Would you like a drink of water?' he said, his voice warm and low.

'Yes, but I don't want to let go of you.'

'Here.' He pulled himself up to lean against the bedhead, and lifted me as well. 'I haven't done this in a while, too weak. Let's see.'

He held one hand out, the other arm still wrapped around me, and a bubble of water appeared in front of us.

'Don't try to drink that, it will drown you, it's the wrong shape,' he said. He flicked his hand and the water changed form to a long narrow cylinder, two centimetres wide and thirty long. 'There. Mineralised. Do you want carbonated? I can make it sparkling.'

I shook my head, pursed my lips as the water approached, and sipped it.

'Damn, that is the hottest thing I have ever seen you do,' he said with wonder.

I took a deep drink and he made a low sound of pleasure. The water was cool and refreshing, sweet with the taste of minerals, and I closed my eyes with bliss as I tasted it.

'I cannot believe I have not done this for you before,' he said. 'I can feel all of that, and it feels ... Oh damn, visitors.' He straightened and the water disappeared.

I felt it too: Simone and Frankie were outside our bedroom door.

'Sorry!' Simone said loudly as Frankie banged on the door.

'What's the matter?' John said. 'Is something wrong?'

'Emma promised me training with the sword *today*,' Frankie said. 'She *promised*.'

I levered myself off the bed. 'He's right, I did.'

John snapped his wrist at the door and it opened. 'How about we all go into the training room and do some sword?' he said. 'As a family?'

Simone grinned broadly. 'Come on, squirt,' she said. 'Let's show you what family is really all about.' She held his hand. 'Daddy, talk to the JE again about taking out this demon essence. I really, *really* want to return to the Mountain for advanced training.'

'Is John as good as Emma?' Frankie asked Simone.

'Nearly,' she said with amusement as she led him down the hall to the training room. 'One day he'll be just as good as she is.'

John shook his head. 'My own son calling me an English name. So wrong.'

'Teach him to call you Xuan,' I said.

'I want him to call me Ba Ba.'

'It will happen.'

33

Er Lang and Guan Yu were already in the hotel conference room when we arrived the next morning. Everybody saluted around, then we sat at the table and waited for the demons.

'What did the Jade Emperor say when he saw my missive?' John asked Er Lang.

'He went very quiet.'

'How quiet?' Guan Yu said with amusement.

'Extremely.'

'You won't have the chance to tell him to go to Hell then,' Guan Yu said to John. 'What a shame.'

'He's still in a world of trouble,' Er Lang said, and we all stood as the demons entered.

Andy had brought Edu, who appeared as a girl of fourteen, still smaller than a natural human. A Duke and a Snake Mother provided an escort. I'd never seen these demons before; they were probably new promotions.

Andy stopped at the table and saluted everybody, and we all saluted back. John gestured for Andy to take a seat, and he gestured for John to sit first. John sat, and everybody on the Celestial side sat as well, carefully in order of seniority.

Andy sat at the table and crossed his legs, relaxed. He gestured towards Edu as she pulled a chair out and clambered onto it like a child. 'My Number One.'

'She destroyed her competition?' John said with interest. 'One so young?'

'I ate them all,' Edu said with a cruel grin. She focused on me. 'You're next.'

'Quiet, Edu, it's treaty time,' Andy said. He gestured towards John. 'Let me see.'

John pushed the copy of the treaty across the table and Andy read it carefully.

I liked being in the Celestial Palace, Edu said to me. *You drove me out of there. You will pay for that. I'm rounding up all the things that my father researched — and when I'm big enough, and I know it all, I will stab this lump of shit in the back and take over as King.* She leaned forward, her grin vicious. *And the first thing I'll do as King is track you down and skin you alive.*

'Leave Emma alone, Edu,' Andy said without looking up from the treaty, sounding bored. 'Nobody has time for your attention-seeking right now.'

She just said that she's gathering your father's research, I said to Andy.

I know, he said. *When she has it all together, I'll eat her.* He smiled, still studying the treaty. *She's in for a surprise when she tries me; a couple of her victories were staged. She's not as strong or as smart as she thinks she is.*

I nodded, satisfied.

Tell me later, John said.

I will.

Andy put his hand on the treaty and looked up at John. 'I want a clause added that says neither of your human kids will ever come to my side of Hell.'

John eyed him appraisingly. 'They scare you that much?'

'Just keep them away.'

'I'm not scared of them,' Edu said.

'Then you're a fucking idiot,' Andy said, and pushed the treaty over to John.

John pulled out his Xuan Wu fountain pen and scribbled the

characters vertically at the end of the treaty. He passed it back to Andy.

Andy studied the addition, nodded, pulled an expensive lacquer fountain pen out of his breast pocket, and signed the treaty with a flourish. He stabbed his thumb with the end of the pen, and marked the treaty with his bloodied thumbprint. He passed the treaty to John.

John signed it, then held his hand out and his Imperial seal, carved with an image of himself in True Form, appeared in it. He stamped the seal over his signature in black ink.

Andy stood and held his hand out. 'Xuan Tian.'

John stood as well and shook his hand. 'Wong Mo.'

'Let me know when you want the formal ceremony,' Andy said. He cocked his head. 'Does the chick play?'

'The *Empress* does not play well. But the Tiger and the Phoenix may.'

'This weekend?'

'My secretary will be in touch.'

Andy saluted him, and John saluted back.

'I will tear your arms off and feed them to you, Emma,' Edu said with relish.

I hesitated for a moment, looking at her, then grinned. 'Bring it.'

They disappeared.

'Thoroughly back to normal,' John said, closing the leather portfolio holding the treaty.

'Teach me to play better. I'd like to play for her hide,' I said.

'I would very much like to be part of that,' Er Lang said, studying where the demons had been.

'Me too,' Guan Yu said. 'Let's get all this rebuilding out of the way as quickly as possible, because teaching this intelligent and merciless woman to play for high stakes sounds like more fun than anything.'

* * *

We stood at the end of the alley that led to the double doors of the Imperial Residence. For a moment I felt I was returning to servitude, and resisted the urge to back away. John saw my face and put his hand on my back, and I nodded to him.

The doors opened and we went through the entry hall and into the Jade Emperor's small meeting room. The Jade Emperor was sitting on the sofa, looking as if he'd never left; but the screen behind the sofa was still gone. The Demon King had sold all the valuables to dealers on the Earthly to pay for the human mercenaries, and many of the treasures were lost forever.

The Emperor had lost weight and become sallow during his incarceration, but he glowed with good humour to see us.

A Palace fairy brought us tea, and clasped me on the shoulder as she left the room.

'Demons first,' the Emperor said. 'What did the Demon King say? How long will it take to finalise the new treaty?'

'Simone and Frankie scared them to such a degree that the new Demon King agreed to everything we presented to him and signed the draft treaty on the spot,' John said, placing the treaty on the coffee table. 'The administrative staff are formalising it, and we'll have the official signing in about three days, depending on which day is the best for such activities.'

'Good,' the Emperor said. 'How are Frankie and Simone?'

'Simone is fine,' I said. 'She was planning to go to university anyway; I think she'll enjoy the opportunity to avoid all her Heavenly duties.'

'But she needs to take her place in the Heavens,' John said. 'We must find a way to restore her status as an Immortal.'

'Don't worry about it; it will happen in its own time,' the Emperor said.

'That's very easy for you to say,' I said. 'I would very much like to live on the Mountain with my husband and family. The Earthly *stinks.*'

'Not husband yet.' He saw my face. 'I know, I know, this is not the time for that particular argument. How about the boy? He's been through a great deal.'

'We'll arrange therapy,' John said. His voice filled with pain. 'Will he ever call me Father?'

'His idea of "father" is someone who is terrifyingly abusive,' the Emperor said. 'He will never call you Father, but one day he will see you as a friend.'

'I thank you,' John said, his voice low.

'Is everyone ready for tomorrow?'

'We are. The flags are in,' John said.

'Good. This will be a great deal of fun; I'm looking forward to it.' His voice changed. 'The three stones in your service that are missing. Has there been any word on them?'

'None at all,' I said. 'All three of them are gone. The Grandmother has no idea. Can you see them?'

'No, they are outside my jurisdiction. They're probably in the European Heavens,' the Emperor said. 'And now that Simone has been converted, we have no way to enter there. So we'll go with the plan. Set a date for the wedding and see where it takes us.'

'I really, really do not like this idea,' John said.

'Are you sure you'll know?' I asked the Emperor. 'John couldn't see them. Only Simone could. They looked like the real thing to me — they glowed like Shen.'

'I am Stone, Lady Emma. I will know.'

'I still hate this idea,' John said. 'They'll try to replace Emma with something I can't sense and can't see. There are so many things that could go wrong!'

'We will continue to search until your wedding day, and then we will set the trap —'

'With Emma as bait!' John said.

'— and find out where the stones are. Is there anything else?'

'I would like to invite the Jade Empress to the wedding,' John said. 'How are the trees?'

'Fortunately the demons did not remove her from the Peach Garden when they took control, so none of the trees were harmed,' the Emperor said. 'When she came down to see Nu Wa, the hour she spent here was nine months in the garden. The watering system failed on one of the trees while she was away, and her staff are repairing it. It will take two days in the garden, which is nearly thirty-five years here. She cannot return here for quite some time.'

'I'm sorry to hear that; I was hoping to finally meet her,' I said.

'She has said the same, but her responsibilities come first.'

'Maybe when things have settled down —' John began.

'— I can take some time and visit her, and you will mind things here,' the Emperor finished for him. 'You've been saying that for a thousand years, Ah Wu, and we both know the likelihood of it happening.'

'Majesty.'

'She really should delegate,' I said.

'We tried that in the past, and look what it achieved,' he said.

'That wasn't delegating; that was postponing having to deal with a pain in the ass,' I said. 'Sending the Monkey King to look after the garden was beyond stupid, particularly when the peaches were close to ripe.'

The Jade Emperor stiffened and glared at me.

I shrugged. 'Well, it was.'

'Dismissed,' the Emperor said with dignified restraint. 'In future, Lord Xuan, I would prefer to see you alone.'

John put his hand on my shoulder and teleported me out. When we arrived back on the Mountain, he fell to sit on the couch, put his hand over his eyes, and laughed until he couldn't breathe.

* * *

Later that afternoon we visited my family at the new farm. The paddocks were lush and green — the grass had grown too long without stock on it. The house was a three-storey village type, with a flat roof holding potted shrubs in an elegant roof garden.

A demon answered the door, then backed away, bowing to us. 'Highnesses, allow me to show you inside. I will tell the Lords and Ladies —'

'Mum, it's us!' I shouted.

The demon's mouth flopped open and he stared at us.

My mother trotted into the entry hall wearing jeans and a T-shirt. 'Well, don't just stand there, come on through! I want to ask you a few questions.' She took John by the arm and reached up to kiss him on the cheek. 'Come and have some tea and biscuits.'

My mother sat us at the dining table in the sunny room that overlooked the paddocks. She busied herself with the kettle and made a pot of Ceylon tea.

'Where is everybody?' I said.

'Your father's out there somewhere checking the fences with Freddo, and the boys are helping them,' my mother said. 'Amanda's on the Mountain with Alan finding out about her new job, and Jen and Greg are upstairs unpacking. Did you find Gold yet?'

'Not yet, but we're working on it,' I said.

Matthew came charging down the stairs and stopped when he saw us. 'I want to play with Frankie. Where's Frankie?'

'I'll tell him you want to play, and I'll see if he wants to come next time,' I said.

'Okay,' Matthew said, and messily tucked into a biscuit.

'No more of them or you won't eat your dinner,' my mother said, closing the biscuit packet.

He made a huffy sound and ran out of the room. He turned the television on in the living room next door.

'And turn that down!' my mother shouted. She lowered her voice. 'There's a few things we want to ask you about the property, Emma.'

'Do anything you want with it and charge it back to me,' John said.

My mother hesitated. 'But I want to buy ponies, and a puppy, and there isn't enough bed linen, things like that. We may not be able to purchase them in Heaven, and I don't want to spend all your money on the Earthly!'

'Mum.' I took her hand. 'I'm sending Jade here to help you the minute she's free, and she'll set up an expense account for you. You can purchase anything you want on the Earthly, up to and including a private jet.'

My mother glanced at John and he nodded.

'Here in the Heavens you can charge purchases back to us,' I said. 'Believe it or not, our expense account is more limited here because of the nature of the Heavenly economy. On the Earthly you have an unlimited account, because if we want more money we just ask the Tiger for some gold.'

'Oh,' she said. She straightened and smiled. 'Well, that's all right then. I was worried I'd be emptying your bank account.'

'Just let me know if you plan to spend more than about a hundred million US dollars, because I'll have to top it up,' John said.

'A hundred million,' she said. 'A hundred. Million.'

He shrugged.

'How much are you worth, John?' she said. 'On the Earthly, I mean?'

'Ask Jade,' he said. 'I have no idea.'

'In the Heavens?'

'All of it.'

'All of what?'

'The Northern Heavens.'

'Oh.'

'Is there anything else you need?' I said.

She rose. 'Come with me and I'll show you what we're planning to do with the stables. Freddo wants to live here when he's not with Simone, and he has some ideas as well. He wants to put a sand arena in, buy some jumps, things like that for when we have the ponies.'

'Actually, Mum, we might do that later,' I said. 'Right now we really need to do something with Jennifer. It's about Colin.'

John concentrated.

'I saw that, it's very rude,' my mother said.

Greg and Jennifer came in, and Greg grabbed one of the biscuits. 'We need to buy some blankets, Jen wasn't warm enough last night.' He saluted John, still holding the biscuit. 'My Lord?'

'Jen and Greg, there's something we need to show you,' I said. 'It's about …' I took a deep breath. 'Colin. Please brace yourselves, this isn't pretty, but you need to see and you need to make a decision.'

I went to John and he put his hand on my shoulder.

'What about Colin?' my mother said weakly.

'We'll explain when we come back,' I said.

John concentrated on Greg, showing him where to go, and Greg put his hand on Jennifer's shoulder.

We landed outside the company building in China. Wind whistled across it, full of dust and smoke, and the air smelled strongly of diesel.

John and I shared a look, and he nodded to me.

'Jennifer, the Demon King was doing some stuff with biological science — genetic manipulation and cloning,' I looked away. 'He cloned Colin. There are twenty-three clones of Colin in here.'

'Colin's alive?' she said, delighted.

'His body is in there too, preserved in ice,' I said.

'We will arrange the funeral,' John said. 'He will receive full hero's honours. He died defending his family.'

Greg put his arm around Jen's shoulders.

'But he's back to life with the clones? *Twenty* of them?' she said. 'Where will we put them all?'

'I don't think Lord Xuan and Lady Emma want to put them anywhere, love,' Greg said sadly.

'How old are they?' Jennifer said. 'Can I see them?'

John gestured towards the double entry doors. 'This way.'

The same young woman was sitting behind the reception desk when we entered. John concentrated on her and her face went blank. He led us through the doors to the lift well.

'Before we go into the clone lab, you need to know,' I said as the lift arrived and we entered it. 'The clones are all snakes.'

'Snakes?' Jennifer said with disbelief.

'They cloned Colin's snake form?' Greg said.

'Yes,' John said. 'It's possible these clones may never be human.'

'Do they talk?' Jennifer said.

'They are starting to say a few words, yes,' I said.

'I feel sick,' Jennifer said. She leaned into Greg. 'I'm not sure I want to see Colin's corpse.'

'You don't have to,' I said.

'I'm not sure I want to see the clones either,' she said weakly. 'Snakes.'

'I'm here,' Greg said, holding her.

The lift doors opened and we went into the lab. Some of the Tiger's children had taken over, and they'd put a sheet over Colin's corpse.

One of them stood waiting for us. 'Lord Xuan, Lady Emma, Lord Bai Jin, Lady Jennifer.'

Jen stopped. 'Is that him?'

'Yes,' I said. I took her hand. 'The demons cut him up. We understand if you don't want to see him. It's a snake; it's not his human form.'

'No. I don't.' She shook her head. 'That's not how I want to remember my son. Show me the clones.'

The Tiger's son led her into the next room, where one of his daughters was waiting for us, wearing a white lab coat and holding a clipboard. The clones were in a room with a large glass viewing window. They had soft mats and balls, and were a black mass of bodies writhing over the floor.

Jennifer put her hand over her mouth at the sight of them, and her shoulders heaved. Greg led her to the side of the room and she vomited into one of the lab sinks, hacking and coughing.

'It's okay, it's okay,' he said gently. 'The staff will take care of it. We understand.'

John and I waited next to the viewing window for her to recover. She leaned against the wall and wiped her eyes, and Greg gave her some tissues. She nodded with her eyes shut, shaking with silent gasps of air.

'Lord Xuan, Lady Emma,' the woman with the clipboard said, 'I'm daughter Ninety-Three.' She looked down at the papers, then back at us. 'The test results have come back. These aren't identical copies to the snake on the autopsy table. These have been modified to be more aggressive and ...' Her voice faded away, and she gathered herself. 'Cruel. They're sadistic little psychopaths. Very strong demon nature.'

Jennifer approached us, obviously scared by the snakes. Two of them saw her and attacked the window, their fangs leaving trails of venom on the glass. Jennifer jumped back and screamed.

One of the larger ones raised itself on its coils. 'Come and play, little human,' it hissed in a voice that held a fragment of Colin's. 'We won't hurt you, we promise.' It lowered its head. 'Come in and join us.'

'We want to play with you,' another one said.

'Oh god,' Jennifer moaned. She glared at John. 'Why are you keeping these monsters alive?'

'The final decision is yours, as mother of the original,' John said. 'They have a great deal of your son in them. It is your choice whether we destroy them or let them live.'

'If they break out, they'll go on a rampage,' Greg said. 'What level are they?'

'As with the black-armoured demons, we're unable to tell,' the Tiger's daughter said. 'But we lost twenty-five demon staff when they hatched — they overpowered everything and nearly killed both of us too. In the end we had to bring in a single-digit warrior daughter to contain them.'

'So it's either destroy them or keep them caged for the rest of their lives,' Greg said.

'That is not Colin,' Jennifer said. 'None of them are Colin. They're *monsters*. Destroy them.'

'Are you sure, love?' Greg said.

'I've never been more sure of anything in my entire life,' she said fiercely. 'They're like the serpent people, but more demon, and Em told us what happens when one of the serpent people go mad: people die. This is what happens. They need to be …' She shook her head. 'They need to be destroyed.'

'Don't do it just yet,' Greg said to John. 'Let her think about it. She may change her mind in a couple of days.'

'Never,' Jennifer said.

'Very well,' John said. 'Let's go back to the farm and talk about buying horses. That will be much more pleasant than dealing with this.'

Jennifer brightened. 'The boys will love having ponies.' She turned away from the snakes; more had gathered at the window and were trying to break the glass to reach her. 'Let's go.'

* * *

The next morning we all gathered at the site of the Demon King's Versailles palace. A crowd of White Horsemen and the Tiger's wives, as well as many residents of the Celestial, stood in front of the palace in the half-finished gardens. A platform had been raised on the gravel drive, similar to the one that John had stood on outside the Northern Palace, but at a height of ten metres. Small surveying flags were set up in a pattern around the site, indicating where the new Western Palace would be built.

I stopped at the base of the platform. 'This is for the Four Winds.'

'You too,' John said.

'Not my place,' I said.

'Empress of the North, absolutely your place,' the Tiger said. He grinned. 'Cannot wait. That will be a *hell* of a party.'

John took my hand and lifted me onto the platform. The Four Winds joined us, and we stood together studying the building.

'Fucking ugly piece of shit,' the Tiger said.

'I don't know, it's rather elegant in its own way,' the Dragon said. 'Have you considered keeping it as a new Residence? It fits your style perfectly.'

The Tiger rounded on the Dragon, then saw his face.

'The Dragon's right, this is very you,' the Phoenix said.

The Tiger opened his mouth, then closed it and turned to face the palace. 'Who's first?'

'Me,' the Dragon said.

He changed to True Form, floating above the platform. His blue and silver scales glittered in the sun as he concentrated. All the trees and shrubs planted by the human slaves lifted out of the ground, their root balls still covered in dirt, and floated a hundred metres behind us to land in a neat pile.

'Take the glass and metal out and I'll see if there's any wood worth saving,' the Dragon said as he changed back to Celestial Form and returned to the platform.

'Very well,' the Phoenix said.

She took True Form, spread her wings and launched herself to float above the platform. She glowed with light and heat that was stronger than the sun, almost uncomfortably hot at such close proximity. She raised her red crested head, opened her beak, then snapped it shut. All of the building's windows shot out of their frames and stopped a metre away from them, suspended in the air. The glass stacked itself and flew to land next to the trees behind us. The roof tiles lifted off the building and landed in a pile with the glass.

The Phoenix shrank to human form and floated down to stand next to us. 'Steel girders holding up the roof. Nothing else in there worth salvaging.'

'All right,' the Tiger said. He raised his arms and the metal girders that had held the roof tiles coalesced into a single shiny blob of steel and floated to land on the ground in front of us. 'Now for the gold. My wives and children were tortured to create this. I don't want it, but I don't know what to do with it. It's not worth anything here on the Celestial.'

'Pass it to me,' I said. 'I'll sell it on the Earthly to create a fund for the mortals whose loved ones were replaced by demons.'

John rubbed my back.

'You have a deal,' the Tiger said. Two dozen kilogram-sized gold bars shot out of the building and stacked themselves behind us. 'Let me know when you go on a demon-destroying sortie. I'll enjoy taking them down.'

'Do any of the human families think the demon copies are the originals?' the Phoenix said.

The Jade Emperor stepped forward, facing the palace. 'Some of them have remained with the demon copies, despite the abuse, because of the love they held for the originals,' he said. 'They think they just need to love them more and the abuse will stop. Destroying the demon copies will free them from fruitlessly trying to make the demons into something they are not.'

He raised one hand towards the palace and flicked his wrist. A piece of stone the size of a house brick slotted out of a wall and floated towards us.

'Ah Bai,' the Emperor said, 'this is sandstone, high silica content, giving its golden colour. The original stones were more iron-heavy, giving them their rich red hue. Which do you prefer?'

'The original red, same as the mountains,' the Tiger said, gesturing towards the crinkled mountains that towered on the western horizon. 'The red colour complements the surrounding environment. This yellow palace looks like a tumour.'

The stone floating in front of us changed colour, becoming more red. 'This?'

'More,' the Tiger said.

The stone went a deeper red.

'Stop,' the Tiger said. 'Damn, Ah Ting, you're breaking my heart. That's it.'

'Do you want this or not?' the Emperor said, glaring at the Tiger over the top of the stone.

The Tiger bowed. 'Celestial Majesty.'

'Asshole,' the Emperor said under his breath. The stone drifted to float at the Jade Emperor's right. The Emperor raised both arms towards the palace, and the air around us went still. 'Taking a video?' he said. 'This will be good.'

'Wait,' the Dragon said, and summoned one of his AI phones. He held his hand out and released the phone so it hovered in front of us. 'Go.'

'Change it to horizontal, you *barbarian*,' I said.

The Dragon smiled and snapped his wrist at the phone. It spun from vertical to horizontal. 'Apologies, my Lady.'

The Jade Emperor stepped to the front of the platform. He removed his hat with the beads that hung in front of his eyes, and passed it to John. He then stood facing the palace and concentrated. The air went still around us and everybody was silenced. The entire building fell vertically into the earth with a massive shockwave that shook the ground. The flags fluttered as the dust settled, and it was gone, only bare red earth where the building had stood.

'Fuck, yeah,' the Tiger said.

'I am putting that up on YouTube!' the Dragon said with delight.

'Do you want a basement?' the Emperor said.

'No, I'll create another purpose-built lab underground elsewhere,' the Tiger said. 'With beefed-up security.'

'I'll help,' the Phoenix said.

'Me too,' the Dragon said.

'We need to keep up with their technology,' John said. 'We'll work together to make the security unbreakable.'

'Very well,' the Jade Emperor said.

He waved one hand, shaking his sleeve out of the way, and the plans for the new Western Palace appeared. They drifted out of his hand to hang at waist level in front of him, next to the red brick. He studied the plans, then looked up. The ground between the flags turned black and shiny in a complex series of rectangles.

'Granite foundation,' the Emperor said. 'It's four metres deep, with recessed service channels through it where they've been marked on the plans. You can cut more channels if needed; it's capable of taking a beating. Put your flooring on top.'

'Nice. Thank you,' the Tiger said. 'Uh ... can you do red, like the stones? Or white? I don't like black.'

Both John and the Jade Emperor glared at the Tiger.

The Jade Emperor flicked his wrist without looking away from the Tiger and the foundations turned white. 'That's not granite, it's marble, and it will be more brittle. You'll have to take care when cutting it.'

The Tiger grinned broadly and crossed his arms in front of his chest. 'Worth it.' He bowed to the Jade Emperor, the grin not shifting. 'I'll polish it and inlay gold detail in the traffic areas. White and gold marble floors will be *sweet*.'

'Now,' the Jade Emperor said, and pulled his sleeves up to his elbows. He took a deep breath, studied the plans in front of him, and raised his arms like a conductor.

The new Western Palace, built of red stone with arched doorways and windows, shot out of the ground without making a sound. It grew upwards, knocking over the marker flags, until it was three storeys high. It spread organically down the hillside into a series of terraces and smaller outbuildings, finishing at the level of the plain that swept from the Palace to the base of the mountains.

The people standing and watching cheered and applauded, some whistling loudly.

'That's bigger than the old one!' John said.

The Tiger tucked his hands into his belt and puffed out his chest. 'I'm always bigger.'

'Not in True Form,' John said under his breath.

'Before you ask, no, I will not extend the Northern Palace purely so you can continue this childish competition with the Tiger,' the Jade Emperor said. He checked the plans and shifted some of the Western Palace around. 'Happy?'

'Fucking ecstatic,' the Tiger said.

'It's ready for the roof,' the Jade Emperor said. He plucked the plans out of the air, rolled them up, and handed them to the Tiger. John passed the Emperor's hat back to him, and he returned it to his head.

John nodded, rose above the platform and took True Form, the Serpent writhing over the Turtle's shell. A couple of people in the audience screamed as a brief rain shower swept over the new Western Palace, washing the stones clean; then the water focused on a small area on the far side of the Palace. The fountains and channels in the gardens filled with water that cascaded down the hill to the ponds at the bottom. John drifted back down onto the platform and retook human form. 'The cistern's full.'

'Thanks,' the Tiger said.

'My turn,' the Dragon said. The plants he'd removed levitated into the courtyards and gardens of the new Palace.

The Phoenix flew up and the glass stacked behind us floated into the air. 'You'll have to add the putty yourself,' she said as the glass panes merged, then separated into arched pieces that fitted into the stones. 'They're in the grooves, but take care: they can fall out before they're fixed, and if they do I'm not replacing them.' She retook human form and joined us on the platform.

'Thanks, Sparrow.' The Tiger held the rolled-up plans behind him without turning away from the Palace, obviously expecting me to take them. I didn't. He pushed them at me, still looking at the Palace. I crossed my arms over my chest.

John made a soft sound of amusement.

The Tiger glanced back at me impatiently, and saw my face.

'Do you mind holding these for a moment, Lady Emma?' he said with forced politeness.

'My pleasure, Lord Bai Hu,' I said, and took the plans from him.

I love you, the Dragon said in my head.

You are wonderful, the Phoenix said at the same time.

John just smiled smugly.

The Tiger turned back to the Palace and concentrated. The lump of steel floated upwards, divided into three-metre beams, and bent to form arched formwork. The beams settled on the walls that the Jade Emperor had created. More iron erupted from the ground, changed to copper, then formed sheets, which the Tiger laid across the iron struts to form copper domed roofs for the buildings.

'Once the plumbers and electricians have been through, we'll have it liveable,' he said. 'Should take a couple of weeks at the most.' He turned to grin at me. 'Where will your mum and dad live?'

'Not with you,' I said. 'So don't even think about making my father wire all of this up.'

'Greg can do it,' the Tiger said, turning back to the new Western Palace. The copper domes glowed in the morning sun. 'Fuck, that's awesome.'

He turned to face us, fell to one knee, and saluted around. 'Celestial Majesty, my Sovereign, Lords and Ladies, this small

Shen thanks you for your care and consideration. This Palace is fucking sick.'

'Lunch at my place,' the Phoenix said. 'Then I'd like your help to do a sweep through the lower levels of the volcano to make sure there's no demons left in there. Oh. Never mind.'

'You three go, I'll stay with Emma,' John said.

'No, go, the volcano needs to be checked,' I said. 'I'll hang around on the Earthly with Simone and Frankie, I've hardly seen them. We might be able to lure the stones out if we're home without you around.'

'You need to choose the stationery as well,' John said. 'And Jade will have an endless list of questions for you.'

'Oh *fuck*,' I said under my breath.

'Do you need me to help you choose the invitations?' he said.

'No, checking the volcano is more important. Go with them, enjoy yourself.' I glared at him. 'Just don't come home drunk and hit cricket balls off the roof again.'

'That sounds like fun,' the Tiger said. 'Let's try some golf balls off the top of the volcano. Bet I can hit them further than you.'

'Not a chance,' John said, and they disappeared.

The Dragon and Phoenix saluted me with huge grins and disappeared as well.

'How about giving me my teleportation back?' I asked the Jade Emperor.

'Never took it from you,' he said, and I landed in the living room of the Peak apartment.

34

I stopped and stared; there was a two-metre-wide circular hole in the living room floor. 'What the *hell*?'

'Oh, hi, Emma,' Simone said from under the hole. 'What do you think?'

'I think there's a huge hole in our living room floor. Were you playing with yin in here? We talked about that!'

There was a clatter and a vertical steel pole appeared in the centre of the hole. Horizontal beams spread from the pole to the hole's edges.

'Jade?' Michael said from under the hole.

There was another clatter and hardwood steps appeared on the beams. They'd created a spiral staircase linking our flat with the one below.

Buffy ran up the stairs wearing a sparkly blue princess tutu and stopped at the top. 'This is so cool, Aunty Emma!'

'Move, Buffy!' Frankie shouted, and ran up behind her. He grinned and waved her wand at me, then ran down again. 'Spiral stairs — woo!'

Simone, Michael and Jade appeared next to me, while Buffy and Frankie chased each other up and down the stairs.

'Slow down before someone's hurt!' I shouted at them. They ignored me.

'Emma, just the bride I wanted to see,' Jade said.

'Oh god,' I said, and tried to teleport out. I failed.

'I saw that,' she said with amusement. 'What appointments do you have this afternoon?'

'Uh … Lots. Plenty. Many, many appointments,' I said. 'Totally busy. Full-time. So many appointments —'

'Good. Come with me down to Mr Li's to try on a few wedding dresses. Do you need a guard?'

'I'll guard,' Michael said.

'I don't need a wedding dress, I'm marrying him in my armour,' I said. 'We *decided* this, Jade. Celestial battle forms and armour!'

'You need a going-away dress, and a dress for the photographs,' she said.

'Mountain uniform. Same as the Dark Lord.'

'Don't you want something pretty?'

I glared at her. 'No!'

'You still need a black and silver robe for under the armour,' she said, smug.

'No, I don't!'

'Yes, you do, you have to match. And you need to choose a design for the invitations. Mr Li has offered to do them as well.'

I was silenced at that.

Leo walked up the stairs. 'Nice job, guys. I'll stay with the kids. Simone, you go with Emma and watch for those stones.'

'I want to go with Simone!' Frankie shouted.

'Hey, Er Hao!' Simone shouted down the hole.

'Ma'am?' Er Hao said from below.

'Do you have to yell like that?' I said, wincing.

'Er Hao, we're all going for lunch together. You don't need to cook,' Simone shouted. 'Tell Yi Hao.'

'Yes, ma'am,' Er Hao replied.

Simone counted around. 'Seven of us — we'll need both cars. Is Martin coming?'

'No, he's stuck in the Northern Heavens,' Leo said. 'We really should buy a van to carry everyone.'

'Good idea,' Simone said.

'We don't have space to park a bus here,' I said with dismay.

'So we make space. I'll drive the small car with Buffy and Jade,' Leo said. 'Michael, take the big one with Simone, Emma and Frankie. Come on, Buffy, you need to change if you're going out as well.'

'Okay, Daddy.'

'Sir,' Michael said to Leo, and opened the front door for us.

'I can take my own car, I don't need a driver!' I said.

'Oh, yes, you do, ma'am,' Jade said, linking her arm in mine. 'Because if we let you drive yourself you'll end up anywhere but Mr Li's.'

Michael stopped and his face went strange.

'Let me order him to back off,' Simone said.

'No, I can handle him,' Michael said.

'He's after you to be Number One again?' I said.

Michael nodded as we waited for the lift.

'You should go,' I said. 'Clarissa will live much longer on the Celestial Plane. It would be good for both of you.'

'I know,' he said. 'It's her choice, not mine. She wants to live an ordinary life on the Earthly.'

'Did you tell him that?' I said as we arrived on the ground floor.

'I did. He told me to man up and make my woman behave.'

'Did you hit him?'

'I killed him.'

'Good.'

* * *

'You can take Frankie and Buffy shopping, you don't need to come to Mr Li's,' I said to Simone when we'd finished lunch at the shopping centre's café.

'Yes, they do,' Jade said. 'We all need to see Mr Li. I want all members of the House of the North to have matching outfits.'

'I have to be flower girl,' Simone said. 'I've been saying I'll do it forever.'

'Since you were four years old,' I said.

'No!' Buffy shouted as we went up the escalators. 'I'm flower girl!'

'Can I be something?' Frankie said.

'You can be page boy,' Simone said, squeezing his hand.

'Do Chinese weddings even *have* a flower girl and page boy?' Leo said.

'This is Xuan Tian Shang Di's Celestial wedding,' Jade said with satisfaction. 'It will have *everything*.'

'Everything?' Leo said. 'What, Eastern and Western both?'

'That will take all day!' Simone said.

'Pretty much,' I said with dismay.

'And you're letting them do this to you, Emma?' Michael said.

'JE's orders.' I shrugged. 'He's put Jade in charge and we have to go along with whatever she decides.' I glared at her. 'If it was our choice, it would be a small family get-together to formalise something that's existed since the day we met.'

'Not happening, Emma,' Jade said, looking smug. 'Deal with it. This will be the biggest and grandest wedding the Celestial has ever seen.' She spread her hands. 'And I'm in charge!'

I moaned quietly as we entered Mr Li's shop. 'I almost hope this Black Jade thing will happen.'

'God, don't say that. The BJ curse could spoil everything,' Simone said.

'Don't worry, we'll keep a close eye on her,' Michael said.

'Zara should stay with you, Emma,' Leo said. 'She can warn us if a stone approaches.'

'The only way she can stay with me is as an item of jewellery, and she won't do it because of her vow.'

'Aren't the demons that could control stones gone?' Michael said as we followed Mr Li to the end of his sunlit workroom where he kept the bolts of silk on display. Half the tables with sewing machines were empty; he'd lost a great many of his demon staff during the war. 'It isn't a problem now, is it?'

'The current Demon King used a stone to hide a conversation we had from the previous King,' I said. 'I think he has just as much control over stones as they did.'

'Enough talk about stones,' Jade said. 'Emma, take Celestial Form and let's choose silk for the robe to go under your armour.'

'Her armour's really ratty,' Simone said. 'Even in Celestial Form there's a huge chip in the breastplate and some of the wires are worn through.'

'The forge is making a new set of dress armour; it will be ready at the end of next week,' Jade said. 'It's black with silver adornment, similar to Lord Xuan's. All we have to do is decide on the design for the under robes.' She turned to study the bolts of silk on the shelves. 'Red is traditional for weddings.'

'Red will make me look anaemic,' I said. 'Black would be better, same as the armour.'

'You can't be married in black!' Jade said. 'How about silver?'

'Silver is grey,' I said. 'I look *dead* in grey. Black is the best choice.'

'And it begins,' Simone said with amusement.

Mr Li interrupted us. 'The Emperor of the East has sent us some bolts of fabric. He's made a few designs in his own silk production facility in Japan that you might find suitable. Mostly black with snakes and turtles, and some with weapons on them. I would prefer "double happiness" or at least flowers and birds, but he insisted.'

'That sounds perfect!' I said. 'Weapons? Let me see.'

'I'm not wearing a robe with swords all over it. I'll wear my stars,' Simone said. 'Find something else for the kids.'

'I want to wear swords as well!' Frankie said. 'I like swords!'

Jade hissed under her breath. 'I will kill that enabler.'

* * *

Simone stopped when we stepped out of the cars under the Peak building. 'What is that demon doing here?' She walked out the gates. 'Two demons. Big ones.'

Michael and Leo readied themselves.

'Come out,' Simone called down the drive. 'I can see you.'

The David Hawkes copy came out of the thick scrub at the side of the drive. He raised his hands. 'Peace. I want to parley.'

'I can see you as well,' Simone shouted. 'The other one.'

One of the black-armoured demons with a tiny face emerged from the other side of the drive, and Buffy shrieked.

It raised its clawed hands. 'I wish to parley under terms of truce.'

'It's okay, honey, you're safe with us,' Leo said to Buffy, and she grabbed his leg.

'Emma, where did Daddy take demons to parley?' Simone said.

'Hennessy Road, when we lived here,' I said. 'Stone Boulder House on the Mountain.'

'We don't have the ownership of Hennessy Road back yet,' she said. 'Jade?'

'There's nowhere secure enough,' Jade said.

John appeared next to us. 'I see.' He gestured with his head. 'Next to the swimming pool. Leo, take the children upstairs. Michael, go with them.'

'I want to stay with Simone!' Frankie shouted.

'This time, Frankie, go with Uncle Leo,' Simone said. 'Don't argue, sweetie, this is dangerous.'

'You too, Simone,' John said. 'Go up with them and guard them.'

She hesitated, then nodded. 'Okay.'

John gestured and the demons walked ahead of us to the block's swimming pool. The elementals that had been acting as water formed four human-shaped watery bodies and floated in the pool cavity. We stopped, and both demons fell to their knees in front of John.

'You first,' John said to the David copy. 'Do you turn?'

'Only if I must,' he said. 'I would prefer to retain my free will.'

'Then why are you here?' John said.

'When I was first assigned to Bridget and the boys, I was cruel to them. But I've learnt better,' the David copy said. He lowered his head. 'I love her, my Lord. I've grown to love all of them.' He glanced up at John, full of hope. 'Allow me to stay with them, I beg you.'

'How do they feel about this?' I said.

'They feel the same way,' he said.

I pulled my phone out of my pocket. 'What if I call Bridget and ask her?'

'She will say the same thing,' the demon said with confidence.

I called Bridget.

'Hello?' she said.

'Hello, Bridget, it's Emma. I have the David copy here, and it's …' I glanced down at the demon. 'He's asking to stay with you. We're in the process of arranging accidents for the copies, because they were torturing the families they were assigned to and corruptly undermining peaceful governance. This one claims that he's been treating you and your boys well and that you want him to stay with you.'

'Is he there?' she said.

'I'm right here, love,' he said.

'Put me on speakerphone,' she said.

'I know I was cruel to you at the start, but when I realised I loved you I never touched you again,' he said. 'Will you have me back? Tell the Dark Lord that I'll treat you right, otherwise he'll destroy me like he did all the others.'

'Let me tell you about David, Emma,' she said. 'The real David.'

'Yes, Bridget?'

'He would give the staff two days off on the weekend instead of one. He gave them Saturday and Sunday, even though he was only obliged by law to give them one day.'

'Well, *that* was stupid,' the demon copy said with scorn.

'And on Saturday and Sunday, he would spend the days with us. One of us would cook, and the other would clean up and wash the dishes. He was a much better cook than I am, and he enjoyed making meals for the family. Often he'd wash the dishes as well, and then we'd spend the evening playing games with the boys.'

'He did servants' jobs?' the copy said with disbelief.

'Would you do that?' she said.

'No, of course not. I don't serve people, people serve me,' the demon copy said.

'If I was to have you back, would you be gentle and caring like he was? He lived to please me. He took me out for dinner cruises on the harbour, just the two of us, and he was so patient and attentive. He was endlessly romantic.'

'Don't be ridiculous. I'm a man, not a child,' the demon copy said.

'You stopped raping me,' she said.

'Yes, when I realised that you are far more than you seem. You might not be beautiful, but you have a good heart. So I stopped forcing you.'

'You stopped raping me. Do you want a medal?'

'No, I want to be with you,' he said, completely missing the sarcasm.

'Emma, is John there?' she said.

'Yes, I am,' John said.

'John, could you cut that monster's head off so it never approaches me or my boys ever again? It was cruel to the family. It beat the boys. It raped me. It took bribes in the business. It is ...' She took a deep breath. 'An absolutely disgusting piece of fucking shit and I never want to see it again. Do me a favour and do your demon-killing thing on it. Fast and hard, so it never comes near me or my boys again.'

'One question,' John said.

'You worthless bitch! I was willing to give you a chance and you destroyed everything!' the demon shouted, and disappeared.

'Yes?' Bridget said.

'Would you like me to change or remove your memories of what happened?'

'You can do that?'

'Yes, I can.'

She hesitated, then, 'Yes,' she breathed. 'Yes. Because that worthless piece of scum is an insult to everything that David stood for. My David was a noble gentle man, and this demon was a travesty of everything about him. I'd rather remember David as a good man who died before his time.'

'I will visit you and the boys as soon as I have tracked down the copy and taken its head,' John said. 'It will take me less than an hour.'

'Can you change the boys' memories as well?'

'Yes, I can,' he said.

'Thank you.' She broke down, weeping into the phone. 'I'll be waiting for you. All of us will be waiting for you. Thank you so much.' She hung up.

'Now you,' John said to the black-armoured demon. 'Are you here to turn?'

'No, my Lord,' the demon said.

'Another one,' I said.

'So why are you here?' John said.

'Look inside me,' the demon said. 'I will open myself to you, and you can see what I am.'

John focused on the demon, and his eyes went wide. 'Holy shit.'

'What?' I said.

'You can look, ma'am, it will not hurt me,' the demon said.

I opened my Inner Eye on it. The tiny face belonged to a child, hanging suspended inside the demon.

'Holy *shit*,' I said. 'Is that a human child?'

'Yes, it is,' John said. 'Every time we destroyed one of you, we destroyed a *human child*?'

'It screams in my head,' the demon said with misery.

'Releasing the child will destroy you,' John said.

'I know that, but I am dead anyway,' the demon said. 'You will track us all down and kill us. The new King does not want us; we are spawn of the West. So I beg you, Dark Lord, destroy me carefully and extract this poor innocent from inside me.'

'What about the others like you?' I said.

'If you agree to do this, I will tell my brothers before you do it. Some may choose to come to you and not fight it; others may choose to flee. Either way they are dead.'

'Kneel,' John said.

The demon fell to its knees. It was so large that its head was level with John's chest.

'Tell your brothers I will make it swift and painless,' John said.

'I am, my Lord. Many will come.'

'Now close your eyes and think compassionate thoughts about the child.'

The demon closed its tiny eyes. 'Thank you, my Lord. Even if you cannot save me, the child will be free.'

John pushed his fingers into the demon's head around the face and ripped the child out. The child screamed. The demon's body dissolved into black demon essence that dissipated quickly.

John lowered the child to the ground and she crumpled. She appeared about four years old, with fair skin and blonde hair through the coating of demon essence.

He concentrated with his hands on either side of her face. 'Not injured, just in shock from the transition.' He conjured a blanket and wrapped her in it. 'Let's take her upstairs and clean her up. How many of these demons did you say there were, Emma?'

'Close on a hundred.'

'Have we found Chang yet?'

'He's on his way home with the rest of the orphans.'

'Good, because we have a great deal more work for him to do.'

The little girl opened her eyes, took a deep breath, and screamed again.

John looked her in the eyes. 'You are free now, little one. You're not a prisoner any more. You're safe.'

She buried her face in her arms.

'The demon was right when it said it was Western,' I said as John picked her up, still wrapped in the blanket, and carried her to the lift lobby. 'Blonde and everything.'

When we were on the eleventh floor we went straight into the flat. The rest of the family crowded around us.

'And she was inside the demon?' Leo said.

'Stay back, give her room. Don't freak her out,' I said.

Michael stood transfixed, staring at her. 'Oh my god. Oh my god.' He repeated the words over and over, his voice thick with emotion. 'Oh my god.'

'Michael?' John said. He carried the child to one of the student rooms. Yi Hao rushed out of the kitchen to help us. 'Do you know her, Michael?'

'That's my *mother*,' Michael said. 'I've seen photos of her when she was young, and that's *her*.'

'That's what the King did with her when she stayed there a week,' John said. 'I suppose we should not be surprised.'

'More clones,' I said with misery.

The Tiger appeared next to us. 'I'll take them. I'll take all of them.' He put his hands out to John. 'Contact me when you free them and I'll care for them.'

'No, you won't,' Michael said fiercely. 'You will groom them to be wives when they're old enough. They're *children*.'

'All of my wives were children at one stage, boy,' the Tiger said. 'Give her to me, Ah Wu. I'll take her and raise her myself.'

'No,' John said. 'Michael's right. They will go to Chang's orphanage, and they will not be introduced to you until they are well and truly old enough to make up their own minds.'

'But —'

'That is an *order*, Bai Hu,' John said. 'Disappear.'

'Humph,' the Tiger said, and disappeared.

John handed the child to Michael. 'I have a demon ... several demons to track down. I am delegating care for these children to you. You will need to find accommodation for all of them. How long before Chang arrives, Emma?'

'He's flying in tonight,' I said.

'Meet with him then and set to work, Michael. You have an unlimited budget to arrange accommodation for them until you find a place to put them all.'

'My Lord,' Michael said, taking the child in his arms. She lay there, unmoving and unblinking. 'We need to clean you up, honey,' he said. He raised his head. 'I'll bring Clarissa in to help.'

'I'll go bring her,' Simone said.

'No, I will,' Michael said. He held the child out to me. 'Can you bathe her? It will be more appropriate and less scary.'

I took the child. 'Sure.'

'I must go. That copy will probably go to Bridget and try to terrorise her into letting it live,' John said. 'I need to reach it first. Call me if more of these child demons arrive.'

'We will, Daddy,' Simone said. 'Go. We can handle this here.'

John disappeared.

35

The wedding was on the first day of winter, the Xuan Wu's seasonal ascension. We stayed in the Imperial Residence in the Northern Heavens the night before the ceremony.

Jade dropped off the boxes containing the robes, and made one last check.

'I need you awake at six thirty so we can start early with the make-up and hair,' she said to me. 'Then we'll take all the photographs with the dignitaries on the front court of the Palace, and after that proceed to the ceremony at the Hall of Dark Justice.'

'What time does the actual ceremony start?' John said.

'Ten.'

He grew pensive.

'No, you cannot meet up with the Tiger and go harass my family,' I said. 'Leave them alone.'

'But the groom and his friends are supposed to take gifts to your family and negotiate a price for you,' Jade said. 'It's traditional.'

'So is the bride wearing red.' I pointed at the boxes. 'Black all the way.'

'Don't worry, Emma,' John said. 'I won't do it.'

'Damn straight you won't,' I growled.

Jade bowed to each of us in turn. 'I'll see you at six thirty in the morning. Lord Xuan, I'm counting on you to ensure that she doesn't make a run for it.'

'I may make a run for it myself,' he said.

She saluted us with a grin and disappeared.

John opened the boxes and took the robes out. He ran them carefully through his fingers, then ran his hands over the interior of the boxes.

'Looking for stones?' I said.

He nodded. 'None here.'

I sighed and sat on the bed. 'I just want this over with so we can start living our lives as a normal family.'

'Normal?' He sat on the bed next to me and held my hand. 'Heaven forbid.'

I leaned into him. 'Bath. Bubbles.'

We lay in the warm water together, the bubbles swirling around us. He pulled me into his lap, and kissed the side of my neck.

'I know this sounds strange,' I said, 'but I'm not interested.'

'In making love?' he said to the side of my throat.

I nodded. 'I'm too concerned. What if I'm replaced? What if you don't know?'

He shrugged behind me. 'Soak. Relax. Sleep. I understand.'

I wriggled against him. 'Some of you doesn't understand.'

'I'm a Turtle, that part will always be interested. But the important part is up here.' He rapped his forehead gently on the back of my head. 'And I will never make you do anything if you don't want it as much as I do.' He pulled me tighter. 'Just be aware: only one demon has ever been human enough to fool me, and that demon is dead.'

'I fooled you,' I said.

He didn't reply, he just held me close.

'Can you see anything in the future?' I said. 'I can't.'

'I don't have any major premonition of disaster. The future seems serene, apart from the usual messy minor catastrophes that occur in any big ceremonial occasion.'

I snuggled into him. 'Thank you.'

He sighed beneath me. 'We will survive this.'

'The most challenging thing that either of us has ever done?'

He nodded into my shoulder.

'How many marriages is this for you? And I don't mean just humans. Have you married Shen before?'

'Let me think,' he said. 'Twenty-five? No, the two at the end of the Qing ... twenty-seven. Twenty-eight including Michelle. You will be my twenty-ninth wife.'

'Damn.'

'And if you take male form ...' He dropped his voice to a whisper. 'My sixteenth husband.'

'*Damn.*'

'None of them were ever as close as we are. What I have with you is unique. There will never be any other for me.'

'I feel the same way.'

'Bedtime, my Empress,' he said, carrying me out of the bath and pulling a towel off the rail. He gently lowered me and wrapped the towel around me. 'Sleep now, and tomorrow will hopefully be the last time I kneel and present tea to the Jade Emperor at my wedding.'

'All I want in life is to be with you and our family,' I said. 'This is an unnecessary formality.'

'I feel the same way,' he said, kissing the side of my neck.

He stopped and listened before we climbed into bed together.

'They okay?' I said.

He nodded. 'Your mother says that Frankie is over-excited. He doesn't really understand what's happening but he's still thrilled. Oh.' His expression cleared. 'The Jade Emperor has lent that ring to Simone. She can come after all.'

'Can she keep it so we can move up here?'

'It's one of the symbols of office; he has to wear it when issuing Edicts. The answer to your question is: no.'

'Is there another artefact that would work similarly? I forgot he had that.'

'No.'

I lowered my voice. 'Any stones nearby?'

He concentrated. 'No.' He sighed and lay back, and I joined him. We pulled the covers over ourselves and snuggled under the warm silk quilt. 'Perhaps destroying the Demon Kings has worked.'

'When we find the stones I'll believe you,' I said.

'Go to sleep,' he said, holding me close. 'Once we have this out of the way we can arrange something just for *us*.'

* * *

There was a rap on the door. 'Emma,' Jade said from the other side, waking me.

'Is it time already?' I said.

The early morning light shone through the shutters, and John was still asleep beside me. I checked the clock: six thirty. I had slept less than an hour. I'd spent most of the night awake, staring at the ceiling and wondering when they'd try to replace me. I could easily have gone straight back to sleep.

John made a soft sound, turned away and pulled the quilt over himself. He'd probably been awake most of the night as well.

'We have your hair and make-up people here,' Jade said. 'I'll give you some time to come out. Bring your robe.'

I kissed John on the hair and he muttered something into the pillow.

'Check me,' I whispered at the back of his head.

He turned to me, smiled, and stroked my cheek. 'It's you. They didn't do anything.'

'I'm glad,' I said, and went into the bathroom to prepare.

When I was ready, wrapped in a simple cotton dressing gown over my underwear, I grabbed the wedding robe and went out. I still felt stupidly fatigued, and it was a dull and grey day, with winter's chill beginning to bite.

Jade smiled and linked her arm in mine. 'Come on, Emma, things to do. Breakfast is ready. What would you like?'

'Coffee,' I said. 'I haven't slept, I was too worried. Toast with peanut butter.'

'I'll have them brought for you.'

I was in a dream as they fussed over my hair and make-up. After an interminable time trying to make me presentable, Jade had me stand and take Celestial Form, and she helped me into the robe and armour. John and I had chosen identical black silk with gold twining snakes and turtles over it, to match the engraving on our dress armour.

'Did you slip a valium into the coffee you gave me so I wouldn't run?' I said. 'I'm wrecked.'

She smiled. 'I would never do anything like that.'

'It certainly feels like it.'

'Probably lack of sleep. Would you like another coffee?'

'How long before the ceremony begins?'

'We'll have the photos in thirty minutes. Then the entourage will arrive for you and Lord Xuan. Have another coffee and then we'll go.' She patted my shoulder. 'I have to put my face on too.'

My mouth tasted of bitter stale coffee as John and I stood side by side and smiled with various groups of Celestial dignitaries.

The Tiger studied me carefully as he joined us with five of his most senior wives. 'You look half-asleep.'

'I am,' I said. 'I didn't sleep at all last night.'

We smiled for the camera and the flash dazzled me again.

'Where's this mysterious honeymoon anyway?' the Tiger said without turning away from the camera.

'Tell him where we're having it, Emma,' John said. 'He can't do anything to ruin it; I won't let him.'

'At home on the Peak with the family,' I said. 'We're not going anywhere because everything we love and need is *right here*.'

'You sure Ah Wu doesn't have something organised?' the Tiger said. He grinned. 'I wouldn't put it past him to surprise you with a snap honeymoon somewhere romantic. And you're so damn clever that you'd know if he did.'

John grunted.

'No,' I said fiercely. 'I would know, and he hasn't. And even if he did, I wouldn't tell *you*.'

The Tiger opened his mouth to argue with me.

'Who's next for photos?' I said. 'Jade?' I pushed the Tiger away. 'We don't have much time left before the ceremony and there are still two dozen people waiting there.'

Jade came up onto the platform and whispered in my ear. 'You're not really going straight back to work on the Earthly, are you?'

'We may take a break when everything settles down,' I said as the Tiger escorted his wives down off the platform and the Dragon brought up the infant tree, which was now in the form of a ten-year-old child. 'But right now we want to spend time with our family and treasure what we have.'

She smiled and squeezed my hand. 'I understand.'

* * *

John looked magnificent as we strode over the arched bridges through the residential side of the Northern Palace. The crowd cheered for us as we passed through the gate into the main square of the administrative side. All the residents of the Northern Heavens were present, with a camera crew at the back transmitting proceedings to the rest of the Celestial.

The cheering intensified when we arrived at the Hall of Dark Justice and walked side by side up the stairs to stand on the platform. The Jade Emperor was there to preside over the ceremony, and he nodded to both of us. I looked around for the rest of the family, but they weren't there. They'd probably join us after the Jade Emperor had finished doing his thing.

I took John's hand and he squeezed it.

'We are here to witness the joining of Lord Xuan Wu of the Northern Heavens and Lady Emma Donahoe of Australia in the bond of marriage,' the Jade Emperor began, and proceeded to make a speech about the war and our part in it, praising both of us for our military ability and intelligence.

'Simone won it for us,' I said under my breath.

'Let him have his fun,' John said.

I zoned out as the Jade Emperor droned interminably about the war and our victory. I swayed on my feet; I really did feel exhausted. John held me close, nearly propping me up.

The Jade Emperor stopped talking, jerking me out of my daze. John patted my back.

'The couple have chosen to make Western-style vows to each other,' the Jade Emperor said. 'Lord Xuan.'

I opened my mouth to protest.

Just go along with it, Jade said. *The Emperor thought that doing this part Western-style would be a nice authentic touch to respect your heritage. I found some standard Western wedding vows and printed them out for him.*

When did he decide to do this without telling us? I said.

Totally last minute. Sorry, Emma.

'Repeat after me,' the Jade Emperor said to John. 'I vow to take you, my Lady Emma, to be my lawfully wedded wife, to have and to hold from this day forward, for better, for worse, for richer, for poorer, in sickness and in health, until death do us part.'

John gazed into my eyes as he repeated the vows.

'Lady Emma Donahoe, repeat after me,' the Jade Emperor said. 'I, Emma Donahoe, vow to take you, my Lord, to be my lawfully wedded husband, to love and obey from this day forward, for better, for worse, for richer, for poorer, in sickness and in health, until death do us part.'

I opened my mouth to say 'Not obey' but the Jade Emperor interrupted me. *Please just go along with this. Don't cause a fuss; everybody in the Heavens is watching you.*

I put my arm out and summoned Dark Heavens, but the sword didn't come. This was wrong. This was completely wrong. John would never expect me to obey him. When I'd pledged allegiance to him and vowed to obey him as a martial arts student, it had broken his heart and he'd performed sword katas for *hours* afterwards. He would never stand there smiling at me, waiting for me to promise to obey.

I had the horrifying realisation — I was Black Jade. I was the copy. The real Emma was stored somewhere and they would use her to blackmail John.

I opened my mouth to yell at John and wake him out of this dream.

'I, Emma Donahoe, vow to take you, my Lord, to be my lawfully wedded husband,' I said, the words coming unbidden. I struggled to stop myself but I couldn't. 'To love and obey from this day forward, for better, for worse, for richer, for poorer, in sickness and in health, until death do us part.'

Thank you, the Jade Emperor said. 'I now pronounce you husband and wife.'

The crowd below went wild. The Jade Emperor turned and sat, then smiled at us benignly. I tried to break whatever was binding me, but they had me. I shook with the effort.

Jade floated up the stairs holding a tray with the teacups on it. John took one and presented it to the Jade Emperor, seemingly oblivious to what was really happening.

The Emperor sipped it, and Jade held the tray out to me. I took a teacup and studied it, then looked up at the Jade Emperor as he continued to smile like a kindly relative.

I stuck all my fingers into the tea, which had gone cold during the interminable ceremony, and screamed in my head at the spirit of the water: *Xuan Wu John I'm Black Jade I'm the copy I'm not the real Emma!*

The water in the teacup changed to ice, and I dropped it. The ice grew and rose from the stones, making the air around us dark and cold. John and the Jade Emperor staggered back, but I held my ground. John had to destroy me and find the real Emma.

The water coalesced into another John, in Celestial Form and holding Seven Stars.

'Yes, you are,' he said, and ran the sword through the Jade Emperor, then through the John next to me. They disintegrated like demons into black essence.

He spun and swung to take Jade's head off, and the world around us changed to something entirely different — a small windowless hall, empty of people — then everything twisted and collapsed.

36

'Totally ruined,' Jade said with exasperation. 'Those robes took *weeks* to make and they're gone. The schedule is wrecked, we don't have time for the martial arts demonstrations, this is a *disaster.*'

'It would be more of a disaster if she hadn't been quick enough to call me,' John said. 'Even controlled by the robe and heavily dosed with opium, she had the wit to contact me through my element.'

'She's still asleep,' the stone said. 'Have you cleared it all?'

'It may take a while to work its way out of her system,' John said.

I opened my eyes. I was lying on the living room couch in our apartments in the Northern Heavens. Jade, John and my stone — in Chinese form, but instantly recognisable — were standing over me. I was under a blanket in my underwear.

I shot upright. 'I'm not the real Emma!' I grabbed John's sleeve. 'John! You have to find her, she's out there ...' It all flooded back to me. 'Did I just marry a demon?'

'Did you say the vows?' the stone said.

'Stone!' I leapt up to hug it, and hesitated. I looked around at them. Were they the real Jade and John and stone?

'Are you *sure* this is the real Emma?' Jade said, studying me.

'It's her,' John said.

'Jade,' I said.

'Ma'am?'

'Have you printed out Western wedding vows for the Jade Emperor?'

'What? You want *Western* wedding vows? Why did you never mention that before?'

'Yes. I want the Western vows,' I said. 'To love, honour and obey Lord Xuan.'

John stepped back, shocked. 'They're still controlling her; it's more than just the robe and the drugs. She would kill herself before vowing to obey me.'

'I wanted to, believe me,' I said.

He summoned Dark Heavens.

'No, wait, I was testing you,' I said. 'The ... whatever they were ... demons, copies, they made me vow to *obey* you. It was like a dream ...' I wiped my eyes. 'Is that really you?'

He put his sword away. 'Go ahead and check for yourself.'

I opened my Inner Eye on him. The Xuan Wu spread before me, vast and dark and cold. 'Okay, that's you. Nothing else could possibly be that ugly.'

'It's absolutely her,' John said.

I turned back to the stone. 'Is that really the Jade Building Block?'

'It is,' John said.

'Where the hell have you *been*?'

'I don't know.' The stone smiled wryly. 'Big chunks of my memory are gone; you'll have to help me.'

'How much do you remember?' I said.

'We don't have time for this,' Jade said. 'They're all waiting in the square outside Dark Justice. Explain after the wedding.'

'Emma,' John said, *'did you say the vows?'*

'Uh ...' I struggled to recall. 'Yes, I did, but under duress.'

'She married BJ,' the stone said.

'BJ was under duress as well,' John said.

'No, she wasn't, my Lord; she seems in control of all her faculties,' the stone said. 'Here is Gold.'

Gold hurried in. I stared at him; he was less than two-thirds his usual height, only just over a metre tall.

He stopped and quickly turned away. 'So sorry, ma'am.'

'What?' I realised I was in my underwear. 'Oh, come *on*, Gold, you're a stone.'

'Well?' John said.

'There is precedent,' Gold said without turning towards me. 'Empress Wu had more than one husband. It's permissible. We'll dissolve the marriage with BJ later. Just go and do the wedding stuff and we'll sort it all out when it's finished.'

'What happened to BJ?' I said, pulling the blanket around me. 'I'm covered up.'

Gold turned back to face me. 'We have her restrained.'

'Six did more than experiment on her,' John said. 'She was one of theirs all along.'

'No, they're just controlling her,' Gold said. 'She can't be one of them. She's my *child*. We'll find a way to free her. We have to.'

'Talk about this later. Wedding now!' Jade said.

'Where's my robe?' I said.

Gold made a soft sound of pain. 'They extracted elemental gold from my stone self and used it as thread in the robes. That's what was controlling you.'

'That silk never came from the Dragon, did it?'

'No,' John said. 'I panicked when Jade tapped on the door — you and the robes were gone. I thought you'd made a run for it. We looked everywhere for you, and I was ready to break things when you spoke to me through my element.'

'We don't have time to talk about this, we have to move!' Jade said. 'I have your armour here, Emma. Change to Celestial Form and I'll help you put it on.'

I changed to Celestial Form wearing my jeans and shirt, and tossed the blanket aside. John changed as well, into his black silk robes and usual dress armour with the Big Dipper on the breastplate.

'Jeans?' Jade said to me as she lifted the dress armour. 'You can't wear jeans! Can you summon a robe?'

'No,' I said. 'This is it.'

'I don't have anything big enough!' she said with exasperation. 'My Lord?'

'I don't do clothes for others, Jade, you know I don't. I can barely do clothes for myself. Can you do a Mountain uniform, Emma?'

'I don't know …' My jeans and shirt changed to the plain black pants and jacket. 'Yes.'

'Quickly,' Jade said, helping me with the dress armour. She fiddled with the buckles. 'We have to hurry.' She stepped back. 'Close enough. Let's go.'

How do you know you can trust Gold and the Building Block if BJ is a demonic agent? I said to John as we went out of the Residence into the courtyard.

The Jade Emperor himself cleared them. He is waiting at Dark Justice.

I nodded. *Okay, I suppose we can trust him. I married BJ?*

The stones were held in demon shells, the same way that child was. They were completely controlled by the demons.

* * *

All the family were waiting for us: Simone, Frankie, Martin and Yue Gui. Simone and Frankie rushed to me and hugged me. Martin and Yue Gui patted my shoulders.

'It's really you,' Simone said. 'I was so worried! You were gone for *hours*.'

'Hurry!' Jade said. 'Everybody into position.'

The dull day from my dream was gone and bright sunshine made the Palace around us shine. The crystalline Celestial sky was clear of clouds; a lovely mild winter's day.

Lucy Chen, the Wudang weapons master, rushed into the courtyard with curlers in her hair and a floral dressing gown over her underwear, her portly figure making the gown bulge.

'Good, you found her,' she said.

'Master Chen, what *are* you doing?' Jade said.

'This is important,' Lucy said. 'Start now or after the ceremony?'

'Now,' Yue said. 'Go.'

Lucy's curlers disappeared and her long black hair fell over her shoulders. She bent forward and tossed it back into a mass of thick curls, then grew into a gorgeous young woman, nearly as tall as John, in a floating red robe. Her hair lifted into small buns on top of her head, and gold pins appeared in it. She held her hand out, Yue tapped her fingertips, and Lucy disappeared.

'What was that about?' Jade said.

'It's a competition,' I said. 'The one with the most … conquests at the end of the party wins.'

'But doesn't Princess Yue have the advantage?' Jade said. 'I mean, she's a …'

'Use your eyes, Jade; Lucy's a turtle as well,' John said. 'She's my weapons master, of course she is.'

'Conquests?' Simone said. 'Seriously?'

I shrugged. 'Turtles.'

'Dragon hunting,' Yue said with grim pleasure.

'Hurry,' Jade said. 'Dark Lord and Lady first, then Prince Ming and Princess Yue, then Princess Simone and Prince Franklin. Swing in from the north, land on the cleared space in front of the hall, and stop to let the photographers do their thing. Then up the stairs to the Jade Emperor. Ming and Yue to the right; Simone and Frankie to the left. Any questions?'

Nobody replied.

'Then go, and I'll see you in the hall! And you two.' She glared and stabbed her index finger at us. 'The Jade Emperor says that if you do a single thing to upset this ceremony, he will free me from your service and you'll have to find someone else to do your books.'

John didn't reply; he just raised his head, took my hand, and floated up and over the north side of the Hall of Dark Justice. I checked behind us: the Number Ones and the children were flying in formation, Frankie grinning like an idiot as he held Simone's hand.

John surrounded us in a bubble of glittering water as we topped over the Hall of Dark Justice and floated to land in front of it. The staff had opened the accordion doors that made up the walls of the hall, revealing its full interior — something that had only happened twice in the hall's lifetime. The Jade Emperor sat on his throne on a dais inside, clearly visible high above the crowd.

We drifted down to the cleared area and John dismissed the water. We stood and waited as the rest of the entourage landed, and gave the photographers plenty of time to take pictures of us. Then John turned, took my hand, and floated us over the central ramp, carved in black marble with a representation of himself in

True Form. We landed at the top and knelt in front of the Jade Emperor. Simone and Frankie knelt to our left, and Martin and Yue to our right.

The Jade Emperor stood to address the crowd.

I had a sudden feeling of déjà vu: he was about to praise us interminably again. At least I didn't feel dull and tired.

I opened my Inner Eye on John again, reassuring myself that it was really him.

Yes, it's really me, he said. *And you are really you, and this whole thing is a circus.*

'The Dark Lord and the Dark Lady are two spirits joined in ways that many of us can only aspire to,' the Jade Emperor said. 'Their chi auras combine and strengthen each other, and their devotion to the Celestial is beyond reproach. When two spirits are so complementary, the wedding ceremony is unnecessary. They have been working as one for many years already.' He nodded to us. 'Xuan Wu and Emma Donahoe. Formalise this bond before all the Celestial and allow us to celebrate your union.' He turned and sat on the throne. 'Don't bother about the tea business; this really has nothing to do with me. You two do your stuff and then we'll all have a big party and about time.'

'Majesty!' Jade said from her spot behind the throne, raising the multi-paged schedule she was holding.

'Rings!' the Jade Emperor said.

We rose and turned.

'Come on, Frankie,' Simone said, and took his hand to guide him up to us.

They gave us the twenty-four-carat pure gold wedding bands, large enough for our Celestial Forms. I checked the one Frankie had given me. It was correct: it had my name etched in English and Chinese around the interior. The one Simone had given John had his name on it too; we would wear rings belonging to each other. Mine was engraved with a snake around the outside; his was engraved with a snake and turtle twining around each other.

'You first,' he said.

I took his hand and slid the ring onto his finger, then looked up into his eyes. His face was so full of adoration that I was speechless.

'If either of you say "Words aren't necessary", I will *murder* you!' Simone hissed in a stage whisper. 'All the Heavens are watching, so say something *awesome*!'

I hesitated, smiling, then said, 'I love you, and I will be proud to call you husband. You're the kindest, most generous and noble man I have ever met.'

He took my hand and put the ring on my finger next to the Jade Building Block. 'I am proud to call you wife. You are courageous, brilliant and full of integrity. You are my only one.'

He gazed into my eyes and we shared a moment of true joy that we were finally here.

'I declare you two finally married, Emperor and Empress of the North, and if you do not kiss each other *right now* this whole thing will be ruined,' the Jade Emperor said.

We smiled and grabbed each other and kissed, ecstatic.

The crowd cheered and clapped below us.

We pulled back, and John smiled at me. 'Yue Gui,' he said.

Yue concentrated and a sword box appeared in her hands. She approached us and gave it to John.

The cheers petered out in the square, and changed to the murmur of voices as people asked each other what was happening.

John opened the box, took the sword out, and gave the box to Yue, who took it and stepped back. John held the sword horizontally in its scabbard out to me with both hands.

For a moment I thought he'd managed to take the Murasame from Frankie. Then I realised that this sword was new, and the tsuba — the guard — had a representation of a snake on it. As the ebony scabbard moved in the sunshine, a textured pattern of scales shifted in colour over its length.

'A gift for you, my Lady Empress. This is the Scales of Wisdom, a blade that took the Mountain forge nearly fifteen years to create. I handed the specifications to them the day you agreed to be my bride. Bear it with valour and as a symbol of my undying love for you.'

I took the sword and removed it from its scabbard. It was a masterpiece of forging: the blade had been folded in such a way that the different grains of the steel formed a rippling finish.

'Exquisite balance,' I said. 'Sharp and deadly, with energy spun through it to make it a more effective demon killer. What

411

a beauty.' I turned it over in my hand. 'Snakeskin wrap on the handle, tortoise-shell tsuba …' I glanced up at him. 'No *way*.'

He shrugged. 'Only the best for my Emma.'

'That was completely unnecessary; you should not have suffered for this,' I said as I held the sword up for the photographers.

'I didn't suffer; it was a simple and painless procedure. I wanted my spirit to be with you whenever you use it.'

'It's wonderful, thank you,' I said as I put it back into its scabbard.

'Take it back out and load it with energy. Show them.'

'Oh, okay.' I drew the sword again, holding the scabbard in my left hand, and filled the sword with chi. Nothing happened. I tried shen. It made a deep bass hum that echoed through the room, and an aura of dark energy formed a cold cloud around the blade.

The crowd went very still and silent.

'That is so awesome,' I said softly. I tuned the shen energy to my top chakra, and the sword's pitch became deep and pure. The aura around it turned rich blue-purple.

I withdrew the energy from the sword and it glittered like ice, the effect gradually fading until it returned to its steel form again.

'As I said, my spirit resides in it,' John said. 'My love for you enhances its power.'

I threw my arm over his shoulder, still holding Scales, and kissed him hard. 'That is the *best*.'

The crowd cheered again. Someone yelled, 'Way to go, Emma!' at the front — probably the Tiger.

I put the sword away and passed it to Simone. 'Ming Gui.'

Martin came to me carrying a jewellery box. I opened it, removed the crown, and returned the box to Martin. I held up the crown. It was platinum with black snakeskin inlay; an elegant slender network of flowing lines, with a gap for his Inner Eye.

I passed it to him and he studied it. 'Beautiful.' He glanced up at me. 'Snakeskin?'

I bowed. 'From my own snake self. Part of my spirit resides in it, as yours does in the sword.' I took the crown back from him and said, 'Duck down a bit.' He lowered his head to oblige and I placed the crown so it wrapped around his forehead and over his temples. 'It will help you keep your hair under control as well.'

He smiled. 'I love it.' He lowered his voice. 'Can I make a matching one for you?'

'I have enough already. I don't need more.'

'I think you should,' Simone said. 'It looks great. Complements your armour. Very *Lord of the Rings*.'

'Open your Inner Eye. Just a touch,' I said. 'And don't turn it on any of us.'

The coronet flared to life, generating a black aura that produced an almost ultraviolet glowing orb over his Inner Eye.

John's face went slack. 'I can see three times further. I can see inside things. I can see more than I've ever seen before.' He closed his Eye and stared at me. 'How did you do that?'

'The Phoenix's materials specialists helped me. I think we've been talking to the same people,' I said. 'No wonder they were so amused when I approached them about the crown. It will do more than just enhance your vision; it will be extremely destructive when you're fully attuned to it, and may have some other capabilities we're yet to discover. You're the most powerful Shen we've ever put one on. This will be most interesting.'

'Best gift *ever*,' he said with awe.

Simone handed me my sword, and John and I turned together to the Jade Emperor and knelt to him.

'Dark Emperor, Dark Empress,' the Jade Emperor said. 'You are married in the eyes of the Celestial. Rule the Northern Heavens with wisdom and justice.'

'Our honour is yours,' John and I said in unison.

We rose and turned to face the crowd.

'Residents of the Northern Heavens,' John said, 'this is your Dark Empress. Obey her as you obey me. Salute your Empress.'

'Salute your Emperor,' I said at similar volume.

Everyone fell to one knee — even the family members — and said the supplication, then stood again.

Jade shuffled through her papers. 'Wait, there were speeches —'

John and I shared a look, and I smiled and nodded.

'Princess Xuan Bei Si Min Simone, present,' John said.

Simone's face went blank and she moved to kneel in front of us.

'Celestial citizens,' the Jade Emperor said from behind us, 'this young woman single-handedly destroyed the Demon King and liberated the Heavens. She sacrificed her ability to live on the Third Platform to free all of you. Northern Heavens?'

'Residents of the Northern Heavens,' John said, 'I present my daughter, the Saviour of the Celestial.' He lowered his voice. 'Stand up and turn around, Simone.'

Simone glared at us, then stood and turned to face the gathered crowd.

'Simone cannot live in the Heavens,' I said. 'It is only by the grace of the Jade Emperor that she is here today. So take this opportunity to show her how you feel about what she's achieved.'

'Simone!' the Tiger roared from below us, and the crowd went completely wild. Some of them had brought streamers and confetti that they threw into the air, and more chi firecrackers went off.

John and I stepped forward and stood either side of Simone as tears ran down her cheeks. We wrapped our arms around her waist and held her. I gestured for Frankie to join us, and he stood in front of me, leaning into Simone.

I raised my sword. 'Let's have a huge party!' I shouted, and the crowd cheered even louder.

* * *

It was very late when we staggered through the door of our room together, and stopped.

'Did you do this?' I said.

'No,' John said. 'I think the Tiger may have sneaked in during the celebrations.'

The modern quilt cover had been replaced by an old-fashioned pink silk one with a large red 'double happiness' character in the centre. Pink and red flowers in red vases covered every surface, and they'd draped the windows with pink silk.

We fell to lie side by side on the bed, staring at the ceiling.

'We made it,' he said.

'We did.' I panted, trying to catch enough air; the combination of being drugged that morning and too much alcohol at the party had made me light-headed. 'I feel so good.'

414

He pulled the covers back, moved us onto the pillows and wrapped himself around me. 'Found, Raised, married. No oaths limit our future; it is ours to make.'

I kissed him, and we lost ourselves into each other. He separated into two male forms, and I was sandwiched between them, surrounded by cool silken skin over taut muscle. I kissed the Serpent as the Turtle held me from behind, and all four of his hands gently roamed my body.

'How exhausted are you?' he said.

'Never too exhausted to celebrate being married to you,' I said, and kissed him again.

I pushed him apart so I could lie on my back, and both of him smiled down at me. The Serpent, fiercer and slimmer and taller, his eyes full of keen intelligence. The Turtle, smaller and darker, the essence of wisdom and kindness.

'I love you so much,' I breathed up at him.

'My Dark Empress, my only one,' he said, and the Serpent kissed me as the Turtle ran his mouth over my neck. He recombined and he was my Dark Lord, gentle and fierce, lying above me and smiling down at me with his tangled hair brushing over us. 'This has been a trying day. I think you need someone to gently love you to sleep.'

I put my arms around his neck. 'Only if I may do the same to you.'

'Always,' he said, and lowered himself onto me.

37

John and I took Frankie and Simone down to the Peak the next morning, then I went to see Black Jade in the Celestial Palace where the Jade Emperor was keeping her.

BJ was sitting on the bed, despondent, and the Jade Emperor and Gold stood on the other side of the invisible barrier that contained her. Two of the Jade Emperor's adult children in their Imperial Elite uniforms stood guard either side of the door.

'Try to think back,' Gold said. 'You were held by Six when you were a baby. Did he do it then?'

'I don't know, Dad,' BJ said.

My stone took human form and stood next to Gold. 'Was it when you were at Lombok? You disappeared for twenty minutes.'

'You were bait, Grandpa,' she said, smiling sadly. 'They needed me back to add new programming. They froze the Dark Lord's assets so Dad would be stuck in Hong Kong sorting it out, and the family had to send me.' Her expression went strange. 'So it is there, in bits and pieces.'

'You were already theirs when you went to Lombok,' Gold said.

'Apparently. I think I've been theirs for a long time.' She wiped her eyes, and her voice went hoarse. 'I'm so sorry. I've failed you all.'

'The current Demon King — he was Number One then — he did this to you?' my stone said.

She nodded. 'You should tell Nanna. She needs to know. The whole stone network needs to know — we're still at risk.'

'The Grandmother will be here in three days to collect you,' the Jade Emperor said. 'She will take you into her heart and attempt to fix what has been done to you.'

BJ bent over her knees with emotion. 'Thank you.'

'Jade Building Block,' the Emperor said, and put his hand out.

My stone took his hand and the Emperor concentrated, examining the stone.

'I see,' the Emperor said. 'I cannot repair this. Have you asked the Grandmother?'

'She can't repair it either,' the stone said, and folded up to return to my ring. 'I want to stay with ... Emma, this is a wedding band! You're married? It *is* Lord Xuan, isn't it? Tell me you two finally made it!'

'No, she married *me*,' BJ said. She stood and her face went fierce; her whole attitude changed from defeat to aggression.

'What?' the stone said. 'You married *Black Jade*?'

'No,' Gold said softly.

'Emma, return to the Northern Heavens,' BJ said. 'Don't tell anyone we're married. Tell them that you ran from the wedding, but you're back now and ready to marry the Dark Lord.' She held her empty hand out to me. 'Take this piece of silk, and keep it with you at all times. I will be in touch shortly with more orders.'

'No,' I said.

'Emma, you vowed to obey me!'

'Under duress,' I said.

'You have to obey me,' she said. 'You *promised*.'

'That may have worked if the Demon King was still in charge,' the Jade Emperor said. 'You could have controlled the Dark Empress. But I have returned to my throne and my Edicts are in force.'

'She's my *wife*!' BJ shouted. 'You have to respect the bonds of marriage. It's one of the basic rights of the Celestial!'

There was a commotion outside.

'Let him in,' the Jade Emperor said.

Justin charged in and stopped, panting. 'It is you.'

BJ sagged with misery and wiped her hand over her face. 'Hi, Justin,' she said. 'Go home. I'm not what you think I am.'

'I think you're cute and smart and funny and extremely cool,' he said.

'And married.' She gestured towards me. 'Meet my wife.'

'I am not your wife,' I growled.

She became aggressive again. 'You said the vows and promised to obey me. I don't know why you're fighting this!'

'BJ, it's *us*,' Gold said. 'Try to remember who you are.'

'You shut up. This is between me and my wife,' BJ said.

'Black Jade,' the Emperor said with a sad smile, 'look at yourself. You identify as female. You have always identified as female, even when under the Demon King's control. And same-sex marriages on the Celestial *are not permitted*. The marriage was invalid, and the vows are void.'

Her eyes widened and she flopped to sit on the bed.

'She's not really controlled, is she?' Justin said. 'She can't be an agent of the Demon King!'

'I'm sorry, Justin,' BJ said. 'I really liked you but I had no choice. They did things to me and I have to obey the programming.'

'The Grandmother of All the Rocks will be here in a few days to take BJ into her heart,' the Jade Emperor said. 'She may be able to return Black Jade's free will.'

'I'll wait for you,' Justin said to BJ.

'It will take some time,' Gold said.

'I'll still wait.'

'*Geological* time, child,' the Jade Emperor said gently.

Justin's face fell. 'Oh.' He looked up at the Jade Emperor. 'Can I go with her?'

'Just leave me,' BJ said.

'No,' the Jade Emperor said. 'But as she said, she has been programmed. I suggest you and the Golden Boy investigate ways to reprogram her — or more accurately, deprogram her. You are a programmer, right?'

'I am,' Justin said.

'You think we can?' Gold said.

'You can fix me?' BJ said, full of hope.

'We can try,' Justin said.

BJ hopped off the bed and approached him carefully. She put her hand up and rested it on the invisible barrier. 'Thanks, Justin.'

He put his hand against hers. 'Whatever it takes.'

Gold put his arm around Justin's shoulders. 'We will fix this.'

'I love you, Dad,' BJ said, her voice hoarse.

The Jade Emperor gestured for me to follow him out of the room, leaving Justin, Gold and BJ to talk under the scrutiny of the Elites.

'Please notify Prince Ming and Lord Leo that the restriction on same-sex marriage has been repealed, and I want to be invited to the wedding,' he said.

I bowed to him. 'Majesty.'

'Dismissed.' He turned away, then turned back. 'Oh. Your teleportation restriction has been lifted as well. You can go where you please.' He disappeared.

'Bastard!' I said, and teleported with no difficulty whatsoever to the Peak apartment to tell Leo and Martin.

I arrived in the kitchen to find John in Turtle form eating cat food out of a bowl on the floor. Frankie was crouched next to him, watching with fascination.

'You teleported yourself?' the Turtle said through a mouthful of pilchards.

'We were right, that bastard restricted me.'

'We will have our revenge later,' he said with relish. 'He didn't keep the Jade Building Block with him?'

'He said nothing could be done for me, my Lord,' the stone said. 'I will just have to live with the damage. Permission to return to duties assisting the Dark Lady.'

'Dark Empress now, old friend,' John said.

'Who's talking, John?' Frankie said.

'The stone in my ring's talking, Frankie, it helps me out,' I said.

'A stone? Like Jade and Richie's dad?'

'Yes.'

'Oh, okay.'

'This is the child!' the stone said. 'Your son! You're married and have your son back? When did this happen? Good Lord, you are too. I missed it! Was I asleep? Wait ... my time stamp says that

I've lost months. I'm seriously damaged.' Its voice went weak with misery. 'What happened to me?'

'You were damaged by the demons, stone,' I said. 'Just take your time and rebuild yourself. We'll look after you. Ask Gold or me what happened if you can't remember.'

'I see. You should replace me, my Lady. The damage will interfere with my ability to perform my duties.'

'Don't be ridiculous,' I said with scorn. 'As long as you wish to be my engagement ring, there's a place for you here.'

'Thank you, Emma. It will take me a while to sort out my matrix. I need to mark the edge of the damage, and link up to the remains of the network to download a summary of events. Give me a day or so, and then I can come back to work for you.'

'Take your time.'

I looked around for everyone. Leo and Martin were downstairs with Buffy; Yi Hao and Er Hao were at the markets, buying for both families and giggling together; and Simone was in Japan. I could even sense Smally, who was keeping the households on the Celestial maintained while we were on the Earthly.

'Where's the Serpent?' I said.

'Wellington Road,' John said.

'Did we regain ownership?'

'Yes. The basement was infested, so I'm clearing it out.'

I stopped for a moment. 'I'm sorely tempted to join you there. I haven't had breakfast yet.'

'Plenty of rats for both of us,' he said.

'No, I have something else to do. You'll like this.' I turned on the kettle and found the teapot.

Frankie pointed at John. 'He says he can give me rides on his shell, Emma.'

'He's too slow to be any fun,' I said as I made the tea. 'Your nanna will have ponies for you to ride with your cousins next week; we'll go and spend a day on their farm.'

He ran to me to lean on my legs. 'Yay!'

Leo, please come up and bring Ming Gui, I said. *I have news.*

Majesty, he said.

Leo, Martin and Buffy came up the stairs and entered the kitchen.

Buffy stopped and her eyes went wide when she saw John. She looked back at Martin, then at John. 'Two of them?'

'That's your Yeh Yeh,' I said as I poured water into the teapot. 'He's a turtle too.'

'Oh, okay,' she said, and went to the fridge. She pulled out a box of lemon tea and stuck the straw in.

'Get one for me too,' Frankie said.

'Okay,' Buffy said.

'No,' I said. 'Frankie, you ask nicely and say *please*.'

'Can I have one too, please?' Frankie said.

Buffy didn't reply, she just pulled another box out for him.

'Yum,' he said as he took it and stuck the straw in.

'Thank you,' I said sternly.

'Thanks, Buffy,' he said. 'When's lunch, Emma? I'm *hungry*.'

'Nothing to do with me,' the Turtle said, at the same time I said, 'It's something to do with your father, I swear.'

'You wanted to see us, my Lady?' Leo said.

'Call me Majesty again and I will inform the Jade Emperor of your blatant disrespect for the Celestial Throne,' I said as I poured tea for him.

'I apologise most sincerely, Your Highness,' he said, bowing to me as he took the teacup.

'That's more like it.' I poured a cup for Martin, and took one myself. 'The restriction on same-sex marriage is rescinded. Don't rush off and do it right away; take your time.'

Leo and Martin both grinned, then embraced and shared a quick kiss.

'Daddy and Ba Ba can get married now?' Buffy said.

I nodded.

She put her little hands on her hips. 'Can I be a flower girl *this time*?' she said with exasperation. 'I want to do it!'

'It will have to be on the Earthly so Buffy can be the flower girl,' Leo said.

'Western-style,' Martin said. 'A celebrant and wedding vows. No tea ceremony.'

'Okay, but on a beach, not in a stuffy hall,' Leo said.

'Pink. Because,' Martin said.

'Cliché,' Leo said with scorn. 'Black for the House.'

'My livery's green and brown.'

'My livery's black.'

'Green and black?'

'Hmm.' Leo went thoughtful. 'I think we can make that work. Jade will kill us if we don't have a bouquet for her to catch.'

'Buffy can carry one.'

'Yeah, that works. But what colour?'

'Go and talk to Jade the Wedding Planner,' I said. 'I'll mind Buffy.'

They didn't need prompting; they both disappeared.

'I'd better be a flower girl *or else*,' Buffy said sternly.

'You shouldn't have sent them off,' John said. He finished the pilchards, changed to human form, and washed his bowl in the sink. 'I wanted to hear the argument about who will be best man.'

'Well, of course it has to be you,' I said.

'Leo will argue that you should be best man. He will want me to give Martin away like an old-fashioned father, and Martin will refuse very loudly.'

'Damn, you're right. That will be the argument of the century.'

'Hey! You were supposed to give us rides,' Frankie said.

'Please,' I said sternly.

'Please, John?' Frankie said.

John grinned at him. 'In the living room.'

'Yay!' both children shouted and raced into the living room.

They'll be fine with me, John said. *Still plenty of rats if you're hungry.*

Deal, I said, and teleported down to Wellington Street.

38

I stepped out of the ensuite into the hotel bedroom and stopped. It was completely quiet; the room was empty. Our suitcases stood unopened where we'd dropped them next to the bed.

I sent my senses out and found John, Simone and Frankie on the beach.

The water here is clean and alive and it was calling him, John said.

I teleported onto the beach. Freddo had joined them, and was standing next to Simone on the sand.

Frankie watched the sea, mesmerised. 'I can feel it.'

'We can all feel it,' Simone said. 'Our daddy is the God of the Sea. That's our element.'

'John is?' Frankie said.

'Please don't call me John,' John said. 'Call me Ba Ba. Or Daddy, like Simone does. Or Father. Or even my true name, Xuan Wu. I'd prefer any of them to John.'

'Emma calls you John.'

'It's my name in her language,' John said. 'You are our son, and you should call her Mother and me Father.'

'I don't want to,' Frankie said, and lowered his head. 'Father was ...'

The water hissed, and pulled away from the shore. I watched with alarm as it receded from us, building into a massive wave ten metres high half a kilometre away. The wave continued to grow and I had a moment of panic — it would destroy everything.

Don't be concerned, I have it, John said.

'Si Shu,' he said to Frankie, 'you are my son and I am the element of water. The beauty of the sea calls to us, but it also has immense destructive power. If you were to release that wave, it would engulf all the buildings behind us and drown everyone in them.'

'Buffy and Mattie, and Nanna and Poppy, and Little Jade and Richie would all die,' I said.

Freddo snorted loudly and shook his head.

Simone squealed. 'All over me! Really? Did you have to? That is so gross!'

'Sorry, Simone,' Freddo said, full of remorse.

'Simone's been slimed,' I said with amusement.

Frankie laughed, and the wave collapsed on itself. The water rushed towards the shore, but John controlled it and it didn't touch us.

'It calls to me, Daddy,' Frankie said.

John stiffened beside me and I patted his back.

'Would you like to go out and see?' John said. 'I can take you.'

Frankie hesitated.

'It's very beautiful,' John said softly. 'There are fish that glow in the deep water. Points of light like Simone's stars.'

'Will we be safe?' Frankie said.

'The water is me, and you will always be safe with me.'

'I'll come too,' Simone said. 'We can go together and see the things I described to you.'

'The big fish?'

'Better than that, there's a pod of dolphins out there playing. Can you hear them?' she said.

Frankie concentrated, then raised his head. 'Let's go.'

John turned to me, his eyes full of the sea. 'Come with us, Emma.'

'No, you three go,' I said. 'I have to help set up the wedding.'

'You don't need us?' Simone said.

424

I gestured towards Frankie. 'Don't make him wait to connect with his element. Just be back by four.'

'I don't have a watch,' John said. 'You'll have to call me.'

'Leave me a scale or a piece of your shell then, so I can contact you.'

'Use your sword,' he said. 'It is linked to me.'

'Oh. Okay.'

He kissed me, then took Frankie's hand and guided him into the water, with Simone beside them. They walked out until the water was waist deep, then dived into it and disappeared.

I sighed gently.

'They are so awesome,' Freddo said.

'I know.'

* * *

A lusciously warm breeze, full of the scent of tropical flowers, lifted the pale green, tan and black silken swags over the bower. Leo and Martin had only invited twenty of their closest friends and family, and they sat on chairs on a raised wooden platform above the sand. Leo's sister, Elise, and her husband, Max, were in the front row, obviously deeply uncomfortable.

The Jade Emperor wore a bright gold tuxedo and managed to look dignified in the intense colour, particularly since he'd left his hair long and in a topknot, and kept his short neat beard. He stood under the bower waiting for the grooms, holding the wedding program in front of him with a satisfied smile.

I stood next to him in a black tuxedo that Mr Li had cut to fit my shape, and John stood on the other side of the Emperor in his black and silver silk robes.

Smooth jazz started somewhere nearby and everybody hushed and turned.

Buffy came up the aisle, her face full of concentration as she held a small bouquet of green, brown and black flowers in front of her similarly coloured dress. Mr Li had done wonders with the livery and the dress looked innocently pretty despite the bold colours. Frankie came behind her, wearing a tiny black tux and holding the rings on a green and brown tortoise-shaped silk cushion. The children walked slowly up the aisle, their little faces serious, and Leo and Martin followed them arm in arm, their expressions full of quiet joy.

Martin wore traditional Tang-style multi-layered robes in green and brown, with a wide belt and a rope over-belt, and they drifted around him in the warm breeze. He had part of his long hair tied in a topknot encased in a gold filigree crown and the rest fell to his waist. Leo wore a Western tuxedo, all in black, with a green bow tie and a brown cummerbund.

Elise's expression softened when she saw Leo and Martin together, and she opened her bag, pulled out tissues and wiped her eyes. Max patted her leg.

Frankie stood next to me, and Buffy stood next to John. She smiled up at him and he returned the grin.

Leo and Martin stood in front of the Jade Emperor and held hands. The warm breeze lifted the silk around us again.

The Jade Emperor opened the portfolio containing the service. 'Never, in my long reign, have I been happier to rescind an Imperial Edict,' he said.

* * *

John eyed the wedding cake suspiciously as the waiter placed it in front of him.

'You don't like fruit cake?' I said.

'I could never understand it; it's very strange,' he said. 'I wonder if they have sliced orange or something a little more normal.' He looked around. 'Maybe one of the children want it.'

Frankie, Buffy, Little Jade and Richie ran up to us, and all four of them hit the table with a bump.

'Yeh Yeh,' Buffy said, 'can I stay with Uncle Gold and Aunty Amy tonight, instead of with you and Aunty Emma?'

'Me too!' Frankie said. 'We want to play with Jade and Richie.'

'Did your fathers say it was okay?' John said.

'And did you ask Gold and Amy first?' I added.

'Yes!' all four of them said in unison.

'They said it's okay,' Buffy said.

'Let me see,' John said. He nodded. 'Just for tonight. We're heading back home tomorrow.'

'Thank you, Yeh Yeh,' Buffy said, serious.

'Thank you, Daddy!' Frankie said, and grinned at me.

'Do you know,' Buffy said conspiratorially to John, 'when I'm grown up, I'll have a big wedding with lots of flowers and cake, just like my daddies.'

Both Frankie and Richie went very still, listening to her.

'Who will you marry?' Richie said.

'Me!' Little Jade shouted, and kissed Buffy on the cheek.

'Yes!' Buffy yelled, and hugged Little Jade so hard she nearly lifted her off her feet. Little Jade hugged her back, and both girls held each other with huge grins.

'Can we stay more than one day?' Frankie said. 'I want to play with my friends!'

'Would you all like to spend a few days at the Peak with us?' I said. 'You can, if your parents say it's okay. We have room.'

'Yes!' Little Jade and Richie said.

'Go ask your parents then.'

'Yay!' Frankie said, and they ran off to find Gold and Amy.

Yi Hao, I said.

Ma'am?

Make up the spare rooms for tomorrow. Gold and Amy's children are staying with us for a few days as well as Buffy.

She was silent.

Yi Hao?

No reply.

Er Hao.

Ma'am?

I just asked Yi Hao something and she went quiet. Is she all right?

Let me check. I'm going up the stairs, here she is ... Ma'am, what did you say to her? She's sitting on the kitchen floor crying her eyes out!

I said that Gold and Amy's children are staying with us —

REALLY? She sounded breathless in my head. *Buffy and Little Jade and Richie will be with us, as well as Frankie? All four children?*

Yes.

For how long?

A few days, that's all.

That is so wonderful! Oh, ma'am, I'm crying too now. Thank you! We cannot wait. Oh, oh ... Her voice disappeared for a moment. *Yi Hao is hugging me. We need to go shopping, and make up the rooms, and ... so many things to be done!*

I'll see you tomorrow, dear ladies, I said.

'All organised?' John said.

I nodded. 'My demons are thrilled to bits.'

'They adore children.'

'They may not be as enthusiastic after a few days,' I said.

'Even worse — they won't want to say goodbye.' John went thoughtful. 'I wonder if Amy and Gold would like to live in the other downstairs flat while Amy's doing her law degree.'

I smiled at him. 'I am so glad you are back, Serpent. That is the best idea ever.'

When the speeches were done and the grooms had been sent on their way, we wandered out of the hotel's ballroom and onto the beach. The chairs and bower were still there, the silk flapping in the evening breeze, and the stars were beginning to show in the violet sky.

We removed our shoes and left them on the platform, then held hands and stepped onto the sand together. We walked along the shoreline, enjoying the closeness, then stopped and held each other around the waist as we looked out over the water. I rubbed my hand over his back, enjoying the feeling of his silk robes sliding over his skin.

'Frankie's with Amy and Gold,' he said. 'We have the whole evening to ourselves. Would you like to go out with me?'

'I would love to.'

Hoofbeats sounded on the beach — a galloping horse was approaching. We turned, alarmed, to see Simone and Frankie riding Freddo bareback, still in their wedding outfits.

'Woohoo!' Frankie yelled, his arms in the air, as they thundered past us.

'You will fall off!' I shouted at them as Freddo splashed through the shallow water, making Frankie squeal.

'Hold on!' Freddo shouted. He made a wide turn and cantered back, then stopped in front of us, his sides heaving. 'I am so out of shape,' he said ruefully. 'Definitely need more cardio.'

'Watch this, watch *this*!' Frankie shouted. 'Do it, Freddo, do it!'

'You holding on tight, squirt?' Simone said.

Frankie grabbed Freddo's mane. 'I got it!'

'Okay, ready?' Freddo said. 'Go!'

He made a small half-rear and Frankie yelled with delight. 'Higher! Higher!'

'That is incredibly dangerous!' I said. 'What if you lose your balance and fall backwards? You'd land on them!'

'Only on a non-sentient horse. Please give me some credit, Emma,' Freddo said. He reared again.

'Yay!' Frankie yelled. 'Now run!'

'Will you be all right if your father and I go into the ocean together for a while?' I asked them.

'Go,' Simone said. 'Little Jade and Richie are waiting for us, they want a ride.'

'Buffy too,' Frankie said. 'Everybody wants rides.'

'Pony rides two dollars,' Freddo said. 'I wish I could change into a cranky Shetland.'

'Be careful,' I said.

'It's okay, I hold them,' Simone said.

'I always am, ma'am,' Freddo said. He made another small rear, spun on his hindquarters and cantered back towards the hotel.

* * *

I was wrapped around the Serpent on top of the Turtle's shell as we sped through the water. I rubbed my tail against his, then extended the stroking to the rest of him. My scent filled the water and the Turtle stopped.

'You know how I said I'm always interested?'

'Oh.' I pulled myself upright on his shell. 'You're taking me to see the Dragon King to pay our respects. I should have realised.'

The Turtle started swimming again, thrusting through the water beneath me. 'You ruined the surprise.'

'I've been dying to see his Palace,' I said. 'Ever since you mentioned that it's the finest underwater one in existence.' I pulled myself tighter around him. 'Cannot wait.'

'He's not as close as the Dragon is, so no private room for us when we get there,' he said ruefully.

'Frankie is safe with Gold and Amy, and Simone is with them,' I said. 'We have all night, all of the ocean, and a luxury hotel suite.'

The Turtle lowered its head and pushed harder through the water. 'That is a fine idea.'

John shared his night vision with me and I saw the ocean bed become shallower in front of us. It lifted into a gentle slope covered in a mass of coral, teeming with fish. The Turtle stopped at the edge of the reef, then raised itself and floated above the surface. The sea bed inclined to a sand-covered coral atoll, circular with a central lagoon that was five kilometres across. The shallow lagoon water was almost invisible against the white sandy bottom.

'When we land, change to your human form,' he said. 'No need for a weapon. Here they come to escort us in.'

Two dragons rose out of the lagoon, their scales shimmering in the tropical moonlight. They approached us and lowered their heads. It was Jade, glittering green and gold, and her daughter Jackie, who was sapphire blue with green fins and tail.

'Xuan Tian Shang Di,' Jade said. 'Xuan Tian Nu Huang. Welcome to Longjia, Dragonhome.'

'We thank you for your hospitality and enter the King's domain in peace and fraternity,' John said. The Turtle bobbed its head. 'Please escort us to the presence of the King of Dragons.'

Jade and Jackie turned away. 'This way, Highnesses.'

'Aren't I just Xuan Tian Huang Hou?' I said. 'Nu Huang means "ruler", not "consort".'

'The Dark Lord himself decreed your title, ma'am,' Jade said.

'Do you always have to piss off the entire Celestial, John?' I said.

Jackie hissed with serpent laughter.

I sighed. 'Yeah, silly question.'

John followed them as they flew over the low sandy atoll and dived into the water. I gripped him tightly, expecting to hit the bottom, but we didn't; instead we plunged through the water and into air. I made a loud sound of astonishment and the dragons chuckled.

'No warning, my Lord?' Jade said. 'That was cruel.'

'Worth it to see her face,' John said.

We flew three hundred metres above the floor of the town inhabiting the bowl-shaped interior of the atoll. The full moon shone through the water as if it wasn't there; we were still close enough to the surface to see fish swimming above us. We flew over the town through a fresh fragrance-filled breeze towards what was obviously the Dragon King's own Palace on one side of the bowl-shaped valley.

The bottom of the valley was a deep blue lake, almost perfectly circular with white paved edges. Dragons splashed and played in the water and tumbled through the air above it.

The town spread and rose along the sides of the valley; and streams and waterfalls cascaded down between the houses, reflecting the street and house lights to cause rainbows through the air. The sides of the valley were terraced to hold the whitewashed houses with blue and green tiled upturning roofs, and gleaming white pagodas with large balconies around the top. A riot of tropical plants flourished between the houses: bougainvillea, hibiscus and tall flame-flowered trees in shades of red, purple and orange, reflecting the light of many red and gold lanterns. Dragons flew among the houses, diving through the waterfalls and playing in the air.

The King's Palace followed the slope up the hillside to a multi-storeyed white pagoda near the surface of the water above. The Palace was mostly single storey, similar to the Celestial Palace and our own Dark North, but water cascaded between the buildings, over the walls and sometimes the roofs, lit from beneath by coloured lights. Trees grew out of the water as well, towering and green, their leaves rustling in the fresh undersea breeze.

Only dragons are permitted in Dragonhome, John said. *No other creatures know of its location. He honours us as fellow reptiles.*

I'm glad he's let us visit, I said. *It's lovely.*

We landed at the entrance court in front of the Palace, and took human form. An honour guard of six dragons in human form, carrying halberds, approached and bowed to us.

The biggest one spoke. 'Dark Lord, Dark Lady, welcome to Dragonhome. The King is waiting for you.' He turned and gestured towards the Palace. 'This way.'

'Dear Lord — Silver!' I hugged him, and he smiled and wrapped his arms around me. 'You disappeared! What happened to you? I thought you were dead.'

The other dragons in the escort group grinned broadly.

'I was severely injured at the Northern Heavens, and they brought me back here,' he said, releasing me and putting his hand on my back to guide me to the Palace. He tapped his left leg. 'This is gone from the thigh down, and the other one from the calf down. The prosthetics are good, but I can't do any more Arts.'

'Don't be ridiculous, that is not a reason to stop,' John said. 'We have eleven students and two Masters who are all disabled, not including Master Leo.'

'Tell them the truth,' one of the other dragons said.

'And the King ordered me back to lead the Royal Guard,' Silver said sheepishly. He bobbed his head. 'Apologies for not informing the Mountain of my reassignment.'

'That's more like it,' John said with satisfaction.

Jade bowed to John. 'If I may accompany you, my Lord? My Lady?'

'Of course,' John said.

She changed to human form in her green robes, and shooed Jackie away. 'Meet up with us after.'

'Okay, Mama,' Jackie said, and flew into the air.

Our guards guided us to the King's main audience hall, with Jade walking at our right as Retainer. The ramp was crystalline blue stone, carved in the form of a dragon and inlaid with gold. We walked up the stairs at the right of the ramp to the veranda around the hall, and stopped at the entrance. The honour guard moved to flank the door, and we entered the hall.

Status? I said.

Equal and informal, John said. *Once all of the formal stuff is out of the way, he's a great guy.*

I relaxed with relief, and he smiled as he saw it.

The hall's roof was ten metres above us, and the walls and floor were tiled with white ceramic. Dragon motifs in translucent blue and green enamel were inlaid into the pillars holding up the roof. The Dragon King sat on a wide gold throne at the other end of the hall, in human form with his golden dragon head. We walked up a green carpet to meet him.

John saluted him first. 'Long Huang Di. Ten thousand years.'

The Dragon King nodded to John. 'Xuan Tian Shang Di. Ten thousand years.'

He turned his green eyes onto me and I saluted him as well. 'Long Huang Di. Ten thousand times ten thousand years.'

He nodded to me. 'Xuan Nu Huang. Welcome to Longjia. Please allow me to show you the hospitality of dragonkind, reptile to reptile.'

'We are honoured by your welcome,' John said.

'May I offer you refreshment? Have you eaten?'

'We have, my Lord,' John said. 'We need for nothing.'

He cocked his head, studying us.

'No, seriously,' I said. 'We're not insulting you. We just had a massive wedding banquet and couldn't possibly fit another thing in.'

'Some grapes or orange would be good though,' John said. 'They had that weird wedding cake that Westerners are so fond of.'

'That dried grape thing? Truly strange.' The King drew himself to his feet, put his hands behind his back and paced towards us. 'Come and have some fruit and tea in the gardens with me then. And I'd appreciate it if you could lay a wreath at a memorial to those who lost their lives in the recent conflict.'

John nodded to him. 'We would be honoured.'

'Jade, wait for us at the memorial,' the King said.

Jade hesitated, then bowed to him. 'Majesty.' She disappeared.

'Lady Emma,' the Dragon King said, gesturing towards me, 'walk with us, honoured lady, and tell us of your magnificent children.'

'Only Frankie is mine,' I said. 'Simone is the Dark Lord's.'

'You helped him to raise her, my Lady.'

I nodded. 'That I did.'

'They're right,' he said with wonder. 'You do sound like him.'

He led us through a courtyard that held a formal garden with a pond and small flowering shrubs, and was lit by strings of lanterns along the walls and the pavilions.

It's not like him to be this formal. Normally he's way more relaxed, John said. *I wonder what's coming.*

'There was much consternation at your choice to remain on the Earthly with your first human wife, my Lord, but none can argue that you made the wrong decision,' the King said. 'Si Min, the child you had with her, saved the Heavens. And now there are two of these powerful children.'

We sat at a table together, and the Dragon King poured tea for us. John took a slice of orange and watched the King as he ate it. The King's dragon face made it difficult to see his thoughts.

'It is a very special feeling when our children surpass us, isn't it?' he said.

'My children fill me with great joy,' John said, putting the rind down. 'Emma's training has made her something unique and powerful, and she has passed that strength to our son. It will be very interesting to see how Si Sha grows.'

'How old is he?'

'Nearly three years old, but because of his nature he appears about twelve,' I said.

'He appears much older than his true age,' the Dragon King said grimly. 'And he has claimed the Murasame.'

'Yes. It speaks to him,' I said.

He turned to face the pond, and the koi glided to the surface in hopes of a meal. 'Truly terrifying.'

John and I shared a look.

'We will teach him to restrain his power, and he already controls the sword well,' I said.

'I have no doubt,' he said. He hesitated, and we waited for it. He tapped the table. 'I have a request.'

'You have but to name it, my Lord,' John said. 'The Northern Heavens treasure their close ties with Longjia.'

'Would you foster one of my children in your household, to grow and learn with yours?'

We relaxed.

'We already have the Jade Girl,' John said.

'Another child of age with your son,' the King said. 'To grow in friendship together.'

'Sure,' I said. 'Frankie's still settling into life as a Celestial, so maybe wait a couple of years and then we can arrange something. We have stacks of room in our apartment on the Peak. I don't think it would be the best for a child to be with us full-time, but send a kid over every now and then and we'll be happy to include them in the family.'

'You really are living on the Earthly?'

'We shuttle backwards and forwards,' I said. 'But since Simone and Buffy are both stuck on the Earthly, we've decided to keep the family together.'

'May I visit and see these exceptional children?'

'Of course,' I said. 'Do you have a fully human form?'

He changed to human form, shrinking in his robes. He lost the dragon head and his human face was youthfully ageless, androgynous and divinely beautiful. His long green and gold hair fell to his waist.

I stared at him for a long moment, and he smiled at my reaction.

'I think you may need to take a form that is a little less ...' I was lost for words.

'Dragon,' John growled.

I glanced up at John; his face was rigid with restraint. I took his hand and squeezed it.

Not you, he said. *That's much younger than his usual human form, and if he makes a single move towards Simone I will take his head myself.*

I'll help you, I said. *And if he sends a boy of Simone's age, I'll send him straight back again.*

John nodded without looking away from the Dragon King.

The King regained his dragon head. 'I'll work on it.' He pushed away from the table. 'Come. Let's lay these wreaths, and then my daughter wants to show you something.' We rose as well, and he led us through the garden. 'Please talk to Jade about marrying Qing Long. She really does love him, and he has renounced his false façade and decided to live true to his own gentle self. They are a fine match.'

'You just want a daughter of yours as Empress of the East,' I said.

The Dragon King chuckled. 'I know, politics politics. But they are still a fine match.'

We went through a small side gate in the Palace's external wall and arrived on the lawn next to the lake. A three-metre-tall statue of a dragon carved from white marble stood in the centre of the lawn facing the water, and a number of dragons in both human and True Form stood around it, waiting for us. Jade and Jackie stood to one side, both of them with tears running down their faces, as they studied the wall behind the statue that held the names of those who had died in the conflict. The statue was surrounded by funereal wreaths, each a circular flower arrangement composed of white and gold chrysanthemums with the name of the donor written on a card in the centre.

The King gestured towards the statue. 'My Lord. My Lady.'

John held his hand out and a flowered wreath appeared in it. I held the wreath as well, and we stepped forward together and placed it at the base of the memorial.

Please say something for us, John said. *It will cement your seniority.*

I nodded, and looked up at the elegant carved dragon.

'The Demon Kings took advantage of the high principles of the Celestial in an attack without honour. They imprisoned helpless humans and innocent children, and many Celestials died in the fight to protect them. As long as dragons such as those of Dragonhome are willing to give their lives to defend the citizens of the Celestial, it will never fall again. We honour those who died, and those who were injured, those who were physically and mentally traumatised by the conflict, and those who suffered even though they had no part in it. Wudang regathers, and we will rebuild our armies to ensure that the Heavens are never threatened like this again.'

The dragons applauded politely.

'You have chosen extremely well, my Lord,' the Dragon King said.

'I did not choose Lady Emma,' John said. 'Fate chose us for each other.'

The King nodded his dragon head. 'I'll be in touch about the fostering. I look forward to forging closer ties with the House of the North. Now I believe that my daughter wished to see you. After you have spoken to her, you may depart with our best wishes. She can be our liaison.' He bowed to John, then to me. 'Lord Xuan, Lady Emma.' And he swept away from us, through the gates back into his Palace.

Jade came out of the crowd in human form. 'There you are. I have something to show you. Come and see.'

'Are you okay?' I said. 'You can stop if you want to.'

'No, no, it's fine, she said, wiping her eyes with her sleeve. 'Every time I think about Frannie and Hinnie I'm sad, but I have something for you to see. I'm fine.'

She led us around the lake towards the houses. A small temple stood on the lawn next to the lake, and a few dragons were gathered around it in True Form, their bright scales shining in the moonlight.

'Did my father give you a hard time, Emma?' Jade said as we walked.

'He was impeccably polite,' I said. 'You're allowed back home now? He disowned you.'

'The Blue Dragon revealed his true nature during the conflict, and Father is horrified that the "strong manly" dragon is a ... what was the word he used? "Pussy". He has forbidden me from seeing Qing Long ever again.'

'He's using reverse psychology,' I said.

'I know,' she said. 'It's in this temple. You'll like this.'

'What is dragonkind's reaction to Qing Long revealing his true nature?' John said with interest. 'Was there much hilarity at his expense? He has been very quiet.'

'The other dragons seem more relieved than anything. They're happy that Qing Long seems to have mellowed after suffering so much during the war.'

'I'm glad,' I said. 'And you? Now that he's no longer living a lie, will you give him a chance?'

'I won't act purely to defy my father, but I'll think about it. General Ma knows how I feel about Qing Long, and keeps suggesting that I go back to him. But I'm loath to leave Hua Guang. He's a fine companion and a generous partner, and we have something very good together.'

'Just marry both of them,' John said. 'Talk to them about it. They're good friends and would probably be happy to share.'

Jade smiled. 'Now that's an idea that would *really* piss my father off. I'll definitely think about it.'

'Reptiles,' I said under my breath.

'Dragons,' Jade said with grim pleasure.

We stopped at the entrance to the small temple, and the dragons around us grinned. We went in to find two statues sitting on the altar, each about half life-size. The statue on the right was obviously John: fierce face, wild hair, Seven Stars across his knees, and a snake and turtle under his bare feet. I couldn't place the one on the left. She was sitting as well, holding a sword vertically in her right hand, and the back of her throne was a black cobra hood. Her skin was pure white, her hair brown and as wild as his, and her eyes were dotted blue ...

'Holy shit,' I said softly. 'No *way*.'

Jade collapsed over her knees laughing.

'Was this your idea?' John said, obviously delighted.

'No, my Lord,' she said through the gasps, wiping her eyes again. 'It was here when I returned. The dragons placed it after the war ended.'

'I should not be in here, I'm not a Sh—' I began, and stopped. John chuckled.

'That statue should be of *me*,' the stone said. 'Nobody ever acknowledges my contribution.'

'No,' I said. 'It should be of Simone.'

'She has her own temple further up the hill,' Jade said. 'Would you like to see?'

I pulled out my mobile phone. 'Hell, yeah. I want to take a photo and show it to her. She'll probably have the same reaction I just did.' I checked the phone settings. 'But she completely deserves it, and I hope many more temples are built with her effigy in them.'

'I'll make sure they are,' John said.

* * *

'Who won last time?' he said as we lifted out of the atoll.

'Me.'

438

'You cheated.'

'Oh, that's very good coming from you, Mr Fertility God.'

'So your choice. Where and what?'

'Back at the hotel room, and I'll tell you when we get there.'

When we'd been in bed for a while, he pulled back to see me, the room's lights glowing in his eyes. 'You have yet to tell me how you want me, my Lady, and if you don't make a choice soon the decision will be made for you. You are pushing me very hard here.'

'I thought I was pulling,' I said, and stroked him again.

He shivered and closed his eyes. 'Last chance, Emma,' he growled. 'Otherwise I'll let it go.'

'But I love it when you let it go,' I breathed into the side of his throat.

'If that's what you want, you can have it, but I must warn you: it won't be gentle.'

'No,' I said, and levered myself off the bed to stand next to it. I studied him as he lay there in his human form, completely at my mercy. He reclined, showing himself off. I admired him, then gathered myself and pointed at the bedhead. 'Serpent, human form, up that end.'

He separated, and the Serpent, in male human form, scooted up to the top of the bed. The Turtle, also in male human form, remained lying in the middle.

'Female, please, Serpent,' I said.

The Serpent bobbed his head. 'As my Lady wishes.' He changed to female.

I cocked my head. 'Do you want it male, John?'

'Tonight is what you want, and I can see what you're doing in wanting me female. But I will win anyway, and then next time you will do what *I* want,' the Serpent said intensely. 'And my choice will be for *you* to be the male one.'

'Uh,' I said, breathless at the idea, then, 'No. I know what I want.' I pointed at the Turtle. 'True Form.'

The Turtle didn't argue, it just changed for me. I couldn't resist the urge to sit on the bed and run my hands over its smooth shell. It raised its head with bliss.

The Serpent threw her head back as well, her face full of rapture. 'This again. I *love* this.' She smiled at me. 'I will win.'

I climbed onto the bed on all fours between them, enjoying her reaction as she watched me. 'I'll make sure you don't.'

'Not a chance,' the Turtle said. 'The only uncertainty is whether you have eight or nine.'

'If I have nine, you can choose the next two,' I said. I rested my cheek against the top of the Serpent's thigh and smiled up at her.

She stroked my face and her eyes roamed my features. 'Before we are lost in it: I love you, my Emma. My wife. You have always been my only one.'

'My only one,' the Turtle said behind me.

'And you are —'

I lost the ability to speak when the Turtle touched me without physically making contact. I was unable to move as he slid over me, cool and slick, then gasped as his touch became firmer and more demanding.

'Oh, you are so ready,' he said, husky.

The Serpent slid down the bed so she was under me, and kissed me, her hands brushing over my skin. She mouthed my nipples as the Turtle teased me into quivering readiness.

'Up,' I said, my voice hoarse. 'I want you. Both of you.'

The Serpent smiled into my eyes, kissed me, and moved up again. 'Whatever my Lady wishes.'

I gently pushed her thighs apart and buried my face into her as the Turtle slid into me, and the world lifted into a blinding explosion of pleasure.

Three hours later I was too exhausted to lift my head. 'You win: I was first. You have the next two,' I said, muffled by the pillow.

'Nine?' he said.

'No.' I gasped a few times. 'Ten.'

I heard a slap and looked up. He was in two human forms and he'd high-fived himself. He slid under the covers on either side of me, then wrapped his arms around me and held me tight between both of him.

'You are the *best*,' the Serpent said, half-asleep.

'And so are you.'

The Turtle chuckled and his chest shook against my back. 'I know.'

39

'Just remember,' I said as I stopped the van at the entrance to the new school, 'if you feel the charm slipping, let us know and we'll fix it.'

'I'm so short,' Frankie grumbled. 'It feels really weird.'

'And don't forget, you're five years old and you can't do anything that Buffy can't,' Leo said. 'And no talking about weapons.'

'And tell the Murasame to stay away,' I said. 'Even if you get mad or get hurt, it's not allowed to come.'

'I won't remember everything!' he protested.

'That's why your mother and I are here,' Leo said. 'We'll be here all day, so you can ask us anything any time.'

'I'll help too,' Buffy said.

'If it's too hard, let us know,' I said. 'You're not really old enough yet, so you can wait a year and start with Matthew. It's okay.'

'No, I want to start now.'

'We'll help him,' Richie said. 'It's fine, Aunty Emma.'

The security guard stood in the middle of the car park entrance and I lowered the window to speak to him.

'No parking,' he said.

'I have a special permit,' I said, handing him the letter from the principal. 'We're allowed to park here for the first two weeks.'

He checked the letter, and nodded. 'Oh, yes, they told us about you.' He stepped back and gestured towards an empty space. 'That one's for you, Mrs Chen.'

'No, I'm not —' I said, and stopped. I blinked at him, then grinned broadly, my heart lifting. 'Thank you.'

'Mrs Chen,' Leo said softly with affection from the seat behind me.

I parked the van, and the children bolted out and ran up the stairs to the entrance, having a quick tussle as they tried to open the locked door.

'Cut that out,' Gold said as he followed them. 'You need to press the button to open the door.'

'Hurry up, Daddy, open it for us!' Richie said.

I checked that the children hadn't left anything behind in the van as they argued over who would press the button.

'Who forgot their bag?' I called, raising the one they'd left behind.

Gold checked them. 'Buffy? Where's your bag?'

I looked at the bag I was holding. 'This is Frankie's.'

'Frankie, you have Buffy's bag,' Leo said, taking the bag Frankie was carrying.

Gold checked his own children's bags. 'These are the right ones.'

'We all set?' I said, handing the bag to Frankie.

'Yes!' they all said, jumping up and down with excitement.

I helped Frankie put the bag on his back as Buffy unlocked the door, and Richie opened it. They charged through and ran into the school yard.

'Hurry up, hurry *up*,' Frankie said to me as we struggled with the straps. 'Come on, Mummy, they're gone!'

He finally had the bag sorted and ran after them. I couldn't stop the huge grin: he'd called me Mummy.

Leo patted me on the shoulder. 'Time to be parents, Mrs Chen. I think your life is about to become way less interesting.'

'You haven't seen her in-tray, Mr Alexander-Chen,' the stone said as I followed the excited children through the door.

Characters

Andrew (Emma's Nephew): middle son of Emma's sister Jennifer.

Andy Ho: husband of Emma's friend April; later turned out to be a demon and promoted to the Demon King's Number One.

Bai Hu: the White Tiger, God of the West. His element is Metal.

Barbara Donahoe: Emma's mother.

Black Jade (BJ): stone Shen, child of Gold, created when he was damaged in battle.

Blue Dragon: Qing Long, God of the East. His element is Wood. Father to Jade's three dragon children.

Brendan Donahoe: Emma's father.

Bridget Hawkes: wife of David Hawkes, who was an executive in a large Hong Kong company until he was replaced by a demon.

Chang: human, ex-Shaolin monk. Manages the orphanages supported by John and Emma.

Clarissa Huang: human woman, engaged to Michael MacLaren, held and tortured by demons in the past.

Colin (Emma's Nephew): oldest son of Emma's sister Jennifer.

Da Shih Yeh: the Little Grandfather; ancient mystical blue-skinned demon who wanders the Halls of Hell comforting those who are in most need. Rumoured to be a demonic incarnation of Kwan Yin.

David (Emma's Nephew): younger son of Emma's sister Amanda.

David Hawkes: human executive director of one of Hong Kong's large family-owned companies; husband to Bridget. Replaced by a demon copy.

Demon King (East): calls himself George. Has several male and female human forms, one of which is Kitty Kwok. His True Form is similar to a Snake Mother (human front end, snake back end) but red instead of black.

Demon King (West): calls himself Francis. Has teamed up with the Eastern Demon King and they are building an army together.

Edwin: Wudang Mountain's staff doctor.

Elise Alexander: Leo's sister from Chicago.

Emma Donahoe: human Australian woman who can change into a snake; engaged to Xuan Wu.

Er Hao: tame demon, major domo of the Imperial Residence on Celestial Wudang.

Er Lang: Second Heavenly General, the Jade Emperor's left hand and John's assistant in defence of the Heavenly realm. Has a third eye in the centre of his forehead and is most often seen in the company of his Celestial Dog.

Francis: see Demon King (West).

Frankie: John and Emma's son; aborted when he was three months old and brought to term in a demon egg by the King of the Demons, who adopted him.

Freddo: Freddo Frog, Simone's half-demon horse.

George: see Demon King (East).

Gold: stone Shen, child of the Jade Building Block. Works as the Academy's legal adviser. Husband to Amy, stone parent to BJ, and human father to Richard and Jade Leong.

Grandmother of All the Rocks: Uluru, the massive stone in the centre of Australia. Spiritual mother of all the stone Shen in the world.

Greg White: human Immortal husband to Emma's sister Jennifer. Used to be the White Tiger's Number One son; resigned to marry Jennifer.

Guan Yu: also called 'Guan Gong', Marshal of the True Spirit and Guardian of the Gates of Heaven; one of the Thirty-Six.

Jade Emperor: supreme ruler of Taoist Heaven, God of the Centre and the element of Earth.

Jade Girl: daughter of the King of the Dragons; John's earthly accountant, now Wudang PR Director.

Jennifer: Emma's sister, mother to Colin and Andrew with her first husband, Leonard. Divorced, and remarried the White Tiger's previous Number One son, Greg. They have a son called Matthew.

John Chen: Xuan Wu, the Dark Emperor of the Northern Heavens; God of the North and Martial Arts. His True Form is a snake and turtle combined together. His element is Water.

Justin: a son of the Dragon of the East who specialises in IT. Dated Simone for about two weeks.

Kitty Kwok: Emma's previous employer, who ran kindergartens in Hong Kong; revealed to be the Eastern Demon King in female human form.

Kwan Yin: a Buddha, one who has attained enlightenment and has returned to Earth to help others. Goddess of Mercy and Compassion.

Leo Alexander: African-American bodyguard to Simone when she was a child; now a Taoist Immortal. Engaged to Prince Martin Ming Gui, son of Xuan Wu.

Liu, Cheng Rong: the Academy's Immortal Shaolin Master; married to Master Meredith Liu.

LK Pak: previous Wudang Demon Master.

Louise: Emma's good friend for many years; married the White Tiger and became wife number ninety-seven. Died in a demon attack on the Western Palace.

Ma Hua Guang: vanguard of the Thirty-Six; one of the Thirty-Six (now Thirty-Five) Heavenly Generals and John's right hand.

Mark (Emma's Nephew): older son of Emma's sister Amanda. Martin Ming Gui: turtle Shen, son of Xuan Wu, elder brother to Simone, younger brother to Yue Gui; Prince of the Northern Heavens and John's Number One son. Engaged to Leo Alexander.

Master (Miss) Lucy Chen: Wudang Weapons Master.

Matthew (Emma's Nephew): younger son of Emma's sister Jennifer.

Meredith Liu: the Academy's Energy Master; a European Immortal; married to Liu Cheng Rong, the Academy's Shaolin Master.

Michael MacLaren: Number One son of the White Tiger.

Michelle LeBlanc: Xuan Wu's first human wife, Simone's mother. Killed by demons when Simone was two years old.

Number One: an honorary title given to the most senior son (or daughter). Most rulers have a Number One to assist them in running their realms, and a Number One has precedence second only to their father/mother.

Nu Wa: ancient Chinese Goddess, believed to have originally created humanity and used the Stone Building Blocks (one of which was Emma's stone) to hold up the sky when it fell.

Pao Qing Tian: Celestial Judge of the Tenth Level of Hell. Responsible for releasing Immortals back to the world when they're killed; also makes the decision on who is Worthy to be Raised to Immortal.

Peony: the Serpent Concubine. John's concubine during the Qing Dynasty; became mentally ill, murdered her servants, and was executed.

Qing Long: the Blue Dragon, God of the East. His element is Wood.

Red Phoenix: Zhu Que, Goddess of the South. Her element is Fire.

Ronnie Wong: half-demon son of the Demon King, worked as a Fung Shui Master and expert on demon seals until he Ascended to a new human life.

Simone: Simone Chen, Princess of the Dark Northern Heavens; daughter of Xuan Wu and his human wife, Michelle LeBlanc.

Stone: the Jade Building Block of the World; the stone that sits in Emma's engagement ring. One of the stones created by Nu Wa to hold up the Heavens when the Pillars were damaged by an angry god, but was never used for this purpose. The ring Emma wears was created for the Yellow Empress.

White Tiger: Bai Hu, God of the Western Heavens. His element is Metal. Michael MacLaren's father, and husband to more than a hundred wives.

Xuan Wu: Dark Emperor of the Northern Heavens, God of the North and Martial Arts. His True Form is a snake combined with a turtle. His element is Water. English name: John Chen Wu.

Yellow Empress: wife of the Yellow Emperor, a fabled ruler from ancient times who taught humanity the basics of civilisation.

Yi Hao: tame demon, Emma's secretary on Celestial Wudang.

Yue Gui: turtle Shen; Xuan Wu's older daughter, older sister to Simone and Martin Ming Gui, mother to Sang Shen. Manages the Northern Heavens' administrative side.

Zhu Que: the Red Phoenix, Goddess of the South. Her element is Fire.

Acknowledgements

Well, here I am. Fifteen years ago, I threw away my life in Hong Kong and returned to Australia. I had no friends and no extended family, and didn't want to go back into an IT cubicle, so I decided to write a best-seller and support myself that way. At the time, I knew nothing about writing fiction, or the publishing industry, and didn't know that it doesn't work like that. My original idea for three novels turned into nine, and I've gained a whole new life on the way.

I would not be where I am today without the help of a very large number of super generous people, that I am proud to call friends, and I'm thanking everybody in kind-of chronological order but not really.

My kids, who put up with the whole business start to finish, and who will remain unnamed to avoid excessive eye-rolling. My sister Fiona and the rest of the Canberra family.

Alana Rottler, who suggested I read some how-to-write books that turned my novels from amateur to pro.

Louise Cusack, who did a manuscript assessment of the first draft of 'White Tiger', and helped me to make it something remotely publishable.

All the guys at the Queensland Writer's Centre: it was through an editorial consultancy there that I met up with Stephanie Smith in the first place.

Stephanie Smith, who read my awful rough first draft of 'White Tiger' and decided to take a risk with it.

Nicola O'Shea, my long-suffering editor who's put up with me through the entire series.

Queenie Chan, my (not really) twin sister, who did the artwork for the wonderful 'Small Shen' and doesn't receive nearly as much recognition as she deserves.

Rowena Cory Daniells, who is a shining light for all speculative fiction writers in Queensland.

Marianne de Pierres, who invited me along for a joint signing when I was a tiny baby author, and helped me with infinite amounts of supremely wise advice.

Trent Jamieson, who jumped up at a Supanova where he was supposed to be signing, and proceeded to help the sales staff behind the cash register.

Chris Tatzenko, my Wing Chun Sifu, who double-checked all the martial arts.

Alex Adsett, who rescued me from some bad contracts and business arrangements, and represents me tirelessly, and her husband Paul who knows exactly the right thing to say at exactly the right time.

Rochelle Fernandez, who stepped into some big shoes and took off running at Voyager HarperCollins, and who has been fantastic support. A special shout-out to all the guys at Voyager Australia, who are tirelessly awesome.

Ineke Prochazka of Supanova, and yes that is her as the bad guy in book 7 and she's much more evil than that character.

Isobelle Carmody, who helped me with genius ideas at my UQ study.

Trudi Canavan, always there with a Polaroid camera and an evil grin.

Kathleen Jennings, who brought my visions to life.

Lea Greenaway and Cynthia Rohner (Edu's name was originally Cynthia), who gave me sugar packets and infinite amounts of support right at the start and helped me to spread my little author wings.

Sean Williams and Rob Hoge, who helped me join the Visions writers' group.

The Brisbane spec fic community: the guys at Avid Reader and Pulp Fiction, Nicky and Damon Cavalchini-Strickland, the magnificent Valkyrie Kim Wilkins, Peter Ball, Aimee Lindorff, Rosemary of her Romance Bookshop.

The Comic Con guys — Carissa and Rand, Amanda Bacchi, Paul Mason, Stew and Wendy McKenny, Cordy and Kate.

The other friends I've made along the way: Tom Taylor, Colin Taber, Donna Maree Hansen and her fantastic husband Matt Farrer, Helen Stubbs, Glenda Larke, Tansy Rayner Roberts, Katie Taylor, Robin Hobb (more nostril, Ian Irvine!), Tad Williams (EGG, TAD), Jana Oliver (come back Jana we love you!), and Jim Butcher.

In 2002 I came to Australia with no friends. Now I have not only friends, but fans. Thank you, everybody.

The next things will be Dragons in Space, and Simone on Earth. To work!

AN EPIC SAGA OF
MARTIAL ARTS, MYTH, AND MAGIC

KYLIE
CHAN

WHITE TIGER
978-0-06-199405-0

Emma Donahoe has just started her new job as nanny to Simone, the daughter of John Chen, a very rich Hong Kong businessman. But when John and his American bodyguard, Leo, teach Emma their particular style of martial arts, she's drawn into a world of magic and extreme danger, where both gods and demons can exist in the mortal domain.

RED PHOENIX
978-0-06-199409-8

When Emma took the position of nanny to John Chen's daughter, she never expected to be caring for the child of a Chinese god, or that demons would want him dead. Nor has moving from nanny to partner in his heavenly realm made Emma's life any easier. Now a powerful race of demons has been created to hunt her and her family.

BLUE DRAGON
978-0-06-199413-5

John is becoming weaker as demons pursue him relentlessly, hoping to use Emma and his child, Simone, as bargaining tools against him. Now Emma must find the courage to defend Simone as John's energy is drained by the effort of both living in the mortal world and protecting them.

KYC1 0616